W9-BZV-768

Two Worlds Walking

TWO WORLDS WALKING

Short Stories, Essays,
& Poetry by
Writers with
Mixed Heritages

Edited by
Diane Glancy *&* C. W. Truesdale

New Rivers Press 1994

Copyright © 1994 New Rivers Press
Library of Congress Catalog Card Number 93-83972
ISBN 0-89823-149-3
All Rights Reserved

Editorial Assistance by Paul J. Hintz
Cover artwork by Marce Wood
Book Design and Typesetting by Peregrine Graphics Services

New Rivers Press is a non-profit literary press dedicated to publishing the very best emerging writers in our region, nation, and world.

The publication of *Two Worlds Walking* has been made possible by a generous grant from the National Endowment for the Arts (with funds appropriated by the Congress of the United States).

Additional support has been provided by the General Mills Foundation, Land o' Lakes, Inc., Liberty State Bank, the McKnight Foundation, the Minnesota State Arts Board (through an appropriation by the Minnesota State Legislature), the Star Tribune/Cowles Media Company, the Tennant Company Foundation, and the contributing members of New Rivers Press. New Rivers Press is a member agency of United Arts.

New Rivers Press books are distributed by The Talman Company, 131 Spring Street, Suite 201 E-N, New York, NY 10012 (1-800-537-8894).

Two Worlds Walking has been manufactured in the United States of America for New Rivers Press, 420 North Fifth Street/Suite 910, Minneapolis, MN 55401. First Edition.

Acknowledgements

"Blood Ties" first appeared in *Westworld/4*.

"Child Christ at the Top of the Stairs" and "Standing at Pasternak's Table, Peredelkino" originally appeared in *Womb-Weary* (Carol Publishing).

"Fabrique de Tabac" first appeared in *Images cadiennes* (Ridgeway Press).

"Family Album" first appeared in *The Georgia Review*.

"Flounder" first appeared in *Callaloo*.

"Half" first appeared, in a slightly different version, in *Parents' Press*.

"Henri Toussaints" appeared in *The Worcester Review*, in *An Ear to the Ground* (University of Georgia Press), and in *Home Country* (Alice James Books).

"Huckster at Noontime" originally appeared in *In the Talking Hours* (Edenhall).

Excerpts from "*Italianità* in a World Made of Love and Need" appeared in *Sinetar and Associates: Human Development Resources*.

"Kukutis's Trip on the Samogitian Highway" appeared in *Writ*.

"The Left Eye of Odin" first appeared in *Hoofbeats on the Door* (Helicon Nine Editions).

"Lemon Ice" first appeared in *Voices in Italian Americana*.

"Les fils" first appeared in *Je me souviens de la Louisiane* (March Street).

"Living in Two Languages" was published as "The Language du Jour" in *The Christian Science Monitor* and in *Cupids Wild Arrows* (Bergli Books).

"Looking for Indians," "Like the Trails of Ndakinna," and "To Human Skin" appeared in *Home Country* (Alice James Books).

"Looking for St. Joe" was first published in *Special Report: Fiction*.

"Rue de Rosiers: To My Brother Fred" was first published in *Song for Our Voices* (Judah Magnes Musuem).

"Sister Death" first appeared in *The Price of Admission*.

"Spécialité Provençal" appeared in an earlier version in *The Albany Review* and *Offshoots*.

"Teatime in Leningrad" is abridged from a larger story which appeared in *Flying Time: Stories and Half-Stories* (Signal Books).

"Trees" and "At the Powwow" appeared in *SAIL* and in *Home Country* (Alice James Books).

"Tulip" first appeared in *5 a.m.*.

"Turtle Blessing" first appeared in *Stockpot*.

"Two Voices," "Inside Green Eyes, Black Eyes," and "Mixed Marriages" all appeared in *Selected Poems of Diana Der-Hovanessian* (Sheep Meadow Press).

"White Lies" first appeared in *The Seattle Review*.

"Zebra" first appeared in *First Things*.

Table of Contents

Introductory Note

Diane Glancy

I THOUGHT *Two Worlds Walking* would be a matter of blood. Anyone who had parents of different races. But the theme turned many ways. I guess like any project. And *Two Worlds Walking* became an *eisegesis* (the opposite of *exegesis*–a reading of one's voice into the text). And whatever came from it.

We live in America. The Melting Pot. But we've found that character and culture don't melt. Maybe under some conditions. But not ordinary life. Our strength is in our diversity. Which is a theme now emerging everywhere.

But diversity has its limits too. And there's been a movement back toward *Wholeness of the Parts*, at the same time of identification with one's own tribe. Within the Native community, for instance, it's called *Revitalization*. In other words, we maintain our individual tribes, while realizing the power of the united groups. So, individuality within the group is another interpretation of *Two Worlds Walking*.

Thus the premise of this anthology: a series of writings that examines and expresses the worlds we walk in, and the worlds that walk within us. A new order of migration, in which *the going* is the journey itself, rather than arrival at a *destination*.

I think, in the end, the theme of Two Worlds Walking also encompasses the act of writing itself. The different worlds of genres. Prose and poetry. Essays and novel parts. Experimentation within these categories. Even the making of new genres. Genres *re-gen-er-a-ting*.

Maybe there are even more dimensions of two worlds walking two by two. Things aren't so cut and dried anymore. Not so linear as rows in our western wheat fields. But, one hopes, there's a succession of migrations in the orbits of these voices.

Introductory Note

C. W. Truesdale

DIANE GLANCY, my co-editor of this anthology (and a contributor as well), is of Cherokee and German ancestry. And though basically English in origin, I became aware early on of the multiplicity, complexity, and internationality of this cultural mixing and of the issues, conflicts, and insights arising from it. My father was born in Minneapolis in 1891 of English ancestry. His grandfather, who had the venerable English surname of Langdon, was named after the great Scottish warrior-king Robert the Bruce. My mother was born in Chile. Her father was a Scottish mining engineer from Edinburgh; her mother was an American from San Francisco. She had an Indian governess from Venezuela who in turn was brought up to the States to become governess of me and my brothers and sisters in St. Louis. My father's family had a carriage driver/chauffeur named Fred Boettiger, probably of German ancestry, who had fought in the Indian Wars and was also brought to St. Louis to act as a chauffeur for the founder of the school where my father taught. So, as a young man, I became aware of an international heritage–with all its tensions and creative possibilities.

From the beginning, we decided to attract as much excellent writing as we could from individuals as diverse in background as Native American and Anglo, or French and Korean, and so forth. Many, many cultures are represented here, including Jewish, Hispanic, Lithuanian, German, English, Italian, African American, Native American, Korean, Japanese, and Indian. (It is interesting to note that Native Americans with as little as one-eighth tribal blood can be registered as Ojibwa, Navajo, Cherokee, Sioux, etc. This in itself is a recognition of the inevitability of mixed heritages.)

One of the major problems that emerges from the material submitted to us–though by no means all the writers included are directly concerned with it–is identity. As an epigraph to her poem "Two Voices," the poet Diana Der-Hovenessian quotes something said by D. M. Thomas: "Do you think of yourself as an Armenian? Or an American? Or hyphenated American?" Identity is often complicated by having to decide which blood-line is really "me." And, as Der-Hovanessian suggests, whether that "me" is really "American" too.

Thus Ana L. Ortiz de Montellano in her poignant essay "In Which I Speak My Name," deconstructs her own very complex name into its many components in a search for her real identity. (Her family came from Mexico.) "When I was nine," she says, "my best friend's father, el Señor Darreda . . . told me, '*Qué chasco, gringuita.* You use your name wrong, sabes. Ana Ortiz de Montellano means you are Ana Ortiz married to a man by the name of Montellano. You should say Ana Ortiz Lamb, your mother's name linked to your father's. That's how we do it here.' " She goes on to say that "He could not take my name away. As much as I longed for a simple name, I knew my last name was Ortiz de Montellano Lamb and not Ortiz Lamb no matter what he said. A picture of a girl with wistful eyes dressed as a *charra* and sitting on a wooden carousel horse taken when I was eight is signed Ana O. at the top, Ana Ortiz de M. at the bottom, and Ana Ortiz de Montellano on the back. Identity was already a problem for me." At the very end of this essay, she speaks her full name–with pride: "Ana Luisa Flor de Maria Ortiz de Montellano Lamb."

Catherine Houser in her autobiographical essay called "Floating" shows us that not only is identity a problem in itself but so are the slurs and stereotypes often associated with being a person of mixed blood. Native Americans are always "drunken Indians" (as indeed many of her relatives were). She resents the fact that "White boys in docksiders who grew up playing in the snow of the eastern seaboard were writing stories about mythical cowboys of the Southwest and the wild and wildly dangerous Indians they fought to conquer and civilize." In her writing class, Houser "set about writing the truth of my people. Following the first rule of writing, I wrote about what I knew. What came out were stories about drunken Indians. No cowboys, just Indians in contemporary situations who had pervasive problems with alcohol." Eventually, she gave up writing about Native Americans altogether to do "airy stories of people void of cultural identity–Americans–and their individual and cultural angst." It took her nearly thirty years to come to terms with these issues and to write honestly and truthfully and with considerable sympathy about the Native American half of her identity: "My ancestors were people who blew west in the dust that blanketed Cherokee land in Oklahoma in the twenties. They were Indians looking for a land that would feed them. They were headed for California, but their borrowed car broke down in Phoenix and in an instant they were Cherokees without a community, without a reservation, focused solely on survival. That is how I know them—isolated and poor, struggling both to rage over what was lost to them when they left Oklahoma and to make peace with that loss. I see my father's thick hands, calloused from field work and bloodied from barroom brawls, and I remember my grandmother's hands, translucent and shimmering, as they worked a beaded leather strap into a belt that would be sold to tourists, and the truth resonates in me finally." She ends her essay ambiguously, the essential question of identity not quite resolved (as it seldom really is): "Sitting here surrounded by water, some three thousand miles away from that unforgiving desert, I float between the two worlds, connected by a solid bridge here, a causeway there, but still, always, floating."

Susan K. Ito, half-Japanese and half-Anglo, writes in her memoir "Origami" about trying to practice, unsuccessfully, that ancient Japanese art. Her failure leads her to surmise "That I'm not really Japanese. That I'm just an imposter, a fake, a watered-down, inauthentic K-mart version of the real thing." She recalls a time when, as a teenager, she worked in an "authentic" Japanese restaurant in upstate New York and was challenged by one of the patrons: "'This is supposedly a Japanese restaurant.' He swept his arm in a wide circle, and I could see a ring of perspiration soaked into his shirt. 'I read that brochure in the bar. It's supposed to be an antique farmhouse that was built in Japan.'

"'The farmhouse is authentic,' I murmured. My face was getting hot. 'It was shipped here directly from Osaka.'

"And what about you?' he demanded. 'Where were *you* shipped from?'

"I felt the blush draining out of my face, and my fear became so intense I thought my body would fail me. I imagined the blood pooling at my feet and then completely seeping out my soles, leaving me standing in a puddle of my own blood, my half authentic, tainted blood.

"I nearly lost my balance. I stood there, holding the tray of heaped up towels, tottering on my *geta*. 'I'm half-Japanese.' Just a whisper.

"'Half?' he scoffed. 'Hey, I come to a Japanese restaurant, I expect to have a Japanese waitress.' He gestured toward the petite, silky-haired Kim passing out bowls of rice at the next table. He didn't have a clue, and I didn't tell him, that she was from Korea, and no more Japanese than he was."

And, finally, Nancy Lee's "Pandora" is a really dark story about a woman half-Korean, half-Anglo who settles for a time in Tokyo to teach English to Japanese students and eventually goes to visit her "aunt" (her "*ajumeoni*"–not a "blood" relative) in Seoul. While there, she sees a man being beaten outside a stationery shop (where she purchases a blank book with the odd–but hugely significant in terms of this story–title of *Pandora*) and recalls some similar incidents in Tokyo. Lee had her degree in teaching English as a "second language" at the time, from a very prestigious American university), but she soon discovers how difficult it is not just to learn a foreign language but to get "inside" an alien culture.

That time in Tokyo I was walking to the subway station at Ikebukura. The intersection in front of the Morinaga Love Burger stand at the entrance to the subway was blocked, not by traffic, but by human bodies. A huge crowd, a huge crowd even by Tokyo standards, all very orderly and polite of course. All nodding and bowing their heads to each other as they jockeyed for a better view. '*Gomenasai.*' '*Gomenasai.*' '*Do itashimashito.*' 'Excuse me.' 'Beg your pardon.' 'Not at all.' I bowed and gomenasai'd my way into the crowd.

At the center of the crowd two young men with wooden clubs were beating a man in a business suit. The wooden clubs had obviously been specially designed for this purpose. They had long paddles and short handles like cricket bats, with cord wound around the handles to give a better grip.

They beat the man. They beat him methodically, taking turns, as if they were driving in a railroad spike. He was crouched down to protect his head so they beat him across his back. Every time a club came down across his back his body flopped with a groan.

And all the time, like a typical American, I was thinking 'Where is the six o'clock news mini-cam? Why doesn't someone call the police?' I looked around wildly for a phone booth but the Japanese class I'd taken back in the States hadn't taught me how to say 'Help,' 'Police.' 'This is an emergency.' At the moment all I could remember was 'My, isn't this a pretty ashtray?'

The two young men tucked their clubs up under their arms and climbed into the back of a small delivery truck. This looked rather like a milk truck or an ice cream truck, except that instead of white it was painted a shiny black, with white *kanji* scrawled across the side. I knew how to read *katakana* and *hiragana* but only a handful of *kanji*–not these. I thought of copying them down on something but before my hand reached my purse the crowd parted and the small black truck drove away to disappear into Tokyo traffic.

At what point had it become too late to do anything?

I remember a weeping woman in a polyester dress and high heels struggling to raise the beaten man to his feet. I remember a burger-flipper from the Morinaga Love Burger stand, with his white paper burger-flipper hat, helping her to drag the man out of the street and prop him up against a telephone pole. I remember the crowd dispersing. Very politely and apologetically. '*Gomenasai.*' 'Am I in your way?' 'Not at all.'

The whole time not a single voice had been raised.

I got on the subway and took the train home. 'Home' meaning the room where I kept my suitcase. The room where I was raped.

The rest of her story deals with the subject of her being raped in Tokyo and her inability to report that to the police: "I didn't know the Japanese for 'I want to report a rape.' I don't think I could have said it in English. It was just another one of those things that don't happen, that somehow kept happening." And she concludes with this bitter paragraph: "My fate was written long before he rammed his cock up my raw insides, before he even opened that door, before I rented that room with the door that wouldn't lock, before I came to the country where that would be the only room I could rent. My fate was written from the moment I asked *who am I and where did I come from?*: the moment I opened the box that can't be shut."

These five examples all show some version of the problem of identity, which is beautifully summarized in a brief statement by Nancy Lee from the story just discussed: "'. . . identity' is just a name you give to a collection of protections and privileges you take for granted–until you leave your country, and leave them all behind." Or leave the comfortable environment of your childhood–if it was indeed comfortable–and face the realities of the actual world with all its disturbances. But these five pieces also show the wide range of feeling, intonation, and mood that is magnified in so many different ways by all of the writers included in this anthology.

We at New Rivers are very pleased to offer this selection of writing on "mixed heritages" to the reading public. It is only a sampling (we received enough excellent submissions to fill at least two or three anthologies) but a sampling which we hope goes a long way toward opening a discussion of one of the most important aspects of cultural diversity and one that probably encompasses half or more of the people of this country and Canada. And yet the particular issues raised have not–to our knowledge–ever been so broadly represented as they are here.

MEMOIR

Family Album

Siv Cedering

THIS IS THEIR wedding picture. Pappa is wearing a tuxedo and Mamma a white satin dress. She is smiling at the white lilies. This is the house Pappa built for Mamma, when they were engaged. Then this house, then that; they were always making blueprints together.

Mamma came from Lapland. She was quite poor and dreamed of pretty dresses. Her mother died when Mamma was small. Pappa met her when he came to Lapland as a conscientious objector. He preached in her church. There he is with his banjo.

Pappa was quite poor too; everyone was in those days. He told me that one spring he didn't have any shoes that fit him. He had to borrow his father's large shoes. Pappa said he was so ashamed that he walked in the ditch all the way to school.

Pappa was one of eleven children, but only five of them grew up. The others died of tuberculosis or diphtheria. Three died in a six-week period. Pappa says death was accepted then, just like changes in the weather and a bad crop of potatoes. His parents were religious. I remember Grandfather Anton rocking in the rocker and riding on the reaper, and I remember Grandmother Maria, though I was just two when she died. The funeral was like a party: birch saplings decorated the yard, relatives came from all around, and my sister and I wore new white dresses. Listen to the names of Maria's eleven children:

Anna Viktoria, Karl Sigurd, Johan Martin, Hulda Maria, Signe Sofia,

Bror Hilding, Judit Friedeborg, Brynhild Elisabet, John Rudolf, Tore Adils, and Clary Torborg.

Victoria was fat and never got married. Tore was the youngest son. I remember sitting next to him, outside by the flagpole, eating blood pancakes after a slaughter, and calf-dance, a baked custard made from the first milk a cow gives after it has calved. Tore recently left his wife and took a new one. He once told me that when he was a boy, he used to ski out in the dark afternoons of the North and stand still, just watching the sky and feeling himself grow smaller and smaller.

This is Uncle Rudolf in his uniform, and this is Torborg, Pappa's youngest sister. Her fiance tried to make love to her once, before they were married, and—Mamma told me—Torborg tore the engagement ring off her finger, threw it on the floor of the large farmhouse kitchen, and hollered, loud enough for everyone to hear: "What does that whoring bastard think I am?" He was the son of a big-city mayor and well-educated, but you can bet he married a virgin. Don't they look good in this picture? All their children are beautiful and well-educated. They say that Torborg got her temper from great-grandfather. When he got drunk he cussed and brought the horse into the kitchen.

These are the Kell people from the Kell farm. I am told I have the Kell eyes. Everyone on this side of the family hears ghosts and dreams prophecies. To us it isn't supernatural; it is natural.

Mamma's oldest brother Karl went to America when he was eighteen. There he is chopping down a redwood tree, and there he is working in a gold mine. He married a woman named Vivian, and she visited us in Sweden. Let me tell you, the village had never seen anyone like her. Not only had she been divorced and remarried, but her hair was bobbed, and she wore make-up and dresses with padded shoulders, matching shoes, and purses. Vanity of all vanities was quoted from the Bible. So of course everyone knew the marriage wouldn't last—besides they didn't have any children. Uncle Karl is now old and fat, the darling and benefactor of a Swedish Old Folks Home in Canada. Silver mines help him.

This is Mamma's second brother. He was in a mining accident and had to have a leg amputated. I used to think about that leg, all alone in heaven. This is Aunt Edith. When I was little, she gave me a silver spoon with my name engraved on it. And this is Aunt Elsa who has a large birthmark on her face. I used to wonder what mark I had, to prove my birthright.

Mamma's father was a communist. He was a ships engineer, but his wife didn't want to be married to a sailor, so he came to Lapland to help build the railroad and then the power plant that supplies most of Sweden's electricity. Once he told me that he ate snake when he was young and worked on the railroad. His wife Emma was a beauty and a lady, and when the household money permitted, she washed her face with heavy cream and her hair with beer or egg whites. My hair? Both grandmothers had hair long enough to sit on.

I am talking about my inheritance—the family jewelry I wear in my hair, so to speak, the birthmark that stays on my face forever. I am motherless in Lapland, brought down to size by the vastness of the sky. I rock in the rocker of old age and ride the reaper, while some part of me has already preceded me to heaven. I change one husband for another, and toss my ring, furiously moral at any indignation. I am a pacifist, I am a communist, I am a preacher coddling my father's language and abandoning my mother tongue forever. I eat blood pancakes, calf-dance, snake, and I bring the horse into the kitchen. I build new houses, dream of new dresses, bury my parents and my children. I hear ghosts, see the future and know what will happen. If I step on a crack and break my mother's back, I can say the shoes are too large for my feet, for I know, I know: these are the fairy tales that grieve us. And save us.

Starry, Starry Night

I AM AN ADULT. I can read. I have studied the universe. I know the earth is a planet afloat in space. I know what the starry sky is, the starry sky under which I walk. I know it is not just a starry cap for our little earth, but the beginning of a vastness that stretches beyond the formulae of expanding space. It is winter. It is dark. The light from the stars in the arm of our galaxy shows its Milky Way. The constellations are almost as familiar as Father, Mother, Grandfather. It doesn't matter if, some night, the serpentine northern lights snake across the sky spitting fire, like dragons, or if the moon is sickled, cradling an oval void, or if an enormous ring circles the moon so that someone will predict snow. This is my world: a starry sky and five people walking.

My mother is wearing her black Persian lamb coat; my father his beaver hat. She has her left arm hooked in his right arm. Her right hand holds my brother's hand. The sheepskin-lined flaps of his leather cap are tied under his chin. My sister and I walk a few steps in front of them, or behind them. Our white lamb jackets are trimmed with red wool. The circle around the moon is enclosing almost all the heavens.

What does it matter if I am in San Francisco or New York, if it is night or day, if I am alone or not, because we are always walking there, and it is always winter. Down the Milky Way we go, with the Swan, toward the Bear. The Pleiades mirror us. My sister and I count and recount them. Five? Six? Seven? There were six of us before the baby died. Will we become seven? We do not doubt the correspondence. Or will yet another star fall out of our constellation, to shoot across the sky, giving someone a chance to make a wish? And if one of us dies, would we still be walking down the Milky Way on this snow-covered road?

The elevated road crosses the flooding plain. Nothing obstructs the view. Then the road climbs, past a house, another house, some trees, two more houses, woods. The sky shrinks to a slender canal above the road. Mamma says, "Did you have to go inside?"

"I just went inside the door."

"Inside!"

The quotes are not exact; they have been obliterated by stars, but the image is clear. I can see my father, just inside the door. He is holding his hat in his hand, looking embarrassed. The woman he is facing has long brown hair, worn in a net-covered snood, like my mother. She is beautiful in the same way my mother is beautiful. She is living in a white house, similar to the white house in which we used to live, on the same side of the road as we lived, as we live.

I am an adult. I know about the theory of relativity. Time does not pass absolutely. The ticking of the clock is related to the motion of worlds, tumbling through space. Years and minutes might have passed between the image of the dark woman with the snood and the blond one I conjure up as my father says, "She came riding on a bicycle."

I can see her—blond, twenty-two, just out of teaching college. She has come to the country for her first job. She is renting a room. She is riding a borrowed bicycle with a basket, say, with a loaf of bread and a women's magazine with an easy crossword puzzle. He is tall, dark, and handsome. He is forty. He used to live in this town, did well, moved to America. His brand new convertible rolls to a stop.

It is summer. Her skirt flutters as she rides. The gravel crunches under the tires and under the sole of her sandal as it slips off the pedal and slides to a stop. And suddenly she is pregnant. Words like *divorce* and *remarriage* enter the language.

Time is relative. My first wristwatch had been my father's. It was a man's watch. The fourteen carat Gruen my first lover gave me on my fifteenth birthday was left unrepaired when it stopped. I was ashamed. I was too young.

I am an adult. I can count. I know when numbers do not add up right. At eighteen, I am seven months pregnant, not married, and thousands of miles away from my mother, thousands of miles away from my father. But I must answer when a man asks, "What happened?"

While I try to explain, he looks at the clouds racing past the moon and says, "Tonight the sky has character."

I'm an adult. I can create my own life. I am thirty-seven. We have driven the old car right out into the overgrown field. "You've got to stop crying," he says. "You're hyperventilating."

But I can't stop. We've been lovers for a year. My husband knows all about it. It has torn what was left of our family apart. The air is full of fireflies. Above us, below us, they blink, on and off, on and off, infiltrating the constellations, confusing what is earth and sky, insect and star, moving through space. "Stop crying!"

How can I stop? I blink, a twinned pulse, we are breaking up. I have ridden the destruction past falling, past passion, to the end, knowing, on some level, this is not what I want, not this world where stars tumble out of heaven to wander, will o' the wisp, in a dark space above a field overgrown with milkweed.

I am an adult. I can read. I know letters both as sound and symbol. It makes sense that the Chinese ideogram for *happiness* is a combination of woman and son, the symbol of home is a pig under a roof. If I were Sequoia, I would device an alphabet of pictographs, that could be shaped by cat-hair brush or hog bristle—or chiseled in stone, each letter a picture of something familiar. The symbol for family would be five people walking under a starry sky. The symbol for the future, a mirror held up to the past.

My Uncle's Numbers

E STER HALLMAN was the best. We never had words. Never. Not a single bad word. But I knocked her up.

I didn't know I knocked her up. When my mother was in the hospital in Jokkmokk, Ester visited her every day. Guess she was stuck on me from the beginning. Me? When I was up there racing. Skis. Sure, I was good. Came in 3rd that time. I was just 16. Usually I was first. In Lapland.

I was working on the railroad. Could lay 53 ties a day. That was the record in Sweden. But 10 years later, when I was in Canada, someone beat it, they say. 57. But while I was in Sweden, I held the record. So when this bastard told the boss I was goofing off, and got me fired–just because I had left work early one day–I beat the bastard up. I hadn't left my job. I was working on contract, and I had already laid the 40 ties, the fool!

Sure I was drunk when I beat him up. So they put me in jail. For 7 days. When I got out, I went right to the railroad station, where that bastard's father was stationmaster. He sat behind the glass window, and when he looked up and asked me what I wanted–pow! Right through the window. I didn't really knock him out. But did he fly back? And the glass! You should have seen it.

I knew they'd be after me. And that the police would be smart enough to check the train station. So I walked through the woods to a place where the train had to slow down. When it came, I waited for the last car and swung myself aboard. I went to Gällivare, where my mother had a sister. But I was afraid they would catch up with me there, so after 3 days, I took the train all the way down to Ystad, where mother had another sister, Hanna.

Hanna was not neat, like my mother. But never mind. She was good, the whole family was, and they helped me get a job digging potatoes. But digging potatoes was no job for someone like me. So I went to stay with another aunt, in Göteborg. Her husband got me a job as a longshoreman.

We were supposed to shovel up coal and carry it in boxes, and I thought, well, that's easy. I was strong. And fast. Everybody noticed. But when I was almost done, I saw the smaller pieces were left and had to be picked up by hand. The other guys laughed, but one man, who was a good one, said, "I can see you're a greenhorn. Let me show you." And he did.

Then I got a job mixing cement, which I already knew how to do, so I made good money. 7 crowns an hour. Not 7 crowns a day but seven an hour. That's more than a dollar. That was a lot in the '20s.

And when I had enough, I took a boat to America.

My mother died when I was 2 days out at sea—or was it 2 days after I got to New York? I can't remember. I can't remember everything. Her hair was so long she could sit on it. She was so kind. It makes me want to cry when I think of her. They say our dog Jeck missed her so much that he howled on her grave every night. They had to shoot him.

But my father. That was a son-of-a-bitch. I had to start working when I was 6. 6! I had to do the rowing when he went fishing, and in the winter I had to push the sled full of fish all the way home. 20 kilometers! Sometimes I did it on my skates. 20 kilometers there and 20 kilometers back is too far for a kid. And I had to carry in all the wood for heating the house and for cooking. And stack it. And chop it.

I was supposed to work on a farm in North Dakota, but I jumped off the train outside Chicago and went to Canada. And then west. I wasn't made to shovel shit.

First I logged. Right after the first week, I did everything on contract. I saw what the other guys got done and I knew how much they got paid, so I went to the boss and told him I wanted to be paid per tree. I had seen him watching me work. So when he said no, I said I'd quit. So of course he kept me on, on contract. He was no fool.

I logged all over the Yukon and British Columbia. Sometimes it was 50 below 0. You know how to survive when it's 50 below 0? You dig a large hole in the snow and cover it with logs. On top of them, you put branches, spruce is nice, to sleep on. Then you build a fire under the logs, so the heat slants toward the place where you sleep. That's how you keep warm. And keep the wolves away, too.

I mined, all along. And for 3 years I was on a fishing boat. As a cook. Those guys never ate better. Sure, things were tough. Nothing's easy. During the depression I had no money for food for 12 days. For 12 days I walked across Vancouver Island. Ate whatever I could find. Worms. I can eat anything. Seagulls don't taste very good. But you can eat them, if you have to.

I figured Sweden couldn't be much worse, so I beat a freight from

Vancouver to Montreal. On top of the box cars. Me and another guy. Then on to Halifax. When we got to Stockholm, we went right to the pace where Ester worked. Dahlberg's Restaurant. I had the address. Smalgränd 2. I can still remember the meal we had. Filet of beef with horse-radish sauce. You bet it tasted good!

Ester and I had some good times. Only good times. She liked to dance, too. I remember we went to The Grand Hotel and danced and danced. They were playing the Charleston, and when my legs were good, I just couldn't keep them still. Everybody wanted to know who I was, and all the elegant ladies wanted me to teach them the new steps. But I danced mostly with Ester. You should have seen us!

But the *fjärdingsman,* what's the word in English? He was after me to sign up in the army. So I took off. People were starving all over America, but that was better than being in the service, or in jail. I had been in Stockholm for six months.

She wrote me. But I didn't get the letter for months. I had moved 3 times looking for work. When I finally got the letter, it was too late. She had gone to a midwife and gotten rid of it. And then she moved. I couldn't get hold of her. She had wanted to come to Canada.

I was her first. I know. I saw the blood. She was a good girl.

Then? I began making beer. And hard stuff. Got very busy. Hell, I made the best stuff in all of Canada, just like it said in that newspaper clipping you saw. It was shipped all over the country, to the United States, too. This was during Prohibition. I supplied all the bootleggers around Vancouver, that's for sure. It was the purest stuff made in the whole country, like the damned paper said.

They looked for me for the longest time! I had a house on a hill in West Vancouver, with the still upstairs so the booze could run down and be bottled downstairs. One day when I was driving off on a delivery with the trunk full, the car too, I saw this car in the rearview mirror. And gunned it. You should have seen us, up and down the hills and speeding around curves. It was a hell of a chase!

Yeah, sure, I did some time. But not too long. A lot of people were going thirsty.

Al Capone was all right. He never dealt with drugs. They should shoot the drug dealers, just like that. That's bad stuff But Capone never bothered with drugs. Or women. Just bootlegging. No, I didn't meet him myself, but someone did on my behalf. Said he was a civil man. Polite. And you could trust him. But I did meet Bing Crosby.

He was a fine man. You could see it in his face. We were talking horse shit. I was trying to corner the horse shit market on the West Coast and Crosby needed some. He was raising mushrooms. I went there twice. To Hollywood. The second time he wasn't there. He was sharp and kind. But his sons—that's another matter. Stuck-up and empty-headed no-goods. I also met Victor Mature. A big phony.

This was after me and Vivian split. So you met her when she came to Sweden, huh? In '46, was it? I don't know if you know, but my brother came to Göteborg to meet her at the boat—and saw her kissing this other guy. But that wasn't the only problem. I had been working up in the Yukon and had sent her all the money I earned, to put in the bank. She did, but in only her name. She sold the house, too, and bought another one, instead, in only her name. And she bought a restaurant in Seattle. She was no dummy. And she was a good dresser. Nothing fancy, just good, classy stuff. Anyway, when I got back and found out that she had been putting everything in her name—well. We were out for dinner. And she was showing off, talking about it in front of others. So when we got outside and were standing by the car, I smacked her. Just like this. Right in the face. That was that.

No, I'm not sorry I smacked her. I had trusted her and she had double-crossed me. She had taken everything. All I had left was my truck. That's why I started the cement business. Built that warehouse you saw, and made foundations and sidewalks and driveways. I built my share of Vancouver.

And I continued to mine. All over British Columbia. I staked 18 claims in Lilloette. It's a Crown grant, registered with the Queen. We've put in a 392-foot tunnel, and there's ore there that gets 2 percent gold. Of every ton, don't you understand? And silver and zinc and lead. The main vein runs, visibly for 500 feet. And there are other veins. We've cut a road in, over the hump of the mountain. It's 6,000 feet high. The road is 15 miles long.

I have a claim near the Alberta border, too. It used to be only partly mine, but now I own it all by myself. And I got a mine up in the Yukon, near Alaska. In the Keno Mountains, near Keno City.

Vivian had a restaurant up north, too. Did quite well. She was smart, except when it came to me. And could she sing! Her voice was so sweet. There was one song she sang over and over. "The Blue Bird of Happiness." You know it? "So be like I, hold your head up high, 'til you find the Blue Bird. . . ." When she sung it, everybody cried. She would sing it at parties. They wanted her to sing it on stage, but she had terrible stage fright. Too bad she had stage fright.

She wanted us to remarry later. But I married once, and that was that. She died of cancer, when she was 63. I used to go up and see her.

Now, Ester Hallman, she was different. We never had a word. Never. I didn't know I had knocked her up. When I finally got her letter, it was too late. I want to send her some money. 5,000 or 10,000 dollars. Maybe 20,000.

I saw her in Boden in 1983. She is married. Has a husband and children. And grandchildren. I visited them at their summer place.

No, we didn't talk about it! That happened in 1932, for God's sake. So what's there to talk about?

I mention her in my will, but I'm going to ask the lawyer to change it. I don't want her husband to get it, if she dies first. I want *her* to have it. She was the best woman I ever knew. Be sure to write her for me. Say that in the letter. Tell her I am sorry for what I did. Tell her I didn't get her letter until it was too late. Tell her about the stroke, so she knows I can't write.

Or read. Except the numbers in the stock market report. I used to read all the time. I liked to read Marx and Spinoza and Schopenhauer and my *History of the World*. I have read them many, many times, and my book on Einstein.

Pain? I'm in pain all the time. But that is that. It's feeling so weak that I can't stand. And worrying if anyone will find me if I die. I don't want to lie here and rot. I told the accountant that if I die, the body might be in the room stinking for days, so he has promised to phone me every day. I told him about the place in North Vancouver, the place where they burn people. I told him what to do. Throw the ashes in the garbage can. Or in English Bay.

But if I get over the operation, who knows, I might be around for another 77 years. And when I get too bad, I know what to do. I can do it myself.

Like I cut off that goddamned finger. I had cut off a part of it logging, and the goddamned stump was in the way all the time, so I chopped it off. On purpose. With just a little whiskey to help. Or maybe not so little.

I still like whiskey, but I don't drink much anymore. My legs are giving me trouble. If I could just chop them off and be done with the pain!

After the stroke, I was in the hospital for a week. When they let me out, I didn't know where I was, and I couldn't read the street signs. But

I knew I had to go toward the mountains. So I walked. I didn't remember my address. But I walked, block by block. First I found the way to my office. And then eventually to my apartment building. It took me all day.

Yes, this place is nice. SuperValu and Safeway, the bank and the fish market, all within a block. And the park just 4 blocks away. And 2 down to English Bay. When I'm up, I can count the freighters waiting in the harbor. Sometimes I can count 12 or 15. From all over the world.

I don't want to be in no graveyard. I want to burn. Put the ashes in the garbage can, what do I care? Or throw them in English Bay. Salt shock. I don't want no funeral arrangements. Scattering the ashes in Lilloette? No, don't you understand it doesn't matter what happens to the goddamned ashes? What's the difference? You're dead, you're dead.

No, I don't have anybody. Except the accountant. And the lawyer. And I talk to the broker almost every day. No, I don't want a nurse. I have managed by myself this long. Have lived alone all my life, except those years in the '40s, with Vivian. But you can call me. Call me. I don't want to lie here and rot. And that shoe box with the pictures, you keep it. I don't want anybody else to have them.

And send that letter. To the address I gave you. Tell her I'm sorry for what I did in 1932, before Christmas. Tell her I didn't get her letter until it was too late. Tell her I've thought about her all these years.

Snow

Regina deCormier

My father sits at the kitchen table.
That night I huddled on the stair,
he says, I heard my mother's *merde*
and I knew she didn't mean *good luck*.
She was watching the moon rise
on the hook of an old wishbone, how
it pulled the world around the hoop of itself.
In this uncivilized land
something, she cried, rocks in my belly
like a child wanting to be born,
and there is no knife
strong enough to cut the blood root. *Ecouté!*

she cried to the inattentive night.
This is my vow: in this house
my children will speak only the language of our people.
We will pray, daily, the old prayers.
We will break bread with the ancestors.
People will say we walk in mismatched shoes,
but we will turn a deaf ear to their catcalls,
and not one of us will ever forget
where we came from, or who we are . . .

That night, the night I was ten,
as I crouched in the curve of the stair,
I watched my mother step out of her dress.
She pulled pins like knives from her hair.
A torrent of hair
spilled down her back. Naked, she leaned
her face against the glass, and I watched
the moon caress her with light,

until the snow blew out of nowhere
and darkened the room . . .

My father lowers his face to a plate,
picks up the knife and peels Christmas oranges
pulled from the toes of wool stockings
made for mismatched shoes, our shoes.
We, his children, stare past his face.
Like smoke, snow whirls past the window.
Neige, neige, the gritty cry at the door.

Grandmother

Seasons are spirits, you said, each
to be acknowledged, each to be honored.
Today, I remember your words,
mormor, and because I live now
by the Hudson where the Lenapes lived
long before the Europeans thought of sailing
up the river, I remember, too,
what the Lenapes say: when the world began

there were four grandparents:
three grandfathers–they came
from the north, the east, and the west,
and one grandmother–she
came from the south, warm, and soft,
humming, chasing the dark
and the cold away. Grandmother,

mormor, you, too, came humming,
although you did not come here from the south
but from Sweden,
land, you said, of long winters,
and the miracle of midsummer
when day and night become one
in that shimmering marriage of light,
and flowers grow fat as cabbages,
and blood leaps like a mountain goat
beneath the triumphant shout of the sun

as the ancestors clap hands, and dance.
How can I forget you – how
your words colored the air of my childhood,
how, when you sat in the Morris chair
by the window that cradled the sun
you loved, your head bent to a book,
your lips moved as if, I thought,
in some mysterious Swedish prayer you knew
would lead you back home. Mormor,

all those summer nights, sharing your bed
carved with mahogany leaves and grapes
round and fat as desire,
I saw your long braids, unbound, brushed loose,
how your hair fell like a young girl's
below your waist, and I knew, then, it was
true that you were young once,
untamed, the aunts said, with a love child,
whistling birds out of trees, and writing poems
you kept in the bottom drawer of your dresser
beneath stockings and underwear. Then

when morning came, you were mormor again,
your braids coiled on your head,
your slippers whispering through the house
as the cardamom-spiked bread rose,
and you spoke, again, of the seasons, as if
they were somehow ours . . . Today,

all these years later, I understand.
I understand, and I acknowledge, but
cannot honor the spirit of winter who has
shouldered his unexpected way, horned and dark-
tongued into our lives. In our pockets
last night's knives, we drink bitter coffee,
and are afraid, today, to ask

when, grandmother you will return.

Mormor is Swedish for grandmother, your mother's mother

The Left Eye of Odin

for my mother

1.

She knows them all. Urchins. Beggars
on crutches trundling downhill.
Fools peddling dreams.
The dog-faced baboons of fear. Treasonous
raconteurs–mummers, all of them.
This morning, the sun waits, tangled
like a goat, or a virgin, in the thicket.

2.

The braided loaves of bread keep warm
on the table, shrouded with white linen.
She walks away from the table
and stands at the window facing
the garden, which is, she thinks, where
she always stands. There is a sound
of clocks, something else
coming up through the floorboards. Perhaps
it is her father singing the smörgåsbord
menu to the dead. She stuffs her ears

with runes she hauled from the stone
mouths of Sweden, hauled all the way
over the bristling Atlantic
and over the Berkshires to the shores
of the Hudson. The wrong words were
stuck in her mouth, bits of pickled salt
herring and schnapps in her father's moustache
which hung, twitching, over his unruly
mouth. Remember, he said, the sun

is the left eye of Odin and the hands of Odin
know the green limbs of Yggdrasil.
She hides her hand, the one with the twisted
finger, in the pocket of her apron.
The piano has needed tuning for seven years.
Ten years. She does not know
how to survive this day. Her hand gropes
in the empty pocket. She tears the sun
from its nail in the sky, and moves away
from the window.
And watches them come.

3.

In twos and threes, the mummers come.
Their shoes on fire, mouse-bitten masks, tin
trumpets and drums. Bells of antimony
ring their legs, their velvet arms
coaxing bears. The bears perform, dragging
their heavy shadows around the circle.
Ropes, red ropes of spittle embroider
the circle. Their eyes go small. Their eyes
measure the circle. The mummers

dance. She tips her hat and their randy tongues
go slack with joy. The Fool, a purple
tulip in his mouth, waves his stick, shakes
his bag behind their backs. They are stealing
the maps. And the horses, all the runic knots
hidden in the drawers above the bed.
Their gloved hands are swift, and unerring; one
gold tooth each hangs out to shine,
"Tell the truth, and run," they say. And
wave. And smile their gold. She turns

away. The bears stand, tailless; their circle
a dark forest. There is a moon, a crescent moon
engraved in the middle of the forehead
of the tallest. He turns, they turn, taking
the circle, their ropes of red. They walk upright, up
over the humpback bridge of the sky, their fur

thick with light, their feet soft
unmistakable good-byes.

4.

The earth pivots on its axis, leans
toward the sun. The sun
sighs, spinning and dancing
to the applause of planets, the shifting
impulses. Inconsequential desires knot
her hands. She rubs her hands. She mutters
a Swedish word, and pulls the shrouds
from the risen bread.

Ten

Simone Poirier-Bures

E VENINGS, after supper, her father immerses himself in the big arm-chair with the broken springs. Nicole watches him. His head tilts back, his jaw hangs loose with absorption. From the radio Carmen sings about love–*L'Amour, L'Amour*–her voice rising and falling in serrated passion. Nicole knows the music well; it is one of the four opera records her father plays over and over until her mother comes in and says all that shrieking is getting on her nerves.

The music catches Nicole in its hooks, that song in particular with its seductive ups and downs. With a sofa pillow for her partner, she prances and pirouettes through the room, stretching her neck like a swan. *See how I was made to dance!* She eyes her father. *Do you see me? See how my body moves!* She tilts her head and lowers her eyes. *I am on stage. I am in the movies. Everyone who sees me is struck by my great beauty and sadness. Do you see me, Dad?*

André and Claude come in. "Oh look at that," they say, their mouths ugly with laughter. They grab the other pillows and flap at the air with their gangly arms and big feet. She is too noble to notice them, her dance too beautiful, too tragic. A pillow smacks against her head. She shrieks. Her father's face turns red. He hoists himself out of his chair: "Get out of here all of you! Can't I have a moment's peace?"

* * *

I am ten. She draws the numbers on a patch of bare earth in the back yard, digging with the toe of her shoe. One, zero. Double digits. The world is opening like a clam. The world is sucking at her feet like the ocean.

* * *

Sunday noon. "No, I am not going to dry dishes anymore. This is IT! I've had it. No more. The boys don't do anything. Annette will never let me wash. I'm not drying anymore." "Yes you are," from her mother. "NO. NO. NO. NO." "Charles, do something." "Do as your mother tells you!" "NO. NO. NO." Her father's face gets red like the inside of a watermelon. The veins at his temple bulge. His words come with a little shower of spit. "Yes you will!" He lunges heavily toward her. She is small and agile and runs to the bathroom, her refuge. The lock is broken and part of the door jam is missing from the many times she or Annette or André or Claude have crashed through in pursuit of someone fleeing there, but she goes there anyway. It's the only place.

She anchors her feet against the edge of the cast iron bathtub and puts the full weight of her body against the door. *I am a flying buttress. I am a steel post. I am eighty-seven pounds of levered strength.* Her father bangs on the door with his fists. "Come out of there right now!" She doesn't answer, saving her strength. He rams his body against the door. It moves a few inches, then slams shut again. She feels the blow in her legs, her arms, her lower back. "You WILL come out! You'll do as your mother tells you!" Again the door shudders violently. She pictures the red face, the flying spit. Her legs hold but she doesn't know for how much longer. "Come away, Charles," she hears her mother say. "She'll come out eventually."

Nicole sits on the edge of the tub. How long will she have to stay in here? What will happen when she comes out? The house gets quiet. There's nothing for her to do. Someone comes toward the door. She wedges herself between the tub and the door again. "It's me," André says. "I have to do a number two." "Is it safe to come out now?" she asks. "Yes," he says. She tiptoes down the hall and peeps into the kitchen. No one is around. The dishes are stacked in the draining tray and spread out all over the counter. Drip-drying. She wipes the ones that are still wet and puts them all away.

* * *

I am ten. I could be like Marilyn Monroe. She practices the throaty voice: It's whanderful, it's mahvelous. She combs her yellow hair over her eyes.

* * *

Annette is acting mysteriously. She won't let Nicole into the bathroom to wash her hands or look in the mirror while she's peeing. She always used to. She goes into their parents' bedroom and closes the door. Peculiar. "What are you doing in there?" she asks. "Sneaking Mom's makeup?" Nicole sometimes does, and puts on her mother's earrings and necklaces and opens the vanity drawers to feel the balled up stockings and lace handkerchiefs and sweaters. "No, I'm not," Annette says. "I'm allowed in here. Mom knows I'm here." "What are you doing, then?" she asks again. Annette is leaning over the vanity closing the bottom right drawer. "Nothing," she says, holding something behind her. "Nothing!"

What could it be, that thing wrapped in newspaper Annette won't show her? Is she sending secret messages to a boy? There are clues here. It must be boys. Why else would she look so suspicious? She thinks no one is looking. She slips the little packet into the waste basket by the basement stairs. When she leaves, Nicole hurries over, picks up the small bundle and slips down to the basement to unwrap it. Inside: a rectangular wad of cotton soaked with brownish-red blood. Oh.

* * *

I am ten. The moon is a big flat coin she wants to put in her pocket. The world pulls at her heart like the tide.

* * *

Her mother is going around talking in French again. Refusing to answer unless they at least *try* it in French. They are going to Digby County for the Acadian Festival. Two hundred years since the Deportation. There will be a mass and a parade; some girl will get to be Evangeline; some boy, Gabriel.

Her mother is getting costumes ready. Flared skirts with white blouses and black vests that lace up for her and Annette. And little white starched hats that look like nurses' caps. The boys will wear vests, too, and pull their socks up over the bottoms of their pants to make them look like knickers. They have big hats. André found a seagull feather to put in his.

Tantes Yolande and Isabelle and Élise have been cooking all week. On Tante Yolande's kitchen table are huge pans of *pâté à la râpure* for the church supper after the parade. One is made with chicken, one with beef, the other with rabbit. "Sometimes they used venison, too," her mother says. "The Acadians had to survive on whatever was available, *ce qu'il y avait.* There were plenty of deer and rabbit in the woods, and potatoes and shallots to grow, and salt pork for flavor." Nicole looks at the brown crusts dotted with small cooked cubes of salt pork and salivates. Chicken *râpure* is her favorite.

Tante Yolande has made vests for her boys, too. Pierre, who has red cheeks and dark glinting eyes, walks around the kitchen in his. He wears tall black boots, and has hung a small pouch from his belt. Nicole looks at him shyly. He is the cutest boy she has ever seen, except that he is her cousin.

Soon they are all pulling things out of the closets and *le grenier* to put on the floats. An old spinning wheel, the butter churn from when Tante Isabelle and her mother were girls. Everyone is excited. Even frail old Grandmère, who sits in her rocker by the window, is smiling and eager. *"C'est une grande fête pour notre peuple,"* she says.

"It was horrible what the English did to the Acadians," her mother says. "We must never forget." Nicole has heard the story over and over, but today she pays more attention. They seem larger, more real, these ancestors, now that they are getting a parade to celebrate them.

"The soldiers separated families, sent people off on ships to any-where that would take them," her mother continues. "Thousands died. Many never saw their loved ones again."

"How did we all get back?"

"Some who survived the Deportation came back, years later, when things had settled down. Others, who had gone into hiding in New Brunswick, Prince Edward Island, and parts of Cape Breton did too. When they arrived, after years of hardship, they found their lands confiscated, their homes burned. They had to start all over, here, along St. Mary's Bay. Can you imagine what that must have been like?"

Her mother's face grows bitter with remembering, as if it had hap-pened to her, personally, just a few years before.

"And Evangeline, did she ever come back?"

"No. She spent her whole life looking for Gabriel. She was young and beautiful, and he was the handsomest young man in the village. They were very much in love when they were separated, so she wanted desperately to find him. She followed his trail all over the United States, from New England to Louisiana to the Great Lakes. Though many young men begged her to marry them, she never would. She never gave up hope that she would find Gabriel. Finally, she became a Sister of Mercy, and one day, when she was nursing the sick in an almshouse, she recognized him. He died in her arms."

Each time her mother tells the story it is sadder, more beautiful; her mother's face softer, more wistful. Her mother has read them Longfellow's poem with its stirring first line–"This is the forest primeval"–but Nicole prefers the way her mother tells it. It's the most romantic story Nicole has ever heard. Even more romantic than *Carmen*. It's a story of True Love. And some girl would get to be Evangeline. Some boy, Gabriel.

"Her real name was Emmeline La Biche," her mother says. "She's buried in Louisiana."

* * *

I am ten. The old apple tree in the yard, the wedge of blue ocean at the horizon pierce her with their beauty.

* * *

So many people have come! Already they line the highway where the parade will pass. Oncle Louie harnesses the two big work horses to the haywagon which he has decorated with several Acadian flags–the tricolor with the star of Mary–and a sign that reads: *L'Acadie 1755–1955*. Old Monsieur Boudreau brings out his two black oxen, and winds wild roses around their horns. And all the priests are there, even the Monseigneur in his scarlet vestments. During mass, he stands on a raised platform and moves his eyes over the crowd. "We must never forget our church, our language, and our history," he says. "They are what make us *Les Acadiens*. We have suffered as a people, but we have triumphed over our suffering."

Everyone who owns a car has it clean and decorated, ready for the parade. And the floats–some show the church in Grande Pré where the Acadians were rounded up; others with dikes show the lands along the Minas Basin the Acadians reclaimed from the sea before the English seized them. Several men and boys, dressed like British soldiers, pretend to guard a group of Acadians. Their expressions are rough and hateful. The Acadians look brave and sad.

What is her mother saying? *She* is to be Evangeline! And Pierre is to be Gabriel! They are to sit here, on this float, under these *papier mâché* trees that represent the Forest Primeval–*l'Acadie* in its happiest days. Could this really be happening?

The parade is starting. Everyone is singing, *Ave, Maris Stella, Dei Mater alma* . . . the national anthem of the Acadians. Hundreds of Acadians line the highway, all looking at her and Pierre as they pass, their mouths open in song. Her mother, her father, even her brothers are singing. Many of the old people are crying.

She looks at Pierre beside her, his hand almost touching hers. She sees herself following him through the woods, her heart sick with longing, knowing that he, too, searches for her. Other boys would ask for her hand but she would turn away, faithful and true. She finds him on a hospital bed, dying. She holds him in her arms and they kiss good-bye. Music swells.

* * *

I am ten. She tilts her head to one side, her face tragic. *I am an Acadian.*

Les Fils
(Sons)

Beverly Matherne

When June came back from Spain in '66,
and didn't get killed in Vietnam,
Daddy cooked jambalaya and red beans
and invited the whole town to celebrate.

As the band played "Blueberry Hill,"
and Dixie Beer and mistletoe hung in the air,
June whisked me to the dance floor,
said how pretty and smart I was,
I drank his words, like everyone else,
wanted to know all about Spain, bullfights,
and long legs under red flamenco skirts.

Outside, firecrackers sparked and shot,
cherry bombs exploded, cars blew their horns
bumper to bumper, the levee blazed
with bonfires, all the way to New Orleans.

After midnight mass, while Mama filled our bowls
with *andouille gumbo,** June was heading home
on a country lane, his high-school friend whizzing
skunk-ass drunk on Highway 61, he didn't see June coming.
The sheriff broke the news, nobody cared for hot *gumbo,*
dirty rice, candied yams, or pralines.

---

*French: A spicy "soup-like" dish of African-American origin made with *andouille* sausage (beef and pork), oysters, and *filé.* The use of *filé,* ground sassafras leaves, is of Native American origin.

The day after Christmas, mourners came, we drank black coffee
and stayed up with June's body through the night.
Ernie Boy, just learning to play pitch and catch with June,
cried, and threw up, and finally fell asleep
among the other little ones at the foot of the coffin.
My sister Shirley and I knelt beside June and prayed
and whispered about the smell of death in his body
and wondered whether everybody smelled it, but dared not say.

The next day, the pallbearers slid June's coffin into the mausoleum,
the way you slide a pan of bread into an oven.
The rain was cold and damp and drenched the scarlet ribbons
on the great sprays of red roses at the wall.

That spring, Mama started checking out books
on death and suffering. She devoted
herself to sorrow, the way she did
the stations of the cross during Lent.
She wore black, and put sorrow
in June's baby buggy, tucked his
quilt at its neck, and pushed
the buggy out of her bedroom,
through the kitchen, down the back steps,
through tobacco fields, and pastures,
into swamp waters, among wild, orange irises.

She dredged the buggy from the swamp,
pushed it back to the house, down the driveway,
onto Grand Point Lane, to River Road,
to St. Joseph's Church. She heaved, she sweated,
the wrinkles in her face stood taut.
She pulled the buggy up the church steps,
to the thick oak portal, up the aisle, to the altar,
did not genuflect, stared God straight in the eye,
and said "*Fils de putain!*" "You son of a bitch!"

The congregation froze, she turned
and waved her arms wildly,
"*Au diable avec tous de vous-autres!*"

"To hell with all of you!" She banged the buggy
down the altar steps, down the aisle to the Pietà,
Mary holding the dead Christ in her arms,
and in her supplicating hand, a crystal rosary
that fractured swords of light from the rose window above.

"You, you . . ." her voice cracked. She hurled
her arms around the neck of the sorrowful mother,
sobbed and sobbed, crumpled, as if suddenly shot.
Daddy ran to her, gathered her in his arms.

"It's okay, Mama. Let's go home, Mama."

Ten years later, when melanoma tumors
covered Ernie Boy's body, Mama got restless again,
she got that wild look in her eyes,
and searched closets and barns and fields.

"What are you looking for?" asked Daddy.
"Le maudit boghei de bébé,"
"That goddamned buggy," she said.

La Fabrique de Tabac
(Tobacco Harvest)

The late summer rain crashes
against the galvanized roof
of our old tobacco barn.
We draw in the silence
as we continue
to harvest.

Brothers, bare-chested in blue jeans,
beat fistfuls of withered leaves
against heavy oak barrels,

then rub the bouquet tips
to remove the last dust.

Rat-tat, rat-tat, rat-tat.
Tish-tish-tish, tish-tish-tish.
Rat-tat, tat-tat,
tish-tish-tish,
in time with the rain,
    the rhythm,
        and the custom.

Daddy wets the brittle leaves
with a fine mist,
to make them pliable.
Shpeare-shpeare-shpeare.

I sit with my aunts and sisters
around the deep *chaland**
piled with pungent tobacco.
Wearing pedal-pushers
and old T-shirts,
we take the tip of each leaf,
break the stem, rip it out,
making great spirals,
right hands over left,
    keeping the rhythm
        and the custom.

Good leaf halves
drape over our wrists,
like mops of hair
combed to one side;
discarded stems build
spaghetti mounds
on the ground.

---

*French: A deep, canoe-like structure into which damp tobacco leaves are arranged
for stem removal and leaf bundling.

Snap-swirl-plunk,
snap-swirl-plunk,
filling our barrels with

red beans and rice,
school shoes,
new underwear.

Our dirty faces
stream with sweat,
we swallow dust
and tobacco juice,
our raw fingers
will not heal
'til harvest is over.

Mama comes to the barn
with black coffee
and *beignets*,* big
with her twelfth child.

In this limbo,
lightning brings into focus
plough shafts
in the corners
of our family past;
our tractors,
        keeping the rhythm
                and the custom.

Outside,
the rain nourishes
the cypresses,
as it has done for millennia,
but I do defy
        this great con-form-ation:

---

*French: Fried dough covered with powdered sugar (New Orleans doughnuts).

"No, no, no,
never to marry,
never to know,

my Mama's silences,
her cries in the night.
     Hell,
          on the rhythm
             and the custom."

Half-

Julia Park Rodrigues

I am half, my children half again,
our blood thinning as our skin whitens,
the half-life of my culture one generation long.
My sisters don't recognize in me
the long cry back to the high hills
where I watched my sheep,
I wove bright patterns in wool,
a warm cape for the chill night.
They do not hear my strange song.
I have no accent now;
I look to my father to find it.
He rolls the words in his mouth
like a caress, a tiger licking its fur.
My children learn to dance as I never did.
They are patchwork creations—
blue eyes odd against the olive skin,
blonde hair sweeping over black eyes.
I hold them in the circle of my arms
and show them pictures of home.

La Frontera

Sheila Ortiz Taylor

A chapter from a memoir-in-progress

No," my mother would say, her eyes turning to black olives, "we're not Mexican. We're early Californians."

As proof, she could not speak Spanish. As proof, she married a gringo lawyer and left the familial house alongside the concrete bed of the Los Angeles River and went to live in the hills overlooking her mother's house.

Curiously enough this gringo lawyer had grown up in Tejas, developing an inexplicable and insatiable fondness for *la lengua*, which he learned from books and whoever would stop to talk with him either in Tejas or Nuestra Ciudad, and for *la comida*, which he ate in his mother-in-law's kitchen and in every Mexican restaurant in greater Los Angeles County.

Therefore, it was my gringo father who taught me and my sister a little Spanish, though he never had much success with my mother. Every evening they would sit down at the dining room table for Spanish lessons. My mother would read simpleminded stories out loud. Until she came to the word *hay,* which she always pronounced as if it meant horse fodder in English.

I remember the still of the evenings shattering like a plate against the wall when my father would shout in exasperation his pitiable mnenomic device. "That ain't hay!"

Where religion was concerned, there was another curious reversal.

My mother was a Catholic and never went to mass; my father was an atheist with a passionate interest in religions of all kinds, including even Rosicrucianism. It was he who took me to mass, when I went, though he would never kneel, let alone strike his breast lightly and humbly. No, he simply looked interested.

My mother had a grievance against the Pope because he did not believe in second marriages and she did. Once she told me the Pope fully believed my sister and I were illegitimate.

This was easier to comprehend than the part about being early Californians. How early, might have been the question. But we never asked questions when our mother's eyes turned to black olives, though, in fact, I had seen eyes like those before.

I am thinking of the eyes of my great-grandmother, Theresa Cabares Ortiz, as she stares out of a silver frame on a table in the house of my Aunt Frances. At four it seems clear to me my great-grandmother was an Indian, and when my Aunt Frances says with a faraway look that she was over six feet tall, I quietly take her as my ancestor and protector.

My mother is not looking at these photographs but is in the kitchen helping Aunt Maggie fix coffee. These aunts are my mother's aunts, daughters of the Indian maiden, my protector, who bore—with the assistance of my great-grandfather, Miguel—eight children: Della, my grandmother, Gullape, Julia, Frances, Madeline, Margaret, Florencio, and Ovaldo. They are all represented here, in this forest of silver frames.

But the two helping me to cookies and milk are Aunt Frances and Aunt Maggie, who have lived together all their lives in this little white frame house nestled onto all that is left of the Ortiz land grant, a small plot of ground near Chavez Ravine that in twenty years will seem essential to the developers of Dodger Stadium.

We eat our warm cookies. Aunt Maggie cooks; Aunt Frances tends the yard. Without Maggie, Frances would starve and without Frances, Maggie would be consumed by their flourishing garden. They sit side by side on the horsehair sofa. My mother sits in a dining room chair pulled up next to Aunt Frances, her favorite. They look alike.

My mother has told me the story of the day Aunt Frances arrived at her sister Della's house, the house of my grandmother, to ask a favor. "You have so many children," she said to her sister. "And I have none. Give me Juanita. She can have her own room, and sometimes a new dress from the Sears and Roebuck."

There was silence in the little house. My grandmother breathed in. "It is true I have many children," she said.

"Thirteen," reminded my aunt.

"Yes," agreed my grandmother. Her eye must have wandered over to Juanita, observed the dress made of a feed sack ("At least it's clean," she always said), marked the tense beautiful face about to flower into what even she could not guess. "But I do not have too many."

"She looks like me," said my Aunt Frances irrelevantly.

My mother sat quietly, in her relief and in her disappointment.

She passes the cookies to her aunt. Their lovely, brown flower faces shine in their pleasure at one another, while Aunt Maggie, her own brown face obliterated in chalk white face powder, beams. The sharp contrast between the white of her cheeks and the dark around her eyes makes her look like a benevolent owl. She hands me the cookies, says, "Oh honey girl."

Later we stand on their small porch, saying good-bye. Aunt Frances breaks off a twig from a hibiscus, hands it to my mother. "Put this in water," she tells her. "It will grow." From the car we look back at the two sisters: one brown, one white.

democracy

w. r. rodriguez

it was decided by the noisier of the people who are delegated such powers by those who just don't give a damn that america was not such a bad place after all it being july and who needs heat or hot water in this weather anyway and at night when everyone is out the tenements don't look quite so bad and who sees them in the daytime when everyone is sleeping away the heat and the war was good for the economy reducing unemployment by sending the men to war and creating jobs for the women who could work for the guys who did not go to war and who were making big bucks and the underground economy was providing enough luxury items to go round and so it was decided by the noisier of the people who are delegated such powers by those who just don't give a damn that america was not such a bad place after all to celebrate by doing what would have been done anyway as it had become a tradition for the fourth of july so each side sent out its scouts to chinatown and little italy to gather up as much firepower as could be bought or stolen and to smuggle it and stockpile it and to distribute it at just the right time which was sunset on the fourth of july when it was decided by the noisier of the people who are delegated such powers by those who just don't give a damn that america was not such a bad place after all to celebrate by doing what would have been done anyway as it had become a tradition and so the two armies of teenagers too young for draftcards or too mean by means of their criminal records for military service assumed positions on their respective rooftops the ruddy irish above their red-bricked tenements and the swarthy puerto ricans and leftover italians above their brown-bricked tenements and it was decided by the noisier of the people who are delegated such powers by those who just don't give a damn that america was not such a bad place after all to celebrate by doing what would have been done anyway as it had become a tradition that the war at home had begun which was signaled by a single rocket's red glare which began the shooting of bottle rockets and m-80s and strings of firecrackers and sizzlers which went on for hour after hour keeping the old ladies and babies awake and driving the dogs crazy they cowered in corners like shell-shocked veterans though casualties were light as the street was wide and nothing more than a sputtering rocket ever hit the other side mostly everything landed in the street which was by mutual decision a free fire zone and anyone or anything in it an enemy to both sides and mostly there was no one in it except a few unfortunate passersby unaware of this great fourth of july tradition and a line of parked cars which would be pockmarked by morning when the sidewalks were covered with red white and blue paper and the air reeked of sulfur and it was decided that everyone should cease fire and get some chow and shuteye and rest up for the night when it was decided by the noisier of the people who are delegated such powers by those who just don't give a damn that america was not such a bad place after all to celebrate by doing what would have been done anyway as it had become a tradition and the sun went up and down on the ceasefire and the irish and the puerto ricans and the leftover italian guys and their girls and their mothers and fathers and sisters and brothers got back out on our street to hang out to rock babies to gamble to play loud music to drink to gossip to party and to wait to wait to wait for a job for a baby for a draft notice which had become a tradition in not such a bad place after all

In Which I Speak My Name

Ana L. Ortiz de Montellano

W HEN I WAS nine my best friend's father, el Señor Barreda, a wine-maker who lived with his family in the elegant Polanco section of Mexico City, told me, *"Qué chasco, gringuita.* You use your name wrong, *sabes.* Ana Ortiz de Montellano means you are Ana Ortiz married to a man by the name of Montellano. You should say Ana Ortiz Lamb, your mother's name linked to your father's. That's how we do it here."

Something in me believed him. I had often sensed a hesitation when I said my name, a void that was covered over with ordinary politeness. The imposing man standing in front of me who seemed so sure of himself had filled the void with his set of words: "You use your name wrong."

Deep in the pit of my stomach something else stood up to him. Something pushed back. Something nameless and wordless.

He could not take my name away. As much as I longed for a simple name, I knew my last name was Ortiz de Montellano Lamb and not Ortiz Lamb no matter what he said. A picture of a girl with wistful eyes dressed as a *charra* and sitting on a wooden carousel horse taken when I was eight is signed Ana O. at the top, Ana Ortiz de M. at the bottom, and Ana Ortiz de Montellano on the back. Identity was already a problem for me.

From the height of my forty-six years, I call myself my father's grandfather's name. He's the one who brought "Ortiz de Montellano" from Andalucía. The town of Montellano stands immutable in stone between the mountain (Monte) and the plain (llano), though I remember only flat fields undulating with olive trees and a dusty street.

My mother and I walked to the church through the haze our feet kicked up. "There are no records," the sacristan shook his head. "Everything burned in the civil war. The castle of the duques de Montellano? Yes, see, what's left of it's over there."

It was only two walls of age-browned stone, shoulder high. The present inhabitants squawked at us from inside their aristocratic barnyard.

"Nonsense," my second cousin sniffed years later. "It's not a noble name. Nonsense."

I felt relief, but only for a minute. In this democratic age a noble name is an embarrassment. Yet the name speaks for itself. Its shape and origin are clear.

Ortiz de Montellano, Ortiz of Monte "hill or mountain," llano "plain." Ortiz of the mountain plains. My great-grandfather's name, I like it. I always have. Apt yet elusive. It fired my blood. After twenty years of using my husband's name, Taylor, I consciously took as mine the name I've had for generations. Because it fits.

Ortiz just stands. It has no "meaning." Montellano points to the foothills of the blue mountain ranges of Spain. And to the mountain plain, the plateau of my Native American ancestors whose names Montellano simulates because it is a riddle like their own names, a metaphor that joins a people to the land.

Simulates, but does not encompass. A chasm separates the two. I do not know a single one of my native names. Guadalupe Ruiz Ruiz, my grandmother, is as close as I come. Her parents, both surnamed Ruiz, called her Guadalupe after the mestiza incarnation of the Virgin Mary, the patroness of Mexico.

Like my own name Montellano, the Virgin of Guadalupe both opens the door to America's native people and blocks their origins. Her sacredness subsumes and hides that of our native mother Tonantzin and her many aspects.

Behind my grandmother rumors fly: "India, india," an identity my father affirms in his unpublished *Recuerdos de la infancia*, his mother's purported "memoires." Remembered fragments? Invented story? I'll never know.

Native roots? Yes. The brown-skinned, green-eyed Zapoteca great-great-grandmother called Acacia of my father's account? Why not.

My mother's family came from England. I've never been Ann Lamb.

My mother, yes–Thelma Milnes Lamb. Her mother was Violet Kilby, her grandmother Mercy Marshall, who migrated with her husband, Richard Kilby, from Somersetshire to Kansas.

Where the name Lamb leads, beyond its obvious meaning, is a mystery. My grandfather, John Lamb, raised by the same Aunt Loe that raised his father, forbade my mother to trace her roots which, so they say, are Scottish, French, and British. Ironically, the only family name I bear from my British side belongs to the one person I never met. My grandfather died before I was born.

I don't need to name my father to claim his name. For me it was mine before it was his. He was "papá." I was Ana Ortiz.

My mother is different. She mediated her culture and her family for me. When I pull on the name she comes with it. Or else it is an incongruous tag, Ortiz de Montellano Lamb. I almost lost it. Like losing a part of myself. So I struggle to hold it, to contain or be contained by Lamb. Sometimes it swallows me up and I am gone. Sometimes I lose track of it. Sometimes it shows up in unexpected places–like China. I was born in the Chinese year of the Lamb.

Ortiz de Montellano Lamb. Surely the name passes in the United States. The English language easily embraces foreign names just as American cuisine has embraced foreign foods–pizza, taco, croissant, sushi. We are the melting pot. We eat tacos.

Wait a minute. A taco at Taco John's is no longer a taco. It is a tahcoh, American chopped meat masquerading as Mexican, a pseudo-taco that comes wrapped in a picture of a little fat guy eternally wearing a sombrero twice as big as he is.

Like the stereotypical lazy Mexican, my mail leers back at me: Ana Oritz, Orpiz, de Montilino, de Montalban, Amantillado, Ortiz Demon Tellano, Ann Elland, and my favorites, Ana O. de la Marée (Ana of the Tides in French) and Ana Ode. No, the English language and the English world do not accept: they deform other cultures.

Ortiz de Montellano Lamb. The Spanish language fights off Lamb as one more sign of American imperialism attempting to take over the culture. It fights in vain. After all, a Lamb did subvert the ancient native religions, at least on the surface, just as "the American way" is slowly subverting Mexican culture.

This divided self, this map of islands held together by a shifting sea, the sea itself. This divided self, the mountain cleft in which I fall. I name you. You are me.

There is more. Ana lives here, the one who responded when others called, "Ana," the one who came to call herself Ana. I say Ana, a grandmother's name–not my grandmother–Jesus' grandmother, the mother of Mary.

Anita, I remember you now. Anita was my name for years. My old piano teacher says it just like she always has, "Anita, nena," the tender name that celebrates, holds, and loves me still. Anita, nena preciosa, you bless me when I'm open to you.

Ana Luisa. I discovered my middle name when I was a teenager. I called myself Anna Louise for a time. Louise sounds like Luis, the Mexican equivalent for Lewis. Maybe I needed that secret link to the male side of me, the side that would help me want to be me enough to endure the loneliness of separation. Welcome, Luis.

It is harder to welcome the bossy, superior side of Luis, the flip side of the coin. Painfully I acknowledge Luis after many years of splitting him off, of seeing him in my husband, my neighbor, my child, in all the self-righteous winemakers of the world. Now Luis and I battle it out. Sometimes we are at peace.

Flor de María is the unspoken part of my name embedded between the given names, Ana Luisa, and the surnames, Ortiz de Montellano Lamb. Place beyond pride, source of wonder, Flor de Maria, Flower of Mary, does not belong to me. She is God's and Goddess's child named for the obscure saint that graced the calendar on the day of her birth, October 5th, or perhaps for the Virgin herself.

Mary's flower, she is me and not me. She is my essence and the absence of what other people call me. And yet . . .

A name behind my name arises unbidden in my dreams. The cave beneath the "Monte," the "llano," and the Christian names opens. My native ancestors emerge. They name me in dreams, in the ancient language of symbols. In one dream, the small creature with the brown and green octagons etched on her shell escapes from the refrigerator of the frozen unconscious. In another, she speaks to me from a grocery store shelf. I turn her over. She will lay the eggs within her belly if I claim her.

Outside my dreams now, my kin do not scatter as they feed below me on the sandy bottom of the Caribbean. At the edge of a pond near my home one pauses, paw lifted, a muddy-colored one, to name me with her look before she dives deep. She is me when I swim in the air.

I speak my name that can be spoken: Ana Luisa Flor de María Ortiz de Montellano Lamb.

Spanish in Black

Beth Harry

W E HAVE one more day of salt and sand, and belly-fulls of deep-fried corn or plantain stuffed with peppered crab, the Spanish names for all these delicacies merging one into the other, the double *ll*s and double *rr*s interchangeable in the midst of a swirl of vowels. Except of course for coco, and I succeed in asking for a coconut with soft jelly; the word *suave* seems to work as the vendor we have approached smiles broadly from his round, shiny blackness and tells me in slow, clear Puerto Rican Spanish that he will be happy to search for the right coconut for me.

Sorting rapidly through a couple of dozen nuts piled into a large sink, he pauses to examine one heavily flecked with brown. Two or three expert swipes with his machete and he holds the nut up for me to see: *"Tá bien?"* ("Is this okay?") I have no idea really, but say, "sí, sí," and hope that the next and final swipe will prove his expert judgment. And so it does, revealing the soft, transparent jelly nestled around the jagged edges of the hole he has made in the top of the nut. He echoes my laughter as I grasp the nut in both hands and lift it to my face, refusing the striped red and white straw he offers.

The sweet, cool water brings a rush of nostalgia, and I am once more on the beach in Ocho Rios, with its frills of palm and the round green of almond, or at a row of coconut carts in Port of Spain, the Poui's brilliant yellow flaming its short-lived glory against the dry brownish-green of the savanna in May.

In a moment the scent of saltfish assails me, and, piling the juicy stew of bacalao, onion, and tomato sauce onto a large round fried bread, the vendor offers it to me open-faced, asking if I would prefer another slice on top to make a sandwich. I say no, but only because I crave the taste of the fish more than that of bread. He laughs again, saying that since I refused the straw for my coconut he guessed I would want my bacalao in the native style. I say, *¡"Sí, como no!"* ("Yes, of course!"), not admitting the happy coincidence.

We have just come from Loiza Aldea, the island's much ostracized enclave of its Black heritage. We had hoped to see some of the masquerade on this Saturday afternoon of the carnival week, but in the central plaza of the town dozens of festive kiosks stood bright and empty beneath the gradually blackening sky. The round-faced coconut vendor explains that we have already missed the parade, which took place on Thursday, but that the village will come alive tonight for the final festivities. He advises us to arrive before nine o'clock if we want to gain a parking spot anywhere near the central plaza of the town. We plan to follow his advice (God willing, rain permitting).

Headed for San Juan, Loiza well behind us, I try to describe to my American friend, Gloria, the spectacle we have missed—the thread of Africa woven into the soul of our islands, shining its power through the sounds and symbols of colonial centuries. In all the territories the heart of the carnival is the same—African gods with French, Spanish, or English names, their fiercely masked blackness embellished in a storm of color, on foot or on supple bamboo stilts, carrying the music on their shoulders, flowing to the rhythm of joy-in-life, in the name of the Father, Son, and Holy Spirit.

* * *

The sea curves to our right, the coastline alternating between small bays and long stretches of open sand. Soon we are in *Piñones*, an area known for its dance clubs, and on our left we notice several small concrete buildings with festive signs and large ads for Medalla beer and Bacardi rum. We mark one whose dance floor opens, wall-less, to a large, upwardly sloping yard.

We return to our small room at the guest house, and the rain pours until well after ten o'clock. When there is only drizzle left, we head once more for the rented Escort, agreeing to settle for the club in

Piñones, instead of trying to deal with Loiza's open-air festival in all this rain and mud.

Cars parked bumper to bumper along the sandy edge of the road, and the lilt of *"sí, sí, sí–sí yo quiero bailar"*, ("Yes, yes, yes, I do want to dance") announce the small, open-sided building where a hundred or more people stand in the yard, lean against the pillars, sit sideways on the low walls, and sway in never-ending circles around an uneven concrete floor. We find a spot to park, and, walking back about a hundred yards, weave through the scattered crowd toward the long, low building. The center of activity is the dance floor, while to one side an enclosed room holds the bar.

We head first for the bar, then, rum and Cokes in hand, go in search of a spot in the crowd that stands facing the dance floor. Gloria takes the lone chair at a table littered with half-empty bottles, and I settle for an edge of the low concrete wall that borders the dance floor. One leg propped up, the other stretching loosely down, I am at home in the soft, sharp swirl of bodies circling to the rapid merengue, at home in the flow of Spanish blackness.

I am here to dance, and two bodies on the floor catch my attention, both in soft white pants that sway with a more than common crispness to the swift merengue. The crispness of the merengue comes from the hips or not at all. It is the hips that lead, shoulders and feet follow.

As always, I am impatient. I need only to know whether the white pants are accompanied by a partner for the evening, and quickly discover that one is, the other is not. The one who is attached would have been my choice, a loose tank-top emphasizing the heavy blackness of his back and shoulders, his hips circling instead of moving sharply from left to right. He is all earth and flesh, and in love with his woman. The other is much younger–neat, black beard settled like feathers against round black cheeks, and his starched black cotton shirt says that he is here to impress. For me, he will be the perfect dancing partner, a show-off, skilled, and proud of it. He sees me, but looks away, and I know he is not really interested. I am too old for him. I let him be until the rum starts to burn in my veins, and then–to hell with it!

Catching his eye again, I mouth lightly across the three or four people who stand between us–*"¿Quiere bailar?"* ("Want to dance?") He smiles and nods, head tilted lightly to one side. There is a mild mockery in his smile. He is not surprised at my invitation; he knows I have been watching him and considers himself no less than worthy. Fine with me. All I want is to dance with someone who likes to perform, someone who is my equal.

We step toward each other, his hand reaching for mine, and move onto the floor. A perfectionist, and, no doubt, unsure of my abilities, he pauses for a couple of bars, waiting for the beginning of the phrase, then steps gently into the simplest of left-right paces. But, *tú sabes* (you know), all you have to do is set me to music and my hundred and fifty pounds is worth all of a feather! He learns this in an instant, and, smiling, moves quickly into a turn. Seeing that he does not have to guide me, and looking into my eyes for the first and only time, he laughs, *"Tá bien!"* ("Good!") I laugh with him.

The floor empties after each dance, and by the second or third bar of the next piece, is filled again. My partner in the black and white decides to alternate between me, his drink, and a buxom young woman; every fourth or fifth dance, he comes back to look for me. He is an impeccable partner, but we are both interested only in the dance. We share nothing else, not eyes, not breasts, not sentiments. Between dances, I scan the room for other possibilities.

He appears in the doorway of the bar, the glossy green of his shirt catching my eye. Glancing up, I see the hard, high cheekbones carved in leathery light-brown against rough borders of black beard.

My habit is simply to make sure the man has seen me, then wait for him to come to me. Nowadays it hurts that this is often no longer enough. I catch his eye and give a brief, half smiling nod, which he returns. Still he looks away, continuing to search the floor for the dancer that will interest him. He comes and goes from the room a couple of times and finally I decide, once more, to take the initiative. Two quick steps and I am unobtrusively by his side:

"¿Quiere bailar?"

A moment of surprise shows in his face, and then:

"¡Sí, como no!"

He is polite at least, not like the man in a touristy dance club two nights before who actually turned me down. He encircles me, a moment's pause for the bar he wants, and we begin the precise yet soft shift of hips that leads our feet into the turn. Immediately the deep-down structure of the dance flows through us, indescribable, defying analysis. His eyebrows and the corners of his mouth go sharply up in surprise as he nods admiringly at my skill. Turn now, swing out to the full length of his arm, under, once to the right, now to the left, then easy back into his arms:

"Tú eres una bailarina!"	("You're a ballerina!")
"Sí! Y tú también!"	("Yes, and you too!")
"¡No, solo por ti!"	("No, only because of you!")

These *"ti"*'s and *"tú"*'s *me encanta* (delight me), so intimate, so warm, yet I know that here in Puerto Rico they are commonplace. No matter, *me encanta tanto!* As the music ends, we step apart, prepared to return to our separate corners of the dance floor as is customary, but he hesitates, saying something. I do not catch the words, but recognize them as an invitation to continue.

"¡Ah, sí, como no!"

Como no, indeed! And we are off again–perhaps two more pieces, until, laughing at the sweat on both our faces and the pounding efforts of our hearts to keep pace with the rapid rhythm, we agree to part. I expect that he will return, since it was so perfect, but as I watch him step back through the doorway of the bar, then out into the yard, it comes to me that he will not. Later I see him standing, face averted, slightly hidden by the crowd, along the far side of the rectangle. I look away also, knowing that no matter how perfect my mastery of the merengue, he has seen the pockets of puffy flesh around my eyes and will not be back.

Soon I am in the commanding arms of a tall barrel-chested man, who I know, somehow, will not care about my eyes; perhaps he is not handsome enough. (I begin to note that, these days, the men who choose me are usually not those I would have chosen.) I relax in his arms since he does not allow the six or so inches of space between our bodies that would respect our strangeness, but holds me hard against his chest, his large, firm belly pressing against my breasts as we circle easily through the turns. As the music ends we step apart, and he promises to return.

Next, a tall, light-skinned man in a dark suit flashes the whiteness of polished dentures at me as we dance. He keeps time well and moves from the waist, but Africa is missing from his hips. He has learned this the way I am learning Spanish, from the mind, not from the heart and soul–not the way I learned to dance, standing on my father's feet, his movement flowing through me effortlessly.

As we circle to the far end of the dance floor, I exchange glances with my heavy-set, moustached partner from the previous dance, and we nod in mutual agreement that we will dance again. He understands the message of my muted smile—this one is too white for me!

The damp, salt air blends with my sweat and the night is mine. Here Spain has wound its way around our blackness—*iy me encanta, me encanta, me encanta!*

* * *

Two days later, at Consuela's house, I am on the other side of Puerto Rico. No more than fifteen miles from Loiza Aldea and the sea-side concrete club, I am in another world.

It hurts to hear the clearly enunciated tones of cultured, colonial Spanish in which my kind, silver-haired host, *tan bien educado* (so well educated), repudiates the people he does not know are mine. For him I am the *trigueña* (light-skinned one) whose class and education remove me from such darkness.

> *"La gente de Loiza Aldea es una gente muy vaga, no les gusta trabahar, solo les gustaes bailar y cantar y jugar por la playa. . . ."* ("The people of Loiza Aldea are a very lazy people, they don't like to work or do anything but dance and sing and play at the beach. . . .")

I succeed in pressing him for an explanation of their history, and learn the legend of Loiza Aldea:

> *The people of Loiza Aldea had been slaves to the Spaniards. They escaped from their masters in Old San Juan, and, fleeing through Condado and Isla Verde they arrived by river to the forests of Loiza where they hid, leaving behind forever the servitude of Spain. When their masters came to get them some huddled in a church, certain that* respeto a Dios *(respect for God) would not allow them to invade that sacred place. In truth, the Spaniards would not commit such sacrilege. Instead, they set fire to the old wooden house of God. Now there are nights when you can hear the screams of burning souls borne on the winds of Loiza Aldea. Meanwhile, those who lived remained for years in the woods of Loiza, hiding for their lives from the men who claimed ownership of their flesh. Today it is the rare person from Loiza Aldea who leaves the only sanctuary his people have known.*

My kindly host concedes that their years in hiding, their knowledge that the land they succeeded in holding on this island was their only security, and their rejection by the rest of society, might explain their otherwise inexplicable self-imposed isolation.

* * *

I am the polite guest, *tan bien educada como él* (as well educated as he), at his hospitable table, my skin still caressed by the warm Atlantic breeze that fills my ears not with screams of burning souls, but with the soft crisp rhythm of *"Sí, sí, sí–sí yo quiero bailar,"* and my soul with the binding blackness that, above all else in my colonial psyche, defines me.

Gotlib, Bombero

Barbara Mujica

E RNESTO GOTLIB lit a cigarette and put it to his lips. He inhaled fit-
fully then coughed. The cigarette tasted bitter. He rapped on the
side of the table with his right hand–an edgy little rap–and mashed
the cigarette in an ashtray.

"Rebeca!"

Rebeca knew what he was going to say.

"You think they've got to me yet?"

"You just asked me that two minutes ago."

"So? That was two minutes ago. What about now? You think
they've got to my name yet?"

"How could I know?"

Gotlib got up and looked out the window, but he did not see the
brown and gray rocks clutching at the sky like gnarled hands. The
rugged coastline extended in either direction in front of him. Waves
smashed against craggy knuckles, then shattered. Slivers of sea water
caught the fading light as they sprayed upward. Gotlib sat down in a
different chair and lit a new cigarette.

"Just tell me what you think."

Miriam came in with dishes and started to set the table.

"Move your arm, please, papá. It's in the way."

Gotlib moved his arm off the table so that Miriam could put down
a dish.

"I don't feel like having tea today," he said.

"Teolinda baked *alfajores*."

"I know, sweetheart. I'm just not in the mood. My mind's not on food."

"But you should eat something, papá."

Gotlib shook his head.

Miriam set a teacup by his dish anyway. He would change his mind, she thought. Papá loved the sticky, nut-filled cookies that the Argentine cook prepared.

"Come on, papá," she coaxed. "It's five o'clock."

Miriam finished setting the table and went back into the kitchen.

"Eat something," said Rebeca. "Whether you have a cup of tea or not won't influence their decision either way."

Ernesto sighed. "You think they've got to me yet?"

Rebeca shook her head. "God knows. How many of you were there?"

"Seven, I think. . . . Me, López . . . let's see . . . Martinelli . . . that's three . . . Valenzuela . . . that's four. . . ."

"What about Tomich? Wasn't he coming up this time?"

Miriam had come back with a plate of *alfajores*. "Marcela Tomich told me they were going back to Santiago, mamá. She said her father wasn't a candidate."

"So that's only four," said Rebeca. She tried to make her voice soothing as she reached over and squeezed her husband's hand. "One less to worry about."

"No," said Gotlib. "I never counted Tomich. I knew they were leaving Antofagasta. His brother is in Santiago. They have a business there."

"Well, so . . . four. López, Martinelli, Valenzuela, and you."

"There's Petersen. He'll have a good chance. They're always impressed with an English name."

"Swedish."

"Whatever. Just as long as it's not Jewish. Just as long as it's not Rosental or Vainberg or Gotlib or something."

"Ernesto, stop it. This is Antofagasta, Chile. This is not Nazi Germany."

"They've never elected a Jew. Never!"

It was true. There had never been a Jew in the Volunteer Fire Department of Antofagasta.

"Papá, don't get yourself worked up!"

But Gotlib was worked up. Tonight the entire department had met to vote. Only the most respected men in the city were invited to join the brigade, and since boyhood Gotlib had dreamed of being a fireman, a *bombero*.

As a child he had watched the incandescent fire engines racing down the streets. On either side, the proud flame tamers stood tense and bold. When they reached the burning building, they yanked out their hoses and shoved their ladders up against the blistering walls, then hurled themselves into the asphyxiating black haze to pull out endangered men, women, children, even pets. It was like a movie.

Don Mauro Mujica had been head of the brigade for as long as Gotlib could remember. A successful businessman who had rebuilt the family fortune that his mother had squandered on horses, Don Mauro had a reputation for tough-mindedness and hard-dealing. At work and at the club he was reserved. He wore English-cut suits and smoked imported cigarettes. But the sound of the siren transformed him. The mask fell and the cool caution that characterized his business style gave way to temerity. He rushed into the flames, balancing on teetering beams, yanking out victims, securing walls, hauling up hose, yelling orders. At a fire, old Don Mauro–he had seemed old to Gotlib back then, although he must have been in his forties–turned bold and resolute. He had grit. He led his men into the most vicious fires. They respected him, and they elected him chief term after term.

After a victory, the fire trucks would return to the station, moving slowly now, but sirens screeching, as the townspeople gathered on corners to wave white handkerchiefs and hail the fire fighters as heroes.

On September 18, Independence Day, and on other festive occasions as well, the firemen paraded through town in their gleaming engines, led by the fire chief in his bright red car. Don Mauro was at the height of glory as he led the noisy train with his young son seated beside him. Sometimes Maurito would ride with his father to a fire on an engine. Gotlib was about eight or ten when he began to envy Maurito, who was the same age as he. Gotlib had longed to sit on one of those huge, gleaming trucks just once–not beside his father, of course, for his own father could never be a fireman. But by that time, he had already realized that he was not of the same breed as the tall, fair, slim boy with the wide smile, whose admittance into the elite brigade was a foregone conclusion.

Sometimes Gotlib hung around the fire station on a Sunday. Mauro Senior would have the victrola on, and the firemen, many of them of Italian extraction, would listen to a tenor sing "Santa Lucia." Don Mauro was at ease on those Sunday afternoons, surrounded by his men. He poured burgundy from his uncle's vineyards while Maurito, in those silly shorts that all schoolboys wore and unanimously hated, galloped around the station house. Then someone would coax, *"¡Canta, Maurito!"* and the others would chant, *"¡Canta! ¡Canta!"* They kept a huge Mexican hat with silver trimmings on a peg in the office and Maurito would put it on and sing *"Jalisco, no te rajes."* All the men would laugh, not only because they thought Mexican songs were hilarious, but because Maurito was the fire chief's son and he was a great little clown. Ernestito would laugh with them, but he would keep to the side, a little out of the way. No one ever told him to go home, but no one ever invited him to come again next Sunday, either. Someday, he thought, Maurito would be a fire chief just like his father.

"I suppose there isn't much of a chance," Gotlib was saying.

"It's an honor even to be a candidate, Ernesto. And to have been nominated by Mauro Mujica, the chief's son!"

"That's right, papá," said Miriam. "I'd say you stand a very good chance."

"So what do you think? You think they've got to me yet?"

Rebeca would have preferred to have her tea and *alfajores* and not talk about it anymore, but she knew that her husband's self-esteem was riding on this vote and that his nerves would not let his mind off the subject.

"Let's see . . . Tomich is going to Santiago . . . Santamaría . . . He'll get in . . . He's Don Mauro's son-in-law, and his father has been a *bombero* for years . . . That makes six . . ."

"What about Carrera?" asked Miriam.

"That's it, Carrera! Good girl, Miriam. How could I forget Carrera?"

Rebeca smiled at her husband. His daughters were the most important thing in his life, far more important than this ridiculous vote. That's why, Rebeca thought, it was a shame he was making himself so sick over this business.

And yet, she understood. To be a fireman was to be one of them.

"Well, if they went in alphabetical order, they took Carrera first, then Gotlib, then López, Santamaría, no, Martinelli, Petersen, Santamaría, Valenzuela. They started at three thirty . . . It's after five now . . . They've already considered your candidacy, Ernesto. They've probably all gone home for tea. . . ."

"Sometimes the debates go on into the night. . . ."

Rebeca sighed.

"What if they didn't go in alphabetical order?" Gotlib said.

Rebeca stood up and went to call her other two daughters. "Tea, girls! Teolinda made *alfajores!*"

She sat down again and turned to her husband.

"If they didn't go in alphabetical order, then I don't know."

"So," said Gotlib heavily, "maybe it's already been decided."

"Maybe. So go ahead and eat."

She poured tea into his cup. Two giggling teenage girls collided with each other and the railing on the stairs. They tumbled into the dining room. One kissed Gotlib on the forehead, the other, on the cheek.

"*¡Hola, papá!* How's the future fire chief?"

"Don't make jokes, Emi," said Miriam. "Papá's nervous."

"Nothing to be nervous about," said Emilia. "You're as good as elected."

"They probably laughed themselves silly, to think a Jew wanted to be a fireman," said Gotlib.

Miriam suppressed a guffaw. "C'mon, papá," said Sara. "Don't get melodramatic."

This time Miriam laughed out loud. "After all this family has been through, papá! Do you really think the Gotlibs of Antofagasta will fall apart if you don't get elected to the fire brigade?"

Gotlib smiled and squeezed her hand. He knew she was right.

Logic told him she was right. But there was more to it than that.

* * *

The Gotlibs had been in Antofagasta for over forty years. Ernesto's father Joseph Gottlieb had come to Chile right before the war. Hitler was showing his fangs, and Joseph's brother Herman, who had seen his neighbors slashed with broken glass, insisted that to wait would be fatal. Joseph didn't think so. He had started out as a tailor, but had expanded into ready-to-wear. He had a shrewd head for money and had built up a thriving business, importing cheap goods from Italy and turning huge profits. He had six stores in Munich alone. To up and leave everything behind would be devastating. Herman said that if Joseph didn't go, he would go alone. He had friends in Switzerland, and he could get false documents.

Herman did not need to harp. Events convinced Joseph that his brother was right. Late one night in September hoodlums hurled a bottle filled with blood through Herman's front window. The crash was deafening. Shards of glass flew crazily through the room. They mixed with crimson on the opposite wall and slid, carried by streams of blood, down the painted surface onto the floor, where red and glass formed splintery pools that glistened eerily. Trembling, Herman called for his brother. Joseph stood and looked for a long time. Then he held his brother Herman in his arms and both men cried.

Joseph returned home and helped his pregnant wife pack two light bags. They took a change of clothes, a few items of jewelry that had been in the family for generations, and pictures of their parents. Joseph went to the store on Winkler Street and took the money out of the safe. Then he straightened lovingly the stacks of sweaters, the rows of jackets, the scarves, the wool stockings. Before he left, he turned out the light. Joseph felt as though a cleaver were lodged in his chest.

There was hardly time to say good-bye to cousins and friends.

In the train, Joseph's wrists went limp and he felt nauseated, as though he were sinking into a sea of vomit. Eventually his wretchedness became so intense that he stopped feeling it. He looked out the window at the tiny farms and drab sky, and allowed himself to be lulled to sleep by the monotony of the movement and the landscape.

Herman, Joseph, and Joseph's wife Constanza arrived in Le Havre before dawn. They got on the first ship crossing the Atlantic in which there were accommodations available. They did not ask where it was going because it didn't matter. Later, they found out that they were headed for South America, and thought that this was as good a destination as any.

The crossing was smooth, but Constanza's pregnancy made it tedious. Constanza was at the stage in which even the smell of fresh cooked vegetables made her ill. The odor of fuel and seawater sickened her to the point of paralysis. The cramped cabin and the rocking of the vessel–slight though it was–made her feel as though she were caught in a rapidly spinning canister. She did not complain, but in those rare moments in which her head was clear, she saw herself running through a pasture hand in hand with the child that would soon be born. Under her feet she imagined the grass to be soft and dry.

The first port of call was Rio de Janeiro. There was a crowd of dark faces at the docks and Joseph thought that maybe they had detoured to Africa, although the steward assured him that he was in Brazil. The swarm of black and red and green and yellow seemed foreign and frightening to Joseph. Multitudes of Negroes in brightly colored shirts . . . ripe produce in crates and baskets . . . throbbing rhythms of portside musicians . . . smells both pungent and rancid . . . Joseph knew that Constanza needed fresh air and solid ground, but he and Herman decided to stay on board until the next stop: Buenos Aires.

Argentina appealed to them. There was already a German-speaking Jewish population there. There would be synagogues and schools for the children. But a man on the boat named Eisenberg said that there was more money to be made in Chile, and besides, Chileans were tolerant of Jews. Argentina was full of Italians, and who knew what to expect of them? There were Italians in Chile, too, but they were a small minority and besides, most of them were from earlier immigrations and so had fewer ties to the homeland. In Buenos Aires, according to Eisenberg, not only were there more Italian surnames than Spanish, but there were sections where the only language spoken was Italian.

Joseph and Herman considered the situation. Mussolini had helped Hitler bolster Franco in the Spanish Civil War, and now there was talk of a formal Rome-Berlin Axis. Where there were Italians with close and recent ties to Italy, there would be anti-Semitism, the brothers reasoned. Eisenberg said that he had a cousin in the north of Chile, where there were lucrative copper mines. It was an area of vast wealth that attracted thousands of Chileans from other cities every year, and this new, affluent population needed goods: clothes, food, furniture, medicines. There was plenty of cash, but nothing grew or was manufactured in the north. Everything had to be brought in from outside. It was, Eisenberg said, a land of opportunity for a shrewd businessman.

Joseph and Herman disembarked in Valparaíso. There, they contacted relatives of friends who recommended them to a German wholesaler in Antofagasta who supplied the mines at Chuquicamata. His name was Uwe Rissel.

Joseph went to work for Herr Rissel, but Herman, who had been trained as an engineer, found work at the mines. Joseph was an excellent salesman, with years of experience, and although he was not pleased with the idea of working for another man, news from relatives in Europe made it clear that he was lucky to be alive and working at all.

Rissel had access to a huge inventory; he sold everything from radios to toothpaste, from refrigerators to perfume, from auto parts to ladies' panties, from penny novels to screw drivers. His orders tripled and quadrupled within a year of hiring Joseph. By then, Constanza had had a baby girl named Ana Noemí, and Joseph was glad of the increased commission that Rissel gave him.

Joseph learned Spanish quickly. At night he listened to soap operas on the radio and practiced pronouncing the names of the characters in front of the mirror: Roberto . . . Rrroberto . . . Raúl . . . Rrraúl . . . He bought a dictionary and read lists of words out loud to Ana Noemí. (When she started babbling, he discontinued the practice for fear she would imitate his imperfect pronunciation.) He went to the local school and offered to pay a young teacher by the hour to give him lessons. The fellow gave him a child's book of grammar exercises and every afternoon during *siesta,* Joseph would write them out, letter by letter: *Tú vas. Quiero que tú vayas. Tú vienes. Quiero que tú vengas.*

Joseph had a knack for convincing the miners that they desperately needed products that they had never even heard of. He sent neighborhood children to the mine stores to ask for Milagro de Lourdes Elexir or Melena de Oro Shampoo, products unknown in Antofagasta. A few days later, he appeared at the store announcing that he was the sole representative for Milagro de Lourdes and Melena de Oro.

In the meantime, Herman had begun investing in the mines. With the demand for metals caused by the war, he was soon making money by the fistful. He was the first of the two brothers to buy a home–a small, pink villa by the beach, with a spectacular view of the sea from the living room and a spectacular view of the mountains from the master bedroom. Within a few years, he married a Chilean-born girl named Ester Anita Shapiro, and they had two children, Jaime and Meyer.

Joseph's son Ernst was born a year and a half after Ana Noemí and a month after his brother's son Jaime. Joseph and Constanza named their son Ernst Heinrich: Ernst after Constanza's father, who had died of cancer years before, and Heinrich, after a Nazi torturer.

The child's middle name was a compromise. Rissel admired Hitler, although that did not prevent him from hiring shrewd Jews to make money for him. When he heard that Gottlieb's wife was expecting, he demanded that his employee name the baby Adolph. Joseph refused, arguing that tradition dictated that he name their son after a deceased relative. Rissel's color rose. It was a little thing to ask in return for all he had done for Gottlieb, he said. He might just have to look for another sales manager. Gottlieb thought that Rissel was bluffing. The German had never made as much money as now. But Joseph Gottlieb could not take a chance. As a conciliatory gesture, he gave the boy a middle name that was acceptable to his boss.

Heinrich Himmler was just beginning to make a name for himself in Europe as head of the *Schutzstaffel,* or "Black Shirts," but with luck, not even the boy himself would ever associate the Nazi's name with his own. Joseph had had an Uncle Heinrich who had died years before. Officially, Ernst Heinrich was named after him.

By the time he was four, Ernst was accompanying his father to Rissel's. By the time he was seven, it was he who went pestering store managers for the products that his father was promoting. At nine, Ernst Gottlieb had mastered one of the fundamental principles of business: create a need.

Joseph got his big chance when Chile broke relations with the Axis in 1943. German nationals were being forced out of the country and Rissel had to sell cheap. Joseph got a loan from his brother and took over Rissel, S. A. He renamed the firm Antofagasta Wholesalers, the most neutral, un-Germanic tag he could think of. Constanza stayed home and took care of the children and kept the books while Joseph hustled. By the late 1950s, Gottlieb had built Antofagasta Wholesalers into one of the biggest companies in the country.

Herman prospered as well. He had invested his earnings in beach-front property and was now the owner of houses, apartment buildings, and a hotel. He urged Joseph to put his money into land, but Joseph preferred to stuff cash into the mattress. "Where I can get at it easily if I need it," he said. Herman thought his brother was thinking like a Chilean peasant instead of like a clever European businessman, but nothing he said made Joseph change his mind.

"This isn't Germany," Herman prodded. "It's not like you'll have to make a quick getaway."

Joseph accumulated sacks and sacks of *escudos*. Soon there were too many to fit in the mattress, so he hid money behind pictures, under floorboards, in wells, in holes dug beside trees, and in a secret compartment under the roosts in the chicken coop. When Chile went into an economic crisis and changed from *escudos* to *pesos,* Joseph was left with bags of money that wasn't worth the paper it was printed on.

Joseph's son Ernst was a teenager when he started writing his name G-o-t-l-i-b to make it conform to its Spanish pronunciation. At the same time, he changed his given names to Ernesto Enrique. Joseph did not put up a fight. In fact, he was glad. At last, he was done with Himmler once and for all.

Ernesto was articulate about his identity. He was a Chilean, he said, not a German, and he didn't want anyone mistaking him for a foreigner. He was proud of Chile, which had taken in thousands of Jewish immigrants before, during, and after the war. It was thanks to Chile's open-arms policy toward refugees that, instead of being thrown into a gas chamber, he had been educated in good private schools and had studied business at the Catholic University of Valparaíso. (Wealthy Jews, like wealthy masons and other renegades, had a tacit working relationship with the Jesuit fathers. The Catholic schools were the best in the country. Jews and Masons supported them generously; in return, the priests educated the infidels' sons. Each side kept out of the other's hair and neither asked too many questions.)

By the early sixties Ernesto had completed his degree and gone into his father's business. He no longer loved Chile because it had taken in immigrants during perilous times; he loved Chile because he was Chilean. Unlike his father, he spoke Spanish without an accent and with dialectal variants; he said *uté* instead of *usted,* *etái* instead of *estás, paco* instead of *policía, porotos* instead of *frijoles,* and *living* instead of *sala.* He ate *empanadas* on Sunday afternoons and had tea every day at five. Yet, Ernesto Gotlib sensed that he didn't quite fit in. No one had ever said anything to him about being Jewish, but at Colegio San Luis he had felt pangs of embarrassment in the locker room, when his circumcised penis was in full view. He felt awkward at Mass and in religion class. The part of the Credo about "the one true faith . . ." mortified him. The first time he had to line up with the other little boys for confession with Father Reblando, he lost his composure and had to be sent home. He was certain that Father Reblando was going to call him an anti-Christ and blame him for the death of Jesus. After that, Joseph arranged for his son to be excused from some of the rites. Joseph had made sizable contributions to the school, and the fathers agreed to the arrangement. They were a tolerant bunch.

As a university student, Ernesto had been invited to parties, and friends often had him to dinner—and sometimes even to baptisms, first communions, and weddings. But whenever a classmate introduced him to his parents, he suspected that they were thinking, "Ah . . . Ernesto Gotlib, the Jew."

Ernesto noticed, or thought he noticed, that his friends never presented him to their sisters.

After college, when young men began to join their fathers' clubs—the Club de la Nación, the Auto Club, the Club Italiano—he began to feel excluded. Joseph belonged to the Unión Hebraica, and that was all right, but Ernesto yearned to attend dances at the Alianza Italo-Española, where the fire chief's pretty daughter Graciela rocked and rolled with the sons of the men who formed the elite of Antofagasta: the firemen. To Ernesto's mind, those boys were real Chileans. Some of them had foreign grandparents—Martinelli, Petersen, López (whose grandmother was Yugoslavian)—but Gotlib was sure that they never felt like outsiders. Gotlib felt like an outsider because Gotlib was a Jew.

Joseph and Herman Gottlieb did not share Ernesto's discomfort. They knew who they were: German Jews who had fled Germany in order to save their lives. They spoke German or Yiddish at home and walked down the street with yarmulkes on their heads on Friday nights. On the sabbath their wives lit candles. They were grateful to their new country for taking them in, but they knew that they were foreigners. They were perfectly content to have dinner at the Unión Hebraica on Sunday night, and they encouraged their sons to attend dances there, make friends with Jewish girls, and settle down.

After the switch from *escudos* to *pesos* Herman lent Joseph money to rebuild his financial base. This time, he invested in gold. Herman was rich and Joseph would eventually be rich again, but what was money for, Joseph asked Herman, if not to pass on to children and grandchildren? The Gottliebs looked at their progeny and smiled.

But in 1970 the world of Joseph and Herman Gottlieb shattered.

Salvador Allende was a candidate for president. At first, Joseph supported Allende. He thought that the socialists would revitalize Chilean politics, clearing out the old guard and making way for a new, more progressive government. But Herman was wary of the talk of nationalization. When Allende was elected president by a narrow plurality, Herman's fears mushroomed. Although the majority of the voters had not supported Allende, the new chief of state set out to revamp Chilean society, expropriating industries–including the mines.

Herman lost everything. He had invested heavily in copper and now, although the government had promised compensation, he was bankrupt. Joseph would have been pleased to give his brother money, but money was not the real problem. Herman's life was in shambles. He had started from scratch in Germany and built a business only to lose it. He had started from scratch again in Chile, and now the prospect of starting over was overwhelming. Herman was no longer a young man. The sleeplessness was wearing him down. The strain showed on his brow and in his voice, which frequently cracked and trailed off. Herman was sinking into depression.

Violence erupted. Rock-throwing mobs attacked anyone wearing a business suit. Herman and Joseph Gottlieb did not consider themselves perpetrators of economic crimes. They had not inherited their fortunes; they had earned them through sweat and ingenuity. But the rabble-rousers saw no difference between Joseph and Herman Gottlieb and the idle rich.

Rumors spread of government hit lists. Herman and Joseph had the impression that they were reliving a nightmare. Herman became afraid to go outside, not only because thugs and hoodlums threw potatoes with razor blades embedded in them at passers-by, but because squatters were taking over homes. It was dangerous to leave a house unguarded, even for a few hours. And who knew if you could trust your servants?

In the coming months, inflation soared, strikes spread. In the stores, there was no kosher meat or any other kind of meat. For a ration of rice, housewives queued up from five o'clock in the morning once a week, on Thursdays. Before long, women were beating their empty pots in the plaza to protest the scarcity of food. Toilet paper became a luxury item. Shoes were unbuyable. Reports spread that Chile, an important manufacturer of leather goods, was sending its shoes to Cuba. Herman bowed his head and with a meat cleaver slashed the toes out of the shoes of his grandson, Jacobo. Meyer's boy was growing, Herman explained as though he had to justify his actions. Jacobo's little foot needed room.

It was a September night when a bottle filled with blood crashed through Herman's front window and shattered against the opposite wall, splashing crimson over the lamp, the sofa, the cream-colored carpet. Herman had been sitting at the piano, picking out a polka he remembered from childhood.

Herman did not move. He sat for a long, long time and watched the blood stream down the wall before he felt his muscles contract and his throat grow tight and dry. His head ached terribly. He had lived this scene before. He wanted to cry, but he didn't. He just sat, watching the blood serpent creep slowly, slowly down the wall.

When Herman's wife Ester came back from visiting with Constanza that afternoon, she found the living room a wreck. In the bedroom, she found her husband sprawled over the bed, his head blown to bits, teeth and hair stuck to walls and furniture, and blood, great pools of viscous, black-red blood, seeping through the white bedclothes onto the floor. His note said simply that he had been through it all once before. He couldn't bear to go through it again.

On September 11, 1973, Allende fell. Much of the country rejoiced, but Ernesto Gotlib was in mourning. His father Joseph had died only two days before. The doctors said it was a heart condition, but Ernesto knew it was grief. Joseph and Herman had always been inseparable.

By then, Ernesto was married and all three of his daughters had been born. He, like many others who had opposed Allende, assumed that the country would return to democracy. When it did not, he ranted at the dinner table and drew up protests that he read at meetings of the brotherhood of the Unión Hebraica. But with time, his furor cooled. Pinochet was a dictator, but the country was prospering. Store shelves were filled with imported goods and there was a huge demand for everything from radios to toothpaste, from refrigerators to perfume. . . . Pinochet wouldn't last, he told himself, and in the meantime he, Ernesto, was cleaning up. He had inherited his father's business, and ran it with the expertise of a person who knew how to sell before he knew how to walk.

Gotlib was a rich man. He owned not only Antofagasta Wholesalers, but retail stores as well. And he did not hide his money in the mattress. He invested it. Over the years, he accumulated houses, office buildings, an interest in a shipping company, and a tourist boat. He had three beautiful daughters and a wonderful wife. But still, something was missing.

Gotlib had influence because he had money, but the pangs of the locker room had never subsided. Did those men who were recognized as the city leaders appreciate his merits, he wondered, or did they consider him a pushy, crafty, upstart Jew? In the middle of the night, as the waves rolled softly onto the beach with a steady swish, Ernesto felt the eyes of his classmates on his circumcised penis. . . . He heard the voice of Father Reblando. . . . He saw the soft, blond curls of Graciela, the fire chief's daughter, resting on the lapel of . . . Aníbal López.

Now that his father and uncle were dead, Gotlib had loosened his ties with the Jewish European community in Chile. After the war and during the following years, waves of Jews arrived from Germany, France, England. But they were not like Gotlib. They were foreigners. Gotlib was Chilean born. Not only for himself, he felt, but for his dead father and uncle, he needed to be accepted as a real Chilean. He needed to validate their choice. He needed a sign for all the world to see that he was not only a citizen, but the best of citizens. He needed to be a fireman.

* * *

Miriam put down the tray of breads and cakes and massaged her father's shoulders.

She's a beautiful girl, thought Gotlib. "It's for her, for all of them . . . that I want this so much," he said to himself. "So that they shouldn't feel like outsiders. So that they should be comfortable mingling with the best of them."

Of his three daughters, Miriam was the one to whom he felt closest. Emilia, the eldest, was exotic and talented. She had huge brown eyes and curly chestnut hair that framed her darkish face, and she played the piano like Artur Rubinstein. (Well, Gotlib conceded privately, maybe not quite like Artur Rubinstein.) Gotlib smiled at his first-born child, and she smiled back at him.

Sara, the youngest, was pert and sassy. The beneficiary of the battles Gotlib had fought with Emilia and Miriam and lost, Sara was allowed to wear make-up at thirteen and go on overnights with the Girl

Scouts of Antofagasta. Her sisters had wanted to do those things; he and Rebeca had said no, but wound up giving in. By the time Sara was a senior member of Antofagasta Troop 1034 and began wearing lipstick, her parents had stopped resisting. Even so, Sara had grown into a fairly well-behaved girl, although more spirited and stronger-willed than her sisters. She had long light-brown hair that she refused to cut, although Rebeca said it looked messy, and a few barely-there freckles that she tried to cover up with make-up, even though Gotlib said they were cute.

Miriam was taller and thinner than her sisters. She had soft, blond, shoulder-length hair and eyes whose irises were blue on the rim and amber within. Her facial structure was less than perfect, but Miriam had an incandescence that brightened a room. Gotlib felt her fingers knead and sooth the tight muscles of his neck, and knew that God had truly blessed him. It was, perhaps, too much to want to be a fireman, too.

Sara was speaking: "It's not the end of the world if you don't get in."

"She's right, of course, papá," confirmed Miriam.

"Anyhow," said Emi, "if you don't make it this time, maybe somebody will nominate you again next year."

Gotlib basked in his children's love for a moment.

"You know," he said, shaking his head, "it gives me a funny feeling to think that at this very moment they may be talking about me. They may be deciding about me."

"Probably not," said Rebeca. "They probably decided hours ago."

But Rebeca was wrong. At the station house, Don Mauro had just presented Gotlib's name.

"Any discussion?"

"A good man," said Don Dionisio. "In spirit he's been one of us for a long time. Since he was a kid, really."

"Anything else?" prodded Don Mauro.

No one made a move to speak. Don Ricardo looked rather sour. He was getting hungry and he wanted to go home.

Don Héctor scratched his eyebrow out of boredom.

Don Ignacio shook his head, but said nothing.

Don Mauro waited in silence for someone to come forward. Don Agustín yawned. They had been at it for a long time.

"Then let's vote."

The men placed their ballots in the box. When they were done, Don Alejandro, the brigade secretary, read them aloud, one by one.

* * *

Gotlib had finished tea, but he and Miriam remained at the table talking. Rebeca sat with them a while, then got up to get her sewing; with three girls in the family, there was always something to mend. Teolinda was clearing the table. Sara and Emilia had gone upstairs, but bolted down when they heard the knock at the door.

Gotlib jumped up, then forced himself to sit back down. One of the servants would get it.

Virginia, Teolinda's niece, came into the room.

"Señor," she said, "there are two gentlemen here to see you."

"Who?" Gotlib's voice was controlled. He was making a very great effort not to appear upset.

"Don Mauro and his son."

Gotlib took a short, tight breath. He hadn't expected a visit. He had expected a telephone call.

"Have them come in," said Rebeca.

"I'll see them in my study," said Gotlib.

But Don Mauro was peeping through the dining-room door.

It was an indecorous thing for the fire chief to do, and Gotlib was confused. But Don Mauro was grinning widely and the younger Mujica was bounding toward Gotlib as though he couldn't wait another instant. Mauro–the son–embraced Gotlib before a word was spoken.

"Congratulations, Ernesto," said Don Mauro.

"Congratulations, *compadre!* Welcome to the *bomberos!*" The younger Mauro's smile was even bigger and warmer than his father's.

Gotlib was fighting back the tears, but Miriam was making no pretense to self-control. She was crying openly. Sara and Emilia were laughing.

"See, papá?" giggled Sara. "What did I tell you?"

Emilia, then Sara, then Miriam kissed their father. Rebeca was last of all.

Gotlib hugged his wife close as he turned to Don Mauro and his son.

He opened his mouth to speak, but his throat was tight. Finally he said, "Thank you . . . thank you . . ."

Rebeca was the first one to regain her composure.

"May I offer you some tea and *alfajores?*"

"Thank you, but we can't stay," said Don Mauro.

"Can you . . . can you tell me if there was a lot of discussion?" asked Gotlib.

"No," said Don Mauro. "There was no discussion."

"Everyone knows you, Ernesto. Christ, you've been hanging around the station since you were in short pants. You've always been part of the *bomberos*. That's what they said . . . that you've always been one of us. It was unanimous."

"Unanimous! But didn't they mention . . . anything else?"

"No."

"Nobody brought up . . . anything else?"

Father and son both looked puzzled.

"No," said the younger Mauro. "Nothing."

Rebeca felt a new surge of joy. She got up, excused herself and went into the kitchen. She did not want to cry in front of her guests. Miriam got up, too, to keep from laughing. "Silly old papá," she said to herself.

Gotlib smiled, but a new worry was gnawing at his brain. I wonder if they really wanted me, he thought, or if they just thought a token Jewish name would look nice on the roster.

ESSAY

Exotic

or

"What Beach Do You Hang Out on?"

Tara L. Masih

WHEN YOU are of mixed parentage–one parent dark-skinned, one light–you come out looking like café au lait, something people struggle with–their compulsion to categorize you, label you, and place you neatly on the shelf in a safe spot, safe because the species is one that has already been identified. Yet while humans have always feared the unfamiliar and foreign, times are forcing us to change.

"Your look is in," I'm told by friends. "I like exotic-looking women," I'm told by men. I still have not learned how to react to these well-meaning comments. I bite my lip, smile, and nod vaguely, hoping they'll take my expression as a thank you.

What that expression really reflects is a reaction to my own struggle, a reluctance to be placed in any category to satisfy the comfort of others. Now I am labeled, and they can rest easy. Everything's safe.

Fear of the stranger goes back centuries. In her essay, Susan Sontag uses this metaphor to explain the fear of AIDS victims: "The fact that illness is associated with the poor–who are, from the perspective of the privileged, aliens in one's midst–reinforces the association of illness with the foreign: with an *exotic* place" [my italics].

There is no doubt that words have power, or rather, we imbue them with power. As the Bible proclaims, the word is flesh and dwells among us. Like humans, words are either accepted or rejected, synthesized into culture or banished. For instance, during the McCarthy era, the term *communist*, like the person it labeled, was claimed to be

64

evil and therefore every effort was made to eradicate it from the American vocabulary.

What many people may not realize is that the word *exotic* is derived from the Greek word *exō,* meaning "outside." "Exotic" itself carries several meanings in modern times, and as cultural and collective views change terms and phrases, chameleon-like, are made to reflect and adapt. (*Communism* is no longer an evil word, communists no longer exist in an "evil empire.") According to *Webster's Ninth Collegiate,* there are four modern definitions of *exotic.*

1. *Introduced from another country: not native to the place where found*

It is amazing what a short-term memory we Americans have. Our history begins with the discovery, by Italian explorer Cristofero Colombo, of this land and its exotic American Indians (and we all know he was looking for a quicker trade route to my ancestors, those other exotics in India proper). But by definition it was Colombo and his followers, religious refugees and convicts, who were the exotics. In essence, all Americans are exotic. Our history, riddled with convenient lapses in memory, takes a great leap to the American Revolution, discounting the fact that the non-native Europeans, with "savage-like" enthusiasm, slaughtered the natives (now rightly referred to as Native Americans). Our fear of foreigners is no doubt a projection of our fear of ourselves.

2. *archaic: outlandish, alien*

By this definition, *exotic* is hardly a compliment. The word again addresses the fear of the unfamiliar. (The *Oxford English Dictionary* uses the words *barbarous, strange, uncouth* as synonymous with foreigners.) It's why we seek to erase differences in this culture. By covering our bodily smells with the same scents, by following the current trends in hair styles (now that Di and Fergie are old hat, who will women follow? Hillary and Tipper?), by spending all our energy/time/money to wear the same clothes during the same season, and by keeping up with the latest profanity, we are saying to our compatriots: "Hey, I'm just like you, therefore I'm *safe* and *familiar.*" (Note how these two adjectives are often paired.) It is no accident that most of the women and men accused of witchcraft during the hysteria of the seventeenth and eighteenth centuries were citizens who lived by themselves, outside of the community–social lepers. In our own century, Michael Jackson is the epitome of one who has tried, literally, to erase his exotic features, even going so far as to erase his gender–he is generic in every sense, and therefore can be marketed to a broader audience. His attempts, nevertheless, backfired. In erasing all differences he has become that which he tried to avoid. A true alien, living a solitary life away from society, he is like the witches of old–a target for outlandish rumors and supernatural speculation.

3. *Strikingly or excitingly different or unusual*

The word's own definitions contradict each other. While the unfamiliar can be frightening, it can also be exciting. As psychologists have discovered, love and lust are heightened in the presence of fear. Now we know how to make someone fall in love with us–take them on a walk over a shaky bridge. And as fear and excitement appear to be in opposition, so do different cultures' concepts of beauty. In the States it is considered an asset to be tan, though the tan shouldn't be natural. It should be achieved through leisurely hours of sunning on tropical beaches or through the assistance of artificial means. Americans brave melanoma, carcinoma, early aging for this brief stain of color. I enjoy being the barometer every summer for my friends to measure their tan by. With what glee some of them greet their achieved goal–to be darker than I am. But only in the summer, when it's acceptable. Or if they've been to Florida. I went to the beach once with a friend. "Look how everyone's staring at me," she said. "Black people aren't supposed to go to the beach, it's only for whites trying to look black."

I find it ironic that meanwhile, on the other side of the earth, people are doing their best to appear light-skinned. Hindu gods are rendered by artists with a blue tint to their skin, and Indian movie stars are lighter than many Europeans. I was appalled to find my own cousin, in preparation for her wedding, spreading hair bleach all over her amber-tinted face and neck. "I'm too dark," she said. "It's not pretty."

If we go beyond the outward schizophrenia of these opposing ideals, we find a sad explanation–it is class related. In the States, a tan is a sign of wealth. It takes money and leisure time to be able to noticeably tan–not burn, but tan, like the model in the Bain de Soleil advertisements.

But in equatorial countries such as India, a tan is a sign of the lower caste. The wealthy stay indoors, cooling themselves under rotating ceiling fans, while the rest of society works beneath a branding sun.

4. *of or relating to striptease*

This meaning is so repugnant it's comical. Is an exotic woman expected to dance her version of the seven veils for the edification (or destruction) of men? Visions of Salome arise, and again that fear of what is different, or man's fear of woman. As Jung noted, we give women all the characteristics that "swarm in the male Eros." Because of the sexual connotations, it has become de rigeur for a man to be seen with a foreign-looking woman. The advertising community, taking note of this, has littered their ads with exotic women, the cosmetics industry is cashing in on their growing number, and the film industry is giving more roles to women who don't look like Christie Brinkley, beautiful as she is.

Which brings me to the real definition of *exotic*.

A growing segment of the U. S. population being targeted for consumerism

As the discussions of the previous definitions reveal, in our society industry and consumerism build the foundation from which change evolves. The foundation for consumerism began with the colonists' revolt against taxation. A growing consumerism held our country together, forcing a civil war: according to some social historians, the North didn't want to lose the South's textile or agricultural contributions, which fed the Northern industries. It met the demands of the civil rights and the women's movement during the sixties, when the work force was in dire need of replenishment. Today, consumerism is behind the efforts to manufacture environmentally safe products, fake fur, and to provide dolphin-safe nets.

And it now causes publishers to compete against each other so that they may proudly announce that thirty-five percent of their authors are minorities; it causes politicians to include minority policies in their political platforms; it's behind the slight darkening of the skin and rearranging of models' features; and it drives fashion designers to steal other cultures' traditional attire, reproduce it, and sell it for a criminal price. Are women aware that they're wearing a mini sarong from Africa? Or *shalwars* from India? These pants cost as much as $200 in the States, but in India, depending on how well you can bargain, you can get them for $5. Westerners don't see the women sitting cross-legged in dark rooms and on thin mats, a useless protection from damp floors, embroidering or weaving their own fallen hair into the materials. And they never haggle with a street vendor for 5 rupees (the equivalent of about 25¢), until the boy says earnestly, with that tilt of the head peculiar to Indians, "Look, miss, to you 5 rupees is nothing–to me it is everything." True.

The melting pot is recognized as an anachronistic term. The new buzz-word for the nineties is *multicultural* or *multinational*, because we know that soon minorities will be the majority. They are gaining economic independence and buying their way into acceptance. So out of fear, our culture is adopting their clothing and jewelry, eating their foods in restaurants with purple decors, and taking up their causes to the point where we will forget who it all really belongs to. But I hope that we will fight the desire to have these groups assimilate, and that the prefix *multi* will begin to take power, allowing this country to exist as many rather than as one generic, incestuous mass. May the words of "M*A*S*H's Frank Burns be banished to an unenlightened past: "Individuality is fine. As long as we do it together."

No one should be labeled and shelved. I hope that we open our minds to learn from other cultures, accept what each has to offer, not because we can make a profit from them but because it will enrich our own culture. As Richard Rodriguez writes, "Diversity which is not shared is no virtue. Diversity which is not shared is a parody nation."

Perhaps the real definition of *exotic* should be "A recognition of that which is especially unique to each culture." For if someone calling me exotic meant a recognition of a proud people who persevere in the face of terrible poverty and disease, if they saw in me even a spark of Paul, a disfigured leper who, every evening, sits on the leprosarium stairs to take in the beauty of the Himalayan foothills during sunset, with no bitterness at his lot, then I would smile widely and say, "Thank you."

STORIES

Vignettes from a Certain Source

Black and White

My mother dishes out steaming rice in large snowy heaps. I get the courage to ask.

"Mommy, what's a nigger?"

"A nigger?" She bangs the serving spoon against the iron pot to unstick some kernels. She makes gluey rice. "There's no such thing as a nigger. It's a bad word that people use for Negroes. Don't use it, you'll hurt someone's feelings. Why do you want to know?"

My brother eats his broccoli. He's the only kid I know who likes the stuff. My father tells him to wait until my mother sits down.

"Someone at school called me that today."

An expression crosses my father's face that I am too young to read. My mother's face is definitely angry.

"You tell those people you're half-Indian, not Negro."

"What's a Negro?"

"They're people from Africa with dark skin, like your father. Some people call them black, but that's not right either. Their skin's not black, mine's not white. They're really Africans."

My father is still quiet. My brother listens, fork in hand.

"So you say you're Indian, okay? And any time you hear someone else say nigger or black to you or anyone else, you tell them that's not right."

"Okay." The rice and chicken are good.

* * *

"I'm half-Indian," I tell a group of friends. Tina raises her left hand behind her head to make a V and makes Indian noises with her right hand.

"*No*," I say, "I'm *East*-Indian, not American Indian." It's important they understand.

"What's the difference?" Joey asks. Joey makes me blush when he stares at me during class.

"My dad's from India. We're the *real* Indians, the ones Columbus was looking for when he ran into America by mistake. He just called them Indians, too." I want them to learn this, so my brother and I aren't looked at in the wrong light. I think they are beginning to understand.

When I take my seat after recess is over, wet my finger and rub off a stray pen mark on the desk's surface so the blue expands and disappears, I wonder what it would be like to be a Negro and be called a nigger and not be able to say that that is not what I am, and be able to dismiss the ignorant.

A Brief Attempt at Becoming Bilingual

"I want my children to learn Hindi," my father tells my mother at dinner.

"Sure," she says, "good idea."

"While they're young."

"Sure."

My brother and I groan and roll our eyes at each other. Now we have to learn at home?

"Stop it, it's important to your father." We stop; we always listen to our parents, there is no thought of disobeying at this age.

"How about every night at dinner, we learn a new word. That way I get to learn, too." My mother is the always-enthusiastic-about-life peacemaker and cheerleader in our family.

The word for tonight is "Toothpaste": *dant manjan.* A practical word. Tomorrow it will be milk: *doodh,* another practical word for children. After that, everyone will lose interest and my brother and I will know two words of Hindi.

Media Mind Play

The media is powerful—we all know that. I learn of its subjectivity the night we take an Indian girl (daughter of my parents' friends) to see

Death on the Nile. We all laugh at the comedic relief–an actor who plays the role of a bumbling Indian.

It is nice to be sharing a room with someone. She sleeps on a cot at the foot of my bed. She is quiet tonight, unlike other nights when we talked until we fell asleep, midsentence. I know she's not asleep, her breathing is wide-awake breathing.

"Did you like the movie?" I ask.

"No." Silence.

"Why not?"

"I didn't like the way they made fun of that Indian. It made me feel embarrassed for him . . . for me."

This is a new concept. To be embarrassed about being Indian? And I realize that just as there is a difference between me and Anglo-Saxons, there is a gulf just as wide between me and full-blooded Indians. With no more to say, we drift off to the sounds of each other's measured breathing.

The Balcony Overlooking

My first boyfriend calls my father Anwar Sadat. "Hey, Anwar, how ya doing?" I find out years later that this hurts my father, but what youth knows her parents share similar feelings?

For now, I see it as an endearment, an acceptance of who I am. My first boyfriend also loves Mahatma Gandhi and I see this as a connection. He takes me to see the movie *Gandhi* at the local 99-cent theater. My parents, who never go to the movies, go the same night but sit below, while we sit above in the forbidden balcony with other couples, breathing heavily. My mother once told me to watch a man and see what he laughs or cries at and if you're doing the same at the same time, it's a good sign. I watch Jeff's face as the epic movie flashes its brilliant Indian panorama of color, despair, survival, spirituality, and triumph across his sharp features. He laughs at the right moments, he clutches my hand at the assassination. I decide the theater is a place of karma.

The Myth of the Monkey's Paw

Manohar Singh, a leprologist and my grandfather's teacher, traveled to China one summer to attend a conference and a celebration in his honor. At dinner, a plate was placed before him. On the china lay a shriveled, baked, child's hand garnished with greens and fruit in the shape of flowers. In horror he stared, then realized he must eat—it was China after all, and his hosts had presented him with a great delicacy. He was saved by his neighbor who whispered that it was just a monkey's paw. Westerners would not understand his relief, as, ever the gentleman, he ate.

"Your grandfather went to a dinner given for him in Bombay. They served him something that looked like a child's hand, and it was a great honor. Dada almost fainted but then they said it was only a monkey's paw. He still had to eat it so as not to offend his friends." This from my aunt.

And this is how family myths are born.

My Brother Is Made from the Same

I know of only two other families on the whole of Long Island that share my heritage: My parents have friends in Stony Brook whose children are Indian and Swedish; in high school, my brother and I discover two sisters in our city who are Indian and Japanese. But all of us look very different. The only similarity is in varying degrees of dark skin and hair. So my brother and I become tolerant of being mistaken for Italian, Greek, Jewish. At least he and I look alike, and do remember a few people in our lives who have guessed correctly. He remembers a woman he taught how to hit a better forehand; I remember my gentle art teacher, who knew I was Indian because of my eyes.

We have this romantic vision of ourselves, my brother and I, as dark rebels. We plan how we're going to make our entrance. It's Thanksgiving and the dinner is to be held at the club this year. My grandmother's club is exclusive, white, and did I say exclusive? Not even Jews or Italians are allowed in. We picture old men with shiny white hair and plaid pants, leaning on wives with silver perms and brooches clasping silk scarves around their surgically smoothed throats. We picture me, dark eyes lined in black eyeliner, mimicking kohl, and my brother, long brown hair flowing over his suit jacket, looking like a civilized Tarzan. Tarzan in a suit, in my grandmother's club. What fun, we laugh. It's always better to laugh at yourself first.

Imagining a Hero

There is no one in the media that I can identify myself with, no star I can emulate. My hair does its own thing–curly and straight where it wishes; my skin looks wrong with Coty's rouge. One day I listen to Cher singing "Half-Breed" on my bedside radio. Through the summer and into ninth grade I wear hip-hugging bell bottoms, Indian beads, grow my hair long (though it never hangs straight). I stand in front of a mirror and wish for small breasts, boyish hips, and high cheekbones. I take guitar lessons and try to learn her songs. I try to forget she's American Indian. It doesn't matter–she understands, and I like the look of my braless right breast nestled in the instrument's curve, of the image I'm trying to be.

My parents are appalled.

Two Men on Opposite Sides of the World

Dada, my father's father, was a minister and a doctor. I hear tales of his dedication, of being offered many women to be his wife, of traveling throughout India on horseback, trailed by tigers and mountain lions. He worked with lepers in a leprosarium, a gentle group of patients. He was afraid of cobras. My brother and I made friends with a leper once, a discharged patient Dada had worked with.

Grandaddy, my mother's father, worked for Singer Corporation and was very successful. He traveled all over the world by plane and by boat, meeting the natives of every country. He spoke with the Masai and ate and drank with Alaskan Eskimos. He was afraid of heights. We went fishing with Grandaddy, and I named a pet spider after him.

They both had snow-white hair and could never sit still.

A Drop in a Bucket

"I can't do this," my doubles partner hesitates at the gate to the tennis park. We are entered in women's doubles at this city tournament. To our mutual shock, we are the only whites in the draw and in the audience.

"C'mon, what's wrong?"

"I feel weird, don't you?"

I have to think for a moment. "Half of my relatives look like this. I feel more anxiety in a room full of white men in business suits for some reason. C'mon," I pull her arm. Her racket sticks out stiffly. "It'll be an experience. Now you know how they feel every day of their lives."

We have a bye in the first round and she plays poorly so we lose in the second. I am disappointed and she is relieved. She walks quickly to her Firebird, takes off just a quickly so her tires leave a trail of roadside dust.

The Kindness of Friends

I am fixing myself a single person's dinner (one plain pork chop, some plain rice, some frozen vegetables) when the phone rings. I only have one phone, and it is two rooms from the kitchen. The phone always rings when I am cooking.

"Hi, Tara? It's Mary. Listen, I have this new co-worker you just *have* to meet."

"Aww, Mary . . ."

"No, I'm serious. He's great. He's an editor, he plays tennis and the drums, and he's cute. He's really together, too. *I'd* be interested if I wasn't married."

"Well . . ."

"C'mon. I told him all about you. He said sure, give me her number, but I thought I'd better check with you first. Okay? He's really great. I told him you were Indian and he said he likes exotic women."

The smell of burning rice cuts through the conversation–acrid and foretelling of another ruined solitary dinner.

"I'll think about it. Gotta go–my dinner's burning." This is one of my best friends, I think in astonishment, as I hang up the phone.

Brown

"Are my nipples a different color than other women's?" I ask Brian. We are lying in bed. The flannel sheet is below my breasts, fallen to the sides.

"Is this a trick question?" he wonders, fearing a trap about other women and his knowledge of them.

"No, I really am curious. I've seen my friends' breasts but don't look long enough to see. So?"

"Yes, other women's nipples have more pink in them."

"So these are browner?"

"Yes."

"Oh, just wondering." I stare at them a moment longer, watch them swell as he kisses my ear. A stupid thought, but I wonder if he minds the less innocent tint of a darker color than pink.

An Indian Legend

"Gandhi's that little bald guy in a diaper, right?"

"It's called a *dhoti*."

"Yeah, whatever, a diaper."

"It's not a diaper, it's what men wear, like pants."

"Sorry, did I piss you off by saying diaper? I mean it looks like a diaper to me."

"No, it's okay." Passive, I think. It's in the blood I'm sure, mixed with anger to result in this feeling that I should punch the guy in the nose, or that I should smile. Can I do both? I know what Mahatma would say. I picture the beatific smile.

A Father's Confusion

My father tries to bridge the gap with his children. Respect is not something American kids grant their parents unconditionally, and respect is something my father needs. He will accept children less interested in schooling, and children who curse, fight with each other, and dress badly. But he will never accept a small child who talks back to him from below belt-level. We say "When in Rome . . ." He says, though more eloquently, "Bullshit." "We are American," we say. "He says, "Don't talk back to me, I'm your father. There are things that other countries do better." It takes years for him to gain our respect, the way it's done in America–conditionally and hopefully before it's too late.

Reality

The sun makes a brief appearance after a day of dark rain. The pale, watery light, not strong enough to warm us, slowly spreads itself to the porch where we sit. It is Dana, Mike, David, Joe, and Joe's girl-friend and I, eating sandwiches and chips and fruit and washing it all down with beer. It is Mike's house, his front porch we are sitting on.

I perch on the rail, saying I always wanted to perch myself on the rail of a proper Victorian house, watch the neighbors stroll by, just a few feet away. I have always wanted to be in an era other than my own, not realizing that I wouldn't exist as I am, who I am, in any other time than this.

Italianità in a World Made of Love and Need

Thom Tammaro

"Amore e eruduzione annobiliscono la vita"
"Love and learning ennoble life"
– Italian Proverb

I AM AN Italian-American, the grandson of three Italian immigrants who, upon arriving in this country in the early 1900s from their south central Italian village of Sepino near Campobasso (described in one recent guidebook as the "Akron of Italy") in Molise, walked through the Great Hall at Ellis Island. Like thousands before them who did not know the language of the new world, they stood mute in front of customs and immigration officials. But with papers in order and, perhaps, with the help of a bilingual staff worker, they eventually found their way to the steel mills of western Pennsylvania. My fourth grandparent, my paternal grandmother, was American-born. However, she returned with her mother and father to their Italian village shortly after her birth, where she lived most of her childhood and early adolescence until the family returned once again to western Pennsylvania. I do not know why they came to the United States, though I have no reason to think their reasons were any different from more than two million others who made the journey from their Italian homeland to the U.S. in the first decade of the 1900s: economic, social, political, health, and, for some, sheer adventure.

I was born, raised, schooled, and churched in an Italian-American neighborhood and culture. From a map I once sketched of the three-square-block neighborhood of my childhood, I recognized only fourteen non-Italian households from among the 107 families living there. Thirty-three of the Italian households were three-generational. Not

until I studied a map of Italy, some time during high school, did I real-
ize that many of my friends and neighbors carried the name of their
Italian village with them in their American surnames: the Costas, the
Ferraras, the Gardas, the Genovas, the Melfis, the Riccios, the Taran-
tos, the Venezis. Even my surname carries the name of the river that
flows through my ancestral village.

Forty-eight first cousins and aunts and uncles lived within walking
distance of my house, all within a mile radius of the Tammaro and
DeTullio homesteads. We lived a kind of village life then. My father's
ten brothers and sisters and my mother's eight brothers and sisters
provided me with a bevy of blood-cousin playmates. Back doors were
always open: for uncles and aunts, who dropped by to visit, found no
one home, then helped themselves to coffee and biscotti; for cousins
who looked for a cool glass of water to quench their thirst from a
hard day of play; for a neighbor, who left a tomato, bell pepper, or
freshly cut flowers on the kitchen table; and for the insurance man,
who knew where my father kept the quarterly premium when he
came around to collect and found no one at home.

Except those of Grandmother Tammaro, I have few memories of
my grandparents—mostly they remain shadowy and vague figures in
my life, though their presence looms large. Grandmother DeTullio
died when my mother was a child of nine, so her image comes to me
through old photographs, especially a formal wedding photograph, a
kind of "Italian Gothic" portrait, that makes her look uncomfortable,
stern, and obedient. I am told she was gentle and loving until the day
the tumor in her brain exploded and she hemorrhaged to death. Of
Grandfather DeTullio—who brought with him to this industrial coun-
try the pre-industrial skill of a stonecutter—I have only one blurred
memory: as a three-year-old crawling onto his lap, the stiff gray can-
vas of his work clothes scraping my hands and cheeks, and the sharp
smell of shaving lather piercing my nostrils. When I travel home now,
I see and feel his presence in the quarried and hand-cut limestone
grotto shrine in front of St. Agatha Church, and in the WPA-built
school in Ellport that he and a group of Italian immigrant stonecutters
sculpted with chisel and hammer. He, like Grandfather Tammaro,
would die before I reached my fourth birthday. Of Grandfather Tam-
maro, I remember most strongly his deathbed: him sitting up and
Grandmother Tammaro holding a cigarette to his lips, emphysema
sucking his last breath away, the result of too many days and nights

standing in front of the huge industrial fans used to cool workers in summer and winter from the heat of the blast furnaces at the U. S. Steel Tube Mill Plant where he worked.

Memories of Grandmother Tammaro, though she was dead before I reached the age of ten, remain the strongest: because on Sundays after twelve o'clock mass we headed directly for her house and dinner–homemade breads and pastas, rich tomato sauces and, of course, cousins and uncles and aunts who gathered there throughout the raucous afternoons; because I passed her house most summer days on my way to the playground, visiting her in her garden where she trained thick tomatoes up thin poles, and I walked through her gnarled grape arbor and plucked thick purple grapes to eat then spit out the seeds and tough skins; because I listened to her in the kitchen, singing and humming country-western songs from the radio– WWVA, Wheeling, West Virginia–songs sung in broken Italian and English by this Italian grandmother, an auditory memory that remains for me at once surreal and charming; and because I sat on her aproned lap, and she sang me Italian lullabies while stroking my forehead and hair with her gentle hand.

Only when I ventured from my neighborhood did I hear people speak *without* Italian accents. Later, in my late twenties, I would lament the failure of my grandparents and parents to preserve the Italian language in their households, though I do understand their strong desire to drop any hints of the Old Country, if not in their accents, at least in the accents of their children and grandchildren. Even though my grandparents did not permit Italian to be spoken in their houses, I absorbed enough Italian from the surrounding neighborhood culture so years later on the train from Rapallo to Genoa, to my surprise, I could carry on what I think was an intelligible conversation with a wonderful Italian woman who knew no English. Words came flooding back to me from some long forgotten reservoir of memory, though sometimes I wonder if Signora Fermenti's bright laughter that sweltering July afternoon was really caused by the silly and outrageous combination of words I struggled to string together.

By the time I was enrolled in a Catholic school kindergarten in 1956, only a few of my classmates spoke with an Italian accent, their parents being recent immigrants. Most of us were second and third generation Italian-Americans, whose vowels and stresses had long been smoothed and Americanized. By the time I graduated from eighth grade, the once prominent accents of my Italian-speaking classmates had vanished, their talk stripped of any residue of their native language. A sure sign that American education had triumphed.

My eight years of Catholic school education were more nightmare–and a Kafkaesque nightmare at that–than dream. And while I believe the nuns were well-intentioned–and I do not doubt nor question for a moment their dedication to their vocations and devotion to their vows–I also have been, over the years, bitter and angry with their pedagogy built on fear and punishment, pain and suffering, humiliation and embarrassment. From that period, roughly 1956–1965, I have few memories of the pleasure that I now associate with learning. My time there was more captivity, filled with nervousness, anxiety, and tension, feelings and associations one shouldn't have about learning. I have tried to keep in mind the possibility that my experiences there were the idiosyncratic, malformed experiences of a disturbed or troubled child. But when I have compared notes with others over the years, I have confirmed my often doubted perceptions. If forgiveness is one of the themes and lessons of Christianity, then it is one I have learned, for I have forgiven those who trespassed against me, those responsible for the slaps in the face, the constant terror and threat of corporal punishment, the screaming voices ringing in the ear, the humiliations of failure, the expositions of frailty. *Basta!*

Even though I was an altar boy for eight years, dutifully serving my share of dawn weekday masses, baptisms, weddings, funerals, confirmations, and whatever else we black and white cassocked and surpliced boys were required to serve, I carry with me into adulthood only one memory of a truly spiritual moment. This occurred in Holy Week, during the "Forty Hours of Devotion," a time of intense prayer and devotion when the altar is stripped bare and church statuary is covered in purple cloth, symbolizing Christ's passion, death, burial, and resurrection. For this most solemn ceremony our parish invited monks from a nearby monastery to participate. Their participation in the "Litany of the Saints," a call and response invocation petitioning dozens of saints on our behalf, was especially moving. For me, hearing the Litany–the priest's calls to *"Santa Lucia"* and *"Santa Regina"* and a hundred other Saints, followed by the responses of *Miserere Nobis*–sung in Latin, Gregorian chant-style, by forty or fifty Benedictine baritone-voiced monks, came closest to the ecstatic moments I read about in books on saints whose hearts were pierced with spears of divine love.

Hard as I tried, I could never conjure the passion or spirit the nuns and priests said should be moving through me during the hundreds of holy services I attended, masses I served, and sacraments I received. It was a train I eagerly awaited but it never arrived at my soul station. But one cannot–should not–feel something simply because he or she is told to do so. All the years of my youth submerged in the daily practice and rituals of Roman Catholicism and I locate that one spiritually charged moment. Perhaps one ecstatic moment is all a person is entitled to in this lifetime? Perhaps I should be thankful for that? I do not want to sound irreverent, nor do I want to suggest that others didn't feel such passion. Never once have I doubted the passion and belief I saw every day in the faces and eyes of those old Italian women at 6:45 A.M. mass. Never once when I was the altar boy standing at the marble altar rail and holding the paten to their chins to catch a falling Host during Holy Communion did I doubt their devotion. But thirty years after the fact, I dredge up only feelings of indifference and ambivalence from that past.

Within my family and the neighborhood where I grew up, I remember few, if any, models of professionalism–no doctors, no lawyers, no dentists, no CPAs, CEOs, or MBAs or PhDs. We were low-to-middle class Italian blue-collar steel mill laborers. I remember an old immigrant saying that goes something like this: "They told us the streets of America were paved with gold, but when we got there we discovered that the streets were paved with bricks, and we did the paving!" To me, becoming a doctor or lawyer or CPA was as distant from my reality as the homeland of many of my neighbors. We were the ones paving the streets, so to speak. My father's second-oldest brother was an exception. He attended Pittsburgh's Carnegie Institute of Technology (now Carnegie-Mellon) from 1936–1940 on a football scholarship. He quarterbacked the team in their 1940 New Year's Day Sugar Bowl appearance against TCU. Upon graduation that same year with an engineering degree, he worked as an engineer until his retirement at the same steel fabricating plant–four blocks from the Tammaro homestead–where my father and uncles worked as laborers. Had he not been able to throw or run with a football with some skill, attending college would have been an economic impossibility for him in 1936.

The centrality of the family in the Italian-American experience is difficult to deny. In the May 15, 1983, cover story for *The New York Times Magazine*, Stephen B. Hall writes: "Inherited responsibilities, moral as well as economic and practical, were so overwhelming that second generation Italians grew up with a heightened sense of familial responsibility that occasioned unusual anxiety when it comes to separation from family." Sons felt a natural obligation to follow in their father's footsteps to the mills; daughters were destined to follow their mother's path that often led to the house rather than away from it. And guilt often followed those who decided otherwise. Census Bureau data from the late 1970s show that educational levels among individuals with two Italian parents rank near the bottom among ethnic groups, as opposed to individuals with one Italian parent.

For many of the Italians in my neighborhood, survivalism was a way of life. Motivation beyond that which allowed for week-to-week survival was difficult to find. Children grew up with a constricted view of the future, with horizons extended not much further than the chain link fences that surrounded the mills. Where I grew up, most second and third generation Italian-Americans were content with supporting a family with jobs that offered good pay and benefits, usually jobs in the steel mills and their off-shoot industries. Paycheck-to-paycheck living became the gauge against which I measured the good life. This short-sightedness is something I still struggle with today. And the good life meant the basics: food on your table, a roof over your head, and clothes on your back. And maybe a little left over, but not much. It was mainly about providing for your family. Does anyone have the right to ask for more? This survival mentality is consistent with what I have read about immigrants from the *mezzagiorno* or middle region of Italy–the region from which most of my family and neighbors emigrated. My childhood horizon extended to the three square blocks of my neighborhood. I don't remember families having such luxuries as "savings accounts for college," since college was never really thought of as being part of our future. I saw many relatives and neighbors return from their daily work indifferent and numbed by that which made their lives possible. Until I was fifteen or sixteen, I believed that people were not supposed to enjoy or find reward and satisfaction in their life's work. If those workers found enjoyment and satisfaction in their work, they certainly did not express it to anyone. So, at an early age, I understood that whatever my life's work was to be, I was not supposed to enjoy it. I understood it as one of life's irrevocable tenets.

But there are always forces working their magic on you, whether or not you are conscious of them. For me, those forces, that magic, came in the form of three women, all English teachers at my high school. And I am forever grateful to them. Like a child in a fairy tale who journeys through dark forests or under mountains guided by benevolent feminine forces, I was guided by these women who recognized my desire to move beyond the constricted view of the future from which they, too, had emerged. How wonderful that they had come back to help others along the same journey! Each woman, in her own way, offered me a new measure of possibility: Ms. DeMark, who offered unconditional support and nurturing of my newly found love of writing—how I admired her strength and courage to live by a creed that claimed books and language as equally vital to life as jobs and money; Ms. Gibbons, who listened carefully to my talk about writing but, more importantly, challenged me to get it down on paper, which taught me that words on paper were commitments; and Mrs. Ionta, who taught me that the job of poems and stories—mine as well as others'—was not complete until something changed inside.

The way these women moved through the world, the way they thought and talked and envisioned the world, their vitality and liveliness, their joy in their own lives, their "differentness," suggested possibilities I had never imagined. Being in the presence of these women was their gift to me. Perhaps that is the gift of the true teacher: to invite you into their world and suggest possibilities where limitations rule.

And so I accepted their invitations; I followed and trusted their guidance. Because of them, I believed I could step from the patterns of my ancestors and culture and make my own way. And perhaps I could step from those patterns because one April afternoon in 1968 we read Robert Frost's poem "Two Tramps in Mud Time," a poem I'm sure rooted in my unconscious but only revealed its meaning to me many years later. It is a poem about work and the proper relationship to it. The woodchopper who speaks in the poem suspects that the two tramps coming along might be after his job. The last stanza, I think, not only resolves the woodchopper's dilemma about his relationship to his work, but also suggests Frost's bold assertion about his own life's work—writing and poetry:

> But yield who will to their separation,
> My object in living is to unite
> My avocation and my vocation

As my two eyes make one in sight.
Only where love and need are one,
And the work is play for mortal stakes,
Is the deed ever really done
For Heaven and the future's sake.

With these words impressed in my mind—and with parents who knew that college was now affordable to their son because of President Kennedy's plan to create a "democracy of opportunity" by providing guaranteed student loans at low interest rates to the needy, I left the neighborhood. But early in my freshman year of college, I discovered the true meaning of an old Italian proverb, *Chi lascia la via vecchia per la nuova, sa quel che perde e non squel che trova*: "Whoever forsakes the old way for the new knows what he is leaving but not what he will find."

In 1969 it would have been easy for me to walk directly from high school into the steel mills, as my younger brother did a few years later, and make $18,000 or $20,000 a year, for those were the boom years in the smoke stack communities that spilled out along the Ohio and Beaver Rivers of the industrial valley of western Pennsylvania. I could have stayed in those towns, made "good money," as they used to say, got married, fathered children, owned a home and cars, and planned hunting and fishing trips and two-week summer vacations. Instead I delayed those dreams and in the early summer of 1969 found myself speeding north on Interstate 79, in search of the Albion-Edinboro Exit and one of Pennsylvania's people's colleges.

Like my immigrant grandparents before me, I was journeying to a new world. But I was an immigrant on a different voyage. I arrived with my blue collar tucked beneath my khakis and cotton shirts. I was only an hour or two away from home, ninety-three miles if I correctly remember the odometer, but distance cannot always be measured by time or miles. What I found waiting for me at college was a world like no other I had known. I might as well have been a million miles away from the blast furnaces and open hearths of U. S. Steel and Jones & Laughlin, around which the lives of friends and families revolved as they toiled through the long days and nights of their lives; for I toiled near another fire then, one that burned deep and bright and does so still today.

Arriving at college with a vision of the future that didn't include steel mills or union strikes in the winter, I, like so many other first-generation college students, found myself a stranger in a strange land. Lacking the social graces that come with two or three generations of middle class breeding and finishing, I stumbled through my first years of college, stumbled not academically, but emotionally, socially, and psychologically. I lacked the savvy that comes from having parents and siblings who before me moved through the new, strange rituals and codes of academic culture and then passed along that savvy to me–through a kind of cultural osmosis–so I, too, could feel at home and move nimbly through that privileged class.

In her intelligent and important book *Errors and Expectations*, the late Mina Shaughnessy, a wonderful educator, speaking of underprepared students, wrote: "college both beckons and threatens them, offering to teach them useful ways of thinking about the world, promising to improve the quality of their lives, but threatening at the same time to take them from their distinctive ways of interpreting the world, to assimilate them into a culture of academia without acknowledging their experiences as outsiders." And somewhere Freud writes that moving up two steps in the social class hierarchy results in neurosis. I certainly recognize neurosis during my early college days. After fifteen years of university teaching, I know that underpreparation means more than academic underpreparation. I understand how emotional, social, cultural, and psychological underpreparation camouflages intellect and potential. Perhaps this accounts for part of the high attrition rate among first-generation college students? In many ways, we are all underprepared–outsiders if you will. We come to whatever new experiences before us at once excited by the prospects that lie ahead, yet threatened by those very forces that can liberate us.

So how do we journey through dark forests and venture across forbidden zones? How do we reconcile that which at once beckons and threatens? Perhaps this is what true education of the Self is all about. In the dark forest of college and graduate school, once again I was guided–but this time by three male English professors, each of whom led me through intellectual territories where my father did not travel. Again, I am grateful for their mentoring, for their showing me new measures of possibility, for their recognition of my struggles (which later I discovered were once their own struggles) in this new world. They provided a kind of safety zone against the threats of stepping from old world limitations to new world possibilities. I am grateful to

Professors Carothers, Heffernan, and Koontz for their good counsel, for their open hearts and their generosity of spirit and intellect.

I consider myself fortunate that between the ages of fifteen and thirty I found a wonderful balance of feminine and masculine guides. Looking back at those years, what I remember above all else about those three women and three men who guided me along my journey was the intensity with which they lived and loved their lives. At the center of their lives, each possessed a love, a passion if you will, for their life's work: teaching literature and writing poetry. And I do not think it is a coincidence that nearly twenty-five years along the journey, I, too, teach literature and writing and write poetry. Remember Frost: *Only where love and need are one, / And the work is play for mortal stakes, / Is the deed ever really done.*

We all possess the power to guide. And now as someone teaching writing and literature to others, I hope to give back the gift that was given to me: to offer my students new measures of possibility; to guide the lost stranger along his or her own way; to help others find a passion to place at the center of their lives, for I truly believe that one passion often leads to other passions. If we can make choices in our lives, striving to keep love and need as one, perhaps we can unite our avocation with our vocation, as Frost says, and come from our jobs not numbed or indifferent but singing the vital song of our lives. "To be a person, identical with myself," the developmental psychologist Erik Erikson writes, "presupposes a basic trust in one's origins–and the courage to emerge from them." Escape was once a word I used to characterize my dissociation from my origins. But it is not a word I use now. It is not so much escape as it is emergence, for we can never really escape those origins. It is not so much rejection as it is acceptance and recognition of how something can be at once nourishing and vital as well as starving and suffocating.

In their book *Ethnicity and Family Therapy*, Giordanno and McGoldritch say that to understand the second and third generation Italian-American we must think that most "trimmed their sails of personal ambition simply to avoid conflict with parents." Moving away from the codes, rituals, mores, patterns, and habits of one's native culture toward those of another is often misunderstood as a rejection or forsaking of that culture. The old bugaboos of "What's the matter? Your father's way of life not good enough for you?" and "What's the matter? You too good for us?" often echo in the minds of those who light out on their own to discover new ways of seeing or thinking. This was certainly true for me. And yet, to some degree, it was that very same independence and spirit that drove so many Italian immigrants to this new world in search of the *via nuova*, which they often found radically different from the lives of their parents and grandparents.

The image of my grandparents standing mute before customs and immigration officials in the Great Hall at Ellis Island because they did not know the language is a stark juxtaposition to the image of their grandson standing in front of his university classroom, talking to and teaching students about the liberation that comes with expressing one's private self and thoughts through language. And while I do not think they could have imagined that life for one of their grandchildren, I am sure they would appreciate and take joy in the irony. How often I have wished they were alive to witness the fruits of their labor.

Italianità is a term used by Italian-American writers, scholars, and critics to characterize the varied ways in which their Italian culture and heritage filters into their life and work. It is a term whose definition is painted with broad strokes, as it should be, for who can truly and surely pin down the ways in which anyone's culture seeps into one's life and work? *Italianità* is the cultural collective that colors and shapes experience, in all of its hues and tones, some bright and lively, others muted and subtle. It is the trickle down theory of heritage; it is the residue of culture that clings to us long after we have moved away from it. The great Russian painter Marc Chagall wrote in his journal "Every painter is born somewhere . . . a certain aroma of his birthplace clings to his work." Is that not true for non-painters as well? We come to discover it is with us, more often than not, and in ways more intricate than simple. It is the way we explain ourselves to others and, most importantly, to ourselves. It is at once the real and mythic identity we have accumulated. *Italianità* is Ariadne's thread that leads us out of the dark cave of our cultural ignorance to recover the light of our own heritage.*

*In her pioneering *The Dream Book: An Anthology of Writings by Italian American Women* (NY: Schocken Books, 1985), Helen Barolini introduces the term in her "Preface." An extended discussion of *italianità* can be found in the "Introduction" to the book *From the Margin: Writings from Italian Americans*, a wonderful anthology of Italian-American writing edited by Anthony J. Tamburri, Paolo A. Giordano, and Fred L. Gardaphé (Purdue University Press, 1991).

Those living *italianità* often embrace the baggage of origin–sometimes heavy and burdensome–of who and what they are and where they come from. Family and place: two aspects of culture we must face if and when we ask ourselves the question "Who am I?" As an Italian American, I live with and accept those tensions that drive my life: of *la via vecchia* and *via nuova,* the old ways and the new; of *l'ordine della famiglia* and *strano paese,* of the ways of the family and the strange ways of the new land. It has not always been easy. However, I would not exchange those experiences of childhood and adolescence for any other in the world. I cherish and value *italianità* and trust in all its goodness; but I also understand its other dimension and try to recognize when it is at work in my life. Once boundaries are drawn, once limits are created, once restrictions are enforced, narrowness of mind and behavior soon follows. And it is narrowness of mind and behavior that restricts and devalues–ourselves as well as others. And that is something I work to avoid in all my actions. In the larger sense, we are all immigrants on the journey. When we find and create our own new world, let it be a world made of love and need.

Lemon Ice

Lewis Turco

P ICK A DAY, just any summer day between 1945 and 1947. The sun is boiling down through the big elm on the corner of Springdale and Windsor Avenues in Meriden, Connecticut, and Lewis is sitting on the front steps of the parsonage looking across Windsor at the run-down corner grocery store, Galluzzo's Market. If he shifts his gaze and looks right, to the northern corner, he will see another grocery–not quite so run-down, not quite so large–Cotrona's.

In the house behind Lewis, his father, Luigi, is hard at work on his English and Italian language sermons for the coming Sunday. Like some scuttler of the deep, he has retreated into the sun porch behind the bookcases he's arranged in such a way as to cut himself a slice of space for his study. If Lewis were standing in the French double doorway of the porch he might watch for a moment the liquid movement of the angelfish among the valisneria in the aquaria that take up the rest of the wall space in the porch. They are Lewis's aquaria. The cries of his brother Gene, out playing somewhere with the neighborhood kids, might swim in the window: "Allee allee infree!"

Lewis's father will deliver his sermons from the pulpit of the white clapboard First Italian Baptist Church behind the house, facing Springdale, surrounded by a wire fence. It is a box of wood without even a steeple, but the churchyard is a large one–Lewis should know, he has to mow the lawn once a week. On it the church each summer holds its Strawberry Festival, the chief attraction of which is not the strawberry shortcake but the Italian pastries sold at the booths manned by large Italian women and patronized by slender Italian men and loud Italian-American children.

The church and parsonage literally and figuratively straddle the corner where Italian and German neighborhoods collide in a melee of great trees and *No Parking* signs. The whispers of the Roman Catholic neighborhood of Springdale have it that these renegade Protestant Italians are holy rollers. The funny little Sicilian priest had wanted to marry some Mayflower queen. They drank real blood, not grape juice, in those shot glasses. They hire a band to praise the Lord—but the band isn't hired, for Elsie plays the new Hammond and old Mr. Parisi brings his fiddle to church on special days. Somebody puffs into his trumpet, somebody else has an accordion, and the noise is always lovely.

In the days of their early childhood, Lewis and his brother Gene used to swing on the church gate made of wire and silver tubing. There always seemed to be a bully around to spoil their fun and to challenge them as they rode the barrier that sealed the churchyard off from the neighborhood. "Let's see you spit on the stairs," he might dare Lewis. "You're scared, punk. Your old man eats snails. Where do you people keep the snakes you kiss on Sunday?"

Lewis's mother is somewhere indoors working on the laundry or the floors, perhaps. She is the unhappy one. A Midwest farm girl who worked her way out of the fields her father let go to seed, who struggled her way through college to become a missionary among the immigrant Italians, she had married one of them and lost the status she had fought and scrambled for.

Lewis's younger brother, Gene, is lurking around somewhere, no doubt planning to horn in on whatever Lew eventually does. What he is planning is getting over to the lemon-ice store. The problem is lack of money, but Lew believes he has solved it.

He gets up and walks slowly across the patch of green lawn under the elm, around the end of the fence at the corner, and cuts across Springdale. Inside Cotrona's it is cool and the smell is of sawdust and salami—the sawdust is sprinkled across the floor, and the salamis hang with the cheeses from wires stretched across the ceiling. There are kegs of olives in the aisle. Behind the counter stands Frank Cotrona minding the store for his father. As usual, the store is otherwise empty of customers.

"Did y' come over to go a couple rounds?" Frankie asks, grinning. Lewis nods. Frank and he are the same age, but Frank is bigger. "Same deal? Three rounds for a nickel bag of chips?" Lew shakes his head. Frankie's smile disappears. "What, then?" He leans his elbow over the counter and looks at Lew, his pompadour flopping over his dark eyes.

"Three rounds for a nickel," Lew says.

"A nickel!" Frank wails and straightens up. "The priest's kid has gone pro!" His eyes are fake wide. Frankie and Lew stand there staring at each other for a minute. "Okay," Frankie says, "it's a deal."

Frank comes around the counter untying his white apron. They square off, hands open. Frank zips one in and taps Lew on the cheek. He laughs. "Come on, Turk, earn your money." Frank has a longer reach..

Lewis gets mad at all the little taps and goes windmilling in. Frankie backs off laughing and defending himself. "Okay, okay, that's your round," he says. He hauls a dime out of his pocket and hands it to his sparring partner. "Six rounds, and I throw in a nickel bag of chips," he says. The match resumes.

"Thanks, Frank," Lew says pocketing the cash at last. They shake. Frankie goes back behind the counter as Lewis goes out and closes the door behind him.

He turns left. There's a house next door on Springdale, then Ponzillo's Tavern, the bone in his father's craw, for it is almost across the street from the church. This is a place that ranks in fable in the Italian community of Springdale, but not in the mythology of the Germans and mixed breeds of Windsor. This is the house and storefront where the Gallicized Ponselle sisters were raised, the only divas Meriden ever produced. Lewis knows this, but he doesn't know why their name is Ponselle, not Ponzillo, and he has never heard them sing, for Rosa Ponselle's years of glory have been over for nearly a decade and a half. She stopped singing at the Metropolitan in 1937, when Lewis was three years old and still living in Buffalo. Luigi loves opera, but Lewis won't listen to it when it is played on the radio or the wind-up phonograph.

Next door is the lemon-ice store. "Agostino's Fish" it says on the dusty window, but Lewis has never seen a fish inside. His throat is as dry as the last leaf, and the sun is hotter than ever. He goes in, the bell on a jiggler over the door makes its Christmas sound—"Allo, boy,"

Mrs. Agostino says, smiling, the faint moustache over her lip arching like the back of a cat. She sits in a chair beside the ice-cream freezer, in front of the window. The candy counter is against the back wall, and behind it is the lemon-ice machine: a wooden bucket containing a smaller metal vat that has a top with a gear. Over this fits another gear on a drive-wheel, the whole thing hooked to an electric motor. Ice, sugar, and lemon go inside, ice and salt go outside, the motor goes round. It is not going round now. Mr. Agostino–large, not terribly friendly–is putting together the ingredients.

It has been many years since this childless couple stepped off the boat to find the fortune to be found in an antique motor and tub, in ice, sugar, and lemons, in paper accordion cups one can squeeze the flavor out of. If you eat too fast the most excruciating headache will momentarily blind you as pain spreads through and across your sinuses. When you are done with the ache and the lemon-ice you throw the cup away on the summer sidewalk outside where the kids have collected maybe to play ball or break a window or go walking down the street full of slat-frame one- or two-decker houses, some with a cat on a strip of earth looking out for the family dog through the spokes of a rusty trike between the weedy steps and the feet of passers-by, the phone poles growing their vines through the leafless breeze scuttling newsprint along the street, the grainy shingles knocked up underneath some old living room turned into a grocery store where all the cornflake boxes on the shelves host banqueting black specks that scatter in the bowl after the rustling has stopped.

"You got a lemon-ice?" Lew asks.

He is out of luck. Mrs. Agostino shakes her head. "We makin' somma now," she says, " 'bout a half hou'. You come back, eh?"

Lewis stands still, deeply hurt, deeply frustrated. How can fate be so unrelenting? Mrs. Agostino understands. "You wanna Milky Way?" she asks. Lewis shakes his head and shows her his single dime. "Well, half-hou'," she says again. "That'sa no so long."

The shadows in the shop gather heat to themselves and smother the corners of the store. In the counter only the hard candies are not in immediate danger of melting–the dots of candy on long strips of paper, the sour balls. All the rest–the jelly hats, the Baby Ruths–may not survive a half hour, no more than Lewis will. He turns to leave just as the bell rings again.

"Oh, no! What do you want?" Lewis asks. It is Gene standing in the doorway.

"Lemon-ice," he says.

"They're out. Let's go." He starts to push by his brother, then stops. "Where'd you get the money?" Gene drops his eyes. "You don't have any, right?"

"Where'd you get yours?" Gene asks.

"Hey, you kids!" Mr. Agostino yells, "Closa da door. Da flies comin' in!"

Lew grabs Gene by the arm and yanks him outside. "You never mind where I got mine," he says. "That's a secret."

"You been boxing with Frankie?"

Lewis can feel the gorge rising in his throat. It's bad enough that he's dry and hurt, now he's mad. He shoves Gene again, hard this time, hard enough to knock him down. Gene scrapes his knee and starts to cry. Lewis crosses the street, opens the church gate and latches it behind him—Gene doesn't know how to get the two halves to go back together right and get the vertical bolt to fit into the round hole in the pavement. Lew glances back and sees Gene picking himself up and heading for the corner to cross toward the front yard. By the time he gets there Lewis will be long gone.

Lew opens the gate again, crosses the street, and starts walking down the block along Springdale, past houses and shops, until he reaches Bonanzinga's Bakery where, if it were autumn, he could loaf on a cool day and watch the bread brown in the stone oven stoked with coal.

The loaves leave the oven on a long wooden spatula as Enrico's arms, like brown loaves themselves, move in and out among the rustlings of the narrow white bags. There is a measured bustle in the bakery. "Eh!" Enrico might say, "make some dough; make some more dough." And so they make some dough—they mix it, they knead it, they cut it, they mold it, then into the oven to bake it. Lew buys it, hot, for a quarter—hot, for they would be waiting at home. "Go!" says Enrico, "go, run! Bread gets cold quick on a cool day."

This, though, is anything but a cool day. On days when it is very hot in the sunny streets like this and the gang languishes after lunch and the morning games, Lew and his friends might continue down the block to Lewis Avenue, sluggish with heat, and turn left. There, parked at the curb, across the street and two storefronts down from where Lewis lived when he was in kindergarten, would be the ice-house on wheels.

When they come to the dreamy door that roars its crystal silence into the sun; where the cubes of sawdust winter rest waiting for the fellows to pick up chips to suck; when they come to that best of quiet doors, there Guido sits with his hat pulled down, and his eyelids pulled down as well, and the shadows down, down to his knees like an awning's ghost. There is no movement, not even of his lips, as Guido says, "Welcome, boys. Come in, get cool. Get cool near the ice, boys," Guido says.

Across Lewis Avenue, on the opposite corner of Springdale, there is the establishment of Louie the barber. When Lew was five all he had to do was cross the street catercorner to get to the barbershop. There, Louie would lower the boom on the boys' cowlicks and locks. As Lew walked in he'd get a snootful of pomade smells—Vitalis, Wild Root Cream Oil, Charley. He'd sit in the leather-upholstered, white porcelain, pneumatic chair, his head bent forward on his chest while Louie snipped and combed. Lew would be thinking, perhaps, of the bats thwacking in the back lot while he sat there itching and the mirror near the chair beckoned him to move . . . just once.

"Well, the Yanks won," Louie would say, "yes, the Yanks won and the Sox lost. What grade you in now, sonny? Steady now, steady your head . . . one more swipe with the comb . . . wish I could comb my hair," said Louie. "See?" He'd lower his bald pate to be patted. "Bene, bene, go home now. You're done, you're ready for church tomorrow. Next man, who's next? Who's next?" asked Louie.

Lewis crosses Springdale and turns back toward home. If he stops at Tomassetti's Market about a third of the way down the block he will find Mr. Tomassetti, the father of Mario and Eddie, two kids from the church who are about Lew's own age, spraying lambchops out from under his snickersnee as though he were some gory potentate mucking his way to empire through the limbs of his enemies. Underfoot the going is unsteady, for the floor is covered with wood shavings that slide up to the showcases that hold a museum of meat. It reminds Lewis of his collections at home. Mr Tomassetti rises in all his charnel glory from behind the chopping block, lays down a bouquet of ribs, perhaps. The bow of his apron ties off his rump where a man's back should start above the buttocks.

"How many you want? the butcher says to a housewife, "how many pork chops you want? These will go nice in a big pot of sauce. That's prime pork, Mrs. Spinelli.

"Here, boy, have some chips and run along, I got work," he might say to Lew when his customer, another parishioner, has left. "Give my respects to your father." He would move, maybe, toward the cold room door, open it, and disappear into its intoxicating coolness.

At last it is time. Lewis drags his feet through the suffocating heat back toward Agostino's candy store. While he has been walking Lew has been thinking about many things: What will it be like when he has gotten to high school finally? What will he turn into at last, a moth or a butterfly? But mostly about the lemon-ice. His lips have puckered and his mouth has tried to water, but his throat is a column of aching parchment.

While he has been waiting, has it gotten cooler? It is almost as though he is inhabiting two different days at the same time, for—yes—he has felt the breath of autumn stirring and rustling among the leaves. He has felt the roughness of gooseflesh upon his arms, and he has shivered. Now, crossing the avenue, jaywalking past the church, he looks down at the pavement and feels as though his eyes are farther from it, as though there is a greater distance between him and the earth. It is as though there were a piece of glass between his vision and the envisioned, a sheet of glass not quite clear, slightly tinted, so subtly colored that he could almost, but not quite, swear there is nothing there at all. He stops to kneel, to bend and tie his shoe—it does not truly need tying, but he wants to see if the distance he is experiencing is physical.

It is not. Nothing changes, although he can feel the movement of change all about him. He shakes his head as though to clear it, rises, and walks on. He comes to the door of the shop and goes in, and then he feels it strongly.

He looks at Mrs. Agostino and notices for the first time what she is wearing—it is a long black dress made of some sort of semi-shiny material, not the usual house dress and apron. On her head there is a close-fitting hat with a black veil falling from it. There is lace trimming here and there about her person—it reminds Lewis of webs.

He looks at Mrs. Agostino, but he cannot tell whether she is returning his gaze. "One lemon-ice, please," he says, holding out his money.

The old woman shakes her head. "We no got," she says, "no got no more. You want some candy, maybe?" She begins to go to the counter, but Lewis shakes his head, an enormous sorrow settling into the pit of his stomach to reside with the hunger and thirst already there. Lewis glances back at the window whose thin film of dust is a deeper tint of the glass he had imagined while he was crossing the street. Now he knows why Mrs. Agostino's veils and laces remind him of webs, for there are webs in the corners of the store, and the floor is littered with scraps of paper, even an empty pop bottle or two.

Lewis looks at the chair behind the counter where Mr. Agostino always sat tending or guarding the machine, but the seat is empty. The flat cushion is faded and threadbare. The machine itself is empty, the gears rusty, the wood dry and stained. Lewis knows but does not understand how he knows, that Mr. Agostino is gone for good. How can that be? He had been in the store barely a half-hour earlier.

Mrs. Agostino shuffles back to her own stool by the window, sits down, and turns her head as though to look into the street. She says nothing more. Lewis sees her hand in her lap lying palm up, the tips of the fingers trembling slightly, every now and again the whole hand giving a fitful jerk. The old lady is more stooped than ever, Lewis thinks. He stands until he begins to feel embarrassed, and then he turns to the door, opens it—the bell makes no sound beyond a small clunk as the door hits it. Lewis looks at it to see what is the matter. It has no tongue.

Outdoors it is autumn. The church and parsonage look the same, but Lewis can feel the difference—no one he knows is inside. The aquaria with his tropical fish in them no longer line the shelves before the windows of the sun porch. The guppies and betas have risen through the glass lids and swum away into thin air. His father writes his sermons no longer in the study where the green-shaded brass lamp stood on his desk throwing a yellow light upon the words about God, words that have long since browned into umber. Who knows where his mother has gone, where his brother is now?

It is autumn. Behind him the candy store stands with its door locked, the window papered over. Cotrona's market is closed, too, and so is Galluzzo's which had used be . . . hadn't it turned into? . . . a pizza palace. Lew's mouth is as dry as the last leaf in a book of leaves. Who knows where he is now? Perhaps it is no longer even autumn.

Black Flower

Walter Pavlich

(Croatia)

A place of suffering, a golgotha.
Each hill is such.

The soldiers don't know what they want.

Each home has at least one dead room.
There is shrapnel in the white sausage
grease of a skillet.

Windows burst like glass lungs.

Paprika, blood and gun powder.

At the church Christ dangles from nails
as usual. But mortar fire has interrupted
his sorrow and his dying.

A hole burst above his hip,
his belly, into his chest.
His entire left arm
a vacant marble wound.

So he hangs on one less nail.

With the black flower
of an explosion
between his lips.

Teatime in Leningrad

Elisavietta Ritchie

O NE OF THE earliest games Babushka, my Russian grandmother, played with me on rainy days was Train: we lined up all the dining room chairs. a flowered armchair became the locomotive and a kitchen stool the caboose. The main difference between our Train Game and those in other homes down the street–in St. Louis, in Lansing, then Chicago–was that our train was Traveling To St. Petersburg To Visit Tyotya Mary.

* * *

Across the river, the Fortress of Peter and Paul reflects its gold spire on the slate-blue ripples. Here, in 1905, my great-uncle Alexander Konstantinovich was imprisoned, along with a dozen other liberal law students from the nobility, when their links with a revolutionary cobbler were discovered. Their cells were located along "the gentlemen's corridor" and they were not ill-treated. On their release, my great-uncle abandoned politics for natural sciences, then became a provincial banker.

This is also where my grandfather, Leonid Konstantinovich, a former general of the Imperial Armies, was imprisoned after the Revolution, a revolution his older brother perhaps helped set in motion.

At moments between boats and ships, when the river is absolutely calm, the image of the Fortress of Peter and Paul is almost perfect, then again falters and ripples. Were I standing on the northern bank of the Neva, I could see the reflections of the Winter Palace stretch across toward the Fortress. As if the mottled reflections from both sides, wavering, never quite touching or superimposed, could hide all their histories. As if by coming here I could discover, recover, mine.

Before World War I and the Revolution, my grandparents knew their way through these palaces. As did their grandparents, great-grandparents and all the way back. How often my father, his brother and sister, walked on this embankment, skipping along in their childhood, and later, too quickly leaving their youth, running bent to avoid blizzards of bullets.

My father last saw his sister Maria Leonidovna (whom the family called Mary, in the manner of their English governess) in Petrograd in 1919. Later that year their brother Ivan was killed near Putivl, a village in southern Russia I can't find on my map. In 1920 my father barely escaped on the last ship from Sebastopol, and came to America.

My aunt Mary stayed in their crowded flat in Leningrad with her mother, my Babushka, and her grandmother, my Pra-Babushka, a witty old countess dying of cancer. In the photo that stood on Babushka's bureau, all three generations of women gaze from a circular frame.

My Babushka's face is long and slender. Her mother's and her daughter's rounder faces resemble each other, the same eyes and smile. But a sad smile from years of extreme hardship, famine, and the special danger to Russians whose origins were an irritant to the new regime. Mary continued her studies in music and history but received no diplomas or formal employment because of that notation on her documents: *nobility*. Like her mother, she lived by teaching and translating. . . .

From America, my father kept trying to get his family out, buy their way out, but always the Soviets raised more obstacles. And my grandfather, Dedushka, could not, did not *want* to leave: "Russia is my country, in time all this turmoil will pass and matters will be set right again."

After years of war, of prison, of malnutrition, in 1932 Dedushka died of a bad heart. Finally Babushka was offered one of the rare exit visas: permanent, no return. Tormented about leaving behind her daughter who could not obtain a passport, she almost abandoned the idea of emigrating.

"You *must* leave," Mary insisted. "*Now* while you have a chance. In

America you will have grandchildren to raise, you must teach them Russian and French. Look, you've been imprisoned twice already, and times will get harder. Don't worry about me, I am young, and strong, and in love with Volodya. We are the new generation, they need us here, we will be all right."

Mary herself had been imprisoned, by accident. Her mother had taken a present of food to some needier friend across Leningrad and didn't return that evening. Given curfews and the dangers of traversing poorly lighted streets, this meant she must have stayed with her friend. But one whole week passed without word. Mary went frantically from the apartment of one family acquaintance to another, whoever she remembered had not fled or been killed, and at last knocked on a door which two militiamen answered.

"Do come in," they insisted. "Your mother *was* indeed here, and she just left." Then, without explaining the whereabouts of the previous tenants, they locked Mary into a room for a week under constant surveillance.

Babushka never told me what had happened to either of them, except "They even watched as we went peepee. . . ."

In later years, after her mother's departure, Mary sometimes wrote that she "had to visit the hospital," which meant, in the code she and her mother had established before their parting, that Mary was called in for questioning by the KGB. Fortunately, she always "recovered in time."

Otherwise, Mary's occasional postcards—whose black and white photos she often hand-painted in color—brought little more than news of Soviet weather, a concert attended, a trip to the Caucasus or Lake Baikal during a break from teaching. She sent Russian children's books to me. She was permitted to receive overseas mail only from her mother, who in turn wrote of my childhood antics and accomplishments, of American weather, a concert attended, and her own travels to the Adirondacks or Lake Champlain. Mary could also receive copies of *National Geographic* and successive snapshots of her American neice. . . .

The early photos of Babushka seemed distant to me. I had trouble matching the tall gracious lady in velvet and silk with my gaunt wrinkled grandmother in a cotton frock. In a formal portrait her lap is full of her babies: my round-faced smiling father and his more serious brother Ivan still in little-boy curls and sailor suits, their chubby baby sister Mary in lace and frills, Then Ivan, about seven, his face longer now, and thin, always serious, standing apart from the other children at a family picnic. He looked too young to be anyone's uncle, and I understood he would never appear to fulfill the avuncular role, but I was always to call him Dyadya Iva. . . .

During World War II, and the eras before and after when millions also disappeared into prison and labor camps, I remained a well-protected American child in Philadelphia. Still, in 1941 mine was one of the few older fathers in our neighborhood who joined the United States Army, and moreover served in several invasions. So although I was too young to understand properly the depths of my Babushka's grief over the loss of her eldest son and many relatives in Russia's Civil War, and her fear for her two distant children in World War II, the battle reports in the *Philadelphia Inquirer* were very real to me.

I asked many questions. Some got no answers. Even early I suffered from the intuition, stronger than guilt, that I had missed my destiny, that I should have been born *over there*, to experience what children *over there* should not have experienced. As a Yugoslav journalist later told me, "You should have been born in Europe, you are a natural *partizanka.*"

So I live history vicariously, and only now this warm July morning in 1986, have I managed the enormous step of a flight to the USSR, the first of several trips. First stop: Moscow, then the night train to Leningrad.

All last night the Red Arrow express swayed and clicked noisily through dark forests and farmland. Other passengers in their various compartments slept or tried to, or gave up and read or drank. I hunched on my bunk and stared out the window.

What if I had been born among birches and barricades, gold domes and gulags, in this dangerous land, familiar and strange from childhood, seen for the first time in a luminous arctic July? Would my hedonistic rebellious nature have been tempered by merciless winters, unseasonal famines, eternal threats of prison and war? With whom would I have fallen in love here?

What if my aunt, who loved travel, had appeared on this train, at this hour, could we have known each other? I peered at every old lady in the corridors, in the stations, as on the street now. To mask her noble origins, blend with the masses, would Tyotya Mary have adopted the peasant white kerchief, like a flag of surrender?

While the train jolted on, I looked through a Soviet book bought in Moscow: World War II in photographs, black-and-white and many shades of gray. In a 1942 photo of the Siege of Leningrad, women are digging an antitank trench, or a mass grave. One girl lifts a spade heavy with rubble, smiles at the camera. Cheekbones wide, eyes too close, untidy curls. Rib-thin. My double, age ten. A lost cousin? Did she survive the Blockade? Would I have?

The train rocketed on between cabbage fields.

It still rockets now as I walk, as when one has spent several days in a boat, and once back on land, one still feels the motion of the sea and stands with legs farther apart than usual, as if to brace oneself against the slant.

I cross over a bridge and from the center look over the parapet to check if the reflections meet, but a navy or militia launch speeds down the Neva, breaking it into a wake and waves.

At last I reach the Finland Station with its absurd statue of Lenin, arm outstretched as if to hail a cab. There are none.

Many trolley tracks converge, people pour off, people queue to struggle aboard. Hundreds of people mill around the station, they all clutch their string bags and bundles, boxes and buckets.

Which train, which direction? A huge board above the ticket windows lists several hundred possible destinations. I spot the name of the—suburb? village? A ticket to that zone costs thirty kopeks. Fortunately I have the change to insert in a machine which yields a flimsy scrap of paper. But which line, and which track, and which stop?

I timidly ask several young people. No one can tell me, or will. At last an old woman in a brown-and-red flowered dress and white peasant kerchief points me to a track, with a waiting train about to leave. Just in time I jump on the end car.

No compartments, just a car full of wooden seats. They fill up with people and their string bags and bundles, boxes and buckets. No other apparent foreigners.

I don't think I look like one today, dressed in an orange-flowered skirt and a white knit blouse that could have been made in East Germany. Old sandals, bare legs. My only jewelry is Babushka's long necklace of white china beads. I too carry a string bag, with a tan sweater which belonged to Babushka, and a gray raincoat that was my father's. Just before leaving home, I had snatched them from the hall closet in case the weather turned cold.

It's possible foreigners are not allowed to go wherever this train is going. Leningrad is a port city, surely naval installations bristle up and down the coast.

I only hope this is the correct train. I sit on the right side, the better to see the names of stations. Who knows how soon mine will come, if at all. My seat-mates are soon dozing, sheltered behind their *Pravdas.*

The train gathers speed, hurtles along, but in three minutes stops at another station, only a minute, then onward again. Stupidly I'm in the last car so I don't see the station names until we're almost past them. If I miss my stop, I'll never know it. What is the end of the line?

We cut through industrial suburbs, dark buildings without windows or half of them broken, blocks of concrete apartments interspersed with small old houses and construction sites whose workers seem always waiting around for some overdue delivery of materials.

Three minutes later, another station, five minutes later, another, ten minutes, five minutes, another, another, station names fly by quickly, increasingly longer names, increasingly longer times between every stop, now we are out in farmland, broad cabbage fields, people get off, people get on, some seem to be going as far as I am, but I don't know how far that may be, or where to go when I get—wherever *there* is..

I remember Babushka describing the journey to her family estate southeast of Moscow. They traveled for two days by train and when it slowed at a certain road, they would signal, and the train would stop to deposit them in a hamlet. The stationmaster would greet them, the coachman was waiting to load all their trunks and boxes and dogs and even the white parrot in his cage into a troika, or a wagon, or several, and off they drove over snowy dirt roads for a day to get home for a season. During the Revolution and Civil War, local peasants protected the estate. The stone manor house became a workers' club. In World War II Nazi officers occupied it, and when they retreated, destroyed it.

Suddenly the right name on a sign. I spring up and jump off as the train is already recommencing its journey wherever.

Not a station, only a siding, in the countryside, somewhere.

Once they had sleighs and carriages here, and farm carts. One cart still, in the weeds. The road between birches and pines is more or less paved, crumbled away at the edges. No sign of a car or a bus, or even a bicycle. No people: they must be at work, or hidden indoors. Two or three lovely old peasant houses with airy intricate wooden trim under the eaves, but it's mostly low one-story barracks like shoe boxes tucked off behind tangles of brambles. At some crossroads there are pumps.

A middle-aged woman in a gray shapeless dress appears with her bucket. I show her the address.

"I'm looking for an old lady . . ."

She frowns, perhaps at my use of the word "lady," I meant to say "woman." She points farther down the road, and I keep going. Several times I turn in a lane to look at house numbers, but I'm barely getting warm. Farther on, the numbers painted on the barracks are closer to that on the envelope. Still, there seems to be little logic or pattern to the numbering. You have to live here to know where you're going.

Strangers aren't welcome, strangers are dangerous, foreigners don't come out here. After my sleepless night, I'm tired, and thirsty, and wonder if this chartless–pilgrimage?–won't land me in jail. I've read too much about the Soviet system of justice, their concern for security.

I try more lanes, paths over hummocks of grass and heaped tree roots protruding from hard-beaten soil. Exploring, I stray from the road, down a winding path. No one around to ask, but I should take a chance and knock at somebody's door. Even as I approach, dogs bark from little fenced yards.

I worry that–even if she has been sent to an old people's home, and I've also read about *them*–my sudden appearance could cause her trouble with the police, KGB. Which is one justification for not having come here in previous years, or tried to contact her ahead.

"But she's old," an ex-Soviet émigré in New York had insisted. "No one will bother her now. Times are changing!"

"Times are changing, yes," warned another ex-Soviet, "but only so much."

Finally an old man feeding a goat escorts me part way down another lane which leads to a yellow barracks with the right number. The tiny garden is a tangle of marigolds, dill, and raspberry vines. The barrack-house, long ago painted yellow, stands on concrete blocks. No cellar, must be cold in winter. The tarpaper roofing shows haphazard patches, the steps are uneven stones. At one end of the building, baby clothes hang on the line, broken toys sprawl across the path. No place for an old lady, she obviously moved on and passed on, then younger people moved in.

No point in it, yet the faint sound of–a sonata?–on the television or radio at least means someone's alive behind one of these doors. I take a deep breath, and knock, and knock.

At last a paunchy man in undershirt and shorts unlocks two thick doors.

"Excuse me, but a Maria Leonidovna once lived around here. Could she still be alive?"

"She was yesterday," he smiles. "Can't you hear, she's at the piano again. At least it's not midnight this time. Go around to the other door."

I knock there. A young man with a mass of brown hair answers the door. He is wearing gray pants and striped blue-and-white shirt. He ushers me in without question.

Inside, the small room is dominated by one wall full of books, and another with what must be fifty years of *National Geographic*. A white dog and gray cat sit on the scarred piano bench beside an old woman.

She stops mid-Scriabin, and exclaims in the King's English, "You are here! From America!"

She bursts into tears as she hugs me. I too. . . .

"Let us have tea," she says, though we are so busy talking—in Russian, in English—that we forget refreshments. Besides, the water is turned off during hours when every able-bodied citizen is supposed to be at work.

Her blouse, navy patterned with small white dots, is stained, and held together at the throat with what looks like a cheap brooch. Her navy skirt is patched, but surely she once was as stylish as anyone here. Her legs are heavy, yet she moves like a princess. Her eyes have a milky cast, but what a straight and delicate profile! More beautiful in fact than Babushka, but yes, there is a family resemblance. When I was a child, people who'd known Babushka in her youth said I favored her, and I dreaded old age. Do I look now as Babushka did when she left Leningrad? I should ask Tyotya Mary, but with her eyesight. . . .

Tyotya Mary takes a navy beret from a nail by the door, adjusts it over her goose-down hair, as if she needed a hat in order to receive guests properly. No, she never wears kerchiefs.

The table is draped with a paisley shawl. A piece of black bread and a half a cucumber sit on a chipped white plate. A young couple who with their two babies occupy two-thirds of the three-room apartment are nervous with strangers, seldom see foreigners. "Did anyone stop you, check on your documents?"

Reassured, they bring out apple pastries. The piano student whose name turns out to be Sasha disappears, then returns with a juice bottle full of his mother's raspberry wine. Other neighbors appear.

"No sugar or coffee in our shops," they complain.

"And the price of black-market sausage!"

"As for vodka–"

"Never mind," Tyotya Mary says, "we will share our rations."

She gropes in a dresser drawer, and under her Bible finds for me a single silver spoon with the family crest. It matches a spoon Babushka smuggled out in her petticoat in 1933.

Without looking, Tyotya Mary cuts the black bread in six exact pieces. Fragrance of . . . stables? Oats, rye, molasses. Dry, but delicious.

"After all," she goes on, "one must *live*, not merely *reside* on this earth. And life will improve after the Nazis and Bolsheviks leave."

"She is old, nearly blind," the young woman whispers as she heaps pastry on my plate.

"She lives in a past best forgotten," the husband adds.

"Troubles enough in the present," says Sasha, pouring thimble glasses full of the raspberry wine.

With a steady hand, Tyotya Mary toasts my arrival. She speaks of ancestral portraits I must see at the Hermitage, and how she met Akhmatova in the park, and walked with Pasternak through the woods. She recites Pushkin, Byron, Lamartine.

We talk for hours and hours. Outside, the sky remains light as day. The faucet finally runs, and the woman from the next apartment brings an enormous teapot painted with yellow flowers. Someone down the hall appears with a crock of gooseberry jam. Glasses and cups are filled and refilled. Neighbors from other houses come and go, a profusion of food and multi-syllabic names.

Tyotya Mary speaks of her brothers as if they were children still. "Only now that I've lived, can I start to know their lives. They have died, and I learn what it is to live."

During an interval while we are alone in her room, Tyotya Mary searches under her mattress, hands me a bundle of school notebooks wrapped in a scrap of oil cloth.

"Take these home," she insists, "I can no longer read."

Two hundred ninety-six pages. Every page, lined or graphed, is covered with neatly slanted handwriting. But the ink—sepia or purple—is faded, the paper browned, and the alphabet is the old pre-Stalinist one I never learned.

And what if they search my luggage again at the airport, accuse me of trying to smuggle out dissident manuscripts? And I always intend to fly light.

But this is the novel my Uncle Ivan wrote at age eighteen. I wrap it back in the oilcloth, then in my string bag.

Next she brings out a box of photos she can no longer see, but tells me about each one. On top is a color print of Babushka in her ninety-fourth year, in a navy polka-dot dress and white china beads, in a Florida garden her final Easter. Then black-and-white photos—some duplicates of those Babushka kept on her dresser—of Dedushka, Pra-Babushka, two little boys in sailor suits, a solemn girl, the handsome Volodya who married her and gave her a less conspicuous name. The many mysterious relatives who have not survived. And snapshots tucked among Babushka's letters: odd to see myself as a child, here, as if through a stained window pane. All must have been hidden throughout the years of searches by nosy neighbors and KGB agents, years of street fighting, air raids, displacements.

Sasha returns with his mother. "Your aunt was a brilliant teacher," she says. "Everyone loved her."

Other neighbors reconvene at the table.

"She still helps everyone in the village," says the neighbor bringing a fresh pot of tea.

"A heroine in the Blockade of Leningrad," nods the man from next door who settles himself in a corner. "See, at her throat is a medal awarded after the Nine Hundred Days."

They make her show off other medals adorned with garish bas-reliefs of Lenin and Stalin.

I ask her about the Blockade.

Sasha warns: "Old people exaggerate."

"No," she says. "You children born since the war cannot imagine the horror. Yet who would believe all we endured? Volodya, my husband, was wounded at the Front the first week of the war. They shipped him to the Urals to mend, but shrapnel splinters stayed in his brain, head pains tormented him the rest of his life.

"For those of us trapped inside the Iron Ring the Nazis flung around Leningrad, bombardments were constant. By night I learned to fire artillery. By day I shoveled rubble into barricades, tore barracks down for fuel, hauled sand bags through the snow. On one slice of fake bread. Some days a thousand died of famine, illness, cold. We tripped on bodies in the street.

"An orphan I adopted perished too . . .

"A truce was set to truck the children north across the frozen Ladoga. Still the Nazis opened fire. Before our eyes children were blown apart. I have outlived tears, but not my hate for Germans. Medals cannot hide scars."

She heaps our plates with piroshki.

"Peace returned. And with peace, returned the old denunciations, midnight arrests, labor camps, more deaths."

Sasha interrupts. "I once overheard my mother say that in the Siege *her* mother, dying from hunger, begged the family to eat her. And when she died," he shudders, "they did."

My aunt sips her tea and–the way you might say, *If it's snowing, of course wear your boots*–she shrugs. "Better they ate than buried her. And all winter the earth is stone."

"You must go," a neighbor exclaims. "The last train . . ."

I rise and because I am suddenly shivering, and she must also be cold, I throw my sweater around Tyotya Mary's shoulders, and the raincoat too. I wind Babushka's beads around her neck. As we embrace, she fills my pocket with chocolates.

With twilight at midnight it doesn't seem late, but the neighbors hurry me out. Sasha will escort me to the railroad siding.

Tyotya Mary remains in the dim doorway, calling out after us, "But where will you hide in the air raid, my dears? And watch your step. Still that awful corpse by the gate."

I grope my way toward the tracks, her candies squashed in my hands, my terrible questions undone.

Two Voices

Diana Der-Hovanessian

"Do you think of yourself as an Armenian: Or an American?
Or hyphenated American?"
– D. M. Thomas

In what language do I pray?

Do I meditate in language?

In what language am I trying
to speak when I wake from dreams?

Do I think of myself as an American,
or simply as woman when I wake?

Or do I think of the date and geography
I wake into, as woman?

Do I think of myself in my clothes
getting wet walking in the rain?

Do I think velvet, or do I think skin?

Am I always conscious of genes and
heredity or merely how to cross my legs
at the ankle like a New England lady?

In a storm do I think of lightning
striking: Or white knives dipped
into my great-aunt's sisters'
sisters' blood?

Do I think of my grandfather telling

about the election at the time
of Teddy Roosevelt's third party,

and riding with Woodrow Wilson
in a Main Street parade
in Worcester?

Or do I think of my grandmother
at Ellis Island,

or as an orphan in an Armenian village?

Or at a black stove in Worcester
baking blueberry pie for my grandfather
who preferred food he had grown
to like in lonely mill town
cafeterias while he studied
for night school?

Do I think of them as Armenian
or as tellers of the thousand and
one wonderful tales in two languages?

Do I think of myself as hyphenated?

No. Most of the time, even as you,
I forget labels.

Unless you cut me.

Then I look at the blood.
It speaks in Armenian.

Inside Green Eyes,
Black Eyes

Inside my eye
is another eye
looking out
seeing inside
your eye
looking in.

Inside my voice
that speaks with
spongy soft words
is another voice
that shouts
Hayasdan! Hayasdan!

Inside my song
is another song
whose words
I never learned.
I sing. I sang.
The song inside
is never done.

Mixed Marriage

He marries the lilac from the Taurus Mountains.
He marries the Cilician Church.
He marries the snows of the Caucasus,
and the Cossacks who will drive
across his dreams. He marries waking
to the sound of the thousand bells of Ani.

He marries the blood sea.
He marries the heart with two million scars
to whom he owes a healing.
He marries unretribution.
He marries village music
and red scarves flying.
He marries pagan dances
and Christian quiet.
He marries the step-child of Russia.

She marries the Mississippi
and Mark Twain,
and the pioneers pushing across the plains.
She marries recipes from Wales.
She marries the blue-eyed West.
She marries Europe's errant son,
the prodigal who made good.

He marries the ashes of Smyrna,
and the dried bones of Dersim.
He marries spring in Kharpert,
the autumn caiques on the Bosphorus.
He marries the Gregorian chant,
a thousand smiling relatives.
He marries a house with an open door.
He marries the knowledge of the fragility
of life. He marries an Armenian.

She marries the red soil of Texas,
and generosity and the blue Navajo turquoise.
She marries Lockheed Aircraft,
Wall Street and the *New York Times,*
Seventh Avenue and East
Main Street and the St. Louis Blues.
She marries the Boston Symphony,
the Cleveland Museum
and popcorn.
She marries Harvard, shrimp boats
in Louisiana and California raisins.
She marries the Great Lakes, psychoanalysis,
the PTA and the great white shopping center,
U.S.A.

Notes In Jerusalem

Nicholas Samaras

Jaffa Gate.
The old sector.
Satchel on cobblestones.
The heaviness of travel.
Wooden bench under stone eaves.
A spindled back.
I wait for the Metropolitan.
Light slanting down and going dusty.
The limestone of the monastery walls softens in shadow.
Vine leaves droop lower, heavy on their hasps.
Their yellow tinges edge the weight of the season.
The turning of October.
Coolness under the stone.
Architecture of worn hands, unplumbed
walls, tilted and uneven.
Cobblestones rounded and smooth
from the footfalls of four thousand Patriarchs.
Iron filigree on beveled windows. The beauty of bars.
Five P.M.
The Arabic call to prayer curls the air.
Many syllables of language hurled to the wind.
Sounds the way of every night here
for a thousand years.
A breeze quickens and chills.
The smell of *jarra* on the wind.
Nearby, the deep sound of a wooden cart squeaking.
A rumble of wheels down Christian Quarter Road.
Alleys curve away into darkness.
Stooped men walk through from the Arab quarter
and you want to hold their shoulders,

lift their grizzled gaze into yours.
The word, *Shokran.*
The word
for loose rocks to fit in a boy's palm.
Consonants that cut the air.
Musical invective.
Fragments of emotion like shrapnel.
Over the rooftop, beyond the barbed wire
and glass chunks imbedded in cement,
you see the New Sector
yellow lamps spotting on in Israeli quarters
and shadows flickering before them.
They move but they stay.
The old buildings and city say *Palestine.*
Brittle books with yellow pages murmur it.
Syllabic wind.
The smell of dust and history.
One who sits in a doorstep, who has learned
the value of listening to stone.
A low flute moans from a radio.
Abuhamed sways his headdress slowly, dangles
the heavy gatekey on his belted shirt, black *kelembia.*
Archways that tunnel to receding archways
that diminish into darkened archways.
The ebbing wail of an unseen cat down them.
Disembodied.
5:15 P.M.
The heaviness of bell-tolls.
They drag the air down low.
A priest glides by, wide black sleeves billowing.
One single, tenor bell-toll lingers.
Substance of the blue wind.
Last sunlight breaking the high windows.
I wait for His Grace.
Abuhamed brings a wet cloth for my shoes.
Slowly, we lose the light for this page.

Crossing the Strait

Behind me, Ovranopolis softens in the distance.
The channel crinkles in the supply-boat's wake
and it is too late to return
to what I know.
Ahead lies the Athos peninsula, a blur of monasteries.
I speak to no one.
The boat creaks on the water, under my boot soles.
Waves cup against the prow.
The backwash fans out, melts into itself.

On the late cusp of winter,
there is a sound to blackness!
A hoarse wind chuffs into my duffel coat.
Whitecaps go manic.
The boat falls on troughed swells, lurches me
back into wooden crates and hemp-twine.
Gulls lilt leeward, the wind unstrings them.
The few oil-gray dolphins that cloyed
the stern submerge with deft fluke strokes.
Slapping each wet hurdle, spray spatters me.
I lick the salt from my knuckles,
give in to reasons for a trip I can't name.

Athos approaches, mute, expectant.
The sea line serrates the beach.
I hesitate to go further, to face
the noise within me
in such silence.
What will my own voice sound like?
The boat smacks the quay
and the captain cleats the line
to a stump of flaking iron and concrete.
I step from briny air.

Leagues above, the monastery juts from the cliff.
Two monks perch on the wooden overhang, grasp the railing.
The fragile slats accentuate the elevation.
The ascetics' black robes billow and fist
their tenuous bodies.
They call down, their voices
drown in the wind.
Their mouths are lost
in massive, darkly-flowing beards,
little mouthing Os.
In contrast, their fingers are spokes of white light.
The monks gesture, wave quickly into their chests.
Grigora, Apano!
But I can't climb and the steps from the sea
are wet, heavy with moss.

After the Children Have Gone to Bed

Lionel, do you remember "Dark Shadows"
when we used to sit on the floor
with a crimson blanket around us,
watching the Vampires suck
the fair ladies with rubies around their necks
and us, sucking the TV screen daily?
Still fresh from England, we were two brothers
who quickly adapted to the Californian shows
The Monsters still march forth, and children grow.
Sepia years now—
and they are bringing back the old programs
for the late hours
and I recall now the in-between
where we somehow grew apart into our own lives
and you stayed young through time
with the dream of drugs and the learned American rhyme.

I laid a dark orchid on your name, Lionel.
You always played Vampires too frantically.
I always thought you were insane.
Yet now, they rerun "Dark Shadows" across my screen
and I cannot resurrect you:
brother smile, darker vision.
So I ask you instead if you remember
while I sit here in the late hours, aglow
with my tuck-me-in liquor,
the room in a blue halo,
still a place for you within my blanket,
up from the great slide of time,
an aging me distantly saying,
Pass the biscuits, Lionel. . . .
Rerunning you here with me
in blue light, stopped
adolescent, over
and over again, laughing at my side.

Elegy for a Professor

It was a small, private school and the walls told
us everything. For seven years, I waxed the dark
mansion floor outside your office, in the great Dowd
Hall. While you taught *Moral Issues* and marked

your way to tenure, blessing your students in classical
languages, I worked the polish in and heard every profane
word behind your door, the reviled names, what you took in vain;
the stringy daughter who left you, the son's transfer to the mental

ward, the students you forced out. All the lives you wrecked.
I smoothed extra wax on your threshold so you'd break your neck.
It never happened. We graduated instead. Outside the gate's
black filigree of bars, invoking your name, the classmate

I would never see again took off his shoes, threw them back
over and walked away barefoot. This is what your name adorns.
Two decades of your legacy, small ruler, in the classical, black
language: Ἀπένθητος θά εἴστε   *You will be unmourned.*

Farasa

Nothing recognizable exists here.

One small, grayed man
rests his long monk's shadow
over the dirt road.
In the town of his parents' stories,
fifty years of expectations
settle on his dusty shoes.

Two hundred kilometers south of Caesaria,
there is one house, one cell he looks for.
He listens for voices in the distance,
for the empty diaspora of his people.
He looks for anyone who can
remember the Farasiotic dialect.

There are a few stone huts, stone walls
marking the boundaries of nothing,
trailing themselves into sod and flowers.
Standing before the rubble,
he has come to find
what of himself was left behind.
Anonymous clothes on the clothesline,
wide turkish trousers wading the air.
Transient faces from the few thresholds.
A stray capon pecking the clay
beneath a Falanga tree.

In an autumn of the harvest and scythe,
they had fled under a crescent moon.
Syllables hurled to the wind.
What could not be carried out on mules
was buried.
Reliquaries relinquished.
Graves given to overgrowth,
the markers effaced and sunken.
Seasons later, what squatters didn't
carry off is left
to the slowness of gravity.

This is the softness of stones.
Time and man crumbling everything,
yet only one is patient.

Although Farasa is inhabited
by field mice, he understands
the need to return,
the tension of past
and present that balances us.
Beyond the tautness we need to live,
he prays for history
and against the tension that may destroy us yet.

Remembering the rote of his father's voice,
he paces off past the alder stand,
curves right over the rise
to the chapel-site:
        It stands. Hobbled. A meditation of ruin.
Mounds of mortar and a minaret's silence
the wind wraps around.
He knows if he were to dig through the floor,
he would rediscover the cellar.

In the buried basement, there is a space
of ancient air, unbreathed for decades.
The air of his parents and three generations.

In one dark corner, there lies
the mute glint of tempered gold.
A benign knife held against the side of waiting.
A chalice holding
darkness,
dust of the earth,
the history of it.

NOTE: Historical political strains between Greece and Turkey resulted in a mutual, mass repatriation of ethnic natives: The Treaty of Lausanne, effecting an Exchange and uprooting of generations amidst a social environment of oppression and persecution. The alternative to this Exodus was genocide, as befell the Armenians. On August 15th, 1924, the forced exile and repatriation descended upon Farasa, Cappadocia.

In 1972, one man briefly returned.

Child Christ
at the Top of the Stairs

James Ragan

How the rain-day froze
the dark walk stair, the ceiling bulb,
the child's avenue of stars,
and the body wood from Infant Prague,

so often to its eye I knelt,
my brother in pajama tops,
the figure of a seal slapping up the palms
to the soddy thorn of its sacred heart.

It was always the same—moonfall, eglantine,
my mother at the head of prayers
I memorized like alphabets in school.
Across the hall, musk-scent, my father's

unstrung beads like a rosary
on the sole of his iron mill shoe,
the skin tongued out, leather
rasping the bed's vestibule.

Nightly to the wood I prayed
for a sign, some miracle, the slightest twitch
on the tincture lip. And just as quick
it shivered, at first the toe, slow-motion,

then the foot, in tapping time and swift gyrations,
it tapdanced wildly down the stair,
somersaulted, kicked the wall like Fred Astaire
and pranced the ceiling. I was in awe

of dancing wood, shapes of metaphor
suggesting idea, and prayer, the dancing shoe
of imagination. I was poet of the body rood,
the Bernadette of Lourdes, praying

for the dark to speak, for the long
shoe tap to the clap of the holy beat.
Each night I danced to words and rhymed my feet.
God was soul and alliteration. In the name

of my father, son, and the hollow ghost,
lead me finally into Hollywood
and into temptation—and into that poetry
we were always praying.

Huckster at Noontime

for Jan Pallach, Czechoslovakia

I

In Humenne, in this time of drought,
when the sun and sky
caress like undulating forms,
slow to love in their callow way,

where poets
with fragile appetites and all-day dreaming
twist their spines through jive-talk parlors
like insects through a hammock,

I think of the chrysalis,
how the moth smothers in a spreading flame,
wings itself to death,
too early for the wind.

And I think of the Huckster,
black as Tatra rock,
his ring-boned haridelles, blinders cocked,
down at Market Square,
crates of fruit dying early in their season.

2

One day in six,
the red rose wilts in his lapel,
jewels turn to glass on his thumbs,
his wheel rims, rolling free-fall in tall air,
stick fast to the customers, ringing bells
like wards of maternity

for the ripe milk of melons
souring like the odor of hoofs and tails.
They have no schedule,
these umbilicates,
exiled in the sleep of their conception.

They save religion for the Friday sale,
for the revolutionary, their *kamelot*,
thief with stolen horses,
huckstering fruit
like news on the anniversary of death.

Celebrant of the extreme
unction, patron of the healing arts,
he spits into nicks of melon bellies,
grinds the sap, the worms,
the spittle of tobacco shreds.
Even corn whiskey turns to gold on his breath.

3

I think of the stench,
the rotted fruit, the cankered skin
like wizened breasts of nuns,
how the juice once flowed,

flesh splitting, wet as lips.
And now this aching
flesh of worms,
blotting the tongue white,
transparent as onions,
the veins like delicate moth wings.

He plays the martyr, liberator,
the huckster out of season,
dropping apple-cores
where now the children lie,
picking roots of rampion
out of the cobblestones of Svermova.
Bodies back at Wenceslaus
rot red beneath the statue's sword.

Standing at Pasternak's Table, Peredelkino

Birch bark, soundings in the linden wood,
ferns ornate as creweled cloth or filigree,
prints of birdscape in pastures and old sod–
these, like May light, he could not spare as easily
as I might, but memorized the Urals
in floats of geraniums unloamed from pots,
vowels of sunlight along the sill.
What the world had named was neither poem not art,
as if to walk in cadence were voiceless, doggerel
laced like shoes to slow his feet.
Words should grow inquisitive, become avowals,
as in birth or naming the unnamed, how brief
their passage of identity, how precious
their fidelity to all nature's voice.

The Ballads of Kukutis
by Marcelijus Martinaitis

Laima Sruoginis

IN THE autumn of 1988 when I traveled to Vilnius, Lithuania, to spend a year studying Lithuanian literature, the power of the Lithuanian Reform Movement "Sajudis" could be felt in every realm of life. You could feel it pulsating everywhere, from the grim woman wearing a "Sajudis" pin who sold you ice cream on the corner, to groups of students and professors discussing ideas and reforms in the university halls. At the university we would be excused from lectures to attend demonstrations. Students passed sign-up sheets during lectures to get people on buses to protest the faulty nuclear power plant operating in Ignalina. That summer women in country villages fainted when they heard students (who had ridden from the cities on bicycles with tri-color flags) speak openly of reforms. Just a few weeks before, one could be imprisoned for such an act. I arrived in Vilnius just as Lithuania was emerging from this magnificent summer of rebirth full of hope, renewed faith, and confidence. The summer had been a carnival of defiance to fifty years of tyranny and suffering.

The key figures behind this miraculous reawakening, which seemed to make even the most devious citizen a better person, were a handful of poets, writers, artists, and musicians who chose the word "Sajudis" to name their organization. They stood for reform, they stood for non-violent resistance toward a super-aggressive military state. One of the key figures in this group was the poet Marcelijus

Martinaitus, a poet and professor of Lithuanian literature at Vilnius University.

I first heard his poetry, particularly *The Ballads of Kukutis*, set to music and performed by the musician Vytautas Kernagis, while I was still a high school student studying at the Lithuanian High School in Germany. Martinaitis's poetry struck a chord in me then, and ever since I've greatly admired his work. I was not the only person deeply affected by Martináitis's poetry. He is beloved by his nation and has an immense following. In Lithuania he is considered a living classic.

During fifty years under the Soviet regime, when Lithuanians were cut off from the church (the nation being ninety percent Catholic) people looked to poets for spiritual guidance. Poetry offered a means of inner resistance to the harsh and brutal world created by the Soviet Union.

"Kukutis" created the opportunity for people to laugh at the regime as well as to examine their own souls.

I found this work so rich and inspiring that I decided to translate it into English so that I might become a "message bearer" as well. I grew up Lithuanian-American and always felt I was on a continual bridge back and forth between two cultures; poetry translation, particularly of a work as powerful as *The Ballads of Kukutis*, was my way of forging in part a bridge between tiny, archaic Lithuania and the United States. However, at the time I made this decision I could not imagine how complex and diverse this work would become and how far it would take me.

INTRODUCTION

The Life and Death of Kukutis

Marcelijus Martinaitis

translated by Laima Sruoginis

SOMETIMES a character out of a book takes on a life of its own. This is what happened with Kukutis, the main character of *The Ballads of Kukutis*. These ballads have been translated into many different languages; in fact, Kukutis has traveled to more countries than I have. I am constantly being offered new themes for Kukutis; I am told of Kukutis's new adventures in foreign lands. However, my work on the book is complete. I am not adding any new motifs, but at the same time the work is not finished. The themes are extended upon by the reading and understanding of the work; the main character is constantly being brought back into new situations, the number of which can be very large. This is why he can become involved in new adventures at any time or in any place. When people ask me how one should interpret this character, I answer: do with him what you wish, understand him however you like, it'll be fine, you won't ruin the ballads, they will become your own adventures.

Kukutis acts as a mythological being, or hero, according to certain readers' or listeners' understanding of archetypal themes. The situations in which those themes are tested can be as diverse as there are readers. That's why I, the poet, in a way distance myself from the reader and almost have nothing more to tell her/him. Texts can be created in a new way, or anew. Much in the same way as this world of myths is the well-spring for many texts.

The Ballads of Kukutis was not written with any format set up in advance. While writing this lyric poem I'd sometimes let my imagination run wild. I'd ponder—what would happen if? . . . Someone else would start speaking in my voice, someone I seemed to know, but had never seen or met.

I grew up in the country, immersed in the Lithuanian villagers' folkloric context of thinking, influenced by their even stronger archetypal understanding of life: the mythological images so prevalent in their lives. This is a powerful phenomenon that still affects contemporary Lithuanian culture. Strange images float in the minds of a person brought up in that culture. These images are inherited through language and tradition, frequently transforming themselves into themes of art and cultural life, becoming characters in works of literature, often gaining a figurative expression.

One feels very close to the archaic Lithuanian world, which survived like a strange island, practically into the twenty-first century, in the very center of Europe.

My nation, which in the last few years has begun to recreate its own state and institutions, has risen up in the world like a myth that cannot be understood merely in political terms. It is like the discovery of a new phenomenon. The Lithuanian nation was considered to be dying, melting into the vast expanses of Eurasia. For half a century her language could not be heard in Europe, nor could the fruits of her labor or creative work be seen. Now she is returning to the world carrying all the complexes acquired by the dying, having felt the chill of near extinction through mass deportations, genocide, and persecution. In this way Kukutis represents my nation's complexes. He returns from the dead, or leaves to join the dead, shows up where he is not wanted, where his presence makes no sense.

It is not accidental that literary scholars often look for Kukutis's roots in Lithuanian folk mythology, in the symbolism of pre-Christian Lithuanian religion, in fairy tales or in the memories of country folk. But the types of myths and occurrences used in the ballads, that type of character, does not exist in this realm. I had only the name to work with–Kukutis. The meaning of the name is not clear. In everyday speech it causes people to crack a smile. Traditionally it has been used in jest, to poke fun at someone. You'd come across it occasionally in one or the other rhymed text. The name itself seems to have a hidden mystical fable programmed into it, and when you use it in certain situations it causes people to laugh. The meaning of that hidden fable came to me much later, after I had written the bulk of the ballads. This confirms the thought that very archaic meanings can be detected in words; certain repetitious archetypal situations help to bring this out.

These archetypal codes come to light during ceremonies, rites, ritualistic trances. Things become apparent at that time that no one had any idea of–stereotypical expressions, words and names, are explained.

The same thing happens during the creative process. Certain conventions, formalities of speech and understanding disappear. For example, one can imagine or feel that no strict border exists between life and death. In this way certain blocks in our thinking are destroyed; therefore the discursive process, like the parade during carnival season, can move in all directions–from death into life or the other way around. Kukutis is given the privileges of the carnival because he can go beyond commonly held beliefs on life, death, youth, old age, masculinity, femininity. Those were the privileges bestowed upon archaic peoples during the time of carnival or other calendar holidays, family or work holidays. Kukutis is a carnival mask. He is someone wearing a costume, into which anyone can fit and acquire the same powers and insight. Kukutis, walking from one non-conventional sphere into another, acquires specific knowledge which, it seems, was almost dictated to me while I was writing the ballads.

That power of knowing, of understanding, belongs to those with a changed exterior: the maimed, one-legged, one-armed, blind or hunchbacked beings who have the characteristics of various animals and folkloric beings. My Kukutis is also one-legged, but that has to do with "one-legged" animals like grass snakes or serpents. These animals are believed to carry magic or god-like powers.

The roots of Kukutis's name can be traced to various Lithuanian words. For example, "kukute" (gegute) means a coo-coo bird, "kukis" means staff, the same word used for hook, or even "kukas" (kiaule), which means pig. Associating my character's name with "kukis," the word for staff, is meaningful because a staff (krivule) is the symbol of the wise man, holy man, or "message bearer" in Lithuanian folk mythology. The staff was especially important as the identifying object of one carrying news or information. Besides that, a certain bird is referred to as "kukutis." The bird is all-knowing and second in knowledge only to the coo-coo bird (possibly he is her husband). Legends recount that the bird Kukutis was a go-between for the Queen of Sheba and Solomon. In Eastern tradition Kukutis (hud hud) is also a go-between, a message bearer.

Sometimes it occurs to me that maybe my Kukutis is a message bearer as well, bringing letters to me from the ancient past so that I may either read them or pass them on. Maybe I've become a message bearer. . . .

This character unexpectedly passed special transcendental powers on to me which usually are represented by shamans, holy people, tricksters, wise men, and a slew of other Lithuanian mythological characters. According to the logic of cultural myths the poet belongs to that same category of archetypal hero, because she/he sometimes acquires knowledge that cannot be acknowledged by everyday profane practice. That unusual experience can be understood by the effort of the collective unconscious or other methods. The poet is often a strange, modern day shaman through his/her creative work. She/he sets the groundwork for the mind to be able to jump over certain conventional barriers. That was especially important for me during the time of the Soviet regime when I had to swallow absurd propaganda and myths created by the bolsheviks. I had to live with a mind inherited from the collective unconscious. That is why I am both the author and persona of these ballads. In the same way every reader of *The Ballads of Kukutis* can become the book's author.

Kukutis's Fruitless Bread

Marcelijus Martinaitis

translated by Laima Sruoginis

–I was born in a dough trough
as the land around me
turned one hundred years old.

Nights, having snuck into the pantry,
I'd suck on the bread,
feeling with my lips for her
naked crusty breasts.
Hollowed out
she would cough dryly
under the blankets
so that the Commonwealth prisoners
would not hear.

I grew well
cared for by the sickly bread.
On good days
the both of us would look out the pantry window
at how in Zuveliskes
from the Vilija to the Neris
the Swedes drag boats.

Mornings I'd awaken healthy
as a hundred potato sacks,
having felt the approach of spring
like a passing woman.

Once
the Prussians set me up nicely in a line
between Klaipeda and Memel*
After that I started passing through hands
like an empire's money:
the kings would use me
to buy silk for the princesses –
this time the Kaisers,
that time the Nicolases.

Unable to share me they grew angry:
they buried me in the ground
in straight lines
from Koenigsberg to Karaliaucius;*
with my body
they measured their kingdoms
or
how many times around the earth I would be
laid down next to myself over and over again.
Summoned again I fought
when they needed to decide
whose rye it was
between the Neris and the Vilija.
So again
I measured the land
between the Nemunas and Memel
marking how many kilometers there are,
and how many it takes to get back
across my entire life.

And there was no time left
to visit the bread.
She remained fruitless,
forgotten,
lonely,

*Memel is the German founder's name for the Lithuanian city of Klaipeda, while
Koenigsberg is the German founder's name for the Lithuanian city of Karaliaucius.

a wrinkled old woman
with a small hunch-back
still waiting for me at the pantry window,
gazing over the world

Kukutis's Lament
under the Heavens

translated by Laima Sruoginis

Kukutis, Kukutis, you good soul,
aren't you afraid of the heavens on such a night?

Oh and the heavens are full of lights–like Paris,
under such skies–a colt and a cross!

Why are you crying, Kukutis, sad like autumn?
It would be better for you to give me your daughter's hand!

It's true, she once was a bullet for me
in Manchuria, it seems, or in the Kursk fields.

A fence was nailed together from my youth–
so it is your farmstead, I see, fenced in.

And these windows were mine long ago–
old blue notebooks from elementary school.

Kukutis, even your daughter isn't the same–
she is buried under the tracks in Silesia.

Never mind! Around the corner: illuminated by the heavens,
we'll both have a drunken cry over our homeland.

Never mind! Above the barn–you see,
a strange worldwide hunchback star is starting to shine.

Kukutis in the Reich's Guard House

translated by Laima Sruoginis

Bird, you sing and sing,
but do you know
what your song's words are?
What would you answer
if they were to ask:
what–are–your–song's–words?

And you, sun,
shine, and don't know
what your light's
words are?

If you didn't answer, sun,
they'd bust your teeth out, sun,
with the butt of a revolver!

Kukutis's Swallow's Hymn

translated by Laima Sruoginis

Spring,
and for you, spring–isn't it spring?
And for you, spring, isn't it beautiful
when it's beautiful?
When it's spring?

How beautiful! How beautiful it is,
when it's beautiful!

Even for the not-beautiful
it's beautiful
when it's spring
when the sun thaws
in the windowpanes!

How beautiful it is to be grass
or smoke
over one's homeland.
Even for the dead
it's beautiful
on earth.

How beautiful it is for you, spring,
when it's spring,
when it's beautiful,
when all of Lithuania returns
to the fields with plows and hoes
after a long winter's exile.

Silly Spring

translated by Laima Sruoginis

What has happened here in Zuveliskes?
Motorcycles fly through the windowpane.
At nine-thirty in the morning airplanes flew by
in underground flight.

Already released from winter's work
Samogitian toads, gods, and mice crawl about.
Three dimwit spoonbrains ride
on Turkish swords to the abode of the dead.

Kukutis's green business,
trampled by goats, will turn green again.

He stares at how on a newspaper, foolishly,
two insects already are breaking God's commandment!

Kukutis's cat saw something move;
the antennas on his eyebrows started to work,
he stretched, got ready to attack,
and his whiskers were full of uranium dust.

Again someone on the ground
lets the airplanes go in underground flight.
A hunchbacked spider scurries across the heavens
and starts to crawl down his spider web onto Pagegiai.

And the long-legged magpie elongates itself
carrying all sorts of foolish talk
above a crookedly plowed field
under the heavens on a fool's hair.
And in the belfry the owl cried so
that crying it went completely blind;
Kukutis's cat skews up his
Chinese
            radioactive eye.

Kukutis's Sermon to the Pigs

translated by Laima Sruoginis

Why do you stare so stupidly?
dirty obese pigs!
You'll burn,
oh you'll burn in hell's fires
fed by hay
and the smoke will rise
reaching England,
stinking up half of Europe.

Hey, Boris,
what do you want now?
After all you've often threatened me
to tell
whom I serve while I sleep
and during the day if I don't pretend
I'm a hanged man.

And you, Victor, how piggish you have become,
informing on me
that I'm hiding one leg from the Reich's work,
and then
that I have relatives in Heaven,
not listed and handed over to the state.
Only, Rolph, I feel sorry for you,
you became a pig so stupidly,
burning Europe's lands,
breaking down doors and windows,
influenced by all sorts of idiots.

Elise, Elise,
what has become of you!
How ugly you are
when you slurp as you eat
and your drool drips down into the trough.
How disgustingly your chin has drooped
and how your calves have knotted.
Oh and I had said to you, be my woman,
when you were still a girl
when I used to carry you
dancing on my accordion.

Oh you pigs!
you've eaten up my best days!
So grow now into hams–
Europe will cram you
into the longest sausage ever!
reaching from Zuveliskes to La Manche!

Unchristened pigs,
eat with your unblessed snouts
what people wouldn't even eat!

Forbid!

translated by Laima Sruoginis

Forbid
Kukutis to drive
with a wagon full of straw
through the open grocery's doors
or to beckon
his hungry pigs
in the cathedral square!

Forbid him
to climb the stepladder into an airplane
with a scythe thrown over his back
or to appear
on color television
barefoot
in a white cloud of chickens!

Forbid him
to spread straw
for his first born calf
in the meeting hall
or to hammer plank beds together
along with newly released prisoners
in the symphony hall!

Forbid him
to hammer his scythe,
or shoe his horses
in the town squares

or to come to *Swan Lake*
wearing his saw as a belt!

Forbid him
to drive past
the jewelry store and
leave horse dung on the street
into which Vilnius's most beautiful
lady might step!

Kukutis's Consciousness Becomes Alienated

translated by Laima Sruoginis

I wake up on my left side,
but on my right side I am still dreaming
with my doors ajar.
On my left side
I go out the door,
while on my right
I still lie
and think with opened eyes.
I think
how on my left,
bent over,
I carry work on my shoulders
through the yard
to the cabbage fields.

Dear God,
what goodness–those
square cabbage fields!

How holy this work is–
alive,
to plant seedlings in straight rows!

All day long with opened eyes
I lie on my side and think about
fingered
greasy money
through opened doors–toward the cabbage fields.
And turning from my left side
to my right
I feel that, instead of me,
there is nothing left–
just a horrible pit
replete with cold.

Kukutis Describes His Hut

translated by Laima Sruoginis

Have I got a hut!
With two ends!
I look through the window–
the sun is rising.
I look through the other–
the sun is already setting.

At one end
the orchard is blossoming;
in the other–
apples are falling.

Through one window
I see
work just started–
through the other
I see it's already rotted.

To one end
I brought home my bride;
in the other I see –
she's already laid out.

At one end
I dance with the young 'uns;
and in the other –
my teeth are falling out.

I have a hut
with two ends;
in one end
I'm walking, still alive,
while in the other –
I lie already dead.

Zuveliskes's Women
Mourn over Kukutis

translated by Laima Sruoginis

–Women! women!
How will we live without Kukutis?
How will the pails ring without Kukutis?

–Who will pair
scythes with rake handles
when the harvest season begins?
Who will pair potato blossoms
with colorful butterflies?

–From whom now
will Zuveliskes's heifers
understand

that it is time for them to marry a young bull:
not understanding anything
they will start to stare
at trucks
and helicopters.

—With what now
will we ferment cabbages?
From what bread-trough sourness
will we take our strength?
Women!
Women!
Without Kukutis
how will we be women?

Kukutis's Sinful Spirit

translated by Laima Sruoginis

When Kukutis falls asleep
his spirit passes through his eyes
and out of his body.
Invisible to everyone,
it roams about Zuveliskes
and no one can understand
who is doing what
is forbidden by the law;
the regulations;
the Ten Commandments.

Kukutis tosses and turns
in his sleep and groans:
who is it brings unto him
all these mortal sins?
and how do so many of them
get into his dreams?

In the morning
he cannot look women and children
in the eyes . . .

Oh and his life is so unsoiled!
How he cleans it every day
by chopping wood,
by carrying hay to the herds
or kneeling with a bucket
beside the well–
he ought to be completely pure
inside!

Released from his body his spirit
bellows drunkenly.
Unshaven,
it enters the sleeping village widows' dreams,
whispers curse words into children's ears;
tempts people drinking at the pub
to denounce
God himself.

On the third day
it returns groveling,
dragging its dirtied
innocent shirt,
crawls up to the Lord God himself,
kisses his hands,
and in a voice ruined by drink asks
that Kukutis be forgiven
the mortal sins
it committed so many of
without him knowing.

Tired out
it returns
through Kukutis's eyes
and gnashing its teeth
falls asleep
for life's long sleep.

A Pony in Kukutis's Ear

translated by Laima Sruoginis

Overnight
a playful pony
emerged inside Kukutis's ear.
Out of joy she jumped about,
whinnied,
and kicked Kukutis's eardrums.

How horrible, Kukutis thought:
I'll go see the doctor,
maybe he can take the pony out of my ear?
But how will I explain
how the pony got into my ear?

How horrible it is
before your acquaintances,
before your children,
before such a beautiful and pure life
where graceful curtains hang
and parquet floors shine!

Kukutis didn't tell anyone,
he procrastinated,
and it became even worse.

He said to himself:
God forbid
I should die–
they'd find such a shameful thing in my ear!

And Kukutis started to fear death:
automobiles,
wheels,
combines,

hay threshers.
God forbid
I should die –
they'd find such a shameful thing in my ear!

Kukutis's Song

translated by Laima Sruoginis

Kukutis broke into song: How fortunate I am
to live and be alive for the sake of living!
I can drive and be happy for the sake of being happy
even when luck deserts me!
A song leaning against a fence heard Kukutis singing
about his good fortune in being fortunate.
The song approached him and patted him on the back:
–You sing the truth and you sing it beautifully, you snake!

The song snuggled up to him and started to harmonize;
the wind blew of itself, scattering the straw.
Kukutis whipped the horses and drove off,
while the song continued singing all alone.

Unhappy Kukutis
in the Potato Patch

translated by Laima Sruoginis

–What should I do!
Where should I go?
When there isn't any money–
there is bread.

The potatoes grew;
their flowers wilted.
A large world
and yet the potatoes are small . . .

Everything tumbles over
onto its other side:
the gnats reproduce
while the cow is barren!

There are so many planes
in the heavens this year,
but next year
there might not be any.

When winter was here—
summer wasn't.
Summer came—
and winter disappeared.

When there was love—
there was no woman.
Look, here's a woman,
but now there's no love!

How it stings one's heart
when the trees chirp,
planes fly,
and potatoes don't.

Kukutis's Trip
on the Samogitian Highway

translated by Laima Sruoginis

While driving, Kukutis exclaims:
How Lithuania resembles Lithuania!
Her birches always resemble birches
just as the heavens
over Lithuania
are always so LIthuanian!

Where does Lithuania's resemblance to Lithuania
come from?
Everything you can remember or think of
resembles Lithuania!

While plowing
he examines a broken clod of earth,
blows grain from his palms,
smells bread baking,
stands barefoot on the ground . . .
What gives Lithuania
her resemblance to Lithuania?
Where does it come from?
Nobody has ever been able to find it or destroy i–
whatever wars may have passed through,
however the land may have been trampled–
Lithuanian skies go on
looking like Lithuania!

And wherever you may travel
or whatever you may think of
will still resemble Lithuania:
her heavens,
her birches,

the warmth of her grain in your palms;
her harvest fields
flowered by women!

Last Farewell to Kukutis

translated by Laima Sruoginis

Burrowing into the grass
small Kukutis dies
curled up like a bee by its hive.
He rests for the last time
breathing in all the good of life.

Kukutis dies, so small—
unseen from airplanes
undetectable on radar screens
unnoticed by submarines.

Kukutis dies quietly,
not interrupting radio waves,
train schedules,
not disturbing airplane flights . . .

Small Kukutis dies
not hurting anyone–like a sigh.
So small, invisible to the entire world,
he dies for all times,
dies wherever there is at least a trace of life,
at least a corner of the heavens,
a handful of earth,
an ant with a fir needle . . .

He dies in bird's nests,
on snow-covered mountain tops,
in fruit seeds, in grain,
he dies in books, in bee hives . . .

He dies where he can never be:
in express train windows, assembly halls:
he dies for words, children, the Antarctic,
Ararat, Australia, the Andes Mountains,
he dies for the entire world . . .

A star risen over the horizon
broadcasts to infinity
his eternal death.

Two Worlds

Julia Older

Spoleto, Italy, 1966

I.

Pound stood at center stage of Caio Melisso.

> He was Ulysses.
> He couldn't go home.

Voice at first like a tired oar feathering water,
he muscled into the storm, a thrash against Circe
and the counter-vortices that protect islands.
Not a whisperer, this one. No susurrus.
The Cantos thundered to the loge.
Cinquecento Doge, he defied them all
with his Greek, Latin, Chinese, Provençal.
Head of the winged Samothrace. Fascist boot.
He learned mistaken identity from the Italians.
Io ho fatto un sbaglio. I made a mistake. *Io. Io.*

II.

Pound wrote to his mistress:

> The scrap of red paper
> attached to this letter
> is to get your attention.

At the reading a beat poet dressed like a hit man from Naples
tore Pound to pieces. A red square of defiance
fluttered in shreds to the stage.

III.

The problem with getting attention, it seems, is to hold it.

    I remember meeting one long-haired American
    waiting for a glimpse of the exiled poet.
    He had scribbled quatrains in the Boboli
    and polished sonnets in the Sistine.
    "Would you like to share a can of spaghetti?" he asked.
    The offer was a flash of red,
    a canto of good will and complete ignorance.

    Many years later, I'm reminded it's easier
    to walk into the Colosseum with a can of spaghetti
    and come out believing you've won
    than to carry a flag, and know you haven't.

Nightlight

Teresa Whitman

BROWNING WILDHORSE is examining his birth certificate. He reads to me what a hospital clerk recorded, thirty-one years ago, in the spaces under *Father's Name, Race,* and *Usual Occupation* with officious typed letters: "MOTHER REFUSES TO TELL. KIOWA. LABORER." Browning and I have lived together for two years. We are sitting on the loveseat turned so that we can watch the logs burning in the fireplace. I'm seven months pregnant.

I ask him, "You've never wanted to find out who your father is?" I say this even though I already know the answer, have been remembering the answer for as long as I've known Browning. A box labeled *Browning's (Odds and Ends)* that his mother, Ruth, has sent up to St. Paul from Norman, Oklahoma, rests between us on the cushion. In addition to his birth certificate, Browning has unpacked news clippings about his high school basketball career, boxes of tiny ornate medals for running track, family snapshots, and for our baby, infant-sized beaded moccasins and a tiny ribbon shirt.

I take a turn studying Browning's birth certificate. My forearms rest on my belly that swells under a rosebud-print bathrobe. I've always had an obsession for history, and now parentage is taking on new significance. Our baby is due in March. Browning hasn't answered my question. I try again, "You're not curious?"

I know what his answer will be before he says it aloud: "Joe was my father. Joe taught me everything I know. He was an Indian gentleman."

Browning repeats this as though it were something he memorized a long time ago. When Browning was three years old, his mother, a Comanche, married Joe Ahnko, a Kiowa. At that time, the three of them lived out in the dusty back country of southwestern Oklahoma.

Browning says, "I can't even measure up to the knuckle on Joe's little finger." He spreads his hands wide. Even though Browning is over six feet tall, he is small boned with long slender fingers. The knuckle of his little finger whorls like the knot on a tree branch.

I lean back against the loveseat. He places his palm on my hand that rests on my belly. From the stereo Bob Dylan sings "Visions of Johanna." Browning sings along with Dylan. Then he says, "How about naming the baby Johanna?" He wants a daughter. He has nine half-brothers. No sisters. I have three sisters, no brothers.

I say, "Johanna? Such a German name?"

"You qualify," he says.

"My ancestors were Irish, English, French."

"Close enough," Browning laughs. He persists. For the moment I agree to the name Johanna only because I know I am carrying a boy. I'd like a daughter too, but I have already seen the baby's face in a dream: a tiny face with smooth brown skin, his eyes, nose, mouth a miniature version of Browning's. There were even traces of a Fu-Manchu moustache.

Browning and I met five years ago. He had come up to St. Paul doing paralegal work on Indian education for the National Indian Youth Council. I was working for a Title IV project, my first job out of school, with Karita Prettyman. Browning and Kirk Poolaw, Karita's boyfriend, came into the Title IV office to take her to lunch. It was Browning's voice, deep and resonant like earth warmed by the sun, that first attracted me to him. Karita teased me, "Don't listen to any Comanche." But there was the way Browning folded his laundry in the Sky Wash laundromat the weekend he asked me to go to Black River Falls for a powwow. Long fingers smoothing a crease into the length of a flannel shirt. The skin on the back of his hands so finely textured that it seemed as cool and moist as spring grass.

We saw each other almost every day for three months, and then Browning went home to Norman for a visit. That first night back in Oklahoma, his younger half-brother Butter was slashed above his eye by a neighbor, Marvin Prichett. Butter and Marvin had been sniffing paint together. Butter stumbled home, his face stained gold, and bloody. Browning cleaned the wound. He left the room to find a bandage. When he came back, Butter was gone and so was Browning's .22 rifle. Browning hurried over to the neighbors. It was dark; there was an argument; the exploding crack of a shot; Marvin was dead.

Browning ended up in prison on a manslaughter charge. I wrote to him in prison. Karita believed that he couldn't have done it, that Butter must have, and Browning was taking the rap.

I waited each week for the clear safe intimacy of his handwriting across sheets of yellow legal paper. Time passed. Browning continued to write once a week, but I wrote less and less.

Then, three years ago, Browning called me. "I'm here. I'm teaching Phy Ed at the Red School House," he said. "Can I see you?"

"You're in prison," I said.

"I won my appeal. I wanted to surprise you."

Maybe in trying to make up for lost time, we've rushed and haven't attended to the three-year gap between us. We try to wall out intrusions from the outside. Browning doesn't like to talk about his three years in prison: "The past doesn't matter," he says. "It's the future that counts." Even though his prison time is the part of his biography I prefer not to remember, a bitter scent, the slight residue of burning that remains after a gun has been shot, hangs somewhere in the background.

We have only two rooms: a bedroom and a long room that serves as kitchen on one end and living room on the other. When we moved in, Browning placed medicine on the ledge over the doorway. An ordinary plastic medicine vial with an inch of red dirt at the bottom. Medicine from Oklahoma to protect the home. We rented this apartment because it has a fireplace. This winter has been a fierce one with a record number of subzero days and inches of snow. Tonight, like most nights, we have built a fire.

I leaf through the family snapshots Ruth has sent and find a photograph of Browning at age twelve: a lanky kid, he stands out in front of the old home place between Joe and Joe's father Samuel. Joe has an army haircut twenty years after his service in the 114th Battalion during the Second World War. Samuel wears two long carefully braided plaits of hair–Kiowa style. This image of fathers and sons moves me. My own father, an Episcopal priest, seemed to cringe from touching me in any affectionate way. Browning strokes my face.

In the photo, he wears a button-down shirt with sleeves too short for his growing twelve-year-old arms; a narrow-boned wrist is exposed. Joe wears a T-shirt; muscles stand up on his arms like bricks. "Because he worked hard out in the fields," Browning says. Joe and Browning worked side by side in the fields–bucking hay, chopping cotton. I imagine Browning sweating a thin sheet of water like he does when we run along the Mississippi River Boulevard together. Not like a white man sweats. Sweat like water with a weak sweet smell.

We stay up late. I listen to him remembering beans simmering and fried potatoes dripping with grease and pepper. Ten boys running wild.

When we finally go to bed, I can't sleep. Browning is behind me, his arms wrapped around my growing belly. I roll out of his embrace to face him. For a moment I wonder how well I really know him. I touch his cheek. It's cool. I roll back into the warm space between us and wrap his arms around me. I close my eyes and listen to his rhythmic breathing. I breathe deeper and slower until my breathing matches his and I fall asleep.

* * *

The next morning, Browning wakes me. It's so cold outside that feathered frost coats the entire bedroom window except for a tiny space at the center. We usually get up with too little time to have much for breakfast besides toast. But this morning he wants me to make him red-eye gravy over fried eggs and grits.

"Red-eye gravy?" I say. "You make it. I don't know what it is."

"Red-eye gravy," he says. "My mom made it as a special treat. You should learn."

He's not exactly sure how to fix red-eye gravy either, but I figure I'll humor this whim since Browning has been humoring the food obsessions of my pregnancy. We've eaten nothing but lamb chops for dinner almost every night this week. Pregnancy has made us needy in quirky ways; I've been asking Browning to brush my hair for me, and he brushes with long attentive strokes: "Your hair reminds me of that shining brown of oak leaves in the fall," he says. I like the self I see in his eyes. So I try to find a recipe. I can't find one in any of my cookbooks.

"What's in it?" I ask him.

He says, "You need ham or spicy sausage."

"We don't have any," I say.

When I set plates of fried eggs-over-easy and grits on the table, Browning doesn't look up. He's reading this morning's *Pioneer Press*. He takes a few bites, then reaches for the bottle of hot peppers. He leaves one small pale-green core after another on his plate; a beaded line of sweat forms across the ridge of his nose.

"What's in the paper?" I say. He holds out a front-page spread of the Reagans' second inaugural ball. Nancy wears a sequined ivory ball-gown this time around.

"White people," he says.

I say, "Am I included in that category this morning?"

Browning glances up at me surprised. "No," he says. "You're different." He studies the newspaper text for a moment. He says, "You don't judge me."

I imagine Ruth, her hands lean and quick, warming breakfast for Joe on a winter morning like this one. Browning is always saying, "Joe was the only one we ever wanted to please." It hits me that in a round-about way it's for Joe that I am to fix red-eye gravy. I say this to Browning.

He says, "Joe's dead—he's been dead for ten years." Joe was killed when the produce truck he was driving hit an escaped bull on the highway at night. The impact of the collision exploded the truck across a field, scattering a wake of onions, cabbages, melons. A few weeks before the accident, someone had come up from behind Joe at a powwow and, fooling around, placed a headdress, a war bonnet, on his head. Joe had been furious. "You don't fool around with that kind of power," he said. Ruth believed that the misplaced headdress caused some evil to find an opening—in the form of a bull on the highway.

After Joe's death, a medicine man came to purify the home. With a wing-feather fan, he had brushed cedar smoke on everyone to protect them—everyone, that is, except Browning who, away at school hadn't made it home yet. It still upset him that he had never been smoked after Joe's death.

I study the photo of Nancy Reagan—over her shoulders, she's looped a feathered boa. The article says the Reagans are eating lobster thermidor at the White House these days. I ask Browning, "How would red-eye gravy taste over poached lobster?"

* * *

All morning I am in the legal library looking up citations for my job as manuscript editor for Mason Legal Publishers. In a federal reporter, I find a citation that Browning has asked me to photocopy: *Wildhorse v. State of Colorado,* a suit brought with the help of the National Indian Youth Council. It concerns Fort Lewis College, a land-grant school that was supposed to be tuition-free for all qualified Indians—a contract in perpetuity that had been faulted on. Then I look up a later citation, *Wild-Horse v. State of Oklahoma,* and read an account of the appeal that Browning had made after his conviction.

After lunch I have an appointment with my obstetrician. My blood pressure is way up. "You're going to have to go straight home and lie down," the doctor says. She says I'm to think only about babies. I'm not to work until after the baby is born. I'm not even to go back that afternoon.

I spend the rest of the day lounging on the loveseat, reading about babies. Browning has made a hammock for the baby that will swing over our bed. He will teach our child how to climb a pecan tree and shake down the hard nuts.

When Browning comes home, I tell him that the book I'm reading calls traditional Indians the parents we should all emulate. They never punished their children physically—it was an unthinkable brutality. Browning picks up some logs and squats before the hearth. He doesn't say anything. I tell him how my father whipped me across my bare back with his belt. I want to know why my Puritan ancestors were beating up their kids, while his Comanche and Kiowa ancestors understood that children don't need shaming.

Browning says, "Because a baby and mother were skin to skin. The grandparents were in charge then. A close community where everyone has equal worth has perspective on things."

He turns toward me and rocks back on the heels of his black boots. "But my mom was forced to go to Indian boarding school. She never even knew her mother. My grandparents were dead—except Samuel, but he lived miles away." Browning prods the fire with an iron poker. "My brothers and I grew up out in the sticks. If a car drove by our house, we scattered into the high weeds."

I saw where Browning grew up when we drove to Oklahoma last summer to see Ruth, who works now as a nurse in Norman. We drove farther south to the old home place ten miles outside the town of Atwater. The land was his grandmother's allotment along the creek, Big Elk they called it. We walked down to the draw of sandy soil that sloped into the creek to look for a melon. Browning told me how his mother used to push his brother in a stroller and he had trotted alongside. They had gone from melon to melon—looking for a big one, a ripe one that split open, cold and sweet. As a child, Browning had loved the wild grass, how green it was, how long. And the wind that blew the grass over and made the fields ripple and soften.

Back then, Joe had tried to farm. Browning remembered him coming in late. The dark. He was dirty and dog-tired. The only light they had was kerosene–kerosene lamps, a kerosene stove. No electricity or running water. Nothing like that. Browning remembered dark nights in the house and the oily smell of kerosene. It was after Browning had left for the university that Joe gave up trying to farm and they moved into Atwater. The old home place had collapsed into a pile of boards, and we found no melons down by the draw.

"I'll tell you one thing," Browning says now. "Anytime anybody did me a favor or just did something for me, a warm feeling started between my shoulder blades and spread over my entire back, made my hair stand up on end, the back of my neck tingle. I could almost close my eyes and go to sleep. I used to have that feeling a lot when I was younger. How come I never have that feeling anymore?"

He comes over and sits next to me on the loveseat. He leans over and puts his ear against my belly. "Maybe Johanna will give me that old feeling."

I feel a small flicker of panic like the fire now burning in the hearth. We both have too much staked on the baby who grows inside of me.

Browning gives me a small wrapped box. "For Johanna," he says. I open the package. It is a porcelain nightlight in the shape of a bear.

"I was afraid of the dark when I was a kid," Browning says. This surprises me. Browning has always struck me as fearless. He plugs the nightlight into an outlet. The thin skin of the bear lights up, a soft beige.

This bear is only the first light. For the next week Browning brings home a nightlight almost every evening: a large oyster covered with tiny shells; an ornate candle; a small spiral of plastic that plugs into an outlet, glowing orange only when the room turns dark. But my favorite is the first round-bellied bear with translucent skin.

Browning doesn't want any of the nightlights in our bedroom. "I got used to the dark," he says. But when we go to bed, he turns on all the nightlights in the long living-kitchen area. The room glows like Christmas. "For the baby," he says.

"The baby can't see these lights," I say.

"It comforts her to know there's light out here for her," he insists. A slender ribbon of light seeps under our bedroom door.

* * *

About two weeks after I'm told to quit my job, Browning hasn't come home by the time I'm ready to put out the fire and get into bed. I turn on all of the nightlights. It has become a habit.

Before I have a chance to fall asleep, I hear Browning coming in. He showers. Wrapped in a towel, he sits on the edge of the bed, his back against the wall. He sets a half-empty can of Budweiser down on the wooden floor.

"I'll sing you to sleep, Clare," he says. The warm earth of his voice presses up against my spine. He sings one of Joe's old peyote songs.

He tells me, "Joe would find an old coffee can and put a few pieces of charcoal in the bottom. He'd stretch a piece of red inner tube real tight over the top; it wasn't hide but it worked; he tied it with a string. He poured water in the can, punched a few holes through the taut rubber top. He thumped and listened. He tuned it by ear. He hit the drum. If he had tuned it just right, when he tipped it, the water moved and caused the sound to warble. Beautiful, oh, it's beautiful, Clare. If you make a little dip, the water will move and put a little waver in the tune."

Now and then, one of Joe's friends walked a mile or two along the creek and came over. The men sat out there on the porch. Browning lay in bed and heard them singing. They chewed peyote; it was brown-green and tough like buttons of dried apricot. Sometimes they crushed and boiled it into a thin-looking tea that smelled and tasted like dust–dry and bitter. They called it speeding. It was a sacred thing. Whoever was there would speed together, pray, partake.

This bedtime story of Browning's lulls me like a familiar melody. But then Browning says, "I quit my job." He says this more to the dark than to me. I'm used to Browning quitting jobs. After the Red School House, he worked for the Native American Leadership Project. Then for the Indian Center. He'd find well-paid administrative jobs–he had a degree in political economy. He worked overtime for the first six months. But then he'd start to resent how hard he was working and quit before eleven months had passed.

But now I'm pregnant and can't work. I sit up, wide awake. "Couldn't you have waited until after the baby is born?"

"They don't like me," he says. "These northern skins don't like southern skins." Once I suggested that we move to Oklahoma where Browning would feel more a part of the community. He refused, saying there were better opportunities in Minnesota.

"Browning," I say.

To the night air he says: "'This is what an Indian gentleman does. At a tribal meeting, don't be pushy. You hang back. No matter what it is, eating or talking. Let everybody else go first. Then you go. Just listen. Listen to it all. If people want to hear what you have to say, they'll ask you. Then you tell them everything that is on your mind. Otherwise don't say anything. Let it go. I let it go.'"

* * *

During the night, it snows—a deep light snow. In the morning neither of us has a job to go to. Browning wants to hunt for cottontails. "I'll make you and Johanna rabbit stew for dinner," he says. He's in a good mood.

"Won't a rabbit be in its burrow today?" I say.

He looks at me surprised. "Cottontails don't dig burrows." Browning has a way of reminding me how little I really know about the world outside.

We drive east, then north along the St. Croix River looking for a place we might stop; all the property along the river is privately owned. The fresh snow dazzles in the sunlight; all the whiteness gives me a headache. He says, "Cottontails sit in the weeds covered with snow. You look for the little hole where their breath melts through. Sometimes you see an eye. Then bap on the head."

We finally stop in a public park outside of Osceola. Browning finds a thick stick. He walks with long elastic strides, then slows down so I can keep up with him. He says, "I'd recognize your gait anywhere. Smooth, like you're walking through thoughts." But my center of gravity is so far forward that I can't keep going; I return to wait in the car.

Browning has told me that when he was twelve, Joe bought him the twenty-two rifle. It was an investment. From then on he was expected to bring meat home for the table. Early in the morning or late in the evening, he went out for squirrels; any time for cottontails. Deer hid in low areas alongside the creek where the grass grew thicker and taller. They never had a license; they poached—it was meat on the table.

One Thanksgiving, Joe said, "God damn it, this is the one day out of the year we're going to have enough to eat." Joe and Browning went out at 4 A.M. when no one else was around to hunt for elk. They walked fifteen miles alongside the creek toward the granite hills of the Wichitas. Joe circled ahead, upwind. Browning stayed downwind as decoy. He moved slowly through the seven-foot-tall Johnson grass that rattled, like reeds, in the breeze.

By the afternoon they had shot only a skinny old doe. They hung it from a tree, bled it, then broke it down to carry on their backs. They walked out to the road. Waiting for them there, a ranger idled in a government-green pickup. Joe sat in the pickup with the ranger for the longest time. Browning stood in the road with the packs of meat.

Browning doesn't know what was said that day: when Joe finally got out of the pickup and the ranger drove off, step-father and son didn't say a word to each other. But Browning saw the smoldering behind Joe's eyeballs and knew that he had begged: You can take me to jail but what good will it do–my kids, they'll still be hungry. Farmers around here kill deer to keep them out of their fields. They're left to rot. Please.

I know this smoldering because I've seen it in Browning's face; sometimes even a slight affront becomes humiliation that he can't bear; and so he does something unexpected like quit a good job. I try to imagine a rabbit's small breathing hole in the snow, the hole that will give it away, that will make it be there for Browning. I feel a growing pressure on my lungs; I'm breathing hard. I open the car door to get out and find him. Bright light reflects off the white ground and for a moment I can't see. Then I hear him coming toward me, cold snow squeaking against his boots. He's empty-handed.

* * *

Browning makes lamb chops again for dinner. He says, "What if Johanna has blond hair? Who ever heard of an Indian with blond hair?" Browning is remembering I'm not Indian.

"Not much chance of that," I say. "Your hair is black. Mine's an autumn brown."

"If you want me to leave, I'll leave," he says.

"Why would I want you to leave?" I say. This is a conversation we have every time Browning quits a job. What he really means is I can leave and go back to my middle class. I don't know what he thinks I'd go back to. He imagines America's white middle class as a chain of free hotels, a huge family that will receive me with no questions asked. I say, "I don't want either of us to go anywhere."

After dinner I take a bath. I hear him on the phone. He talks for a long time and then he comes into the bathroom.

"I did what you wanted," he says.

"What did I want?" I say.

"I called my mother and asked her who my father was. She didn't want to talk about it."

I am in the middle of washing my hair. Pink-purple bubbles slide down my bare breasts.

Browning says, "They say that when squirrels and Indians die, they have red bones. His name was Vincent RedBone. Vincent RedBone. Vin-cent Red-Bone. Four syllables of sound. That's all."

* * *

Early in March, the oldest of Browning's half-brothers, Harmony, comes for a visit. It's snowing again with high winds making for blizzard conditions. I am huge.

Harmony is a lawyer. As a student, he took electives in trust relationships and treaty rights every chance he had, but now he works for General Motors in Oklahoma City. Harmony looks a lot like Browning only he seems built on an entirely different scale; he is a large-boned man. We roast hot dogs in the fireplace and talk about the old home place.

Browning says, "When Clare and I were down there last June, we camped below Tepee Mountain." We had borrowed a domed tent from another brother. We lay awake watching the sky, listening to the cicadas—*soyakis*, Browning called them. I remember the scorched smell of hot granite in the air, but it bothers me that I don't remember how the heat felt against my skin.

"It's funny," I say. "I know it was hot. I know it was humid, but I don't remember sweating or feeling hot." Browning and Harmony look at me and then at each other and laugh. Their eyes are full of land.

Browning says, "I used to sweat out there so much chopping cotton that when my arms dried, salt caked on like powder. In one morning, I'd drink all the water in a cream can—five or six gallons."

Browning and I have calculated that the baby was conceived below Tepee Mountain. I remember only the sunlight and shadows washing through the trees; a warm wind to lean against; the feeling, looking across the plains, that flight was possible. It was only later that Browning told me about fire ants, rattlesnakes, copperheads, barbed wire.

Now he puts his arms around my waist and holds my belly. "When I met you," he says, "you were like a cool drink of well water in the summer." My belly tightens. I've been having preparatory contractions all week. But this contraction pulls sharper than the rushes I've had before.

I go to bed. Harmony and Browning are remembering a tornado cellar. Lying in bed, I can hear their low voices through the thin wall. "We spent half our summers in that cellar," Harmony says.

"Remember when Joe had something to tell us, we sat around the table or out on the front steps. All ten of us. He had an audience, a crowd. He'd say, 'And the law is. You will be here every night. You do not stay out for any reason.' "

"That's exactly what he said. That's why I walked long distances in snow storms and tornado weather, day or night, to get home. They weren't rules or suggestions–they were flat absolute laws."

"Sometimes when one of us messed up, nobody wanted to tell who did it. That pissed Joe off. 'All right,' he said, 'line up.' He lined up the whole crew outside against the house. Then, slap, slap, slap, slap, slap– he went down the line with his belt. Then he said, 'Now I know I got the right one.' Because he was Old Testament. Even though he was traditional in his ways, he didn't think there was anything wrong with the principles in the Bible. He sat us down at the table and read: 'Spare the rod and spoil the child.' He said, 'I'm going to tell you kids right now, you're not going to be spoiled.' "

I can no longer tell whose voice is whose. I try to see the small vial of medicine above the doorjamb; but I can't make it out in the shadows. I fall asleep watching the narrow wedge of light under the door.

I wake up when Browning comes to bed. I realize how dark the room is. "You turned off the nightlights for Harmony?" I ask.

"No," he says. "The power's off."

We lie together in the sudden dark. After a while Harmony begins to snore in the next room. He is sacked out in a sleeping bag in front of the dying firelight. I know Browning isn't falling asleep. He's turned away from me, but every curve of his body has pulled taut.

After a while he says, "Before my mom married Joe, we lived with my aunt Ellen." I know this and I wonder why he is telling me it again now.

He waits, listening to the dark. Then he says, "Sometimes my mom would be gone all day. She worked as a cook then. My cousins, they were teenagers, played Indian boarding school. They locked me in the cellar." Browning turns toward me. "Why would anybody do that to a little kid? I waited hours for my mom to come home. I sat with my cheek pressed against the top step to be near the line of light and air under the door."

I move in as close to his chest as I can get. My belly is in the way. I touch his hair.

He says, "Then Ruth married Joe. He hated that I was afraid of the dark. After a long day of farming without any of the necessary tools, he couldn't deal with hearing my whining. He yanked me out of bed and told me to stop crying. I couldn't. He threw me against the wall. I was three years old. Joe used to beat the dog shit out of me every night until I wasn't afraid of the dark anymore. I was afraid of Joe. Nothing was worse than Joe's beatings—even my terror of the dark."

Browning is crying. "Maybe I should leave before I hurt this baby," he says.

My belly tightens. Our child presses large against my ribs, bladder, and pelvic bone. It is making its presence felt. "Why would you hurt the baby?" I say.

"Sometimes I feel this blind rage that is so intense I'm afraid."

He turns away from me. He's talking to the wall now. "He beat the dog shit out of me. I never knew when it was coming. Once I was eating dinner and he threw a fork at me. It stabbed me in the cheek. Blood was dripping in my potatoes. He made me eat them anyway."

I hold my belly. It hurts to breathe. I try to speak, but my open mouth makes no sound.

"We were out in the boondocks. Joe's own brother said to my mom. 'How can you live with that man? He's so mean.' She said, 'He's not mean to us.' " Browning pulls the blanket closer. "The only thing on our minds was getting enough to eat. We were harassed our entire lives. You won't ever be able to understand that. You can't."

A contraction comes so fast and hard that I sit up. I am sweating. I get out of bed and go stand by the window. I look out at the blizzard. Even with all the power off in the neighborhood, the snow seems brilliant and cruel. Our son, curled inside of me, must plunge into the world head first. He is waiting in my womb, held tight, his rhythmic breathing making a small warm hole in the dark.

Scissortails

I

You speak of back home
    the double blade
    the scissortail in flight

2

We scan the red clay road
that shoots straight into your past
for scissortails.
You give me your world:
Here is the Old Home Place.
Gray boards collapsed under hackberry
and elm. Hot wind. Nothing but the rubbing
of tall grass and unseen insects,
the flat plain and blunt granite hills
you call by name:
Little Bow, Tepee, Saddle Mountain.

3

Listen, you say, *cicadas*,
soy-yakis *we called them.*
You were a child when they tried
to stick a cicada in your mouth
buzzing
to make you a singer.
You cried, hit, pulled back.
You say you can't remember
if they got it past your tongue.
Yet, your mouth is wide,
you sing into me:
I walked these roads in every
kind of weather, a kid
bucking hay, chopping cotton.
The only thing on our minds
was getting enough to eat.

4

On the way to your Aunt Mary's
you point out the patch
of wild plums where you killed

that old rattlesnake. Big cars,
Oldsmobile, Chevy, Continental
fill the road. Mary says,
Come sit by me, white girl.
Laughter buzzes from the house.
The only things on their minds, she says,
drinking since Friday noon.
We want that far horizon
where the sun swells,
the sky's a sharper blue.
Mary waves her arm, gives us Comanche
for star   *ta-tsee-nup-sta*

5

There, you say. Rising skyward,
a small gray bird (white breast,
the long forked tail feathers)–
this fierce resilience after splitting,
crossing and recrossing.
We'll rest here, Corn, Esther says.
Your mother calls you Corn.
I lean against the hot wind
that smells of burning metal.
It holds me. *See this red earth.*
See this creek called Little Elk.
I know it like the back of my hand.
It is clear here. The scissortail
spins, plunges earthward, whistling.
Look: a scissortail in flight.

Looking for Indians

Cheryl Savageau

My head filled with TV images
of cowboys, warbonnets, and renegades,
I ask my father
what kind of Indian are we, anyway.
I want to hear Cheyenne, Apache, Sioux,
words I know from television
but he says instead
Abenaki. I think he says Abernathy
like the man in the comic strip
and I know that's not Indian.

I follow behind him
in the garden
trying to step in his exact footprints,
stretching my stride to his.
His back is brown in the sun
and sweaty. My skin is brown
too, today, deep in midsummer,
but never as brown as his.

I follow behind him like this
from May to September
dropping seeds in the ground,
watering the tender shoots,
tasting the first tomatoes,
plunging my arm, as he does,
deep into the mounded earth beneath
the purple-flowered plant
to feel for potatoes

big enough to eat.
I sit inside the bean teepee
and pick the smallest ones
to munch on. He tests
the corn for ripeness
with a fingernail, its dried silk
the color of my mother's hair.
We watch the winter squash grow hips.

This is what we do together
in summer, besides the fishing
that fills our plates unfailingly
when money is short.

One night
my father brings in a book.
See, he says, Abenaki,
and shows me the map
here and here and here,
he says, all this
is Abenaki country.
I remember asking him
what did they do
these grandparents
and my disappointment
when he said no buffalo
roamed the thick New England forest.
They hunted deer in winter
sometimes moose but mostly
they were farmers
and fishermen.

I didn't want to talk about it.
Each night my father
came home from the factory
to plant and gather,
to cast the line out
over the dark evening pond

with me, walking behind him,
looking for Indians.

Like the Trails of Ndakinna

We're French and Indian like the war
my father said
they fought together
against the English
and although that's true enough
it's still a lie
French and Indian
still fighting in my blood

The Jesuit who traveled up the St. Lawrence
found the people there uncivilized
they will not beat their children
he wrote in his diary by candlelight
and the men listen too much
to their wives

You who taught me to see no borders
to know the northeast as one land
never heard the word *Ndakinna*
but translated without knowing it
our country, Abenaki country

Grandmothers and grandfathers
are roaming in my blood
walking the land of my body
like the trails of Ndakinna
from shore to forest

They are walking restlessly
chased by blue eyes and white skin
surviving underground
invisibility their best defense

Grandmothers, grandfathers,
your blood runs thin in me
I catch sight of you
sideways in a mirror
the lines of nose and chin
startle me, then sink
behind the enemy's colors

You are walking the trail
that declares this body
Abenaki land
and like the dream man
you are speaking my true name
Ndakinna

To Human Skin

My father's eyes were blue
like his grandfather's
but if I trace the line
of nose and chin
it is his grandmother's face
I see. Abenaki woman.

His heart was green and growing,
as if he'd lived for centuries
an old forest tree man
rooted in the rocky soil
now called New England,
as if Gluscabe's arrow
had just pierced the bark
and turned it to human skin.

Ndakinna, I want to tell him now.
Ndakinna. There is a name

for this place you call in English
the home country.

Over the last meal
we'll ever eat together
he tells me, I'm going up north,
up to the old home country,
Abenaki country. He smiles
in anticipation, his feet
already feeling the forest floor,
while my stomach tightens
with the knowledge that he
is going home. I push
the feeling away. But when spirit
talks to spirit, there is no denying.

Through the long days of mourning,
I see my father's spirit
walk into the bright autumn woods.
Red, gold, and evergreen,
they welcome him back,
his relatives, green of heart,
and rooted, like him,
in the soil of this land
called *Ndakinna.*

At the Powwow

my mother, red-haired,
who lived with my father
forty years,
who buried my grandparents,
whose skin was brown, she said,
from age,
watches the feathered dancers
and says, so that's

what real Indians look like.

I wrap the shawl around my shoulders,
and join the circle.

Henri Toussaints

When Henri Toussaints
came down from Quebec
his hands already knew
the fine shape of the world
the hungry feel of earth
eager to be sown
the wet hard flank of a mare
the proper curve of a cradleboard.

His hands had eased the young
from sheep and mares
had freed the bound egg
and women
with no doctor about
with the pains coming close
wanted his hands
to navigate the maze
to bring the child
to first light.

Later the husbands would say
come, Henri, to dinner
eat with us, Henri
and they would sit to table
for the coming of new life
demands great things.

Later, much later,
Rosa had

cried out on the marriage bed
and the blood had come
red and strong and not stopping
as if getting were as hard as birthing.
He had soothed her then as if
she were one of his fine
mares, had crooned
Rosa, ma pauvre, Rosa, ma poule,
till she had quieted
and the bleeding stopped.

She brought him his first son
head so small it barely filled his palm
too small to live, they told him
but in the box behind the stove
next to the steaming kettle
and with Rosa's good milk
the boy had thrived.

Still, when Henri held him
he sang *Il p'tit, Rosa,* he's small,
and so they called him,
though his name was Armand
and he grew to be a man large
of hand and chest,
still they called him Ipsy
from his father.

And others followed:
Marie, called Tootsie, all small,
Eva, *'tipoule,* little chicken,
and Peter who was called Bebe,
though there were more born after him,
eight in all, and Baby Alice,
who was born with red curls
and a hole in her heart.

Cold spring nights
the hole grew grave-size
settled in his own heart
mocked his healer's hands.

In the kitchen at night
with the oil lamp burning
he placed the fine gears
into the ancient watch.

The priests are wrong, Rosa,
it is not in the heart
that the soul lives,
but here, in the hands.

Trees

– for my father, Paul J. Savageau, Sr.

You taught me the land so well
that all through my childhood
I never saw the highway,
the truck stops, lumberyards,
the asphalt works,
but instead saw the hills,
the trees, the ponds on the south end
of Quinsigamond that twined
through the tangled underbrush
where old cars rusted back to earth,
and rubber tires made homes for fish.

Driving down the dirt road home,
it was the trees you saw first,
all New England a forest.
I have seen you get out of a car,
breathe in the sky, the green

of summer maples, listen for the talk
of birds and squirrels, the murmur
of earthworms beneath your feet.
When you looked toward the house,
you had to shift focus,
as if it were something
difficult to see.

Trees filled the yard
until Ma complained
where is the sun.
Now you are gone
she is cutting them down
to fill the yard with azaleas.

The white birch you loved,
we love. Its daughters
are filling the back.
Your grandchildren play
among them. We have taught them
as you taught us, to leave
the peeling bark, to lean
their cheeks against
the powdery white and hear
the heartbeat of the tree.
Sacred, beautiful, companion.

All Night She Dreams

All night she dreams
a panther, a white bear,
a wet moose.
When she wakes
she is on turtle's back.
She can feel the lumbering
movement beneath her.

Here she can talk to fire,
to stone, and people take
many shapes.
She knows one day
her hips will grow heavy
as squash,
she will lie on the earth
and vines will grow
from her arms and legs,
milky kernels will form
on the ears of corn plants
growing skyward from her breasts.
Meanwhile, there is walking in balance,
there is clear thought,
and song
rising from her lips
like smoke, like mist,
like welcome clouds,
like some green and beautiful plant.

Sister Death

Penny Harter

My death grazes just out of sight
over my right shoulder.
I hear the whisper of green
between her lips.
I imagine her as mare
heavy with foal,
tail swishing flies from her strong back,
eyes brown as a farm pond.

Each day I toss a lump of sugar
back into that unseen pasture,
murmur soothing words under my breath.

Wherever I go she migrates with me.
Even in winter
when fodder is scarce,
I feel her warm breath on my neck
and dream of bundled hay in a heated stall.

One day in some field
neither of us has visited
I will forget to toss the sugar
or to dream of hay,
and my death will canter closer
whinnying softly
until her nose finds my palm.

Turtle Blessing

After the boy threw the pregnant turtle
hard against the brick wall
of the courtyard, screaming
"What are you, some kind of
fucking humanitarian?"
to the girl who called him crazy,
the creature bounced off,
crawled a few feet, blood
seeping into the weeds
from her cracked shell,
and stopped.

She died last night,
was buried, her eggs gone
with her into the earth.

This morning in the mist
by Seeley's Pond, an ancient turtle,
huge and black on the wet grass,
turns its blunt head this way, that,
as it crawls up the slope
toward the road, and I bless it
against the crunch of its dark shell,
against the driver who will not swerve.

Tulip

I watched its first green push
through bare dirt, where the builders
had dropped boards, shingles, plaster—
killing everything.
I could not recall what grew there,
what returned each spring,
but the leaves looked tulip,
and one morning it arrived,
a scarlet slash against the aluminum siding.

Mornings, on the way to my car,
I bow to the still bell
of its closed petals; evenings
it greets me, light ringing
at the end of my driveway.

Sometimes I kneel
to stare into the yellow throat,
count the black tongues,
stroke the firm red mouth.
It opens and closes my days.
It has made me weak with love,
this god I didn't know I needed.

Looking for St. Joe

Lise McCloud

W HEN THE HEAD nurse hands us the patient charts, I'm buffaloed. It's the first time I actually looked at one, and all I understand is the little box that says "Born: St. Joe 1892." That explains about my "client," as college-educated nurses call them now.

There is no St. Joe anymore, except in the old people's minds. People today don't know anything of the past. They don't even know enough to write *North Dakota* in the box. The past has been plowed under here, turned into beet fields and wheat fields. I know about St. Joe: I don't know how to be a nurse.

For the present that's my secret. I have no doubt, though, that soon enough someone will give me the accusing look that says: "You're Indian, aren't you? They're paying your way through. That's the only reason you're here." And they might be right.

The head nurse is discussing each of the old people that have been assigned to us. She is one of those old girls who went to a hospital school but tolerate our college ideas. She is talking about my new client, Mrs. Cadotte. "Cleo's just a sweet, lovable little lady who's a little confused now," she says. "She woke up a few nights lately hollering about the Sioux Indians, and she has this buggy thing about being an Indian or a halfbreed. She goes off on that all the time, but her daughter told me she's French Canadian." She punctuates this with her tolerant, cheerful smirk, which is clearly an instructional device. "Anyway, you need to help her with her ADLs . . ."

She goes on, giving me hints about the client's Activities of Daily Living, and I consciously contain the rush of blood that tries to rise to my face. Should I say something or not? There's nothing to give me away. I once had a Sioux friend, a fullblood. "You're a white woman!" she's say, laughing. "It's just your eyes that are Indian." But at an Oklahoma powwow she introduced me as a Turtle Mountain Chippewa. I had to tell everyone that my dad's Indian and my mother's a fullblood—a real white woman.

I say nothing this time. It wouldn't do any good to explain. No, I think, it's hard enough to figure out what to do next, how to do the right thing right now. I'll keep my mouth shut and my eyes open.

I'm thinking that when I get home I'll have to study harder, practice things more, or I could be dangerous. This is the first day I ever had a client that wasn't made out of rubber or plastic.

I got up early this morning, so nervous I felt like I didn't belong in my skin, especially as I put on these crisp white clothes and pantyhose. They feel creepy and electric on me, charged with responsibility. When I looked in the mirror my reflection was like someone else, some neatly contained, tidy individual. Except the eyes.

It seemed as if I'd never get the kids dressed and over to the sitter's. The car felt like it was coming apart all the way to St. Pat's Home—a big old dark brick place down by the river. I took one last deep calming breath of the cold, clean air and opened the door. I almost threw up from the smell that met me in the close, tight hallways. It grew stronger as I descended into the basement—the greasy, soggy, mushy institutional breakfast odors, mingled with the general scent of decay. Our orientation conference is being held in a gloomy corner of the basement called the Fun Room, where the residents play games and work on arts and crafts. A collection of sad clothespin butterflies are shoved to one end of the table.

The Subjective Information on my client's chart is set off in quotes. "I can't breathe. There's no air. Let me go home. I'm a halfbreed. I don't belong in here." The student before me had written it down. The other sheets tell me that my client's daughter left her in this place; that her heart, lungs, limbs, everything is going, and she can't take care of herself anymore; that she has some kind of cancer and "is not a candidate for surgery or therapy." Still, my task is to develop a care plan that includes getting her to take care of herself more and "participate in ADLs."

When I find her room and look in the bed, the first thing I check is whether she's breathing, and how. I hold her thin, papery wrist in my hand and take her pulse. It's slow, feeble, irregular. I think of the river outside: the Red River of the North. The River Rouge. An old story tells how it's named for blood. I think of how it looks now, clogged with breaking ice, flowing slowly in some places and swiftly in others, winding its way north to Lake Winnipeg. I write down in my little pocket pad observations about the old lady and cautiously shake her awake.

"Cleophile," I say on impulse. It's one of my favorites of the old names. "Cleophile, wake up. It's your friend." She comes to in slow motion. With a shaking hand she reaches for her glasses at the bed-side stand, and I help her up and put them on her.

"Eh? Who are you? I don't know who you are." She looks fearful but resigned.

"It's Reine," I say. "I'm going to be coming in to see you every Monday and Wednesday morning. I'm a student nurse."

She drifts for a minute. "Where did you come from?" she says.

"From the university. I'm a student nurse."

She makes no response. Then I look over my shoulder, out the door. All clear. "I'm from St. Joe," I tell her.

She seems to start out of her dream, or into it. "Oh my," she says, a big grin on her face. "How many came with you?"

"It's just me, I'm afraid. No one else could come." She's disappointed. Maybe she thought I'd bring the whole tribe.

I help her into her wheelchair and bring the basin of water and a washcloth. "I can do it," she croaks fiercely. I let her try. She protests when I help her get cleaned up and dressed. She's so stiff I think of just laying her on the bed like a paper doll and dressing her there. Although her gray hair is cut short, she can comb it only with a struggle. Finally she's sitting in her wheelchair next to the bed, all dressed, her shoes and socks on, her bed table in front of her. I go to get her breakfast tray, then fresh sheets. Hers were soaked, even though she wears a diaper.

When I come back, my instructor is there, a questioning look on her face. "I don't know how you motivated her, but Cleo certainly seems alert this morning–excited, in fact. Have you done a cardiac and peripheral vascular assessment today?"

My own heart jumps. "Assessment" is vital to who she is, what she does. Something tells me her little picture of *me* looks like this: single mother, overworked, overstressed, difficulties handling the program, possibly not interested enough, not efficient enough, needs to be weeded out.

I won't let that happen. I haven't checked Cleo's blood pressure, but I nod yes and give her the same figures I read on yesterday's notes. She takes her stethoscope, listens to the old lady's tired heart, and gets out her B/P cuff.

"My readings are higher–see this? You have to make sure the cuff isn't too loose. Don't forget to listen to the heart sounds. There's a splitting sound here I want you to take note of. I'd like to see how you describe it later on today. And I'd say her heart rate is slightly increased. Cleo tells me you're from St. Joe. What does she mean?"

I shrug. "It used to be a little town upriver, up north."

"In Canada?" she asks.

"No, North Dakota." That's all I'll tell her. I don't tell her the significance of that place, this valley, its forgotten people. I won't let on that I have anything on my mind.

"Oh, and it's gone now, your hometown? Funny, I never even heard of it, and I've always lived here." I start making the bed, my skin crawling. Eyes on me do that.

The village is not actually gone, but its name has been different for over a century, since the immigrants named it after *their* version of heaven. Valhalla. But Father Belcourt had named it St. Joseph in 1851, when he brought his mission school there, and the Indian people remained loyal to their memories.

I can't seem to ever get the bedmaking right, especially the part about getting the pillow out of the old pillowcase and into the new one without shaking microorganisms around or hugging it to my contaminated person. My instructor inspects the sheets and tells me to correct them. The corners aren't tight enough. Finally she goes away. Cleo has said nothing this whole time, staring at her food as if she'd started to think of something and then forgotten what it was.

"Cleophile," I tell her, "you need to eat more. How can you dance with the young men if you don't stoke up your furnace? Cleo, eat *sou dezhanhee, li tous, li lawr boukawnee avik li zaef. Meetshou shaenmawk!* Eat your breakfast, the toast, the bacon and eggs! Eat it right now!"

"*Ah baen, en vyay pischpawy-hitouhk niya,*" she says with a toothless grin, her finely carved face cracking into a hundred lines. "I will let the young girls have a chance now." I can see she was a beauty once, *en zhalee fee*. She doesn't seem surprised to hear me speaking the French-Chippewa-Cree language, though she certainly has not heard it in a very long time.

"Oh, you're not an old wreck," I say. "You look to be only about ninety." This makes her cackle.

"I used to love the dance," she tells me. "But now I feel very, very old. Oh, we used to go to the dance, my sisters and I . . . My papa and brothers played the fiddle so beautiful . . ." She trailed off, gone to visit some log house of long ago, nestled in the green, sleepy Beautiful Valley, alive with music and dancing feet, the clear black sky and sparkling stars above, dancing 'til dawn in the lovely, lonely land. I've heard this story many times.

"Why, I bet you can still do the Red River jig," I joke. "I'll bring music next time. Fiddle tapes? I have some."

"No," she says. "I'm pretty near dead. I'm the last one alive. I had eleven brothers and sisters. I had twelve children. They are all gone now except my daughter, and she's a white woman now. She married a man who lives here." She looks up at me suddenly as if she just remembered something. "Are you a halfbreed?" she asks.

"Why sure," I tell her. "I'm a Mechif. Aren't you?" My tribal ID says one-fourth Chippewa, government-certified Indian. Halfbreed has never had exactly to do with ratios, and Mechif has to do with the reservation my dad was from.

"I'm a halfbreed," she says, proudly. It's an honorable distinction to the older generations. Yet all that they built, all the assistance they gave to the early settlers, all their peaceful civilized ways counted for nothing when the land began to fill up. They were just Indians who needed to be removed.

"Well, Cleo," I say. "It's time for your pills. I'll be right back, and then you're going for a spin on those wheels." She smiles and settles back behind the limp toast and greasy gray eggs. Cleo hasn't left this wing in weeks, from what I can tell. No one has time for that, and she can't go by herself.

But first she has to take all her pills. There's a proper procedure for handling and dispensing them, and since I've never done meds before, my instructor has to supervise to see if I learned what I was supposed to. After I'm almost done mixing and sorting the medications correctly, I drop one of the pills on the floor. Now it's contaminated, but my instructor looks the other way. I pick up the pill and put it into the little cup next to the medication's name on the checksheet. These pills are expensive. Still, I messed up, and she won't forget.

Leaving the instructor behind, Cleo and I move out down the hall, off the wing. Most of the residents who have been set out in the hall in their wheelchairs are just sitting there, vacant or unconscious. Others are clumped around the television set.

In the oldest, core part of St. Pat's is a pleasant surprise, a sort of drawing room on the second floor. There's not a soul around. "Hey, how about this," I say to Cleo. "Let's go chat in the parlor." But she has fallen asleep. The room has dark, polished woodwork, bookcases full of old clothbound, gilt-paged volumes, heavy wine-colored embossed drapes, fake Oriental rugs, old-fashioned lamps, and lumpy old couches and chairs. There are framed black and white photographs of women and girls in long white dresses and feather-plumed hats, and men in strict suits and vests, fingering their watch fobs. The room is dark except for a place by two tall windows where the sun shines in. A table with a vase full of cloth flowers catches that golden light in a dappled pattern of curtain lace.

I park Cleo by the table and start playing "Camptown Races" on the piano, watching to see if she's surprised. Slowly, ever so slowly, she wakes up and focuses. Her head wobbles on the way up, and her eyelids flutter heavily. Meds. I finish the tune with a flourish and lean toward her. "How do you like that one?" I ask. "Do you have any requests?"

"Are any of those Sioux here?" she inquires crankily. "They killed my grandma and cut off her scalp. Where are all the girls from St. Joe? How many came with you?"

They call it dementia, but I can easily see her mind is just wandering around, sorting and sifting through nearly a hundred years' worth of memories. After a while she comes back to the present and tells me about when she went to school so long ago with her little brother. He had blond hair and blue eyes and was very small for his age. Cleo defended him as best she could.

"His name was Amable," says Cleo thoughtfully. "I remember one time we were all traveling in the wagon." She pronounces it *waw-ginn*. "We saw a little animal running across the road. 'Papa,' he said, 'what is that little animal? Would you go catch it for me so I can eat it?' Oh, Mama and Papa would do anything for him. We knew he couldn't live much longer. He had TB. So we stopped right there, and Papa went and got that animal for him. It was a little beaver. Mama made a fire and cooked it for him. 'Oh, that was so good,' he said. A few days later he died."

They were roaming and camping on the prairie, going west to the reservation. There were too many settlers and too much sickness in the valley by then. The buffalo were gone. Even the millions upon millions of their bleached bones that had littered the plains had been picked up and sold to buyers who shipped them East for some mysterious thing white people did. A small reservation had been created at Turtle Mountain, but it was over-populated and ravaged by disease. The family went farther west to try their luck in Montana while Cleo stayed behind with a boy she met and married. They moved into a mud-chink cabin, scratched out a livelihood, and made children. The Catholic missionary priests always said you needed twelve to gain the gates of heaven.

"I never would eat a gopher," she muses. "They crawl through the graves and eat dead people, you know. And I would never eat a dog. One time I saw an old Sioux woman. I thought she was playing with the puppies, but then she knocked them on the head and put them in the soup."

The way she says this strikes me as hilarious. I tell her how my grandma used to cook muskrats a certain way so that people thought they were eating something luxurious—like jackrabbit. We're laughing it up.

Just then my instructor comes barreling in with her assessing expression and tells me it's time to report. "There you are! Cleo seems lively today," she says. "You've really got her going. What did you find to talk about?"

"Oh, we're discussing diet, nutrition, stuff like that," I say. Cleo smiles and nods absently. My instructor looks perplexed. I wheel Cleo back to her room and join the group for report. We're required to write down pertinent things in the charts and share our experiences with each other. One by one, our instructor goes through the group and discusses our work and our clients. When it's my turn, the instructor talks about how well Cleo is doing, and she wonders if it's a little "reminiscing therapy." I tell her that we were having a nice talk about the old days. The instructor talks about short-term and long-term loss and senile dementia and about the effects of "polypharmacy."

"Did you hear about the Indians again?" asks the plump girl who's nineteen or twenty, Scandinavian, new; her memory is new, her connection to the land is new, and she no doubt thinks of anything Indian as being unreal, part of the remote past. "The nurses at the station were telling me about her. Pretty wild stories!" She has giggly eyes.

"Perhaps you could keep this in mind while you're working on increasing your client's level of activity and involvement," says the instructor. "Increasing self-esteem and Increasing ADLs go hand in hand. I'm not sure why she chooses to express low self-esteem through calling herself a halfbreed . . ."

Already I can picture the blank, hostile stares I get whenever I open my mouth in a situation like this. Still, I can't seem to stop. "I think she calls herself a halfbreed because she's proud of it. The mixed-blood Indian people have lived around here for centuries, because the early fur traders and trappers intermarried with native tribes. They sort of got left out of history because no one understood what they were about."

My instructor shifts in her chair as if she's going to break in here, but I keep right on. "A lot of these mixed bloods were absorbed into Indian or white culture, into fur-trade society. Others developed their own lifestyle that was a mix of Indian and European ways. In Canada they called themselves the New Nation of the Metís and tried to protect their rights to the land."

They looked shocked now, and suspicious. I continue. "Around 1870, the Metís established their own provincial government, which the Canadian government put down right away. Later, when the Metís lost their farms because of a new survey method, they resisted. They were defeated at the Battle of Batoche, and their leader, Louis Riel, was hanged for treason. These were called the Halfbreed Rebellions."

I'm rolling. I should be a history teacher instead of a nurse. "A bunch of Metís fled to the United States—to the Turtle Mountain Indian Reservation, which was crowded already without them. Some of the Americans of mixed ancestry there called themselves half-breeds, but generally they were a different group than the Riel refugees. Nowadays they're all called Chippewa Indians. But many of the native people were forced to wander—they were never able to receive federal recognition as American Indians or find any place in non-Indian society."

Everyone is silently indicating that I'm being quite the big pain. I'm indulging myself; I'm a smartass. "That's an interesting way of looking at things," says my instructor. "Where did you happen to learn this?"

"Introduction to Indian Studies class," I lie.

"Well, that's one thing I'd like to mention here," says my instructor. "Nothing you ever learn is ever wasted in your nursing careers, you will find. You will integrate it into your knowledge base and apply it to problem-solving situations of the nursing process—Assessment, Nursing Diagnosis, Planning and Implementation of Interventions, Evaluation of Care . . ."

And so the days and weeks go by. Every week we take on more responsibilities, including an extra couple of patients each. I remind myself how easy it is, compared to real nurse's work. Still, no one could blame me for enjoying an escape from the present, from the future, for a few minutes. Cleo and I visit whenever I get time. Sometimes we are back in the buffalo days, swapping the handed-down tales. She believes in the miracles that the early missionary priests are said to have performed. I almost envy her faith, her ability to keep on believing in something. She talks about St. Joe, about the little cabin of her childhood in the woods by the clear running stream where she and her brothers and sisters played and caught speckled trout. There was a fish trap built into the Pembina River by the old mill. She always wanted to go back to St. Joe and have a look. She talks about the families there, about my distant ancestors. I'm amazed to hear these stories again, coming from someone who knew them.

On the last day I'm at St. Pat's, Cleo and I are in the drawing room, and I play "Red River Valley" on the piano. It's not elegant; but when I look at Cleo, she's crying and smiling at the same time in a sudden stream of lace-filtered light. Then I notice that other oldsters are wobbling into the room, drawn by the music. They move like ancient turtles, their heads poked up in curiosity. I play the song again and again, and it's improving. I go right ahead and sing, because no one in this room cares if I sing well. "From this valley they say you are going, we will miss your bright eyes and sweet smile, for they say you are taking the sunshine, that brightens our pathway awhile."

* * *

It's midnight. The children are all asleep. School's out. I can go back in the fall if I want. I'm sitting in front of the TV, drinking whiskey. It's a big old bottle; I should call someone over to help me drink it, but I can't stand the thought of company, anyone's company. I keep pouring the whiskey over the ice cubes and drinking it and waiting for that feeling of relief. You'd think it would just come rushing in. Every time I put new ice and whiskey in, it makes a cracking sound. Snap, crackle, pop.

I think of the river ice breaking up in the early spring, the loud crashing sounds. I think of the big rocks floating along, melting, through the early spring. I wonder if I feel good. I feel my brain cells getting desiccated, popping, bursting, dying–causing this sensation that we interpret as pleasure. Now the TV is crackling and snowing. I start to get up to change channels, but instead the coffee table lurches forward, the bottle tips over. The incandescent screen seeps quickly into the dark and takes on the shape of North Dakota. The righthand side squiggles and blurs and becomes the Red River of the North, and I dissolve back into the couch to note the TV snowing and the whiskey spilling, and I think of the river running and running, toward Pembina, St. Joe, Winnipeg.

See No Indian, Hear No Indian

Victoria Lena Manyarrows

it wasn't so long ago, i tell you in a stream
    of broken words & suppressed anger,
when these lands were not occupied
    they were free
and people lived in harmony

you tell me you don't
    want to hear it, you don't
want to hear what i have to say

i tell you, *what you are doing to me now is*
    killing me
    negating my existence
    denying me my voice, my life.

i tell you how we the indians always listened
    listened to one another and
    talked out our differences.
i tell you this world
    this world strangled & distorted by white men
will die a harsh and bitter early death
    if no one learns to listen
and dream together.

but you don't want to hear this
    you say it's too much for you now
you've already left
    your mind a stone
and the doors have closed.

The Conference Tribe

Heid Ellen Erdrich

THEY WERE hatching a scheme. At first I couldn't figure out what my mom and Ginny's mom were plotting. I knew it involved a pre-fab cabin they had hauled up against a hill facing that little bit of water they call Mushum Lake. Actually, it's not a lake, it's more of a slough—reedy and dark. Still, it's a good spot for that cabin, which looks real nice, sorta like a half-buried soccer ball.

Ginny's mom called me last week, said "Critter, you're such a handy fellow, won't you help us winterize the new place?" Handy just means I'm the kinda guy who never says no.

Well, it did just so happen that I had some time off from work, so I drove the three hours home and took a look at the place. Turned out the cabin came from one of those dome home kits. Of course I'd heard of the things before: geodesic design, Buckminster Fuller. They're shipped on a flatbed. A local crew set it up in just two days. When I first looked at it I couldn't imagine where you'd put insulation. It was all angles and windows, cedar-shingled. I walked round and round the place trying to figure out what I could do to winterproof it and wondering what Ginny's mom and my mom were scheming. Finally I sat down at the edge of Mushum Lake to think.

I'd seen Ginny at a conference two months before and she hadn't said anything about her mom retiring back to the reservation. So naturally I began to wonder just who was supposed to live in this cabin. You see, me and Ginny have known each other our whole lives. Our mothers were best friends before we were born. When it turned out that my mom got a boy and Ginny's mom got a girl, they decided the two of us would end up together. I believe that's why they sent us off to the same college and it was probably the reason they'd bought the dome. Those two would try anything to lure us into a domestic situation.

As I sat there looking from the dome to the water, and back again, seeing how homey it looked, how natural, like a muskrat lodge, I began to wonder when Ginny would think of settling down. And if she did, what would that mean for me?

Ginny works for a scholarship agency. She's lived in four different cities, all in those mid states east of here, the ones that all have names starting with vowels. She would be hard to keep track of if it weren't for the fact that in the three years since we finished college, we've seen each other quite a few times a year at conferences and seminars and the like. The last time we met up with each other was at an Indian Education meeting. A lot of people we both knew were there—it was like a reunion. One of Ginny's uncles sang with the drum at the last-night powwow. When he honored her with a song, she didn't know what to do so I took her twice around the gym. I didn't grow up around traditional dancing, but luckily all the moment required was a social dance, partnered up, like me and Ginny had learned from our friends in college. I remember how the drum went right through us, drawing us into the beat. It was impossible to get it wrong. The fringe on the shawl her uncle gave her swayed in neat waves as Ginny stepped along with me. I could tell she was surprised to have the hang of it. We were so filled with the sound of the drum we had to smile wide to keep it inside. That was a good night, a time that made all the travel worthwhile.

But it wasn't me Ginny took back to her hotel room that night. You see, there was this certain guy she hooked up with on such occasions. Yes, it always bothered me a little (not that I'd ever been clear that I'd want a romance between us) but I wondered if the guy was stringing her along.

I didn't let Ginny's off and on romances distract me. I had to concentrate on the job our moms had put me up to. The funny thing about the dome was that it seemed larger on the inside. All the walls seemed to move outward. There was lots of light from the little portholes set up high. It was just one big room. Ginny's mom had said it was up to me to decide where the partitions would go, and the fixtures and the floor tiles . . . There was a whole lot more to do than just insulate the place. I started making lists and taking measurements.

One day I stopped and looked out across the water. There were several bird boxes on posts, abandoned. Cattail puffs floating in the low white sun looked like snow. Honkers overhead flew so low I could hear the rasp as they inhaled to call: *Hank, hank, hank.* They sounded like they had bad colds. I knew I should talk to Ginny before I did any more work on the dome. But what would I say? *Ginny, your mom and mine put up a new nesting box along Mushum Lake. They got me feathering it and they're just waiting for a mating pair to come on home . . .*

The thing is, I don't ever call Ginny on the phone anymore. She never was the kind to be alone. One or another of her temporary love interests was always hanging around—some professor types, or maybe they were graduate students, I don't know, but the way they'd answered the phone, I could tell they read meaning into how I'd ask to speak to her. It got so I couldn't stand the image I'd get when one of them put me on hold. Being put on hold makes you think of the high-tech phone, its blinking lights, the black plastic receiver and cradle, the narrow black hall table, the futon furniture and so on. It was too strange to get a sense of Ginny's whole other life. Truth is, when we weren't together I liked to think of Ginny as being on hold—like she was just filling up her time until her life brought her back home. Then again, sometimes I worried I didn't know anything about Ginny. She had always been slippery. I feel like I've been looking at her my whole life and right this minute I couldn't tell you the exact color of her hair and eyes, only they are the same color, a color like a satin dress our mothers once shared—somewhere between brown and gold.

You can see the tone my thoughts began to take as I worked on the dome. I began to be sorry my boss hadn't sent me away over break. Out there somewhere, Ginny was probably in some lounge networking for her life while underneath her name tag beat the mysteries of her heart . . .

It was useless trying to manage the other women in my life—all my mom would say was the dome home was an investment she made with Ginny's mom. Investment in what? I wondered. And what was the pay off? Grandchildren? I just listened while Mom told me how much money they had saved to fix it up. Since Ginny's mom lived two hundred miles away, she gave me free rein, saying, "Do up the place like it was your own."

So I went on a buying trip. While I loaded up my uncle's truck with foam panels, lumber, gravel, chicken wire, and drywall, I tried not to feel guilty. Then I tried to figure out *why* I felt guilty. Somehow I felt I owed it to Ginny's mom to get Ginny settled in the place. Then I figured it out. I owed it to Ginny's mom because she got me to go to college.

The spring we were juniors in high school, Ginny's mom arranged to drive me to take my SATs at the university. Afterwards she took me out to eat at a place they advertise a lot on TV: *Smorgasbord–All You Can Eat.* Between the herring rollmops and the cucumber salad, Ginny's mom told me that in the fifties, when she married Ginny's father, there were many states that would have considered their union illegal. Ginny's mom asked me, "Do you know what miscegenation means?" I had just taken my SATs, so I felt I had to answer yes. But it wasn't until years later that I truly understood what she meant as she leaned across our overflowing plates to say, "You must take the advantages your parents were not allowed."

It was around that time I noticed that my mom and Ginny's always bought the same clothes. The shirt she wore that day had ribbons and bandanas sewn to the chest, same as one my mom had. I think they did it on purpose so I'd confuse the two and listen to Ginny's mom the same as my own. Which in fact I always did. That's why I ended up going off to college with Ginny. And seven years later I was a recruiter for Native American students at a college close enough so I could drive home on weekends–which I did pretty regular once I got serious about fixing up the dome home.

Even during workdays my attention wandered. I went to the library and checked out books on geodesics. There were pictures of dozens of styles. Some looked like old-time wigwams. I read how to shore the dome up with properly drained soil banked all around. The crew who put the dome up had left mounds of earth on either side. It was up to me to mix all that earth with gravel and shovel it along the bottom of the house. I was going to make a frame with chicken wire and spread the whole thing with straw so winter wouldn't erode it to sludge.

The books suggested several types of ground cover I could plant come spring. Raspberry bushes seemed the logical choice. My mom grew a fierce patch of them behind her house. Every year it was a struggle just to keep them from taking over the yard. So I knew they'd grow well in that climate. Better yet, I knew Ginny would love them. When we were about eight or nine we spent a lot of time crawling along through the rabbit trails in my mom's raspberry patch. It was cool down there. The thorny branches grew far enough overhead that we could sit up under a shady umbrella eating berries until our tongues stung and the spaces between our teeth were filled with seeds.

As I paged through the nursery catalogs with their lush watercolor illustrations I went back to those days. I found myself thinking of how Ginny would want things. One day, maybe, I'd get courageous enough to explain to her that I'd done all the work on the dome with her in mind. I even constructed a daydream, with vivid images of her gratitude to go with it. But even as I shoveled earth around the dome I began to allow myself to understand that Ginny would probably never live there for good. I knew the truth of the situation, but tell it to her mom, or my own? No way.

Once, holed up in a hotel during a lull in conference activity, Ginny told me she thought of the reservation as home, but she didn't know if she belonged there. When I told her I didn't understand, she tried to illustrate her point. "Do you remember," she had asked me, "how your mom used to tease me every time we came to visit? She would call out from the screen door, 'Hey, what are you doing here, little white girl?' in a real gruff voice."

I remembered that Ginny would answer, "Doncha know me, Bernice? I'm not a little white girl." Then Mom would lean real close to Ginny's face and say, "Oh she's just another little Mix-up." It was an old joke, a play on the name Mechif, that is, our French-Indian way of saying mixed-blood, which is what we all are. But truth is Ginny does look mostly white. The summer sun brought the French copper out in all us kids' hair, but she was the only one who got freckles.

I asked Ginny why she told me that story and she said "Just to let you know I understand why she teased me–so that I would defend myself, so I'd always know I was one of you. But at the same time it taught me that I'd always have to prove myself back home."

Now me, I just never talked about being Indian or about the part of me that's not. The whole subject seemed shameful, like admitting insecurity. Like catching someone chewing a bad hangnail, it made me want to look away. But long ago Ginny said, "Critter, I have to be

able to tell someone the truth about my life." And I knew that some-
one would always be me.

* * *

The best thing about the little dome home was how the water
reflected blue in all the porthole windows. I thought I'd like to get a
red enamel woodstove and ceramic tiles so the floor would be fire-
proof under the stove. I had a million plans. It was all I could do to
stop myself from beginning to think of the cabin as mine. So maybe I
did begin to think it could work out between me and Ginny. Just
because nothing went on between us in college didn't mean we hadn't
grown into each other. And it wasn't like I was such a lousy catch. I
wasn't short and I wasn't skinny. I looked about as good as the aver-
age guy. Maybe there was even a little something cute about me that
made everyone call me Critter. It wasn't like I'd never been the object
of female affection. In college, for a short time, I went with a big and
tall tribal woman named Brenda. We called her Bren and she was
nasty to everybody but me. I remember how skeptical she was of
Ginny when we first stopped by the cultural center. Bren led a whole
couch full of jean-jacketed, wranglers-and-cowboy-boot-wearing
females in giving Ginny the cold eye until I found myself explaining
that Ginny was from my tribe, that she grew up with me. That wasn't
the last time I explained Ginny.

Years later, at conferences, people began to recognize Ginny from
meeting to meeting. Once I heard someone ask what kind of Indian
Ginny was, and she said, "I'm of the Conference Tribe, a nomadic
people who roam from hotel to hotel hunting dough and gathering
leaflets." It was funny, but it was true. There were many in her tribe,
and I was one of them, and so was that certain guy Ginny always
took to her hotel room.

Back in college all of us Native types stuck close together. We went
to a lot of All-Indian basketball tournaments and seminars offered by
Native American students at other colleges. There was a lot of mating
and dating. Every time a guy acted interested in Ginny, Bren would
tease her, saying, "Eh, go with that one and you might get a little
Navajo in you . . ." or "Hey, if you keep snagging–get a little Kiowa,
a little Mohawk–you could be a fullblood by morning!" They both
laughed, of course, but for as long as I was with Bren, I worried Ginny
would get hurt. She had a big heart, as tough as it was sweet. She

never fell apart if a romance hit the skids. In fact she usually had a spare boyfriend or two. Not that she was faithless, it was just that asking Ginny to wait for love was like asking her to hold her breath or stop eating. She just loved all kinds of men. She even dated a cowboy, once. I was never sure what she saw in the guy, except that we were all the way out East, and his rodeo-trophy belt buckle must have reminded her of home.

It was at a Soaring Spirit seminar hosted by our college that Ginny met that certain guy. He came from people whose names had music in them. I remember listening as everyone was introduced: in those many syllables, tones and modulations, I thought maybe I could hear what those names meant. Maybe, like rock 'n' roll or loop-de-loop, they meant the way they sounded. The one Ginny fell for had a name with all of that mystery. And he was good looking too, a big man with a postage stamp kinda plains face.

"For Sale Or Rent," Bren had once hissed in his direction. That was last year when we ran into each other at a conference in New Mexico. Bren was so steamed up that Ginny still went with that guy that she said the worst: "He's the kind who shows up anywhere that pays him, even New Age stuff and charity stuff. He looks good, plays his flute, shakes hands with rich people . . . And he'll never marry her."

"Why not?" I asked, hoping Bren was right.

"Genetic Imperative," she answered, and we had to laugh–that was our phrase for the compelling need to marry someone from your own tribe.

* * *

One weekend, instead of working on the dome, I drove down to Ginny's mom's. I thought I'd discuss a few details with her, show her brochures I'd collected on woodstoves and chemical toilets, and casually find out what all she had said to Ginny about the place. Turns out I had no need to be subtle. Ginny's mom merely glanced at the pamphlets. "Critter," she said, "I'm not so good with decorating, why don't you call Ginny and see what she'd choose." I gave her my most skeptical look, but she insisted. "Ginny took a leave from work, you know, she went to Paris with *her most recent*, but she came back a lot sooner than we thought–and without him."

I dialed Ginny's number with every intention of asking her advice about the dome. Of course, before I could begin she wanted to tell me about Paris.

"It's a very pale city–all those plaster buildings. Hey, Critter, I thought of you when a huge chunk of ice fell off a roof and crushed one of those tiny French cars–it was like the cartoons we used to watch."

She paused for my reaction, but I just hung silent for a few beats. I didn't like to imagine Ginny walking down the street across the ocean, in another world.

"Did you look up any of our French relatives?" I asked to make a joke. But Ginny took me seriously. "No," she said, "but I saw an Indian man in the subway." She told me he was wearing a blanket coat and a black cowboy hat. He had a map and he looked lost.

"I wanted to help him but . . . Critter," she paused, "I couldn't go up to him, what was I going to say? 'Hi, I'm Indian in Paris, too.' I felt all out of context."

"Were you alone, or with *your most recent?*" I teased her.

"I was with my French boyfriend, yes, but he wouldn't turn back. He just pulled me along until we were on one of those moving sidewalks and it speeded me farther and farther away."

The image of the lost Indian man and Ginny gliding away through the train tunnels was too much for me. I asked her if she had been homesick. What I really wanted to know was how it was that she and the French professor had called it quits. Before I could ask she told me.

"I just never felt the same about him after he stopped me from helping that man in the metro station," Ginny said and she sounded surprised at her own words. "I never admitted that, but it must be the truth."

I said, "Hey, I *am* the guy you always tell the truth of your life to, aren't I?"

What she said then really threw me. She said, "Well, you're *one.*"

We ended the call by agreeing to meet at a conference in Oklahoma in a few weeks. The second the phone clicked I realized two things: that I hadn't told her about the cabin and that the other guy she told the truth of her life to must have been him, For-Sale-Or-Rent.

There was nothing more I could do on the cabin until later in the spring, so to keep my mind off Ginny, I hunkered down at work. The idea of gainful employment still thrilled me. I never would have gotten into education if Ginny hadn't convinced me it was the easiest major. I got a million miles out of the "Native-centered" paper topics she would come up with. It seemed she could connect any issue with some part of Native American culture or history. Once she told me she knew everything about being Indian except what it is like to be treated like one.

Finally we met up in Oklahoma City. A quiet moment in which to bring up the subject of the dome home did not present itself right away. The big celebration was going on and Indians from all over the country flooded the streets. When we met in the hotel lobby there was a parade outside with more princesses than you could shake a beaded scepter at. We got on the elevator with some Miss Tribal Nation who was just too darn friendly. She kept extending the good-will of Native People to Ginny, who she assumed was a white bene-factor. As you can imagine that put Ginny in a bad mood. To cheer ourselves up, we went to the powwow.

We sat up in high seats watching the hundreds of dancers enter the arena. There were so many people, so many colors all in one motion, it absorbed us so we couldn't talk at first. Then the jingle-dress dancers began to move into the circle. I'd noticed those dresses had been getting real popular. The emcee said that the style of dress and dance had spread from the north where it started. I asked Ginny what she knew about it and sure enough she could tell me the story.

Below us the women danced in satin hung with rows of shiny sil-ver cones. Ginny explained how the dress had come from a dream and was meant to heal the people. The first cones, the jingles, she said, had been made from the lids of snuff cans. I was thinking of my old grandpa, who had enough of a snoose habit to outfit every woman on the floor, when there in the bleachers beside us, For-Sale-Or-Rent appeared. He wore a beaded belt buckle the size of a license plate. He touched his hat to Ginny, gripped my hand in a brief, warm, manly welcome. It was then that I knew for sure how I felt about Ginny. But right at the minute I was in the way.

Did I bow out gracefully? Yes, indeed. I went off in search of the frybread stands. I sampled them all. I bought matching beaded hats for my mom and Ginny's. Then I peeked back in on her. She was alone, nervously glancing about. I stood there watching her a long time. She looked sad, upset, alone. But I guess I had some pride–I could not bring myself to join her.

Hours later she flopped down on my bed. "He has a girlfriend," she said. I couldn't resist, I had to ask: "What did you expect after you been shacked up with various professors all these years?"

Ginny looked up at me, surprised, maybe even hurt. "Well, I don't mind the girlfriend, except she's here," Ginny explained. "It's just that we could be together at these meetings where people know me, where it's easy for us, where I don't always have to prove myself." She bunched up the flowered bed covers as she spoke.

"I didn't expect he would go off and leave me alone because he was ashamed to be seen with me." There was a cry in her voice. I sat down on the bed and touched her shoulder. I comforted her, told her he must have other reasons. That set her off and there was nothing for it but a good cry.

Years ago, when he visited Ginny at college, I was sure he was jealous of me. I remember how, if me and Ginny talked, he would start singing those forty-nine songs real low, under his breath. I get them all rolled into one in my head, but I know they go something like: *My one and only, even though you're married I still love you, it's always you I'm thinking of dear, even though you got another one, Way yah hey yah hey.* . . .

I don't know what made me do it, I never sing, but there in that hotel, with Ginny in my arms, those little songs came humming out of my throat. She was still crying when she looked up at me, but in the next moment we were making love in that hotel bed.

I dreamed I walked with Ginny to the dome home along Mushum Lake. My words were as eloquent as any of the books I'd read as I explained to her that the shelter could withstand such external forces as heavy snow, wind pressures, earth tremors, vibrations, and impacts from automobiles, airplanes, uprooted trees. . . . I dreamed us inside the dome where the noisy plains wind spread to a background hush. I told her that the strength of the dome came from the same things that made your bones and tendons powerful, the thing that held water in a drop. *Tension and integrity*, I said to her, then I woke for a moment. As I watched the dark wings of Ginny's eyebrows, the fluttering black lashes, I was sure we were together in that same dream: We built around us a huge dome with an aluminum skeleton and a skin of clear plastic. The sun shone on the dome, warmed it within so it began to float like a balloon, like a bubble, like a traveling, enduring nation that was Ginny's and mine alone.

Calling Up the
Spirit of the Lost Child

Maggie Penn

On the Dakota prairie an Indian girl was given many gifts:
    A place in creation, her tribe, her family,
    A strong spirit,
    A heart that soared on the wind,
    Eyes that sparkled with the colors of creation.

The prairie glistened with the flow of life:
    Grandfather Sky, thunderheads soaring gray,
    Mother Earth, myriad greens and grasses,
    Wind, a whispering gentle playmate, secrets,
    Mustard grass six feet tall, foxtails shimmering blue.

A place in creation, a tribe, a family:
    Granmama, the center of the universe, soft and
    Brown, smelling of bread and violets;
    Mama, distant and silent sad beauty, hard and
    Cream, smelling of whiskey and honky tonks.

Then abruptly time fell and the world was broken:
    In a United States, flag flying, office building,
    White women, Christian women,
    Damned to hell for their self-righteousness,
    Decided.

    An Indian girl, laughter stopped in her throat,
    Was taken away,
    Forever lost in the company of whites.
    The colors of life stopped, were taken away.

The wind stopped flowing through her heart.
The colors of creation fell away from her eyes.
Indifferent to the prairie,
Vision deadened to black and white.

Indian child walked away to far down inside herself,
Closed the door, and sat down
In the empty chambers of her heart.

Indian child peers quietly from behind broken dreams,
Broken shards. Tangled in memory, a place in creation:

Hollyhocks and chokecherries.
Tin pails glistening in the sun.
Laughing to Granmama across the prairie grasses.

Floating

Catherine Houser

A S A CHILD growing up in Arizona in the fifties and sixties, I never heard the word *Indian* without the word *drunken* in front of it. My father, one of thirteen children and one of the eight who were alcoholics, was a drunken Indian. My grandfather, who in the twenties moved his growing family from the fruitless dirt relegated to the Cherokees in Oklahoma to a patch of land and a two-room shack on a date farm outside of Phoenix and who died thirty years later passed out face down in two feet of water in an irrigation ditch, was a drunken Indian. My uncle, who after serving in the U.S. Army in Korea came home to do battle in Saturday night brawls outside the Blue Door bar in downtown Phoenix and who died at thirty-six from cirrhosis of the liver, was a drunken Indian.

My mother, wanting something different for me, my sister, and my brothers, raised us to be Americans. I imagine she thought that automatically put us with the majority and as such we'd be better able to handle the epithets attached to American–at least they wouldn't cut deep into bloodlines and we wouldn't have to contend with being "other." Because the Cherokee and Choctaw in us was mixed with Greek and German, we didn't necessarily "look" Indian, and because the only Indians in our house were "drunken Indians," my brothers, my sister, and I were all too happy to be American. And as we grew and began filling out forms for schools and the military, American got translated to "white," a half-truth label that has allowed us to coast a long way and one that is still serving my siblings well. But, for me, somewhere in my second year of graduate school, as I was writing my way through short stories to an MFA in Tempe, Arizona, the wheels on that red, white, and blue American Flyer wagon I'd been whizzing along in broke and I tumbled headlong into what it was to be an Indian in Arizona.

It was in graduate school that I encountered in the flesh easterners writing westerns, complete with all the cliches of a John Wayne movie. White boys in docksiders who grew up playing in the snow of the eastern seaboard were writing stories about mythical cowboys of the Southwest and the wild and wildly dangerous Indians they fought to conquer and civilize—stories that all seemed to be set at about the time my grandparents, real-life Cherokee and Choctaw Indians, were working fourteen hours a day on a date farm in the wilderness at the foot of Camelback Mountain. As we discussed these stories in writing workshops, I found myself fidgeting in my seat, the energy of my ancestry rising up in me, demanding that I give it voice, say aloud, "That's not the way it was." But I didn't; I kept silent. After all, I was not "out" to these people as a Native American. As a woman I already knew well the wrath that speaking out against stereotypes and demeaning portrayals of women in fiction provoked, and I suspected that raising similar issues with regard to Native Americans would inspire the same groans and denials and justifications. The energy of my anger went underground and, as it does quite often in minority writing, resurfaced in my own work.

I set about writing the truth of my people. Following the first rule of writing, I wrote about what I knew. What came out were stories about drunken Indians. No cowboys, just Indians in contemporary situations who had pervasive problems with alcohol. Stereotypes? How could they be—they were real people, the only Native Americans I had ever known. The veil of fiction crystallized the truth of those lives and none of the cultural accouterments could disguise that truth. But I knew what I was writing was no different from the cowboys-and-Indians stories of my fellow students. My depictions were worse, in fact, because I, supposedly, knew better. In effect, what I was doing was updating the stereotype, giving it a contemporary context, making it real now.

My own indignation throttled my passion for the truth and I stopped writing about that half of my cultural identity. I could not find a way to tell the truth of my experience without further denigrating an already fragile society. I stopped "working deep," as my bodyworker might say, and came up, instead, to the surface to write airy stories of people void of cultural identity–Americans–and their individual and collective angst.

Four years ago, after thirty years of living in the Arizona desert, I left the Southwest thinking I might be able to find the distance that would allow me to explore more honestly in my own writing the full range of my experience as a Native American. Now, living on a little island off the coast of Massachusetts, just a stone's throw from where the Europeans who were soon to be Americans first encountered Indians, I am beginning to be able to write the real story of that little patch of dirt in the Arizona desert and the people who called it home. And I am finding there is more than one way to tell the truth. Yes, I am Cherokee and Choctaw and, yes, I come from a family of alcoholics–my father, his brothers, their father–Indians for whom silence and violence served as points of balance. But here, floating on this island three thousand miles away from my immediate family's deep denial of this sullied cultural heritage, the humanity and the struggle for survival buried in that heritage have begun to surface and I'm finding my own points of balance. My ancestors were people who blew west in the dust that blanketed Cherokee land in Oklahoma in the twenties. They were Indians looking for a land that would feed them. They were headed for California, but their borrowed car broke down in Phoenix and in an instant they were Cherokees without a community, without a reservation, focused solely on survival. That is how I know them–isolated and poor, struggling both to rage over what was lost to them when they left Oklahoma and to make peace with that loss. I see my father's thick hands, calloused from field work and bloodied from barroom brawls, and I remember my grandmother's hands, translucent and shimmering, as they worked a beaded leather strap into a belt that would be sold to tourists, and the truth resonates in me finally.

Still, the ironies persist and balance is hard to come by. Upon learning that I am Native American, a colleague at the university where I teach said, "Oh, no wonder you left Arizona. They have absolutely no respect for Native Americans there, what with the commercialism of kachina dolls and Indian jewelry." That same colleague, when I asked about teaching a course in Native American writers, said, "Oh, I don't think there is enough literature to warrant a full course." Another colleague, a screenwriter, knocked on my door recently and asked me to help him "authenticate" a scene in a western he was writing featuring Angelica Huston as the "Indian princess." "They drank a lot, didn't they?" he asked rhetorically. "I want to get a lot of that in. Have them really whoopin' it up."

To those in the white world who identify me as Native American I am a curious anomaly, a mystery, a quota. And to Native Americans I am not Indian enough. After I delivered a paper about Native American literature at a Native American studies conference a few years ago, a man who had sat through the whole presentation with his arms crossed defiantly across his chest approached me and said, "You don't look Indian. How much Indian are you anyway?" To him, apparently, not "looking" Indian meant I wasn't. And a few weeks ago I interviewed a Native American woman for a publication I work for and we were talking about how Native Americans are so inundated with white people's definition of who they are that they begin to believe those definitions. Identifying myself as being "part" Cherokee and Choctaw, I offered as an example my experience as a child thinking all Indians were drunken Indians. Her response was to remark that in an interview earlier that morning the interviewer had "appropriately" waited until after they had completed their interview before identifying himself as having Native American ancestors–clearly implying that she was the only "true" Indian there. She added that when people say they're "part" Indian she often wonders, "What part?" Among Native people I am not Indian enough.

Sitting here surrounded by water, some three thousand miles away from that unforgiving desert, I float between the two worlds, connected to solid land by a bridge here, a causeway there, but still, always, floating.

Landscape Painting

Diane Glancy

*Once the earth and sky were one. There was no room to stand. No light
to see. Everyone crawled around in darkness. A flock of birds thought
they could lift the sky. They flew up into the dark. The sky split and
revealed the sun. That's why birds are first to greet the dawn.*
– from an Aboriginal Myth

(NOTE: On a trip to Central Australia, I saw the Aboriginal dream-
paintings, which tell stories of the land with a series of dots, some-
thing like an early stage of pointillism. I also wanted to tell a story
with clumps of words like the mounds of spinifex grass over the land-
scape I saw from Ayers Rock, which are the genesis of the "dots."
Writing that way was like hearing someone trying to speak after a
long silence. I even tried numbering the paragraphs in a "paint-by-
number" effect, but later removed the numbers.)

The crows cawed. just before. dawn.

He heard them. he thought. at first light. but later. he knew it was ear-
lier. before he woke. when the dream-givers were. still picking up.
their plates. sweeping crumbs. from the table.

The dream givers. came early. when he first entered. the dark sky. of
sleep. their faces painted red and black. lightning. or sun. or a star. or
the moon. on their foreheads.

They walked. without sound.

They had to get. into his head to keep his thoughts. on earth.

Otherwise. he could slip. away forever. from darkness into. true dark.

Maybe the crows. slit the dark. to let the waking in.

He knew the crows. spoke to him.

He tried to listen past. the hush of the dream-givers who. knew he was. awake now. a change. in his breathing. or quick movement. that didn't belong. to sleep.

He rubbed his head. and the sleep. from his eyes.

The dawn was blue. as the shirt pocket. where. the denim hadn't. faded.

He picked up. the shirt from the chair. got dressed.

The dream-givers were. surely gone. now. they'd done. their work. turning the darkness. inside out. spilling him to the floor. like lint. or chaff. from a pocket. or pants-cuff.

The sun was. over the edge. of the last dream-image. in his head. like a memory. that returns.

He knew. he belonged to it.

What kept him. here?

Though the crows. had done their work. he could. still hear them. caw.

They were. darkness. to the light. as the moon was. light. to the dark.

His neck ached from sleep.

His head. felt heavy. wet. as bacon.

He would go through the day. his heart. wrapped in baling-wire.

He wanted to be. with the ancestors. corn-farming. carving pipes from. corncobs.

That's what drinking did. eventually. stopped the dreams. so he could cross. to the other. world.

Maybe his dog would. be. waiting for him. there.

Yes. dreams were. the animals of. nature.

More than ever. now. when he started. his old truck. he wanted the night. when the moon. followed the earth.

He remembered following. his grandma. to the chicken coop.

The hens cackled. a fire just. lit. from kindling.

He remembered his grandma's. patched dress . her large shoes. their tongues. all parched. dust. on them. like something. he was supposed. to remember. but kept getting. away.

He felt. the moon. half-light. half-dark.

The moon was also. light. for the dream-givers. to play cards. at the table.

He thought he heard. hens. cackling. no. that was the dream-giver. with the sun. painted on. his forehead. shuffling cards.

Maybe the crows were. fragments of. blackness broken. because of. light.

The earth was. his grandmother. unable. to take care of him. anymore. because she was sick. now. he followed her. not even knowing. how. to turn. for the sun's warmth. on both sides.

It was the day. that was hard.

Someday. he'd escape. the earth. its bright. light into dark.

Someday. he'd sleep. and not. return. he'd pass from. ordinary dark into. true dark.

The dream-givers. could throw. as many dreams. at him. as they wanted. they could. hit his head. until. it jumped like a sack-full of monkeys.

He wouldn't come back. no. he'd be. gone. there's nothing. they. nor the crows. nor anyone. could do.

What bothered him?

The wife. he'd not. been able. to keep?

Even the animal. chose. to leave.

No. the dog. had been made. to leave.

He remembered. something. kicking. was it his leg. or what?

Sometimes. the crows, yelped like. a hurt dog.

Maybe. the groaning was. from his own. throat.

When he got. to work. he'd be late. in trouble again.

He didn't want. to think. about it.

He remembered. climbing the hill. behind his grandpa's farm. the clumps. of birches between. the narrow fields. the creek that. dried. in summer. the rocks. from the sweat-lodge. spoke. to him.

Sometimes. in his stupor. he tried to turn. to light. but too much. had happened.

Yet. there was something. in him. that resisted. true darkness. too.

Something that sent. the dream-givers.

Maybe. that was the nature. of the landscape. inside. his head.

He had in himself. the struggle of. light. dark.

Maybe. he had to learn. to face. both.

But. where did they. come from?

Was the Creator. a Trickster?

Sometimes. the crows seemed. to laugh.

Or was the Creator. a giving Spirit? who sent light. not the ordinary glare. men brought. into their lives. by their own efforts. and had to live with. no. but true light.

Did he. have to choose between. the possibilities?

All right. then. it was. light for the moment. he'd face. the Creator's light.

But. someday he'd be. through. then he could. follow the ancestors.

He'd go back. to his grandpa's place. climb the hill. behind. the sweatlodge.

Yes. he'd see. the clouds. overhead.

It was only. a step. up. there to the sky.

Bird of Death

Sharon Olinka

for Everette Maddox

In my dream dark wings
brushed the ceiling.
Black bones,
you hold me still.
Little secrets.
Ball of fluff
from hell.

When your drinking
increased, job gone,
you went where no one
else would go,
and the corrupt, shell-pink
flowers of Prytania Street
remained with you.

Your eyes
pools of light
in a skull.
Bone points,
you cut me raw,
pulled me
to the deeper shade.
And I thank you.

People say
to me, I can't place you.
I tell them we're all
from another place, really,
its faint flower odor

of pure release
on our skin.

And I speak a language
without translation,
flawed, but filled
with the gold lights
of sickness
and illumination.

A forbidden door
will free me.
I give you
this touch. This flight.

Me and Fester, Flying

Ian Graham Leask

for Ray

W E'RE GOING to fly, then.
This is how to fly home.
This forgone life is disturbing; to see it again you enter an interior where all the past is stored, not well stored but scattered haphazardly; you enter this interior, this messy storeroom, when something about the present is faulty and you need elements from the past to help keep the present running, to make existence travel straight again.

You've been thinking more and more about Fester, and about home, where it's impossible to be. Sometimes your wife wakes you in the night and asks what's the matter, and you say, "Nothing, nothing at all," while she wipes water from your cheeks. So you relax and put your head on the pillow and close your eyes and the stars return to your vision and through them you gain what was lost in consciousness: comprehension of the presence of The Lake of Flints. And Fester's face, pushing up at you out of the lake of closed moments, this refuge of black light, is completely known to you through all its expressions, through all the time you knew it. You look down on yourself from the stars and are amazed at how old you look lying in the bed beside a woman with her tangled hair spread over the pillow. "Why is this happening now," you mutter, "I don't need this."

At the center of existence is The Lake of Flints. A lake of little carbon deposits, hard slivers of memory, the sum of which somehow convinces us that we've lived life in a continuum. The flints move constantly with the pull of the moon and the moon has exposed your dead friend. It's time to go back and gather the sharp remnants of Fester. This is when the flying starts, in bed, staring through the roof into the stars, staring deep into the impenetrable mystery beyond you. You feel yourself lifting. Oh yes, you remember this, there's nothing to be scared of, it's natural, you've always been able to do it. You drift out of bed and down the stairs.

Out the window, through the garden and down the alley. Chest hair touching pavement–pick up speed, arms back–faster, heading for that clapboard garage, ooh, dodge sideways–frighten hell out of the fat yellow cat. Yes. Soar up, over the lines of trees, whole neighborhoods come into view–lakes, two rivers, two downtowns, confusing ribbons of freeway. You can see the perimeter of the pulsing metropolis shut in by dark countryside beyond.

The higher you go the faster you fly and you follow the call of home until the south shore of Lake Superior comes into view, then the St. Lawrence Seaway and beyond that Newfoundland and the Atlantic; to the north the white spreading fingernails of Greenland. Sea and sea and sea and sea, then the warm scent of the Islands of the Mighty and go faster, faster still, until the old stones rise out of the ocean in their purple mists of nightfall.

If they knew you were coming, if they knew you could come, if they were used to it, prepared, how incredible it would be. "Who will it be this night?" they would whisper to themselves.

"Don't touch my bald spot like that," Fester would say, "leave it alone, it hurts."

Calum would say:

"And what will we see from the future if we press our noses against the windowpane and look out into the dark from the quiet of our bedrooms?"

Fester would reply:

"Cut the poetic crap, you big-headed git."

"Hark at you, talking about big heads! Old Boulder Bonce!"

And we'd wait for the visitor, Fester and Calum, breathless time travelers, until we fell asleep with starlight on our faces. We'd dream the same dream of the stranger, unidentifiable yet familiar, coming late to our slumber party but we can't wake up to greet him because we're dowsed in the dead sleep of metallic smelling boyhood.

* * *

Fly in over Cape Wrath, Scotland's crouching dwarf mountains looking up warrior wild, ready to bite, and down the rigid spine of England, the silent yellow night cities, right and left. Southeast, the glow of London, sulfur and the hot mud smell of estuary as you descend over the flat fields of Essex to one spot of habitation among millions— a tiny pellet of place that opens like an orchid in the dark.

* * *

We used to play a lot of football, and what finally has you flying is that you always made Fester stay in goal. And for some inexplicable reason you never said good-bye—you feel as though he's stuck in goal forever. It's around twenty years ago and you see him against the twelve foot brick wall of the Library Gardens waiting slightly crouched, for you to boot a shot at him. We used to sneak into those gardens in the middle of the night to play. He's waiting for you to shoot the ball between the makeshift goalposts made of keep off the grass signs. He's Gordon Banks. Peter Bonetti. Ray Clements. Peter Shilton.

* * *

The only thing we had in common at first was our Scottish fathers, but there was something else—we both had these wild imaginations. It wasn't only the Cutlas Stone just outside the vestibule of St. Clement's where a devil could be made to pop out of Mary Ellis's tomb and grant a wish if you ran around it once for every midnight chime of the church bell—during the full moon, of course; neither was it the pirate treasure that was hidden in the catacombs hollowed out for centuries by smugglers beneath Elizabethan sepulchers and Jacobean plague pits; it wasn't even the ghosts of furious Iccini warriors who walked on foggy nights over the mud flats in search of the treacherous Romans who stole their brave queen away in chains that bound Fester and me together in imagination—it was football. We wanted to be footballers and play for our favorite teams.

The truth was neither of us could even get on the school eleven. They made you, the arch dreamer, play rugby because you were so big, and poor old Fester was simply the wrong shape. He was a good goalie but that wasn't good enough for him. We kept dreaming though—one day, if we played enough, we could make it into the Football League, into the ultimate dream.

Fester lived with his imagination on the outside and suffered for it. As we grew older and his old man wanted him to start thinking about a trade he became disappointed and bitter with life. He was starting to hate being alive because he didn't look right—even after he left high school, the "Addams Family" theme haunted him in coffee bars and pubs—life wasn't measuring up to his dreams.

You kept your imagination hidden, only your mother knew you had one. You got by, did all right—it irritated you that Fester couldn't take it, life that is, this pathetic network of dreams that so consistently rips open under our struggling weight and lets us fall.

The last time together: a Friday night in Benfleet.

We go to a pub that doesn't ask questions about a man's age. There's a tough kid there that spends the evening talking to us. None of us has much money but at the end of the night the tough kid asks if his new-found mates will lend him five bob. For some reason you want to curry favor with this kid; you don't have any more money so you persuade Fester to part with the five shillings.

We're coming back to Leigh, sitting upstairs in the front of the bus with our feet against the window. "Are you sure I'll get it back," he keeps saying, "I don't believe you're sure I'll get it back."

"You'll get it back. Don't be such a bloody miser."

You watch the drunken traffic ahead on London Road, weaving and overtaking, and you want to be rid of Fester's miserable belly-aching. He gets off the bus at The Elms, your stop isn't until The Cricketers. "Cheerio, mate," you say. "See you next weekend, all right?" He mumbles something and swings down the aisle, his progress blocked by the cautiousness of an old inebriate, a pissed fighter ace, the blazer and moustache type, who insists upon waiting for the bus to come to a complete halt before he'll dodder to the top of the stairs. Fester looks back at you and pulls this face that makes you grin. "Typical," says his face, "bloody typical—it's like this in everything I do."

He's crossing London Road to the fish & chip shop on the corner so you slide the window open and shout some abuse down at him. There are raindrops on the glass and leaves blowing up in swirls. He looks up from the middle of the road and fires two fingers at you.

You remember thinking: *He'll be all right. Yeah, he's okay.*

In Thursday's *Southend Standard* you read that he'd taken an over-dose. It took a long time to understand that it wasn't the loss of five shillings that sank him in The Lake of Flints. He was your friend, the founding member of the Blue Flame Club–he was supposed to be able to take it. That's what it was all about, the Blue Flame Club: to hell with our fathers, our abusive, coercive, narrow-minded war hero fathers who were not going to get us down however hard the bastards tried. You remember thinking: *Fuck that, I ain't going to his bleeding funeral. Don't want to talk to his creepy dad or his bastard of a brother. And his mum and sister'll want to know everything we did on Friday night. Besides, in the Blue Flame Club there's no need for funerals–we burn hot and blue.*

Absurd bravado. Truth is you were numb, couldn't feel a thing. It's that simple, is it, that psychological: you didn't go to the funeral because you were angry at him? He'd tried to do it several times but you hadn't understood, you'd thought he was simply playing life to its limit, living up to the tenets of the Blue Flame Club. You accepted extreme behavior back then–your parents, Fester, Fester's parents, certain teachers at your school–you carried on in the hope that people were okay inside and that they merely needed a little attention. That's hard to do now because you know people can suddenly implode, like Fester did, when you're not expecting it; one realizes then what violent and anachronistic codes we're living by; but, of course, it's always too late to help.

You're in the middle of your life now, a time when the events of childhood resound in all the things you do. You're still Fester's pal, still the same, just a little less fresh–now perhaps you can calm down a bit and say good-bye to him.

You're cooling off, flying home for a while.

* * *

You're hovering over the Library Gardens, but he's not there. When you think of him it's usually here. But sometimes he's at the bottom of Leigh Hill by the railway lines where he tried to decapitate himself. What a game that was: keep your neck on the railway line as long as you can while the train roars toward you. The smooth metal would rumble against the throat. Most of us could stand it to about fifty feet and what a triumph it was if an alert train driver saw a boy draped across the track and slammed on the brakes. What joy to try and run up the steep hill through the bushes, laughing so hard you could scarcely breathe, while the alarmed faces of businessmen and secretaries popped out of the carriage windows to peer like blinking half-wits up and down the track. But there was the day when Fester left his head there, his eyes staring at the oncoming train and it was nearly on top of him when we dragged him aside. He'd wet himself and messed his underpants. We took him to the public toilet at the top of the hill to clean him up.

You see him all too often with his head laid on that track but mostly you see him in the Library Gardens waiting for you to shoot the ball at him. Yes, when in goal he thought he was Gordon Banks, and on the rare occasions he was playing the field he would be Jimmy Greaves, Bobby Charlton, Dennis Law. All his other mates–I suppose there weren't that many of them outside the Blue Flame Club–used to put him in goal, too. None of the others could stand the way his imagination worked–he really was playing in the front four for Spurs or Manchester United against Red Star Belgrade, Moscow Dynamo, Benfica, Inter Milan, Real Madrid, Borussia Munchengladbach. He was at White Heart Lane under the floodlights with the packed crowd singing "Glory Glory Halleluja, Glory Glory Halleluja. Glory Glory Hallelujajaja . . . and the Spurs go marching on."

His dad hated it when Fester got too creative, the old bastard called it lying. It was true that Fester didn't have the same way of looking at things as most people. Maybe it was because he'd been born with such a funny-looking head; it was this almost hydro-cephalic block covered in thick black hair that would shed in great tufts when he was under stress, leaving flaky suppurating sores. So he'd shave his head completely and act crazy and they'd call him Fester from the television show and because he seemed to be festering and leprous; he hated that, he absolutely hated that, but what else could he be called? It stuck. Through his life he'd had a few other names: "Missing Link" by one of the teachers at school; "Tunes" because of his wondrous ability to control flatulence; and when we were younger, "Humpty Dumpty."

* * *

Fester's not at the Library Gardens. He's not by the railway lines. He's not walking home from school. He's not messing about in the boats by Bell Wharf. I'm hovering above Fester's house on the corner of Elm Road. I've just flown across the Atlantic to see if he can play and I can't find the pillock. I don't think a week has gone by in my life when I haven't in some way tried to find him, and here I am hovering above his house where his dad sits in the living room in front of the television, beside his coal fire, brooding like a keg of Celtic gunpowder. He's a police constable and does nothing but sit and brood when he gets off the beat. He sits in his uniform and gets pissed on cheap whiskey.

I descend to Fester's window and look in. He's in there on his bed, wanking. He's already eaten the pills. The bottle's empty beside his bed. He's in the middle of his last wank, the smile of a dolphin on his face, pumping and thrusting up into his own hand. Maybe he's already getting heavy and falling into odd kinds of dreams, like having his old mate float in from the future and hover at the window like a banshee, an angel of short-term memory. When he sees a face at the window he covers up quick. I'm light and futuristic while he's leaden and historical, usable only between goalposts, sinking deeper and deeper into the soft humus of memory.

Fester drags himself to the window and opens it. "What're you doing here?" he says. "I'm not dead yet."

I notice that there's a pack of wolves waiting in the corner of his room, the ones that used to chase him up the stairs. I'd forgotten that. For years those wolves chased him–I wondered even back then, despite being teen-aged and testosterone-blind, what those wolves signified, what they sniffed. What the hell does it mean when a child repeatedly dreams of wolves chasing him up the carpeted stairs of his own home?

I squeeze through the window. I'm huge, bulky, and bald. Fester says, "You look like shit, Leith. The future hasn't been nice to you at all."

I say, "Oh, yes it has."

"You can fly, you lucky bastard. Trust you to get all the luck."

"I got all the brains too, didn't I?"

"No you didn't, you rotten bastard!"

"You wanna play midnight football?"

"Do I look like I wanna play football? I'm trying to top meself and you wanna play football. Selfish sod."

"Come on, you miserable fuck. The Library Gardens! Under the lights! While all the old bastards sleep."

"All right," he says. "I suppose so. But I'm not going in goal."

"You miserable bugger. Get your togs on and bring your ball."

"Why can't we use your ball? We're always using mine. And it's new. Let's use yours, we always use my best stuff."

"I've lost my ball. Let's break in one of your new ones."

"Where did you lose it, liar?"

"It's a long story, mate."

"Oh all right," he says. "You always get your own way."

I snort, say, "Not any more I don't."

He thinks and says, "You remember when we wanted Mary Ellis's ghost to give us bikes. You did all the running around the Cutlas Stone and you only got ten circles to twelve chimes."

"Eleven. I did eleven."

"Liar. I bet you been telling everyone for decades that you did eleven, but I was there and I know you only did ten. I counted."

"You always were a bleeder for detail. I predicted it'd be your downfall."

"I knew exactly how many pills to take. I looked it up in the library—it was easy."

"And you took them, you stupid asshole."

"Yeah, well. I've got my own way for once. I never got no bleeding bike but you did even though you only did ten circuits . . ."

"Eleven."

"You got a bike because your old man caught you coming in the window. And I did my job properly and never got nothing."

Fester's pulling all his sports kit out of the cupboard. The wolves sit lazily in the corner looking at him with their pale eyes. They're unconcerned. No doubt they saw how many pills he took. I think about our first midnight encounter with the Cutlas Stone, which, like he said, didn't result in his getting a bike. And I think about the time his brother told everyone that he'd caught Fester in their mother's bedroom trying on her slinky underwear. Maybe I should pay his brother a little visit—melt through his bedroom window and slit his stinking throat.

Fester's choosing his kit.

He liked teams with beautiful names and hated teams with ugly ones like Middlesborough, Oldham Athletic, Arsenal, Leeds United. All his passions, the teams he'd get crushes on, had lovely old names and were seldom, with a few exceptions, successful on the field: Aberdeen, red shirt white shorts; Heart of Midlothian, purple and white; Tottenham Hotspur, white shirts, navy blue shorts; Queen of the South, blue and white; Exeter City, red and black; Torquay United, gold and blue; Plymouth Argyle, green and white and black; Wolverhampton Wanderers, gold and black. It wouldn't take much to make him fall out of love with them. If they got too successful and were no longer in his category of underdog, or if they advanced luckily in some competition, or if he read in the paper that they'd played dirty. He used to love West Ham United until they won the European Cup Winner's Cup; then he hated them so much that he'd go to their home games and always buy a rosette in the colors of the other team. And Southend United, his home team, his first love; he hated them because he wanted them so badly to be a better team than was ever possible. He owned the playing kit of all these clubs. He'd make the kit himself on his mother's sewing machine to save money.

I'm about to tell him that Southend is in the first division now and doing pretty well, but he probably wouldn't believe me. "You haven't changed," he'd say. "You'll always be a lying git."

He's putting on the red and black outfit–Exeter City circa 1970. He's lacing his football boots. One of the wolves, the big black one with gas-flame eyes, sits up, pricks its ears, blinking, licking its chops.

I get ready on the windowsill. Fester throws me the ball and I put it under my left arm. He vaults the bed and dashes for the window. I stand up on the sill and help him. The wolves are up and after him, snapping at his backside. Our right arms meet, our hands clasp each other's elbows, and I launch myself backwards into the misty midnight sea air of my lovely childhood town. The wolf pack hits the window, yapping and snapping, saliva dripping and smearing the glass.

We dip a little at first, threaten to demolish his dad's garden shed which is always kept locked so the tools will stay in place, but we start ascending just in time and before long we're up over the trees, looking down at the empty roads lit by yellow street lights. It's quite dark up here because the street lights have lids on them and shine downwards. It's quiet and we're up high enough to see the Kent coast and the river opening into the sea, and Southend Pier, the wreck of the Montgomery, the Roots Hall floodlights, our old school, St. Clement's Church, Hadleigh Castle, and the houses of our friends . . . and ahead, our midnight stadium, the Library Gardens.

I let go of him and he flies alone. "This is good," he says, "chuck me the ball." And I do. We throw the ball back and forth as we fly to the Library Gardens.

We fly a couple of times around the church tower, cackling like witches, then dip down into the trees and fly over the wall into the dark, locked interior of the gardens. We hover above the flower beds for a while then land and wait under the fuzzy branches of the monkeytail tree, looking out at the manicured lawn lit up by the yellow street lights of The Broadway. The lights are all out in the flats above the shops. We are there, hidden, hiding and watchful in the shadows.

* * *

A black and white football bounces out of nowhere onto the perfect turf, into the silent yellow light. Two figures walk out of the shadows. A tall deep-chested man, bald and bearded, fully kitted out in the colors of Southend United. And a pear-shaped teenager wearing the colors of Exeter City. Our boots are shining, their cleats tear softly into the immaculate turf–designed for old people to look at. We pull up the please keep off the grass signs and rearrange them as goalposts.

I throw Fester a green jersey; he sighs and puts it on, stands between the signs and lobs the ball out at me as I run backwards into position. I take the ball on my right toe, bounce it on both knees, then volley it in an arc toward the left goalpost. Fester dives and punches the ball out over my head so that I have to chase and trap. I'm Gary Lineker coming out of retirement to play for the team he always had a soft spot for. I turn on the goal and dribble in, swaying through tackles as the crowd roars, and I let fly a shot that sends Fester sprawling.

A bus stops. The two sleepy people in its upper deck, one at the front and one at the back, are capable of seeing me so I walk in toward the goal, get under the cover of the wall.

I hear a fog horn in the estuary.

An owl screeches.

We sit in the flower bed and wait for the bus to go. We can hear its engine idling while the driver waits to catch up with his schedule. I remember the frightening night we watched the black sabbath in the graveyard of St. Clement's. I remember how much marmalade Fester would pile on his toast and how many times he'd say "thank you" to my mother every time he came for tea. I remember him sticking up for a kid called Woodley in school when our idiotic headmaster wanted to cane him for having a nervous smile on his face. I remember when he nearly lost his head on the railway tracks at the bottom of Leigh Hill. I remember the intensity of his laughter, how he'd roll on the floor, infecting all of us with it. And there were his farts. They were great farts—he had names for ten different types, like Eskimo snow.

The Blue Flame Club. Dear God, how I miss the laughter of the Blue Flame Club. I look at Fester beside me, throwing the ball up in the air and catching it—it's amazing he's alive. I thought he was dead.

The bus revs up and pulls away. I trudge out into the middle of the lawn and Fester throws the ball just ahead of me so that I can dash in and head it. It's a great header, low and hard, but not beyond his acrobatic reach. To my surprise, he lets it in; his dive is listless, and he takes a long time to get up. He sits for a while in the goalmouth like that statue I saw somewhere. The Dying Gaul.

"Come on, Fester, chuck us it."

And he moves obediently, rolls the ball out to me. I try to roust him a bit. I trap it and swing in towards him with a breathless commentary: "He's on the attack! He beats one defender, two, three. There's no one to pass to, so he swings into center field, looking for help." In my peripheral vision I can see Fester standing with knees bent, arms by his sides, very unprepared for the rocket I'll send him. "He twists and turns, evading tackles, still no one to pass to—he's going to have to go it alone!" And I pivot and turn, blast the ball toward the goal.

It sails over the wall.

I hear it bounce once in the road and thud against a shop window.

Fester's sitting in the goalmouth again, his head lowered.

In the darkness all around us, under the trees, are red eyes watching.

"Fester!"

The red eyes move closer and the faces of wolves are illuminated by the yellow street lights. Fog horns moan in the estuary. The old owl hoots again. Police officers start entering the gardens, quietly climbing over the wall, dropping down from the trees, creeping out of flower beds. I can hear them marching along The Broadway in their rubber-soled boots. Hundreds of cops climbing out of windows, stepping out of alleys, sliding under hedges, looming up from graves in the rotting uniforms of twenty generations. The peaks of their helmets are pulled down over their eyes to disguise the glowing red. The wolves step cautiously into the full light, followed by those sharp-helmeted agents of extreme coercion.

Fester's mired in the goalmouth.

"Come on!" I yell. "Get up!"

He looks at me, leaden-eyed, saliva forming a string from the side of his mouth to his knee.

The coercers are creeping nearer, so I spring into the air and hover above them lest they infect me. "Fester, come on, fly. Fly! Up and fly!"

He gets up and staggers, then falls back into the flower bed behind him. The police pounce on him. His body absorbs them, they fly up his anus, pointed helmets first, and add weight to him. His mouth is a black hole out of which no sound comes.

The wolves attack.

"Fester!"

Snarling wolves leap at his face and enter his head through his eyes; the weaker ones go in through his ears, nose, and mouth. He's sinking into the flower bed as he becomes filled with police and wolf. He's a small thing of astounding weight, sinking into the rich soil of the flower bed; sinking down among the tulips, sinking . . . sinking into The Lake of Flints, while I hover like a hawk above the whirlpool of coercers that wish to add themselves to his descent.

When I've witnessed the last police officer and the last wolf enter the slight depression in the soft earth that Fester has left I fling myself skyward, toward the stars that never get any nearer. Below, the little park and church become pinpricks of illuminated light. Then I see the old black river, lit up by oil refineries, shining the way to London, and I follow that until I can see the prospect of America glowing in the distance. So I fly there.

Photo Taken in Winter, 1944

Barbara Unger

Collaborators,
naked Vichy women
who gave comfort to the Gestapo,
heads shaved,
ankles manacled
cower in a pit
like the open mouth
of a grave.

Behind them, respectable Frenchwomen
exact their revenge, guarded
by grinning G.I. captors.

It was how I harvested
my first glimpse of the woman's body
I'd soon inhabit, the forbidden body
I'd leap into like a flame,

The treacherous breasts,
their flaccid resistance
easily conquered,
the untrustworthy vagina,
that dark hairy mouth
between the legs,

Inside lay a long red tongue
like the tongues of traitors
and tattle-tales.

I ponder women as both the tortured
and the torturer; drawn to
the still shot, the shaved skull,
the true-to-life shudder.

Observance

Grandma Jenny never learned
to read or write,
never marched or voted,
saw the law
steal her children,
given, taken away,
pushed to the limits
by exile and poverty.

Why was she a faster and atoner
and not you?

This Russian grandmother
who left her children
at the orphanage
to make a living
at the factory?

Why does your tongue,
so agile at fine print,
stumble at *Kaddish?*

Why do you, like Abraham,
still bargain with God
in the desert?

Summer, green and irresponsible,
has not started to rust or yellow.

Like a door opening in a dream,
Grandma enters and sits
in her claw-footed chair.

Her witch hair is coiled
and pinned in place.

You have never been so alive.
Your ignorance flies from you like lice.

You sit in the dark parlor again.
She promises macaroons at sundown.

Rue de Rosiers: To My Brother Fred

Liliane Richman

In summer the Jews of my childhood sit on chairs
raucous kings and queens of the street the sidewalks
their high-pitched voices their guttural syllables
their tongue first cousin to that teutonic language
I am deathly afraid of

In front of the butcher shop
a cloud of feathers rises
devouring the woman with sheitl
her busy plucking hands
her newly koshered hen hidden

from a trio of old men in black hats
their locks and white beards questioning the wind
as they stand in the middle of the narrow street
gesturing with utmost urgency

An outsider I feel except Sundays
when my parents the immigrants
send me to Goldenberg
for pastrami pickles halvah
to the bakery for sweet chalah and rye

and on my way at the corner of Rue des Rosiers
stands Klapish Fish Market
whose name my brother and I always mispronounced
until the made up name became the only one

Years later so much older we laugh
a detour to our childhood

through the Jewish neighborhood
gray mysterious insistent
a chatty maze of streets beckoning
ancient letters stars of David above stores
with fish of all sizes swimming as always
in vast vats through the window at Klapfish forever
the fish market in the street of roses

To Valenton:
Impressions circa 1947

On weekends we climbed the bus out of Paris
the long time it took
like a summer vacation
our whiny impatience to get there,
of course with our parents,
father a snapshot
white shirt white pants,
orchestrating the outing,
mother carrying a big bag
towels snacks the meowing black and white cat
the only pet we ever had
in that cramped apartment in Paris,

and only two of my brothers,
the youngest born years after the war,

when we finally arrived at Valenton
a scraggly beach along a big lake, or was it the sea?
only the map knows,
we took our shoes off
at the entrance of paradise by the gate
where people in long lines paid their money,
and groped with our toes through the warm sand
for fallen coins

and amazingly, we always found some,
that was the best time, and after
in the height of noon
wet and cold from braving waves
like fearless toreadors,
we ate banana sandwiches
and combed seaweed out of each other's hair
while listening to the drone of the members
of the Hungarian Club
their accents
thick as goulash spicy as paprika
till satiated with riches and air
we fell asleep under the sun

The Right Way

Arlene Gralla Feldman

Sam s father, David, sat at the far end of the kitchen table reading *The Jewish Press* as Sam's mother, Ruth, handed him a bowl of oatmeal.

David put aside the newspaper and reached for his coffee cup. "Margaret is a nice girl, Samuel!" he shouted. "But she's not Jewish!" David always shouted when he spoke, being hard of hearing. It really wasn't his fault that he was obnoxious.

"You mean, she's not Jewish enough, don't you, Dad?" Sam shouted in response.

"What I mean!" David yelled, "is that it's not good enough that Margaret's father is Jewish! It's the mother that counts! If the woman who brings forth the child is not Jewish, then the child is not Jewish! Margaret is not considered Jewish! It's as simple as that!" David picked up the newspaper. He was finished.

"What we'll do," Ruth said, reaching for Sam's hand, "is talk to the rabbi and see how we can make it right."

"Whatever you do, her mother still won't be Jewish and that's what counts! But," David shouted, "if the rabbi says it's all right, who am I to question?"

"To make it right," Sam told Maggie, sitting in his father's '57 DeSoto sedan, "would be for you to go to this rabbi–Rabbi Rubin, on Stone Avenue and take lessons."

"What kinda lessons?"

"The Bible. How to keep a kosher home. That stuff."

"My mother is going to hate it. Just hate it."

"She'll get used to it, Mags, just like your father got used to Lizabeth getting baptized and marrying a Catholic."

"Yeah, but my mother is anti-Semitic, you know that. And my father is anti-nothing."

"Believe me, Mags . . . she'll get over it, and it would probably make things simpler down the road when we have kids."

At that she smiled. "Okay . . . tell your parents I'll do whatever has to be done to make it right."

Relieved, Sam hugged her. "God, I love you, Mags!"

* * *

The first thing Maggie noticed about Rabbi Rubin when she entered his study was him. She thought he resembled da Vinci's Jesus Christ in *The Last Supper*—though in better condition. He wore a well-tailored black suit and a cream-colored shirt. The top button of his shirt was undone and from that space tufts of bronze chest hairs sprung out, touching his auburn-colored beard. His russet hair reached his shoulders and blended with that beard. His skin was fair and he wore gold wire-rimmed glasses. Maggie tried to see the color of his eyes, but he avoided that contact, gesturing for her to have a seat.

The rabbi stood up, turned, and walked over to his bookcases. He ran his hand slowly along a row of books. Her eyes followed those long slender fingers until they stopped at a volume. He removed a morocco-covered book, fingered through the pages, and turned suddenly. Maggie shifted her gaze to some far corner of the room. He returned to his chair, and still not looking directly at her, pushed the book slowly across the desk toward her. She noticed his wedding band and wondered how many children he had . . .

"Oh, they have plenty of kids, those Orthodox ones" her mother had said. *"It's all that davening . . . that rocking . . . back and forth, back and forth. Shoulders forward! Pelvis forward! Shaking up those sperm! I swear they're jerking off! Why else would they wear those shawls, the* tallit*? So no one can see what's really going on, that's why. I pity the wives!"*

Maggie reached for the book and placed it on her lap. *Code of*

Jewish Law it was. He slid a small green booklet toward her. She placed *Jewish Family Life–The Duty of the Woman* on top of the *Code*.

"Read these and come to see me again next Wednesday at this same time."

Maggie thumbed through the green book. The words "Why a mikvah and not a bathtub?" sprang up at her. She closed the book.

"That is all for now, unless there are any questions."

Well yes, Rabbi. As a matter of fact. . . . I mean, why a mikvah and not a bathtub? I would like to know that and so would my mother, I'm sure.

"No, no questions. Thank you." Maggie got out of the chair and faked a move toward the door. Abruptly she turned, faced the rabbi and waving the books said, "Thanks for these."

Green. His eyes were green. *Gotcha! she thought.*

* * *

"You're going to what?" Zena demanded, holding the soup ladle in midair.

"Look at it as a baptism, Ma, like Lizabeth's. It's no big deal. You yourself told us a hundred times that you and Daddy decided not to raise us as Jewish or Russian Orthodox because religion was just so much bullshit."

"It is bullshit! Do you think going to a mikvah is going to make you Jewish? It's the mother that counts. And I'm your mother, remember me?"

"What's going on?" Jacob asked as he closed the bathroom door behind him.

"Jake, would you believe, she wants to go to a mikvah," Zena said, pointing the ladle toward him and then at Maggie. "Did Elizabeth Taylor go to a mikvah? Did Marilyn Monroe go? No! Even the women born Jewish don't go to a mikvah anymore!"

"A mikvah, Zee, is no big deal. All it is, is a dip in a pool of water," he said, taking his seat at the table.

"So, if it's no big deal, why is it so important that she go?"

"Why is it so important that she not?" Jacob asked and shrugged.

Zena plunged the ladle into the pot of soup. "Bullshit!"

* * *

Maggie went to see Rabbi Rubin the following Wednesday and the Wednesday after that. At that time the rabbi slid a card toward her. "Memorize this," he said.

She read the words silently. *"Blessed art thou, O Lord our God, King of the Universe who has sanctified us by His commandments and has commanded us to observe the Ritual Immersion."*

"And this," he said, sliding another card.

The first line contained a Hebrew inscription. Directly under that was a phonetic translation. *"Shma Yisroel, Adonoi Elohenu, Adonoi Achod,"* and below that in English, "Hear O Israel, the Lord our God, the Lord is One. Amen."

"This last, you will also say at the time of immersion. It is a prayer you should recall all the days of your life, and before death it should be your last words." He paused and then continued. "As of this day forward, you will no longer be called Margaret. Your name will be Leah."

Lay ah. Lay her . . . Ugh! Maggie thought. She wondered, Rabbi, can I exchange it for maybe a Shoshana, or a Roni?

"And now, Leah, I ask that you answer the following questions: Do you hereby renounce any affiliation with any religion other than Judaism?"

Well, see, I've never been affiliated. Unless you call having a Christmas tree in the house affiliated. But really, that was just for the fun of it. You know toys under the tree, all the decorations, the wonderful scent of pine. Even my father loved it, though he was always afraid it would catch fire.

"Yes," she said aloud.

"And do you renounce any deity other than the Lord, our God of Israel?"

Well you see, somewhere along the way somebody, an aunt, or maybe even it was my mother, taught me the sign of the cross. And every night before I went to sleep I would repeat in Russian, "Vey Mitzah," the three fingers of my right hand clasped together to my forehead, "Sinnah," to my diaphragm, "Shvatuha," to my right breast, "Ducha," to my left breast, and "Amen," to the center of my chest. In the name of the Father, the Son and the Holy Ghost, Amen! I only did it because I was scared as a kid the communists were gonna drop the bomb on Brooklyn. And then it really just became a habit. I can probably stop it. And anyway, I never mentioned Jesus Christ! Maggie nodded, "Yes."

"And do you, Leah, dedicate your life to the joyous anticipation of the coming of the Messiah?"

"Yes."

"And lead a life befitting a Jewish wife and mother according to the *Code*?"

I do. I promise to love, honor, cherish and protect this religion of our God of Israel, until death do us part . . . so help me, Jesus!

"I will," she said.

"That's fine, Leah." He removed his glasses and smiled. "You should go to the mikvah a week before your marriage. On a Sunday . . . three o'clock in the afternoon."

*   *   *

The door opened slowly, quietly.

"Shalom, Leah. We were expecting you," the young matron whispered. She took Maggie by the hand and closed the door noiselessly behind her. The matron wore a white dress covered by a white apron. A white cotton scarf hid her hair. "My name is Taharah," she said.

"That's a beautiful name, Taharah," Maggie said wistfully.

"Thank you, Leah. It means purity," she said serenely.

I wonder, Maggie thought, could you tell me what Leah means, or better still, can you tell me how I could get it changed. I mean, after all, here I was thrown this mane. I had no say in the matter.

"Come with me, Leah."

Maggie followed Taharah through a long, dimly lit corridor. The matron paused before an open door and nodded in the direction of Rabbi Rubin. His back, toward them, was slowly rocking back and forth.

Shoulders forward! Pelvis forward! Shaking up those sperm!

"The rabbi will witness your *tevilah*, your immersion," Taharah said as they walked on. "You will have a sheet around your body while you stand in the water. After you recite the prayer, the rabbi will leave. I will witness the rest, when you release the sheet and submerge."

And then, will I be as pure as you?

They stopped before a door marked TOILET. Taharah motioned for Maggie to walk in.

To Maggie's right was a toilet and a sink with a small oval mirror above it. Beside the sink was a full length mirror and next to that was one of those curved bathtubs on claw legs. The shower curtain matched the blue-tiled walls and floor. There was a towel and all sorts of toiletries piled on a bench before the tub. Taharah pointed to it. "Take your time. Cleanse carefully," she said, and left the room.

Maggie undressed, leaned over the bathtub, adjusted the water temperature and climbed in. She washed her hair and scrubbed her body–twice to be sure. She vaguely thought about her impurities gurgling down the drain.

As she stepped out of the tub, she caught sight of herself in the full length mirror. Her flesh looked beet-red, raw. Her hair, a knotted mess. She gently towel-dried, walked to the sink, and brushed her teeth. Barely finished combing the tangles from her hair, she heard a tap on the door.

Taharah walked in. "Good! You look to be finished," she said, tipping her head slowly from left to right, up and down, carefully looking Maggie over. "Now you washed carefully, and your nails are trimmed?"

"Yes, did them last night." Maggie extended her hands proudly.

Taharah scrutinized Maggie's fingers and then her toes. She reached into her apron pocket, drew forth a small, gleaming scissor and gripped Maggie's right hand. She began to cut and trim her fingernails zealously. She turned the scissors around and with the blunt end of the handle began to dig at Maggie's cuticles, pushing them back, deep into her fingers.

Maggie pulled her hand away and put her throbbing fingertips to her lips. "Oh, God, that hurts so much! Aren't they short enough?"

"We have to be sure that the water has access to every part." Taharah reached for Maggie's left hand, checked it over and gave one last stab to her pinky.

"Your teeth? Did you brush?"

Maggie nodded.

"And your hair–have you combed your hair?"

"Yes," she said, fingering a loose strand, pushing it behind her ears.

"I mean . . . below."

Below! "Below?"

"Yes, below."

Maggie reached for the comb, turned her back to Taharah and combed her pubic hairs.

Below. Sure, so the water has access to every part.

"Fine," Taharah said, handing Maggie a sheet. "Now follow me."

Maggie struggled to keep the sheet around her naked body as she followed Taharah through a door marked MIKVAH.

The room was a small, silent one. The ceiling, walls, and floor were covered with small, white tiles. The floor was a narrow space that edged a pool of dark, steel-gray water. Maggie heard the echo of her breath as she approached the steps leading down into the pool.

"There are seven steps," Taharah coached behind her.

Seven. As the Blessed Sacraments. Seven. Seven steps. Steps . . . stations. Stations of the Cross. Now, how many stations of the Cross were there? Twelve? Or were there ten? No less than ten.

"Seven," Taharah was saying. "Count them as you go so that you don't fall. When you reach the bottom, say the prayer and then, after the rabbi leaves, hand me the sheet."

Maggie took the first step . . . *Eucharist.* She whispered the Hebrew prayer, "Blessed art thou, O Lord, our God–" Then the second step, *Baptism* . . . "–King of the Universe." Three, *Confirmation* . . . "Who has sanctified –" Four . . . "us by His commandments." *Confession.* Five and six . . . "and has commanded . . . " *Marriage* "–us to observe . . ." *Holy Orders.* And finally, *Anointing of the Sick,* the seventh step . . . "–The Ritual Immersion."

The water skimmed the top of Maggie's shoulders. She walked cautiously to the center of the pool and turned to Taharah. Her peripheral vision caught the rabbi standing far to her left. She placed her right hand across her left breast.

"Blessed are Thou . . . " she began. "*Shma Yisroel* . . . " With conviction, she continued, "*Adonoi, Elohenu, Adonoi Achod.*"

As she pulled the corner of the sheet from her left shoulder to hand to Taharah, the rabbi left the room. Maggie slowly drew her arms up and extended them out to either side. She opened her hands, palms resting on the water, and separated her fingers. Parting her legs, she began to crouch into the water when she felt the sheet being pulled by Taharah, who gripped her left ankle and over she went into what seemed like the never-ending depth of the pool. . . .

As she settled to the bottom, Maggie saw Rabbi Rubin swimming above her, his body frantically jerking back and forth, back and forth. As he moved toward her, arms outstretched, his yarmulke floated away, then his tallit. Here and there went his jacket, trousers and underclothes.

His beard and his long hair billowed out, encircling his head, halo-like.

His floating scrotum cradled his penis, which thrust forward, bobbed up and down. Rabbi Rubin sank into Maggie's open arms and then, even further . . . deeper . . . below.

Ah, Heaven! Maggie thought, as she locked her ankles behind him, drowning in his kisses, rocking in unison. Unum. One. One God. In the name of the Father, the Son and the Holy Spirit! One God! One!

Maggie struggled against a force pulling them apart. She mouthed a scream, No! No! as she moved further from her rabbi–NO! She saw him moving away, arms outstretched, reaching–NO! He made one last forward thrust and the water filled with glistening, dancing sperm, rocking back and forth, gaining access to every part of her body.

She tore at the hands gripping her underarms.

In the name of *Shma Yisroel, Vev Mitzah, Sinnah, Shvatuha.* Oh, God! Amen!

"What?" Maggie gasped. "What are you doing?"

"Leah! My God, are you all right? The sheet caught!" said Taharah, who fully dressed, was standing in the pool beside her.

"Yes, I'm all right."

"Would you like to try it again?"

"Yes, again," Maggie sighed. "From the beginning?"

And Maggie did–perfectly, or so Taharah had said afterwards.

Later, when they were both dry and Maggie was ready to leave, Taharah handed her a sealed envelope. "Rabbi Rubin said to give you this."

Maggie carefully opened the envelope and pulled out a letter. Rabbi Rubin's name and address were boldly printed and centered at the top. Just below there was a message, handwritten in Hebrew. There was no phonetic or English translation, but Maggie knew the words made everything right.

I got it. My passport! My passport to Judaism, to matrimony, to maternity and the sacred burial ground.

Like Yesterday

Deborah Stein

T HERE ARE not many who remember being eight years old the
way Dora Taylor remembers it. Like it was yesterday.

Damp Pacific Northwest autumn twenty years ago, Seattle is
wrapped in rain-soaked maple leaves. Dora spends weekends raking
the slopes of her family's front yard, raking random layers of geome-
try and colors. Her big brother J. W. burns the piles and their parents
drum up more chores.

Finishing a last mound of leaves at the lawn's bottom edge, Dora
climbs high to her tree house built with a best friend: their home,
braced by the largest maple in the neighborhood.

On the girls' last climb to their private heaven, they find the
secluded galaxy of boards gaping open. Walls streaked red and boards
wounded by gashes and paint. The door's padlock is forced and
cracked.

Certain their brothers know who, and why, the girls are convinced
the offenders are the boys. The boys refuse to speak.

Now, twenty-five years past, the brothers keep their secret. Still
best friends, the girls stay certain the boys did it.

* * *

Dora remembers nine years old even better. Mixed-race girl of many
worlds, America is segregated, her family is not. She belongs every-
where, yet matches no one in those times without in-betweens.

Fitting nowhere, she feels discarded like the leafy stems of strawberries. Like their soft leaves crushed from being gripped as a handle for its fruit.

J. W. is frantic. Shoves Dora under the front car seat one Sunday, screaming, "Lock the doors! They might take you!"

Dora and her brother wait for their mother on that warm damp Seattle Sunday outside her favored 23rd Street Bakery in the inner-city Central District of the late 1950s. They wait in their mother's faded green Plymouth.

Coiled car seat springs tear Dora's brown-skinned back while J. W. and she pray for sugar donuts and glazed ones too.

Dora hopes more for the seclusion of her tree house.

Living in Two Languages

Susan M. Tiberghien

WHEN I married Pierre, I slowly slipped into a French-speaking pattern—thinking, dreaming, and raising children in French. Only when the children grew up and left home did I have the time and space to venture back to an English-speaking pattern.

It took a while to adjust and make the edges fit, then one day I found myself American once again. Pierre appreciates the variable metamorphosis, like having both wife and mistress. And I have the choice, will I live the coming day in French or in English?

* * *

If I decide for French, I'll greet my husband with *"Bonjour, mon cheri, as-tu bien dormi?"* There will follow an intimate exchange about whether we slept soundly, if we were too hot or too cold, how many times we woke, and so forth. I will dress in a dark skirt and lighter blouse. Our breakfast will be short and precise—coffee, bread and butter. I'll question him about his day, he'll question me, it will all be rather rational, one subject after another, well-constructed, like a dissertation.

And my day will continue as such. In my head I'll make lists of things to do and go about my morning, proceeding methodically, not losing time. I'll avoid odds and ends of conversation with people I meet, especially with people I don't know. At the same time I'll be unfailingly polite, *"Bonjour Madam," "Au revoir Monsieur," "Vous êtes très aimable, Madame,"*

"Je vous remercie, Monsieur," using the same tone of voice, be it with the neighbor, mailman, or butcher.

Back home, in the afternoon, when working at my desk, I may loosen up and temporarily slide out of this French-speaking pattern. But if the telephone rings, I'll sit up straight, pick up the receiver and reply, *"Allo?"*, without the slightest encouragement to whoever is at the other end of the line.

In the evening, I will relate my day to Pierre and ask about his. During dinner we will talk seriously about something in the news, politics, a concert or movie, a book, about our grown children, our friends, the company we wish to soon invite. If we are planning a large dinner party, he will suggest that I send the invitations rather than phone everyone, "It's less familiar." And I will explain that I prefer to call, "It's more personal," even if I sometimes mix up the *"tu"* and *"vous."*

Even today we have certain close friends whom we address with the formal *"vous,"* as we also address Pierre's parents, and his aunts and uncles. Regardless of the relationship–mailman, butcher, close friend, and favorite uncle–they all receive the same *"vous."*

* * *

Now, however, if I decide to live my day in English, I will greet my French husband with something like "Good morning, dear, time to get up," pulling off the covers to make sure he's heard me. I'll dress in a purple track suit and go fix orange juice, which will maybe awaken our appetites for eggs and bacon or pancakes. I'll take my time, talking to Pierre about whatever comes into my mind. He'll try to get up from the table once or twice, but I'll ask him not to rush off, reminding him how I used to love long breakfasts years ago in the States.

And when he's gone, I'll stay right there and reread yesterday's newspaper in English, making myself a second or third cup of coffee, sometimes adding some water. Before doing my work, I'll perhaps call and invite a friend for lunch. When I go shopping, I'll bump into somebody I haven't seen for weeks and stop and chat. By the time I get to the post office, there'll be lots of people waiting in line. I'll smile at whoever looks at me, and then I'll smile and talk with the clerk who's been there for several years. Finally I'll skip the shopping and serve whatever I have in the fridge. My friend won't mind, she's used to my improvised menus.

In the afternoon I'll work at my desk. When the phone rings, I'll lean back in my chair–or take the phone and lie down on my bed–and answer,

"Hi, this is Susan." And I won't look too much at my watch. If the weather's good, I'll go for a short walk, down the road opposite our house, near the empty fields that remind me of New England. I'll find a stone and kick it along for company, I'll say hello to the people I meet, they'll look startled and most likely won't answer, but I'll keep trying.

In the evening, I'll tell Pierre about the acquaintance I met at the shopping center, the clerk in the post office, my friend who came for lunch, the people who telephoned, and then I'll tell him about my afternoon walk and the dog who wagged its tail at me while its owner looked away. I'll laugh and make him laugh.

He'll tell me about the people he met and we'll ramble on this way. I'll interrupt him and ask him questions that have nothing to do with what he was saying. I'll jump from one subject to another, something I read or I heard, something I dreamed. Then I'll go telephone our guests for Saturday evening, and I won't give a hoot about *"tu"* and *"vous."*

* * *

Bilingualism or split personality? Once the two patterns fit, the choice is mine. I wake up and write down my dreams in the language I dreamed them. I read the newspapers in both. I live my day as it comes along. I say either "tu" or "vous," whichever one I wish. And I make "I love you" sound just as beautiful as "Je t'aime."

ESSAY

Spécialité Provençale

IT WAS SUMMERTIME when we arrived in the small village of white walls and red sun-baked roofs, built on a hillside in southern France, where Pierre was assigned to an air force base hidden close by in the fields of lavender.

I was an American bride, learning to be a French housewife. In the fifties in Provence, there were no supermarkets, no Colgate toothpaste, no Coca-Cola, no paper bags. Each day I bought bread at the bakery, cheese at the dairy shop, meat at the butcher's, vegetables and fruit at the open market. And each day I carried it all home in my straw basket.

Nor were there refrigerators. I kept the milk in a pitcher wrapped with a damp dish towel outside on the window sill. The mistral, the strong northerly wind, cooled it even on the hottest of summer days. Nor washing machines. I washed everything in the bathtub, including the sheets and the towels, and hung it all out to dry—in no time at all on the line outside the window, near the milk pitcher.

* * *

During my apprenticeship, I learned to count on my next-door neighbor, Madame Michel, an imposing woman, surely twice my age and twice my size, steel-gray hair in tight ringlets, corpulent and corseted.

Shortly after my arrival I went and rang her doorbell, wanting to introduce myself and coming from the other side of the ocean. Slowly she took me under her wing.

"*Pauvre petite dame*," she'd say, "here all alone, with a husband away day and night at the air base."

My spoken French made her scowl. She tried for over a year to teach me to roll my r's. I found it already difficult to make them guttural, now my next door neighbor wanted me to make them *provençale* at the same time. I tried but I knew I'd never succeed.

* * *

When Madame Michel learned that I was expecting my first baby in the winter, she told me about her first baby—how huge he was and how she thought she was going to die right on the kitchen table in her house. After that she made sure there wouldn't be another.

She told me I should eat garlic, raw garlic, every day. "It will keep your muscles soft, and ease the delivery," she said.

She suggests we go garlic picking every Friday morning. It grew wild in big clumps near the lavender fields. We pulled it up by the armful. On the way home, she'd tear a bunch apart and squeeze out the cloves for me to chew. At first I tried to say I'd wait for lunch and then I just chewed along.

* * *

She found my husband very handsome in his air force uniform and gold-trimmed hat, and invited us to Sunday dinner, requesting that Monsieur come fully dressed. Pierre told me that meant in his full dress uniform. Madame Michel wasn't a churchgoer but said she's hold dinner for us until after Sunday mass.

When we rang at her door, she was dressed in black as usual, but for the occasion she was wearing a polished yellow stone which glowed fiercely on her bosom. In the dining room lingered a musty odor mixed with lavender. Three places were set on the starched white cloth.

"I have made a surprise for you," she called from the kitchen, "*paella provençale.*"

She carried in a large round earthenware dish. The yellow saffron rice was ringed with onions and tomatoes and mushrooms and in the middle rested a rabbit's head, its eyes staring right at me.

"They're the best part of the paella," said Madame Michel. "There's one for each of you."

Pierre and I declined. I quickly looked away, but not soon enough. She had picked up the rabbit's head and was sucking out each round, beady eye.

* * *

It was a very cold winter. Our landlord told us it was an exception. Madame Michel went to call on him, insisting that he install something to heat the apartment and keep us warm.

"Imagine with the baby coming and no heat!" she said.

So our landlord put a wood stove in our kitchen. When Pierre was home, he tended it, and when he was at the air base, Madame Michel tended it. Certain that her American neighbor knew nothing about French wood stoves, she'd watch for when I was alone and then come knocking at our door. She'd poke around in the pot-bellied stove, shoving the wood back and forth, and sure enough the fire would glow for rest of the day.

* * *

One Sunday morning I woke up to a snowstorm. Pierre was away at the air base. Madame Michel was hammering at the kitchen door.

"I thought you'd freeze and never wake up," she said, carrying in an armful of wood.

When I told her I was late for church, she said it didn't matter. People didn't go to church when it snowed.

"Besides," she chided, "you're getting too pregnant to go to church, snow or no snow. In your condition, you shouldn't show yourself so much."

I told her I still was going. She shook her head and said something I didn't understand. I bundled up warmly and trudged up the narrow street to the old stone church built when the village was more prosperous and its people more church-going. With the light snow falling, everything was still.

The church was nearly empty and I huddled up front with a few other churchgoers. The priest arrived late, his black cassock and black beret flecked with snow. He told us we had gained in the grace of the Lord and could now go back home. There would be no mass.

* * *

Shortly after the snowstorm, I started having labor pains and Pierre drove me to the hospital. The birth was very long and laborious in spite of Madame Michel's garlic. Pierre fell asleep while reading Marcel Pagnol aloud. I was no longer listening.

When finally I was wheeled into the delivery room, the doctor had gone home long ago. Only the midwife, short and squat, was still waiting. As the pains shot through me, I pictured Madame Michel on her kitchen table. The midwife told me to push harder. She pushed with me until at last it was over and the baby was there. It was a boy. We named him Pierre, after his father and his grandfather.

Madame Michel came to visit at the hospital. She appeared awed, almost afraid. She said it was the first time she had ever set foot inside a hospital. Staring at the baby swaddled in white in the small crib, she tried to brush away tears without being seen.

"Maybe I should have had another baby," she said. "But not in my kitchen."

* * *

I never learned where her one child lived. He had moved away, that was all Madame Michel told me. And she never told me anything about her husband. Each time she got near, she'd fall silent.

She lived alone in her house with dust covers on the furniture. She must once have had many people at her large table. The sounds and smells were still there, along with the china, crystal, and silver.

"I don't have company any more," she told me. "There's no one left to invite."

"When I'd ask her to come and have supper with us, she always refused, saying she preferred keeping to herself. And every night I'd see her light go out in the kitchen at nine o'clock sharp when she'd disappear into the dark.

* * *

In the springtime, my husband watched her hoe and plant a vegetable garden on her side of the fence. Madame Michel told him he could come and help her. She said he could turn over the earth in the corner and plant whatever he wanted. He asked if she knew anything about planting corn.

"Corn," she repeated, looking at him as if he'd lost his mind. "What are you thinking of doing with corn?"

Pierre said he was thinking of eating it. He explained that he had tasted it for the first time fresh from his father-in-law's garden in the States. It was sweet and tasted a little like fresh green peas.

"Well," she said, shrugging her shoulders in disbelief, "you just try eating the corn that grows around here. Even the cows would prefer fresh green peas."

We wrote to ask my father how he planted his corn. An envelope of pink-colored grains arrived with a long sheet of instructions. Pierre made ready a patch of earth and planted half of the package.

Madame Michel watched as ten cornstalks raised their heads out of the ground. Soon one cob of corn appeared on each stalk. Madame Michel would pull back the husks, when she thought I wasn't looking, and take a good sniff at the kernels.

Once the corn was ripe, she finally accepted an invitation to Sunday dinner. I picked six of the cobs and served them steaming hot. Madame Michel didn't say much, she was too busy chewing every kernel off four of the cobs.

* * *

Before we were to leave the village, Madame Michel wanted to make us another provençal dish.

"No rabbit this time," she promised. "Only fish. I'll make you a real bouillabaisse, *bouillabaisse provençale*. Invite your friends and I'll come make it for you."

This way, she said, I wouldn't need to move the baby and carry him next door. She told me that babies should stay put, especially in the evenings. She scolded me plenty and then hugged me tight.

The day of the bouillabaisse, she arrived early in the morning with bundles of fish, bought at the market and wrapped in newspaper. She undid them all at the sink and started splashing away, slitting open bellies, slashing off heads and tails. Blood, scales, and other odd bits splattered around the sink and over the wall. I disappeared into the bedroom to nurse the baby and closed the door.

Madame Michel was still at the sink when I came back. She held up each cleaned fish and rattled off the names: "*raie, rouget, rascasse . . .*" I wondered if she had purposely chosen fish whose names began with r. She set them aside to be cooked at the last minute, putting everything else into my biggest pot and telling me to let it simmer all day. When she went home at noon, I washed down the wall and opened the windows.

She came back in late afternoon to make the *aioli,* a garlic and red pepper sauce. I opened the windows still wider. When the bouillabaisse was ready, I asked her once again to stay and eat with us. She thanked me but said she wasn't hungry. I understood.

* * *

It was soon time to pack our belongings and leave la Provence. We were moving to Brussels. I was going to find supermarkets once again, Colgate toothpaste, Coca-Cola, and paper bags. I never liked leaving a place, wanting instead to take it with me. And so I wanted to take along Madame Michel, the wood stove, the corn patch, the paella—without the rabbit's head.

Our small car was packed. We still didn't have any furniture, just ourselves and our first baby, along with the straw basket for shopping and a few odds and ends for keeping house that I had bought in the village.

Madame Michel came to say good-bye. She looked at us and sighed heavily.

"Now be off with you."

She hugged little Pierre. She let big Pierre kiss her on each cheek. And then she clasped me close in her strong arms.

"*Adieu, ma petite dame.* I'll miss you. I never had a neighbor before."

White Lies

Natasha Trethewey

The lies I could tell,
when I was growing up–
light-bright, near-white,
high-yellow, red-boned
in a black place–
were just white lies.

I could easily tell the white folks
that we lived "uptown,"
not in that pink and green,
shantyfied, shot-gun section
along the tracks. I could act
like my homemade dresses
came straight out the window
of *Maison Blanche*. I could even
keep quiet, quiet as kept,
like the time a white girl said,
squeezing my hand, "now
we have three of us in our class."

But I paid for it every time
Mama found out. She laid her hands
on me, then washed out my mouth
with Ivory Soap. "This is to purify,"
she said, "and cleanse your lying tongue."
Believing that, I swallowed suds
thinking they'd work
from the inside out.

Flounder

Here, she said, *put this on your head.*
She handed me a hat.
You 'bout as white as your dad,
and you gone stay like that.

Aunt Sugar rolled her nylons down
around each bony ankle.
And I rolled down my white knee socks
letting my thin legs dangle,

swinging them just above water
and silver backs of minnows
flitting here and there between
the sun spots and the shadows.

This is how you grip the pole
to cast your line out straight.
Now put this worm on your hook,
throw it out and wait.

She sat and spit tobacco juice
into a coffee cup,
hunkered down when she felt the bite,
jerked the pole straight up,

reeling and tugging hard at the fish
that wriggled and tried to fight back.
It's a flounder, and you can tell
'cause one of its sides is black.

The other side is white, she said.
It landed with a thump.
I stood there watching that fish flip-flop,
switch sides with every jump.

Zebra

Up and down the one way streets
of houses huddled deep and close
together, sycamores, live oaks
brace up to the concrete, break through,
their dark roots surfacing, disrupting
the order of a New Orleans neighborhood.

A block away the laughter, the games
belong to black children, confident
on a street colored their way.
With light skin and braids hanging
to my waist, a stranger on the block,
I wander past them looking in
through the chain link fence.

Their eyes, like dark and shallow pools,
hold me caged. "Zebra,"
I hear a small voice say.
The red bobos laced on my feet,
that only yesterday I tested for speed,
don't move fast enough.
I am shoved to the pavement
by the boy who yelled "get her."

White children whose street we've invaded,
watch them run away, see me sitting there
untying and tying my shoes. And later,
kicking them off, I decide not to tell
my black mother, my white father,
where I have been.

STORY

The Birthday Party

Marcella Taylor

THE CARIBBEAN island on which I lived as a child was large and sprawling but, until I was twelve and attended a Catholic academy for girls on the far side of downtown, I didn't have any idea of its size. My world included no more than half a mile radius to the west of our house and less than that to the east and the north where, after a few minutes' walk, we could sit on the sea wall and watch the ocean tides move in and out. I imagined that they were like my life–always moving but, as far as I could tell, never changing. Under a stormy sky, they might look gray and dirty rather than aquamarine, but I knew that it was simply appearance.

To the south of us, our world stopped with the houses that faced our own home on Willoughby Street. Beyond these, only blacks lived and, while my father was black, he no longer lived with us. On rare occasions, my mother would entertain a sister-in-law in the front room with the uncarpeted floor that made us all feel self-conscious, but our social lives were lived for the most part within the white community. Black family homes filled the streets just beyond our neighborhood and my mother often stopped to greet some of the women and, after mass on Sundays, people of all colors smiled and chatted with each other and asked about this one who had gone to the States or discussed a booth at the upcoming bazaar that they were managing together. Yet it was always understood that we were two commu-

253

nities superimposed upon one another, sometimes difficult to distinguish. But the fact of the superimposition was always clear.

Then there was our family—three girls with a white mother and a black father who had gone to work in the States and sometimes sent money and sometimes didn't. Although my sisters and I had hair that fell over our cheeks in soft brown curls, our light brown skins were obvious, too obvious, but no one made any remarks, at least not to our faces. Once a schoolmate stroked my arm and said, "You're lucky, you have such a nice tan. I can't tan. I only get freckled."

Except for one family at the end, all the people on our side of the street from corner to corner were white. We were all cordial to one another, taking home a dog that had strayed or bringing eggs or fruit to this neighbor or that. My mother spoke with this one across a fence and that one at the front gate, but the people who lived next door were not so friendly. They were what we called "stand-offish" and we let them be, paying little attention to their behavior at first.

After all, no one on our street did much visiting of each other in their homes—that is, no one except us and the Franklins who lived two houses down, on the other side of the "stand-offish" family, the Carters. The Franklin family was made up of an elderly plump woman who waddled so badly she could scarcely move from one room to another and never went out; her daughter Rosalie; and Rosalie's son, Sammy, who was about the age of my younger sister, Frances. Rosalie's mother was a seamstress but Rosalie didn't seem to do much of anything, except come to visit my mother every day, sometimes twice a day.

When she came, she would call out from the front yard and not wait for an answer but walk right onto the stone portico and through the door that was never locked and sometimes wide open so the sea air could flow all through the house. Rosalie wouldn't sit down but stood as if leaning against the wall that wasn't there to separate the front room and the dining room. My mother may have been ironing in the dining room. When she wasn't in the garden tending her roses, or taking care of the chickens, or in her room reading, she ironed in a spot where she could hear her favorite radio programs, "Our Gal Sunday" and "Helen Trent." So my mother and Rosalie would both stand. Rosalie called my mother "Miz Archer" but my mother called Rosalie "Rosalie" perhaps because it was her mother who was Miz Franklin to us. My mother was probably a bit older than Rosalie but they seemed very much alike to me, women a little over average height, with slim builds, straight backs, and oval faces, both faces having that yellowish cast of island whites, the winter color of those who lived beneath a hot sun year after year with no concern for protecting their skins.

The two women talked standing, as if they were only going to talk for five minutes but sometimes it was three-quarters of an hour before Rosalie said, "I gotta be going" for the fourth time and meant it. My mother never invited her to sit and never offered her tea or cocoa as she did her real visitors and Rosalie never seemed to expect it. She would stand there totally comfortable, her hair pulled back and wound in a bun, some strands of a nondescript color falling over her ears, her kimono-like dress hanging loose on those bony limbs.

Sometimes Rosalie brought my mother something she had baked and sometimes, before she left, my mother walked her through the farm-like kitchen, across the gray stone terrace, into the backyard and picked her a couple of avocados or some grapefruit or lemons.

I was often present during those visits because, when I didn't have school, I spent hours reading, sitting at the dining room table or curled up on the front room couch, my legs tucked under me. Usually I just went on reading, for no amount of talk was ever strong enough to distract me from the words on the page, but if Rosalie addressed me directly, I always heard her and would look up.

I never reflected much about her then, because Rosalie was just a part of our world, like the black shopkeepers across the street and the relatives who came to visit and the pets we kept. But, looking back, I realize now that I was fond of Rosalie because, from the time I was about eight, she talked to me as if I were an adult, not just asking questions people asked children–about school or Christmas gifts, things like that–but she would talk to me about the things she and my mother sometimes discussed. She would say, "Christine, have you been in Mr. Barnes's shop this week? Do ya see how slow he's movin'? Don't look to me like he's goin' be able to keep getting up every morning to open that store. Look like he's ready fer the coffin since he had that stroke." Or, "I hear Flora Adams gone broke up with that man–that's why they sent her off to relatives on the Cay for awhile–until everyone forgets about it. The man must be gone back to England. Some say he had a wife there anyway."

And so by the time I was nine, I knew something of the adult world, or age and sickness and dying and marriage and hoping and being disappointed. I had hopes too. For one thing, I longed for a bicycle. But I knew my mother couldn't give it to me and by then I knew there was no Santa Claus but her, so I would dream of how my father might come home suddenly rich and how we would go to live in one of those fine houses on the beach. Those houses fascinated me. They seemed very romantic as we passed them at night on our walks. The chandeliers would sparkle through the windows with their lace curtains drawn back. I would dream also of how I would be a movie star or a dancer and could come back to the island to buy a house like that if I wished. But I probably wouldn't, because I would live in New York or Paris or Rome.

Despite my glamorous imaginings, I never wanted to reach twenty-one because after that it seemed each bad thing made one walk just a bit more slowly until there you were imprisoned in a hearse and people were hollering and drowning out the Lodge band that was following the hearse playing "Shall We Gather at the River?"

Still, there were no rivers on our island. Rivers went somewhere. They had a beginning and a place to go. We had only the ocean and that was like a wall around the island. It was always the same there, just as it had been the day before.

All the people I knew as a child–I mean adults–seemed to live static lives. I didn't expect anything ever to change for any of them. Rosalie, however, didn't seem to mind that. She was always curious about the world of the neighborhood and never seemed bored. She spent a lot of time worrying about Sammy so that he was a little spoilt, although it was evident that the Franklins didn't have any more money than we did for food or clothes or anything else.

I didn't know anything about Sammy's father and I didn't even ask. I didn't even know if Rosalie had been married like my mother. I never wondered about it. In our neighborhood, only about half of the families were like the families in books–father, mother, a few children. The Carters were like that–Mr. Carter, Mrs. Carter, Irene, and Pandora–but scarcely anyone else. There were grandparents, single mothers, sisters-in-law, and grown-up cousins all living under the same roof. Sometimes there was just a father and a teen-aged son or a woman and her grandchild. Everyone took the shape of each family for granted and if questions were ever asked, it was for the sake of entertainment, a matter of gossip, not a matter of true concern.

When I was ten years old, Rosalie transferred Sammy from the public school to the school Frances and I attended. My mother was a proud woman and wouldn't have us going to the public or parochial schools where most of the children were poor and black. To be fair, it was probably also true that the education was not always very good. Our school cost a shilling a week but we all had our own books, moved at our own pace, and received a lot of individual attention from the elderly, experienced teacher. Except for my sister and me and one other family of children, mixed race like us, the pupils were all white and the very fact that I attended this school seemed to say that I was also white. I was smart and now one of the older children in the school so I had a position of prestige. I knew I was "looked up to" and anything I said was accepted as the "gospel truth."

Rosalie asked if Sammy could walk back and forth to school with me, and I said, "Sure." He walked with me that whole year, but the following year Irene and Pandora Carter joined us and he was more or less in Irene's care. Actually, there were about twenty of us in all. Sammy, Frances, Irene, Pandora, and I brought up the rear and were the last left along Willoughby Street after we had said good-bye to our friends as they turned off at various intersections. We walked together not just for company, though. Part of Willoughby Street between our neighborhood and the school was not a comfortable place to walk alone. It was not truly dangerous, but there were bar-rooms along the way and intoxicated black men often hung about at the entrances and sometimes stood talking and reeling uncertainly in the middle of the street. I had no sense of why they were there or what pains they endured because I thought only of avoiding them as much as possible. Then too, the black children coming from the public schools often teased us and sometimes pushed one or another in our group. So we would move close to each other and become very protective. By the time we reached our own neighborhood, the street had quieted down and we felt no fear.

The Carters' cousin, Teresa, sometimes accompanied us. She was an awkward, often isolated redhead who lived far to the south end of the island, a spot sparsely settled. She had to wait until five o'clock for her father to come by in his truck to pick her up wherever she happened to be. This was usually at her cousins' house. After a few weeks, however, the Carters seemed to tire of this arrangement, and began to encourage Teresa to seek other places to stay. I knew that she was a little weird but I didn't dislike her. Even as a child, I seemed to have greater tolerance for fringe characters than most people I knew. Was this because I recognized in myself someone who, unknowingly, would often be outside the circle instead of inside it?

Thus it was that the day when Teresa turned to me and asked, "Can I come home with you?" I didn't object. I had become friendlier with her than I was with Irene and Pandora, because years of living next door and not acknowledging each others' presence affected our relationships even then. But on this day Irene looked at me with narrowed eyes. "She means to go home with you and have dinner and wait until five o'clock." I appreciated the warning for I had known immediately what Teresa meant. And I knew, too, that my mother would be upset. If she had prepared mutton or fish for the dinner we ate right after school, there would be only one piece of mutton for each of us or one half of a fish, no extras. But I felt sorry for Teresa and annoyed with the mean way some of the others treated her. She seemed poorer than the rest of us. I'm not sure why. Her red hair and green eyes would perhaps make her a beauty later in life, but now she was just an outsider.

If I took time to think, I probably decided that my mother would feel sorry for her too. Behind that rigid exterior there was a great deal of compassion. I was right. So, for awhile Teresa came home with us two or three times a week until her family moved back to live on the island that was their original home.

My relationship with her two cousins became somewhat more comfortable. But they were strange children who never went anywhere except to school and church. They always wore granny-looking dresses that hit their mid-calves like their mother's and their long, straight blond hair always looked slightly uncombed. Later, when I began to watch the Waltons on television, I was reminded of these two girls.

We talked to each other mainly in the presence of other children and after saying good-bye to them, we seldom said anything to each other. This didn't seem strange to me at all, since we had lived so long side-by-side without communicating. I figured that their parents wouldn't want them to talk with us because we weren't white. Perhaps this was true, perhaps it wasn't. Perhaps it was their natural reclusiveness. Their father struck me as being comfortable in society. He was a rather good-looking man who left for work in the morning and came home before suppertime. But the mother looked more like the children's grandmother, her hair tied back and her face pale and lined. It was a sad face, with a sad smile. She reminded me of the images I had seen in books of the Virgin Mary Sorrowing. Her face always seemed to carry the whole pain of her life in it.

One morning, after we had arrived at school, I stood by Sammy's desk and idly picked up his exercise book. Sammy had gone outside to get a drink of water from the outside faucet. I stared for a moment at the name on the outside of the book trying to figure out what was wrong. And then I realized. Sammy had written not "Samuel Franklin" but "Samuel Carter." I stood looking at it puzzled and then realized that Irene was looking at me. As my eyes met hers, she dropped her head and left it hanging there. I quickly walked over to Eunice's desk and stayed there chatting with her until school began.

My older sister, Melanie, was growing up fast and not sharing things with me as she once did. But she was the one I still turned to when I needed advice. That afternoon, as usual, she arrived home from the secondary school she attended an hour later that we did. I waited until she had eaten her dinner and then I followed her upstairs to our room. "Melanie, I saw something funny today," I began. And then I hesitated. Perhaps I really knew the answer to the puzzle. Finally, I told her about the name on the exercise book. "Why does he write the Carter name and not the Franklin?"

Melanie laughed. Her answer was brief and to the point: "Because his name is Carter."

"But how . . . ?" I began.

Melanie stood with her head cocked to one side as if she were intently studying me. Then she sighed, "I guess you're old enough." She walked over to the dresser and opened a drawer, where, hidden beneath some of her panties, was a small blue pamphlet. She handed it to me. I stared at it without taking it from her. The title was *The Virtue of Purity*:

"Here, read it." She shoved it into my hands. "After you've read it, we'll talk again."

Obediently, I curled up on the bed and read it through cover to cover. What I read shocked me. It was a book addressed to young girls and it told how after the age of thirteen or so, every month for several days girls bled from their vaginas. Words like puberty and vagina were new to me but I figured out what the words meant as I read. The book went on to say it was all right, a natural process, because it meant that the girl could now become a mother. In the next chapter, it described how babies were made. The description was impersonal but graphic.

None of it seemed very exciting to me and the text made it sound like a duty, something like having to go to mass every Sunday. But after I read it, I turned to Melanie who was now busy reading in the other corner of the room. "You mean Mr. Carter and Rosalie do this?" I was overawed by the thought.

"Yes, that's why Sammy is a Carter."

"How often do they do it?" I wondered.

"Oh, probably not very often," my wiser sister answered. "Maybe every couple of months."

"And Mr. and Mrs. Carter," I asked. "How often do they do it?"

"Oh, probably once a month."

I returned to school the next day and couldn't look at Sammy or the Carter sisters without remembering that they were brother and sister. This was a new way to see them. Did Irene know? I wondered. I believe I felt some satisfaction. If I did, I must have been sure, long before this, that the Carters, mothers and daughters, ignored us because of our brown skins. Now I was also feeling a bit superior, believing I had knowledge of life the other children did not. When I pulled Eunice over at recess, I said to her, "Do you know how people have babies?" And she answered matter-of-factly, "Yes." I was disappointed. She was a year younger than I was, after all. But I went on and blurted out, "Well, you know, Irene's daddy is Sammy's daddy, too." I said it in a whisper so that the children gathered under the tamarind tree busy eating their lunches would not hear us. It was to be a secret between the two of us.

* * *

During the next few days, I sensed a strain between Sammy and the girls because he trailed behind them as Frances and I turned into our yard, and I whispered, "See ya tomorrow."

It was four days later that I came upon Irene taking an eraser to Sammy's book, trying to eradicate the name Carter. Her ordinarily white face was flushed as she lifted it to Sammy who was just coming inside from recess. She stared at him for a moment and then continued working at the name on the cover so hard that it began to tear.

Sammy just stood there looking beaten and embarrassed and said nothing. Irene looked up again and shouted, "My father is not your father."

Sammy mumbled, "Yes, he is" and started to take the book out of Irene's hand.

Irene repeated over and over, "No, he isn't. No, he isn't."

Now I was standing close to Sammy and I heard myself saying, "Yes, he is." Irene stared at me as if in shock. Perhaps I didn't care. The girls had made it clear by their coldness that we would never be friends. I repeated with emphasis, "He is Sammy's father." Just then, the teacher walked in, and Irene released her hold on the exercise book. We all went silently to our seats. But I was feeling good. After all, my mother and Sammy's mother were friends and he and Frances got along well enough. I felt I had done something for him and I was glad.

*   *   *

A month or so later, I came home to find Rosalie chatting with my mother in great excitement. "It'll be his first birthday party. I've always wanted to give him one and I decided I would do it this year." During the next two weeks, I would often come upon Rosalie talking to my mother about the party, the details—cake, candy, bobbing for apples, the hats for all the children—and so forth. I started wondering whether my mother would let us go. I had been asked to birthday parties before but seldom went. Sometimes it was because there was no money for a gift; other times, I didn't have any dress shoes.

A day or so before the party, I decided to ask my mother. By now, the party was general conversation at recess and all the children seemed to have been asked. I knew it would look strange if we weren't there. "Can Frances and I go to Sammy's party?"

"You know Rosalie never asked you?"

"But maybe she just meant us to go?" My mother only shook her head. I thought she was wrong.

On the day of the party, the children kept saying, "We'll see you at Sammy's party." And I lied, "See you there."

That afternoon, even though it was a sunny day, we stayed indoors and tried to pretend not to hear the children's voices that kept rising and falling from the Franklin's yard. We did not admit to each other how glad we were as evening arrived and the street settled into its accustomed quiet.

When Rosalie came, Melanie had gone upstairs and Frances was as usual sunk in her own world. Rosalie was carrying something–a paper sack that felt cold as she placed it in my hand. I looked inside the sack and saw that there was a huge chunk of cake and some ice cream. Rosalie turned to my mother. "I knew the children wouldn't feel comfortable at the party but I brought some leftover sweets for them," she said.

My mother was standing at the kitchen door and she stayed there without entering the dining room. I noticed that she was a head taller than Rosalie. As she spoke, she seemed to space her words carefully and her voice was much quieter than it usually was. "Take that back," she said, "an' don't ever come into this house again." Rosalie stumbled over what it was she was trying to say. The ice cream was now dripping all over my hand. Once more, my mother said, "Take it back" in that same firm, cold voice.

I looked at Rosalie as she turned to go. "What should I do with this?" I pleaded.

Rosalie flung the words back at me, "Throw it in the garbage." I held the sack gingerly away from my dress as I obediently walked into the kitchen and threw it into the garbage can. I wished we could have eaten it. I thought Rosalie would never know.

*   *   *

I soon transferred to the Academy and, as I moved into my teens, I came to know more of the island and was often not at home. The importance of the neighborhood lessened in my life. Although, at first, Rosalie and my mother did not speak to each other, gradually they began to say "Good morning," which developed into small conversations as months and years passed. But those long, comfortable visits in the dining room were never resumed.

The year before I went away to college, Mr. Carter built a store between his house and the Franklin yard and put Rosalie to manage it. Or perhaps he gave it to her. About this time, or soon after, when Irene was already married at the age of fourteen, Mrs. Carter and Pandora went off to live with relatives on the Cay, and no one on our street ever saw them again.

* * *

After college, I married an Italian seaman who worked on one of the cruise ships visiting our island. I went to live among his relatives in a small Italian town where I would always feel like a foreigner. On my first trip home, I saw Mr. Carter and Rosalie sitting together companionably behind the counter of the store. When I passed walking on my way to my cousins' house, I waved my hand in greeting. It was the first time I had even pretended to greet Mr. Carter. Then my family moved to a new housing development close to the ocean and I forgot about the woman who had been such a familiar fixture in my childhood.

Until one day recently, on a visit back to my mother, my sister drove me past the old neighborhood. The house we lived in had been razed to the ground and a tiny shopping mall stood in its place. But the Carters' house was still there and the shop. I knew that Mr. Carter had died some time before of a heart attack but I could see Rosalie, her hair now gray but still in a bun, her face looking much the same, sitting alone at the door of the shop. Melanie said, "Oh, there's Rosalie. We should have stopped to say hello. Do you want to go back?"

I was thinking of how sad and old she looked and how she was never going anywhere beyond this street. I thought I should have been feeling sympathetic and my sympathy should have inspired me to be friendly. But I hesitated only briefly. "No," I said. "No, I don't. What would I say to her?"

We drove on, following the curve of the road as it neared the ocean. We were now passing those once brightly-lit houses that impelled my dreams. They looked shabby, the shining whiteness of their facades now had a greenish tint and it suddenly occurred to me that the people who once lived here had not been so wealthy after all, that the houses had not been much grander than the ones that now surround my middle-class existence.

STORY

Hair

Nora Reza

THE DRIVER, Ali Aga, was late. Cursing him, Mrs. Aram set out on foot, accompanied by her daughter, Farideh, and Lara. Although Lara had lived in Iran with her friends for several months now, this was the first time she had been allowed to walk anywhere. She had a sensation of freedom as they walked up the mountain, past the high stucco walls that hid terraced villas and gardens. Farther on were vacant lots where wild dogs scrounged in the mud and rocks. Perspiring and breathing heavily, Mrs. Aram stopped before a newly-painted black gate. Next to it was a shiny brass plate inscribed with the name of an American colonel and his wife.

"A hairdresser here?" Lara asked, mystified.

Mrs. Aram nodded.

A servant girl with a checked scarf wrapped around her head and pantaloons under her long-sleeved dress opened the door. Inside was a luxurious garden, so green that for a moment Lara thought she was back in upstate New York, in a rose garden of a park. In order to create this gleaming landscape the sprinklers were shooting spray high into the air. Mrs. Aram's lips compressed in disbelief. Just a week ago she had found Lara brushing her teeth with the tap on and kindly reprimanded her by shutting it off.

The servant girl led them down the stone pathway that ran alongside the glistening driveway, and past a large white Oldsmobile and a Harley-Davidson motorcycle. On the terraced lawns above them, behind rainbow mists, a man was skimming the swimming pool. Nearby an American lady, the colonel's wife, cut roses. She wore gloves, a plaid cotton skirt, white blouse, and white tennis shoes. A straw hat protected her straw-colored hair and freckled skin from the sun. A yellow spaniel followed each of her movements, and a gardener respectfully held a basket in which she placed her roses. She barely glanced at the Iranians as they strolled down the driveway to the lower level of the house, where, to Lara's surprise, there was indeed a hairdresser's shop, furnished with dryers, sinks, and mirrors.

The shop was run by the landlord's wife and daughter. The landlord owned the house and lived in it with his family in a small apartment next to the salon. His was a rare story in Iran and Mrs. Aram delighted in telling it. He began as a poor baker and developed a business of baking and packaging sliced bread, American-style. This bread soon became fashionable among the middle-class, who thought it superior to the traditional fresh-baked, flat loaves of *non*. The baker managed thus to extricate himself from the lower classes and moved into a position where he could afford to buy a large house. With his modest background he was happy to live in the servant's quarters and rent the rest of the house to one of the thousands of American military families in Iran. The hairdressing business was a way to keep his wife busy.

The wife was a large matronly woman who wore cotton pants and a knit top stretched tight over huge breasts. Her hair was cut fashionably short and streaked with peroxide. The idea was to look blond. She smiled and beckoned Mrs. Aram into the chair. Lara and Farideh sat around reading fashion magazines like *Vogue* while the servant who had opened the door brought in a tray of glass teacups. Mrs. Aram's hair was washed and set on tiny rollers, then sprayed until Lara was gasping for air. Once under the dryer Mrs. Aram held out a hand to have each fingernail painted a bright red.

The hairdresser then invited Lara into the chair. By this time Lara's hair was bushy and wild. While she was being "combed" she could see, reflected in the mirror, the colonel's wife cutting her roses. A young man with shoulder-length hair came out to talk to her. The youth began shouting, and she stopped cutting and clutched her shears to her chest. Her son waved his arms toward the car which now streamed with water. The gardener remained nearby holding the basket, his face rigid and immobile, his eyes on the ground. Every now and then Lara caught a word from the boy, who spoke in exasperation, "Keys, Mom, I need the car keys."

She wouldn't give them. "Your father told you no. Besides the driver is taking us to the commissary in a little while. You can get everything you need there." The commissary, next to the American Embassy, was rumored to be the largest in the world. It sold only to Americans and the royal family.

The boy continued to pester his mother. Finally, she turned her back on him, knelt down on the ground and vigorously began building a little wall of dirt around each bush. Her son stalked off, cursing, oblivious of the Persians in the room nearby. The hairdresser laughed and shook her head, muttering, "*shaiton.*" Lara smiled, interested in any boy described as a "*real devil.*"

"You don't know what he has done," the hairdresser exclaimed, hovering over Lara's hair. "He got drunk with his friends and rode his motorcycle into the mosque in Isfahan. He even . . ." and here she took a deep breath, "hit his mother, *pesara devaneh! Curses upon him.*" She and Mrs. Aram shook their heads in mutual disbelief and shock at this last transgression. What kind of son did not believe the Persian saying that paradise is at the foot of the mother? The hairdresser shrugged, "But what can we do? Americans in Iran do anything they want." Under the immunity law, the colonel's son could not be prosecuted for any crime he committed in Iran.

Tilted back in a lounge chair at the sink, Lara enjoyed the luxury of having her hair washed and saturated with creme rinse until a brush could be guided through it. Her hair was then set in large rollers and she was seated under another hot dryer. She kept an eye out for the American boy and was sorry not to see him again. Next to her, Mrs. Aram emerged from her dryer, pink and giggly. The rollers came out and the teasing began. Each swatch of Mrs. Aram's fine black hair was backcombed to a thick frizz. A few hairs on top were kept in reserve so as to cover all this frizz and create the impression of abundance.

Lara did not want her hair teased, but the hairdresser ignored her protests. With pins in her mouth she smiled and jerked Lara's head up and down, telling Lara not to worry, "You will see."

"Don't tease anymore," Lara pleaded. She was beginning to acquire a black pill box on top of her head. The hairdresser brushed and sprayed the strands that refused to obey until she gave up and put in hairclips "temporarily" to mold the hair into position. She smiled in satisfaction as the others complimented her. Lara wondered how Farideh had managed to avoid all but a minimal teasing, emerging unscathed, her ash-colored hair in a casual American-style pageboy.

The mountain of lacquer on top of Lara's head had added a good half foot to her height. Her eyes felt pulled to her temples. She thought she looked hideous, but everyone assured her that her hair was really "styled" now,

"Lara, dear, you've become chic!" Mrs. Aram said.

On the way out the servant girl ran ahead to open the door. The American woman had gone inside. Lara was relieved not to see the son. Surely he would find her ugly. She glanced into the steaming windows of the white Olds. There among the wet reflections of leaves, light, and smoke the youth languished. His eyes were closed. A sweet odor emanated from his rolled cigarette. On the floor of the backseat were copies of the *International Herald Tribune*, a briefcase, and papers he had scattered.

The sprinklers were still going like fountains. By this time a small river flowed out under the gates and down the street. Lara helped Mrs. Aram carefully over it. She felt as though there were eggs balanced in a nest on top of her head.

On the road outside the door, Lara stopped and stared. An American couple was walking up the hill. This in itself was remarkable. But the fact that they were dressed in dirty jeans and workboots was astonishing. Could this blond girl and bearded guy be backpackers or mountain climbers? They were each carrying two water jugs. Lara longed to acquaint herself with them, to convey somehow that she was from America too. In her new beehive, among quintessentially Persian companions, she had a feeling they would not believe her.

"Hi," Lara smiled. They eyed her doubtfully. "Where are you going?"

The bearded man did not stop but the young woman put down her burden and gestured up the hill. "Do you know if buses go up here?" she said by way of reply. Her straight blond hair blew freely in the hot wind, in defiant and enviable contrast to Lara's own imprisoned locks.

"*Autobus?*" Lara turned to Mrs. Aram, who shrugged, disappointed in Lara's eagerness to throw herself at these dirty sweaty people just because they were Americans.

"Come on, Gail," the bearded companion shouted.

"Wait a minute," Gail replied, looking at the water flowing down the hill. "Is this your house?"

"No. There's a hairdresser here," Lara explained.

"Hairdresser?" The woman walked up to the plaque and read the colonel's name. "Wouldn't you know," she exclaimed scornfully. Just then the gates of the driveway flew open and the colonel's son zigzagged past them on his motorcycle, splattering their clothes. The sound of his motor swallowed their feeble protests.

The youth, already far off, was bending into the downcurve of the road, his long hair trailing behind him, when the white Olds pulled out. His mother, seated in the rear, seemed not to see Lara and her companions, but the yellow spaniel barked from the safety of its air-conditioned haven.

The American woman's pale blue eyes met Lara's for a moment, before she kicked a stone with her boot, picked up her water jugs and began trudging up the hill toward her companion.

Lara turned to Farideh, "Who are they?"

"Peace Corps," Farideh sniffed.

"Why don't you like them? They're people who are trying to help Iran," Lara said.

"Peace Corps is CIA," Farideh replied scornfully.

"If they were CIA, why would they live like that?" Despite the disdain Lara had felt in their eyes for her lacquered hair, she wanted to believe they were doing good, living as they did in relative poverty.

They walked in silence, following the stream of water from the colonel's garden until they reached home. It was noon by then. The road was empty except for a man thrashing a donkey.

Untitled

Kip Fulbeck

my relatives wear fur coats that grow hairier and hairier by the second
fox and mink and buck teeth and chandeliers

my relatives are pharmacists that call themselves doctor on wedding
   announcements *aiyaaaa* long time no see *lawrencee pungnow ah
   holang holang holang*

my relatives have hairy furry coats balding heads gold fillings and
   buck teeth the size of small chickens
doctored eyelids and eyelid doctors engineers lawyers and
   pharmacists bustling between round tables covered with white
   covers and champagne and chocolate

in a polished ballroom
buck teeth haystacks wax around me ask how i'm doing how i've
   been how tall i am how beautiful my date is *holang holang holaaaang*

i'm standing sharing blood with two fur-coated relatives that get in
   my nose and eyes (because) "your eyes are so round"
and one asks what i'm doing these days
i answer and one translates and they both laugh and fine hairs float in
   the air (there are many kinds of chinese laughs)
i don't need to know what she translated

on a different stage a band with black tuxedos and electric guitars
   plays too loud to talk comfortably
and surround a singer who flips her blonde hair and has seen too many
fabulous baker boys
her chin almost double as she smiles downward and claps her hands
   silently to the music

why does she try to look so young why doesn't she just clap her
    hands she just taps them taps her hands swings side to side and
    flips her hair claps her hands without any sound
why don't you just clap them bring your hands together make a noise
    stop smugging stop flipping clap your hands clap your hands clap
    them clap them clap them

i keep looking at her
watch her flip her frosted hair swing side to side her downward smile
    a mouth that says "make mine a double" red lipstick and doughy
    chins

clapping her hands silently black nylons and black heels she sees me
    looking and smiles downward coyly back as she sings
damn
she thinks i think she's sexy singing smooth operator somebody tell
    her somebody tell her i don't think you're sexy somebody tell her
she must drive an american red car

we eat white gloved oysters on the half shell and salmon and veal
that gets more tender by the second as the calf gets younger in its
    little pen
and i wait and the meat cools and the gravy hardens and gets more
    rare by the second as i chew and swallow mink and chandeliers
    and relatives
in my black bow tie
at my cousin's hong kong wedding at the four seasons hotel,
beverly hills, california

Number Games

Elaine never wore shoes. She had thick calloused feet with a ring on
one toe and the first time I walked her back from class I kept wonder-
ing if the asphalt was hurting her. Our crush wore off one day so
now when we see each other we just let our dogs play. I still think
she has beautiful hair.

Angi really wanted an A and she got one. I see her doing her economics homework in art class. She doesn't care if I see.

Kathy *giggles*. All the time. I call her on the phone *giggle* she doesn't recognize my voice *giggle* then realizes it's me *giggle giggle giggle*. I found out she was a cheerleader when I saw her saddleshoes in her bag "I have aerobics later today" *giggle giggle*. She tells me her father was in the military. Sometimes I think all our fathers were in the military.

Chris was my wife in Japan. They asked if one bedroom was all right and we didn't want to put them out so we said okay. The next morning the mayor asked us when we were going to get married.

Carol has a boyfriend from Oxnard, he's full Japanese. She wears L.A. Gear hightops with double laces and has one of those "best friend" pendant necklaces that's split down the middle for each of you to wear.

Sang works at his parents' grocery in South Central L.A. He tried to make himself look like a blood one time–put on black Reeboks, red socks, red shirt, bandana, and beeper. But he still looked like Sang.

Leanne is 5'2" and plays pick-up basketball with the best of them. She perms her hair and bleaches it blonde and won't take any crap from anybody.

Elaine was born and left in the naval hospital in San Diego. A Filipino family adopted her as an infant so when she checks the ethnicity box she says she checks Filipino.

Kelly's dad is a butcher and she can talk for hours about anything. She teaches aerobics but carries cigarettes in her purse.

Chris and I didn't know what to do. We realized it would have been disrespectful to have stayed in the same bed if we weren't going out. So for the rest of the month I'd kiss her cheek or hold her hand now and then. The mayor always liked that.

Tamaki's dog died when I met her parents. I wanted to help bury him the next morning but I overslept and all I got to do was shovel the dirt back in–her dad had dug the whole thing himself. I wish I had cut my hair before I met him.

Elaine's apartment is full of marijuana plants and bright lights. She says she gets worried when she coughs up ash.

Leanne got arrested for spray painting red paisleys on buildings (she thought they were too drab). The only time we get to touch each other is when we play basketball. So we play hard.

Chris goes out with my best friend now. Once in awhile she'll get a letter from our host family asking how me and her are doing and she'll sign both our names when she writes back.

Sang had a crush on Angi. He did a performance where he had written a letter saying how much he liked her but he didn't want to embarrass her by pointing her out so he handed a letter out to every girl in the class.

Chris and Kathy are both from Chula Vista and their fathers were both in the navy and they were both cheerleaders but they don't know each other.

Kelly bought me lunch when I forgot my money. She's 25 and her boyfriend's 19. I told her I'm 25 and my girlfriend's 19 and she said that's not the same thing.

I introduced Tamaki and Carol outside. Carol asked Tamaki if her dad was in the military. She said no. I said mine was.

I knew Chris for four years before I found out she's not really half-Japanese, half-white like she says. She's half-white, quarter Japanese, and a quarter Korean.

Tamaki and I went to watch "Cheers" get taped and we met Woody Harrelson. He said "Hey, Tamaki–that's my favorite kind of sushi. The one with the egg right?"

Angi gave Sang a letter at the end of the quarter saying thanks a lot and I'm really flattered and let's just be good friends and so forth. I asked Angi how come she didn't want to go out with him and she told me she doesn't date Asian guys.

Kathy says she never thought of herself as Oriental without laughing.

Kathy says she never thought of herself as Oriental, without laughing.

Angi's mother is Korean so her father must be in the military.

Blood Ties

Thelma Seto

– for my mother's eldest sister who is also my father's second wife.

I.

They measured you like a cup of meal. This much
and no more, not one teaspoon.
I am crying,
not at the battering I sustained from you,
not this time. We were both silenced
by the final word. In the end they buried you
in your dead sister's marriage bed,
halfway around the globe.
You hold yourself by the chest,
hug the brittle bones.

On a sandbar off Padre Island
I waited with my cousins in the tractor tire tubes
for the tide to come in.
You called me out of the water,
ordered me to cook the shrimp.
I didn't want to walk that shore.
I'm sorry. I couldn't see
the ghost of your sixteen-year-old self
staying behind at the farmhouse
longing for hayrides, store-bought dresses,
boys.

I wanted other things,
things you couldn't understand, wanted
to drive the hot melting asphalt
all the way to Tierra del Fuego
in an electric blue 1954 Chevy,

wanted just to eat goat
in Cuernavaca
like you had already done
before I was born,
but mostly I wanted to live simply
on the lip
of a volcano.

II.

The time I surprised you and my father
lying on my mother's white counterpane,
knives I thought meant for me
sliced the air. You were working
on your marriage. You were working on replacing
my mother, your sister.
My heart cried out, even at fourteen,
to think of forty years
without the melting myrrh of desire—
just this clammy
whale's flesh.
I turned and ran.
We pretended it never happened.
Is this what you meant
by "sharing a bed"
in all those mother/daughter sermons?

You taught me to keep my passions secret,
even the one you might have understood:
My son, that flash flood
child of the heart
I planned for two years.
When I told you I was pregnant,
your eyes glazed over,
filled with a deadly light.
There was no reaching into that awful,
private place.
When I wouldn't marry

or give him up for adoption,
you called me a whore.

III.

I fear loving you,
fear calling you back
to the place you lived
when I was four
and you were music,
unabridged,
untamed,
escorting me out of the maze
of the female cattle call.
Coffins come in so many sizes,
styles and shapes.

I am a child of the wind,
my Issei grandmother's
warrior granddaughter, not content
to flap my apron at the chickens
by the sod hut, or make indigo dye
while waiting for the mail train
on the prairie.

Now you are seventy-four,
lost in a darkened corridor,
smiling for someone else to the bitter end.
I am afraid to love you
though it would be so easy
and that is all you want,
all you ever wanted
though you never said it:
The love of your women kin—mother,
sisters, nieces, great-aunts,
stepdaughters.
We were all females at the auction block,
unnecessarily cruel
to each other.

I pass the mirror.
It reflects only the swirling mists
of your eyes
and your sad, brave smile
in the glass.

Jihad

Come, nationals in exile,
like lemmings,
to stand with your brethren
in this honey-combed village,
to reclaim the memories of its shadows
which do not erase
even with torture's persuasion.

Listen, to the sands creep across
the Dashte-Kavir, particle
by particle, the only sound
in sight. Separate out
caravanserai from mirage.
It is an art whose cultivation
asks patience
but affords no mistakes.

When they come at last
with their strange kindness,
when the desert is the black hole
of an air raid,
when the spring rains
turn yellow,
return to the minaret
and the invulnerability
of its purest mirage.

Origami

Susan K. Ito

I TAKE MY PLACE, hesitantly, among the group of Japanese women, I smile back at the ones who look up from their task to nod at me. Their words float around me like alphabet soup, familiar, comforting, but nothing that I clearly understand. The long cafeteria table blooms with folded paper birds of all colors: royal purple, light gray, a small shimmering silver one. They're weaving an origami wreath for Sunday's memorial service, a thousand cranes for the souls of those who died at Tule Lake's internment camp.

I spread the square of sky-blue paper flat under my hands, then fold it in half. So far, this is easy. I'm going to follow all the directions. It's going to be a perfect crane, *tsuru*, flying from my palm. Fold again, then flip that side of the triangle under to make a box. Oh no. What? I didn't get that. I'm lost. The women around me keep creasing, folding, spreading, their fingers moving with easy grace. My thumbs are huge, thick, in the way of these paper wings that are trying to unfold but can't.

My heart rises and flutters, beating against its cage in panic, in confusion. I try to retrace my steps, turn the paper upside down, in reverse. It's not working. I want to crumple the paper into a blue ball, an origami rock.

But instead I unfold the paper with damp, shaking fingers. I persevere. *Gambaro.* Don't give up. I'm going to make this crane if it kills me. I'm going to prove that I can do this thing, this Japanese skill. I'm going to pull the coordination out of my blood, make it flow into my fingers. I have to.

But what if I can't? Then it only proves the thing that I fear the most, don't want to believe. That I'm not really Japanese. That I'm just an impostor, a fake, a watered-down, inauthentic K-mart version of the real thing.

* * *

I remember the summer when I was nineteen years old. Waitressing at the Gasho restaurant in upstate New York, the centuries-old farmhouse brought over, beam by beam, from Japan. It took over forty-five minutes to dress for work each day, from the white Japanese underthings, pure snowy cotton, to the stiff red and gold *obi*. My mother helped me, turning me around in front of the mirror, her pride making her tall as she fussed over me. I put up my hair, an elegant round sculpture full of air, with red lacquered chopsticks holding it all together. I shuffled around the house in my wooden *geta* clogs, practicing small dainty bows toward the dog, my parents, various pieces of furniture.

It didn't matter that I was making less than minimum wage, that I was putting in more time getting dressed and commuting up the New York Thruway than I was actually working. I was proud.

I still remember that one July night, the frogs singing in the garden behind the restaurant, the moonlight shining like wetness on the stone lantern. I stood in the back doorway of the kitchen, listening to the chefs shouting in Japanese, the dishwashers howling in Spanish. The smell of miso soup and green onions floated in the steam of the kitchen.

I passed through the swinging dining room doors and called out to the next party on the waiting list. "Harrison?"

A short woman with champagne-colored curls waved enthusiastically in my direction. I greeted the group of eight people as they milled around the bar, clinking glasses of emerald green Midori on ice. I led them to the horseshoe-shaped table with the flat steel grill in the middle, handed them each a steaming towel.

"Good evening," I said, smiling. "Welcome to Gasho."

The customers took the towels, pressed them into their faces, wiped their hands. They made small sounds of pleasure as the steam softened their skin. One man, wearing a beige polyester jacket, did not unroll his towel. He stared at me with reddened eyes and chewed on the end of a toothpick.

"Wait a minute," he said.

"Yes? Is there something wrong?" Sometimes a towel came out of the steamer cold, or not moist enough.

"You're not Japanese, are you?" The man looked up and down, craned his neck to look at the back of me.

"Pardon?" I faltered.

"This is supposedly a Japanese restaurant." He swept his arm up in a wide circle, and I could see a ring of perspiration soaked into his shirt. "I read that brochure in the bar. It's supposed to be an antique farmhouse that was built in Japan."

"The farmhouse is authentic," I murmured. My face was getting hot. "It was shipped here directly from Osaka."

"And what about you?" he demanded. "Where were *you* shipped from?"

I felt the blush draining out of my face, and my fear became so intense I thought my body would fail me. I imagined the blood pooling at my feet and then completely seeping out my soles, leaving me standing in a puddle of my own blood, my half-authentic, tainted blood.

I nearly lost my balance. I stood there, holding the tray of heaped up towels, tottering on my *geta*. "I'm half-Japanese." Just a whisper.

"Half?" he scoffed. "Hey. I come to a Japanese restaurant, I expect to have a Japanese waitress." He gestured toward petite, silky-haired Kimi passing out bowls of rice at the next table. He didn't have a clue, and I didn't tell him, that she was from Korea, and no more Japanese than he was.

He shook his head in disgust. "No, sir, if I wanted to be served my dinner by someone like you . . ." he looked me up and down again. "I'd have gone to McDonald's."

* * *

I stop, unfold everything, smooth the paper out on the table, take a deep breath, start again. My sweat is starting to make the paper all slick and even more unmanageable.

It must be those paternal genes that make me so klutzy, I tell myself. I take stock of all the ways his shadow marks my body. The dark hair that pushes up, unwanted, through the skin of my forearms, my legs, sometimes my belly, or worse, under my chin. No Japanese has to deal with this. I long for the smooth gold skin of my Nisei adoptive parents, the way they tan like caramels under the sun. My skin reddens into a dusky burnt color, and I know it's those delicate European genes that can't take the heat. Then there are the freckles. The huge flat feet, the bushy eyebrows. I blame him and his ancestors for all the parts of me that I hate.

People ponder my lineage. What *are* you, anyway? they ask. They've guessed my roots to be Puerto Rican, Jewish, Italian, Hawaiian, Irish (the freckles). My pencil hovers over the forms that say, *check one for Ethnicity.* One? I mark ASIAN, defiantly, and then feel guilty, humiliated. It's a lie. A half-lie, anyway.

* * *

I'm ready to give up. Hundreds of origami birds are piled into a mountain of color, spiky wings and beaks poking out like hatching newborns. What difference will it make if I don't complete this one? There are more than plenty for the memorial service.

I look down once again at the failed sculpture in my hands. There are so many folds in the blue paper, the color is starting to wear away at the creases. My would-be crane, still an awkward triangle, is scarred with white lines. I fold it again and again, over into itself, until finally something squat and deformed finally emerges. I shove it into my pocket and get up from the table when I notice the little *oba-san* sitting next to me. Her gray-white head, with its round rice-bowl haircut, the kind little children have, barely reaches my shoulder.

Her knotty, bent fingers are working a piece of pale butter-yellow paper. The folds she makes are gross, awkward, and her eyes are huge with concentration behind her spectacles. She doesn't seem to be having much more success than me, but I know it's not for lack of experience.

Finally she places her lopsided product in front of her and sighs. "This is no *tsuru,*" she mutters. "Looks more like sick chicken."

I take my crane out of my pocket and sit it down next to hers. They make a sort of clumsy, humble symmetry on the table. *Oba-san* looks up at me with a tiny hint of smile behind her round glasses. She reaches for my sleeve, sways a little bit, and I help her to her feet. She and I walk slowly to the kitchen. It's time for tea.

Instructions to All Persons of Japanese Ancestry

Sesshu Foster

Pursuant to the provisions of Civilian Exclusion Order No. 33, this Headquarters, dated 3 May 1942: all persons of Japanese ancestry, both alien and non-alien, will be evacuated by 1200 hours, P.W.T., Saturday 9 May 1942. No Japanese person will be permitted to change residence without obtaining special permission from the representative of the Commanding General, Southern California Sector, at the Civil Control Station located at the Japanese Union Church, 120 N. San Pedro St., Los Angeles, California. This Civil Control Station is equipped to assist the Japanese population in the following ways:

1. Give advice and instructions. (Ah.)

2. Help dispose of property. (Ah.)

3. Provide residence in horse stalls at Santa Anita racetrack until each person and whatever baggage they can carry can be transported to the concentration camp. (Ah.)

The Following Instructions Must Be Observed:

1. A responsible member of each family, preferably the head of the family, or a substitute if such person was already sent to Leavenworth Federal Prison at FBI discretion, or any individual living alone, will report to the Civil Control Station to receive further instructions. This must be done between 0800 and 1700 hours, Monday 4 May 1942, or Tuesday 5 May 1942.

2. Japanese persons seen in public after this date will be reported to the authorities.

3. Evacuees must carry with them on departure for the assembly center the following property:

A. Clothing, forks, spoons, bedding (no mattress), essential personal effects, etc.

B. A drawing on 8½ x 11 paper depicting all family members next to their dream house, pursuing a life they had expected in America.

C. Expressions of human dignity, limited to the following extent: only allowable gestures are to overturn funeral urns and spill ashes on one's head, face, and neck, beating the ashes into skin and clothing as if attacking lice. No other gestures allowed.

4. No pets of any kind will be permitted. (Ah.)

5. They finally got them, that Uchioka family. And that irascible man, K. Uchioka, was taken—not in front of his family—arrested by the FBI at work. He was told it was because he belonged to a suspicious organization/sports league. His family will not see him for a year. He is on the train to Leavenworth. After disposing of the family property, Mama has assembled the family and their suitcases on the section of the train platform where she was told. She went to check on a detail. Grandpa Nakano is watching the kids, talking to Tommy in the hot sun. Her daddy's favorite little girl, April, is sitting on her suitcase with its yellow tag. She's hot in the navy coat she must carry or wear, and is tagged with numbers herself that correspond to the master registry. April, a raven's wing of black hair slanting across her eyes, sees a shadow cross the shining cement. It's a white woman with a black box camera. She takes April's picture.

Go to the Civil Control Station Between the Hours of 0800 and 1700 hours, Monday 4 May 1942, or Between the Hours of 0800 and 1700 hours, Tuesday 5 May 1942.

STORY

Untitled

I DON'T RECALL which war it was. It could have been on a convoy on the road through Bien Hoa. With kids scrambling around a garbage dump, and they would come up on the highway to beg. And she might have been walking there on the roadside, the other way from the ARVN, holding the kid on her hip, trying not to get run off the road. And the guys were flipping C-rations at the kids begging on the roadside, like it was target practice. Some of them got a big kick out of it when the kid took the C-rat real hard in the chest or the face and fell off the road. Bored GIs. It was like shooting gophers. I heard them screaming at the woman up ahead; it was some joke. I don't recall exactly what about. Just a fucking joke. But she was scared you know, all these guys yelling at her. So she didn't look up, just trudged along in the dust kicked up by the trucks, holding her little kid on her hip. So somebody wound up a good one and let fly, and the can caught her right in the face. They cheered, like somebody had just gotten a strike in bowling. The woman and the kid got knocked down into the dirt. Even as we outdistanced her and she stood up, I could see the bright red rose on her face as we went away. I think that was Vietnam. Hell, maybe it was Guatemala, maybe it was some *kaibile* soldier, the jaguar units we were giving special forces training in a covert operation. Maybe it was some Mayan woman wearing an Indian *huipil*, one of them colorful head-rags. Black hair, black eyes, like the Vietnamese. Riding through them strategic villages again. Shit, it could have been Panama, I suppose. On the highway to Panama City, with the sky trying to break open, or trying to rain, trying to decide. The highway shining and wet under a dark sky. Maybe not. It doesn't really matter. The funny thing was to see her in Monterey Park. I was driving down Atlantic Boulevard in my business suit, a world away from camouflage green, the sun glaring through the windshield of my Mercedes. With a contractual obligation to attend to at a Hong Kong bank branch. And there she was, standing on the corner with the kid on her hip, waiting for the light to change. It was red for me, and she crossed right in front of my car. I couldn't see for the glare, but I was sure it was her. Seeing her hit me hard all of a sudden. I could feel it in my hands like I was falling off a cliff. A sinking feeling that fell through my body. I was scared all of a sudden. Because there she was, still holding the kid on her hip, like a ghost in the pedestrian traffic. I gripped the steering wheel real hard and squinted and looked at her. Jesus, it got to me. I don't know what it would do to me if I keep seeing her, you don't know how scared I was. She was still wearing them cheap clothes poor people wear. Still carrying the kid. Like it was just a minute ago she'd gotten hit in the face with the C-ration, and she stood up by the side of that highway and wiped the blood off her face, just stood up and walked right into my sunny day here on the street corner. Like all the action in the armies I've seen was nothing. All the convoys of trucks and APCs, heavy armor, olive-drab-covered trucks full of men holding their automatic weapons, driving all those highways across the world and looking out on a mean green landscape. Like all of that was nothing to her. She still had to get someplace, carrying her kid on her hip.

STORY

Untitled

THE JAPANESE man would not appear riding a horse above the telephone pole like the marlboro man the japanese man strode above the endive kale and parsley weeding the glendale truck garden his life was not picturesque like a hiroshige block print or a flight of golden cranes across a kimono though his cotton clothing absorbed his sweat like the pages of a book absorb the ink of meaning and desire itself formed in his mind something long and cool as his woman a piece of iced celery when he heard a shout in english stood upright and saw the labor contractor standing on the flatbed of the white man's truck waving him over this morning what did it mean? after seeing the billboard in town NO JAPS WANTED THIS IS A WHITE NEIGHBORHOOD/ the old Issei sat in the cluttered livingroom in the boyle heights bungalow with his cigarette in the tin ashtray cradled in the linen napkin his wife always placed on the arm of the couch for him and the marlboro commercial projected from the tv into the stale smoke as the old man lifted the cigarette in his freckled knobby fingers and took a long drag

Pandora

Nancy Lee

S TAMPED ON the spine in letters of gold is the name *Pandora*.
The binding is bone-colored, leather-grained and embossed,
with a clear vinyl dust cover that smells like new toys at Christmas.
On the back cover the publisher's name is stamped in *hanul* along
with the price, fifteen hundred *weon*. The pages are blank, but in
between the signatures are divider sheets printed in sepia ink with
Victorian line engravings.

These are purely decorative, I think, or else so loaded with mean-
ing that I am unable to interpret them. What am I to make, for exam-
ple, of an engraving of a poodle-haired, vaguely Renaissance woman
playing a lute, with the title "Adonis"? Or a portrait of a formidable
young woman, a crowned head of Europe, perhaps, or a young czar-
ina, formally posed in ropes of pearls and a veiled tiara, titled "Eros"?
Or a hoopskirted woman holding a baby in her arms while a ragged
boy kneels at her side, with off in the distance a girl in a white night-
shirt and the Infant Jesus floating in radiance in front of a belfry? "Nar-
cissus," it says. If only I could read Korean.

For though the title of each picture is printed in roman letters,
underneath each title is a paragraph or two printed entirely in *hanul*.
And there, I am sure, is the explanation for everything.

The frontispiece, from which the whole book takes its name, is the
most enigmatic of all. A little girl, perhaps ten years old, in a white
organdy dress with a dotted sash. Long blonde curling tresses flowing

down around her shoulders. The dark stare straight at me, the faintest knowing smile. And the title: *Pandora*.

I stare at the Korean text, willing it to make sense. I know the alphabet but not the language; I can sound out words but I don't know what they mean. All that I recognize are the names: *p'eu* . . . *ro* . . . *me* . . . *t'e* . . . *u* . . . *seu*–something clicks in: Prometheus, the Titan, whose name means Forethought. *E* . . . *p'i* . . . *me* . . . *t'e* . . . *u* . . . *seu*, Epimetheus, his brother, Afterthought. *Je* . . . *u* . . . *seu*, Zeus, king of the gods. And *p'an* . . . *do* . . . *ra*, *p'an-do-ra*, over and over.

I know this story. One of those stories that started out Greek and wound up universal: when I was growing up in Cleveland I read it in an English book of fairytales. Apparently its moral–all the evils of the world are unleashed by a too-curious woman–was sufficiently misogynist to transcend its national origin. Whatever.

There was one colored plate in particular, a picture of the evils erupting from the box like a plume of volcanic ash–smoky, cobwebby creatures with sharp teeth and flapping wings like bats. I remember looking at it and wondering why it was Pandora's fault for opening the box and letting the evils out, and not the fault of the gods for putting such horrible things in there in the first place. I must have been very young.

Anyway, what does a Greek myth have to do with this fey Victorian child, what does either have to do with the Asian country where this unwritten-in book was printed, bound, and sold?

Buying this book was my first venture out of the house unattended. I arrived at Kimp'o Airport a week ago, sick, weak, and hysterical. I was down to my last fifty dollar traveler's check and I had to break it to get the change to make a phone call so I could ask somebody to please pick me up at the airport. My first week in Korea I spent eating oxtail soup and recovering. Perhaps a few years from now I will look back and try to sort out everything that happened in Tokyo, but not now. Now I only feel how good it is to have food and a warm place to sleep.

My aunt has a Western-style bed but she sleeps, Korean-style, on the heated floor beside it. It's warmer that way. My room–the room that I've been sleeping in for the past week, actually her daughter's–has a Western-style bed, too, with an electric heating mattress-liner that imitates a Korean heated floor.

Leaning against the wall is a framed silk embroidery of an albino peacock. I'm looking at it as I lie here writing in my book. It's so large that it all but obscures the window, and the craftsmanship is extraordinary. For every filament of every feather there is a single strand of iridescent white silk, just so. It must have come down in her family. My aunt was born a princess, you see, although they've long since abolished royalty. Her uncle has been under house arrest for twenty years. Still, her family has nice heirlooms.

Anyway she's not really my aunt. She's my *ajumeoni*, a Korean word that means "aunt" without implying blood relation. I have no blood relations in Korea. All my blood relations are political exiles or dead.

But the bed is warm (literally), the thick snow falls outside the window, the white peacock struts on a background of satin as scarlet as the blood soaking the sweater of the man I saw lying in the street.

My thought at the time was, "Here we go again."

It was my first time out of the house by myself. Just down to the corner grocery store to buy a notebook. It was such a short distance, I'd even thought of running out in my houseslippers instead of putting on my boots.

Ajumeoni put money in my hand and wrote a note to the shopkeeper. Just give him the note, give him the money, and wait for the change. Simple.

I heard the screaming before I saw what it was. Then I rounded the corner and saw.

In the street in front of the store a man was lying face down in the snow. It was he who was screaming. I had no way of knowing whether those were words that he was screaming or just meaningless sounds.

Someone went up to him and shook him by the shoulder. He went on screaming. Doors opened. Men and women came out, stuffing their arms into their winter coats. Argued loudly. A little girl sat down in the snow and started to cry.

I could not ask what was happening. No words, no tongue. A man screaming, men and women shouting, a little girl crying. All this was taking place outside any language I might have framed a question in.

I went into the store.

When you can't do anything you do nothing. You do what you would have done anyway. You do what comes next.

It was like that in Tokyo. When he was done raping me I picked up the book I'd dropped, opened it, and started reading on the page where I'd left off when he first broke into my room. Just so. Just like that now.

I went into the store.

The shopkeeper's attention was out on the street, but when I handed him my note he looked at me. He said something in Korean with a rising intonation. "I don't understand," I said in English. "I don't speak Korean." And I pointed at my note.

He handed me the book then, this book, the one I'm writing in now. *Pandora.* I turned it over in my hands, wondering why a book with blank pages should have a title and illustrations, as if the story had already been written somewhere and only needed to be copied down. I wondered at the strangeness of binding it in leatherette and stamping it in gold, then putting it up for sale at a corner grocery store. I wondered if fifteen hundred *weon* was too much of my *ajumeoni's* money to spend when all I really needed was a plain old notebook.

But I had no words with which to ask to see something else. I held out my *ajumeoni's* money. He took the bills and put change in my hand. I nodded and said "Thank you" in English. I left the store.

Out in the street the man was still screaming.

At least I think it was the same man. His head was covered with blood. His hair was wet with it, as if he'd just stepped out of the shower. His eyes were full of it, weeping blood. His sweater was soaked with it. All around him the snow was melting into steaming scarlet pits. He was still screaming.

Around him stood a circle of soldiers dressed in olive drab and carrying M-16s. The shopkeepers were all standing in the doorways of their shops, talking all at once but very loudly, clearly, and distinctly.

I couldn't understand a word.

I turned around and walked back to my aunt's house.

I stamped the snow off, hung up my coat and took off my boots, and gave *ajumeoni* the change. When she asked to see what I'd bought I showed her the blank book. Then I told her what I had seen and asked her what it was all about. She shook her head. "Twenty years I have lived in this neighborhood and I never saw anything like that."

And I believe her when she says "I don't know"; but she doesn't get up from her chair and go outside and take a look. She will live in this neighborhood for another twenty years and still be able to say, "I have never seen anything like that."

White and scarlet. The peacock embroidery covers the window.

My mother told me that See No Evil, Hear No Evil, and Speak No Evil were the Three Wise Monkeys of Japan. I wondered why they weren't the Three Foolish Monkeys, or the Three Ignorant Monkeys, or the Three Monkeys Who Didn't Want To Get Involved.

That time in Tokyo I was walking to the subway station at Ikebukuro. The intersection in front of the Morinaga Love Burger stand at the entrance to the subway was blocked, not by traffic, but by human bodies. A huge crowd, a huge crowd even by Tokyo standards, all very orderly and polite of course. All nodding and bowing their heads to each other as they jockeyed for a better view. "*Gomenasai.*" "*Gomenasai.*" "*Do itashimashite.*" "Excuse me." "Beg your pardon." "Not at all." I bowed and *gomenasai*'d my way into the crowd.

At the center of the crowd two young men with wooden clubs were beating a man in a business suit. The wooden clubs had obviously been specially designed for this purpose. They had long paddles and short handles like cricket bats, with cord wound around the handles to give a better grip.

They beat the man. They beat him methodically, taking turns, as if they were driving in a railroad spike. He was crouched down to protect his head so they beat him across his back. Every time a club came down across his back his body flopped with a groan.

And all the time, like a typical American, I was thinking "Where is the six o'clock news mini-cam? Why doesn't someone call the police?" I looked around wildly for a phone booth but the Japanese class I'd taken back in the States hadn't taught me how to say "Help," "Police," "This is an emergency." At the moment all I could remember was "My, isn't this a pretty ashtray?"

The two young men tucked their clubs up under their arms and climbed into the back of a small delivery truck. This looked rather like a milk truck or an ice cream truck, except that instead of white it was painted a shiny black, with white *kanji* scrawled across the side. I knew how to read *katakana* and *hiragana* but only a handful of *kanji*– not these. I thought of copying them down on something but before my hand reached my purse the crowd parted and the small black truck drove away to disappear into Tokyo traffic.

At what point had it become too late to do anything?

I remember a weeping woman in a polyester dress and high heels struggling to raise the beaten man to his feet. I remember a burger-flipper from the Morinaga Love Burger stand, with his white paper burger-flipper hat, helping her to drag the man out of the street and prop him up against a telephone pole. I remember the crowd dispersing. Very politely and apologetically. "*Gomenasai.*" "Am I in your way?" "Not at all."

The whole time not a single voice had been raised.

I got on the subway and took the train home. "Home" meaning the room where I kept my suitcase. The room where I was raped.

I told the other English-speakers, the Americans, the Brits, Canadians, Australians, what I had seen. They reassured me. "Things like that don't happen here." "There isn't any violence in Tokyo." They quoted comparative homicide statistics for Tokyo and New York City. They told me stories about forgetting a package on the subway and having it returned unopened.

My *ajumeoni* said, "I don't know what you saw." But she didn't say, "You didn't see it."

She knows. She knows. That "identity" is just a name you give to a collection of protections and privileges you take for granted—until you leave your country, and leave them all behind.

She came to America with her husband, a doctor. He deserted her in Cleveland, of all places, which is where and how she became my *ajumeoni.* It didn't matter in America that she'd been educated at one of the top universities in Korea, that she came from the most prominent family in Seoul, that she'd been born a princess. It mattered that it was in Ohio in the fifties and she didn't speak good English.

She begged a passage home on a cargo ship. She was lucky. They had an empty berth.

And now I am lying in the bed of her daughter who has gone to America. I am lucky. They had an empty bed.

In Japan it didn't matter that I'd been educated at one of the top universities in America, that I was *cum laude* with honors, that I'd taught English as a Second Language two summers in a row. It didn't matter that I'd agreed with my college friends that "it doesn't matter whether you're Chinese-American or Japanese-American as long as we all identify as Asian-American."

It doesn't matter what's inside that box as long as you never open it.

My mother packed dried squid legs in my lunch bag, demonstrated the tea ceremony to her church group and laughed afterwards about how the white ladies wore their kimonos wrong-side-out like corpses, could still recite by memory the names and reigns of all the Japanese emperors, and never missed a chance to remind me that she had gotten into a *government* school in Tokyo. She was, in short, just like all the other (Japanese) Asian mothers of my (generic) Asian-American friends–who were, of course, just like me.

It just so happened my mother was born Korean and had a Korean name. A Korean name that is in my passport and stamped, so it seems, on my face.

I have been told that it is a typically Japanese trait to avoid speaking of anything unpleasant. I conclude then that my mother is typically Japanese in that she never told me what it was like to be a Korean in Japan.

I could not get a job teaching English. I could get interviews over the phone. The interviews ended when they saw my face.

And why should that be surprising? If a family in, say, Shaker Heights wanted their daughter to have a private tutor in French, would they hire a Lebanese woman who speaks the language fluently? Or someone who looks as classically Anglo as the engravings in my book? And do I have any idea what happens to that Lebanese woman after she doesn't get that job?

For twenty years I have lived in America, and–"I don't know." I don't have to know, I'm an American. Of course I'm an American. Who else but an American would go to a foreign country and expect to be welcomed and handed a job?

Foreigners the right color think they've stumbled on paradise. They make easy money "teaching" (exhibiting their whiteness) and spend it on Kitaro tapes and flower-arranging lessons. The Japanese are such a spiritual people. There's no violence in Tokyo. There's no racism. How can there be racism when I'm still white?

They will hear no evil. They don't have to. Foreigners the right color can afford Walkmans.

I could afford a room. A place to keep my suitcase, that was all. No heat. No lock. A room with a door that wouldn't lock.

"Things like that don't happen here."

Afterwards I picked up my book.

I didn't know the Japanese for "I want to report a rape." I don't think I could have said it in English. It was just another one of those things that don't happen, that somehow kept happening.

All the evils of the world are unleashed by a too-curious woman.

I screamed. I hit out. I pressed my knees together. It happened anyway. It was too late.

My fate was written long before he rammed his cock up my raw insides, before he even opened that door, before I rented that room with the door that wouldn't lock, before I came to the country where that would be the only room I could rent. My fate was written from the moment I asked *who am I and where did I come from?*: the moment I opened the box that can't be shut.

Brahms's New World Variations

Joan Lindgren

T HE TAIWANESE violin soloist has just launched the solo passages of the first movement of the Brahms concerto. In a minute the violins will come sweeping back in and the cellos, all rosy and burnished, will tenderly saw out the supports. The principals in the string section are all Chinese, too, from Beijing and polished at USC. How can they know Brahms, I ask myself, they who grew up on pagodas and Imperial duck, delicate foot bridges in the mist and blossoming fruit trees?

* * *

Brahms composed the concerto in 1878 in Austria in the summertime. There are, he says, so many melodies afoot there in the Tyrolean meadows and lakeshores that he is afraid lest he step on them. Brahms wears dark bulky clothes, high-top shoes, not sandals or slippers, and he drinks heavy malt brew or *kaffe mit schlag.* Sauerbraten and strudel are his staples. He is five times the size of the Taiwanese soloist; he is hirsute, in contrast to this smooth and lustrous, weightless Oriental youth, and he very likely suffers from dandruff.

Though not polished at USC, Brahms could have had honorary degrees from New England universities, being the kind of man offered honorary degrees. But he refused them. Did he disdain Americans? North Americans? Or was it fear of the sea? Or of finding on our shores the same ruffians and renegades that had terrified him as a boy when forced by his father to play his fiddle for money amongst the dregs of Hamburg. Unlike the Playboy of the Western World, Brahms never even said he killed his father. He was a middle-of-the-road man, wary of wanderers. Like my eastern-seaboard stepfather, who, when visiting California and encountering poor service in a restaurant, would grump to my mother, "What can you expect? They are all transients here." What about the Pilgrims, I always wanted to retort.

* * *

I am in the living room of my parents' house when I am listening to Brahms. It is Sunday afternoon and I am wearing a velvet dress and patent leather shoes. An army of cellos overcomes my callowness as I sit on the sofa with my library book. John Charles Thomas has just sung "Macushla." A few years later Japan will bomb Pearl Harbor while John Charles Thomas is singing on the "Bell Telephone Hour." But today there is peace, and in our house this is rare. My father is always agreeable when there is opera or its cousins on the radio, though he doesn't care to talk to us—as of course he does not when there is a baseball game or Walter Winchell. We listen, too, eventually by choice. My mother is in the kitchen parboiling the potatoes that in a few minutes will be arranged around the roast beef. Auntie Flo and Uncle Percy are coming out from the city to have dinner with us. The presence of Auntie Flo—not our "real aunt," we had no real aunts or cousins—nourishes my mother, who therefore is less apt to erupt into her bouts of operatic hysteria, though there is never a guarantee. My father has shoveled the snow, thereby earning the right to hear the "Telephone Hour" and Evelyn and her Magic Violin, as well. Sometimes he reads the *New York Times* and listens like a lord all day Sunday and cuts the grass by the headlights of the car; then our mother, her visions of ideal family life aborted, throws things at him, or anybody who happens to be in her way, and my brother and I stop our endless quarreling and try to look as small as possible.

* * *

But today Fritz Kreisler is going to play Brahms or maybe "Humoresque," or maybe it's Paderewski or Andre Kostelanetz who will star—those exotic unpronounceable names, regal in the domain of music, but unwelcome on our street. Years later my father will take me to the Met to hear the wife of Kostelanetz, Lily Pons, sing Lucia DiLamermoor in a tiny kilt and a velvet jacket, and there will be a mad scene that, although set in a Scottish castle on the moors, is not in the least unfamiliar to me, if more melodic and less mundane, of course. Not that our mother can't sing. English lullabies about golliwogs or Blanket Bay, and when Frank, who knows how to play the piano, is over, "Along Came Bill" from *Showboat*, or "Vilja" from *The Merry Widow*. A product of the Irish/English wars, Mama has an untold variety of international personae within her, all subject to come alive at the drop of a beautiful song. At such times they may even dance together, our parents—they've won best dancer at the Couples' Club—and our mother is beyond peaceful, she's our fairy godmother and will overlook every sin, large or small. Her voice is quavery and sweet and, our defenses down, we indulge our yearning to trust her.

* * *

The cellos are coming in now to back up the melody that begins the second movement, the andante, and cellos playing Brahms always spell roast beef for me, the substantial fare of Sunday, holiday, any ritual endeavor to define ourselves as a family, whatever the drawbacks, and to celebrate, I suppose, that in those Depression or post-Depression years, we had the amenities, even though we lost our house once and had to live in a rented one. But rented or not, rats in the basement or not, that ramshackle house had nine porches and a neighborhood community of kids who functioned at a high level. That is, we played Sardines and Ringalevio for hours during long spring and summer dusks, games that were worth putting aside *The Secret Garden* for, or the million other volumes available through the local public library, thanks to that Scot, Carnegie. Besides we kids measured gloss not by who owned the mortgage but by the level of contentment of our parents and by the attention given to ritual. Spanish olives and French Roquefort cheese-stuffed celery sticks for company dinners, for example, and when I would reach my quota, our Cousin Ettie would pass me olives on the sly under the table while Dad was preoccupied with carving, a feat he never mastered, and Mama was mashing the potatoes by hand. Cousin Ettie was an ally among adults, and power politics, however veiled, bespoke an undeclared need for reserve allies. Gloss was also the presence of a piano in our house and complete liberty to play—even "Chopsticks" was tolerated.

* * *

"Chopsticks"? Wherever did this two-fingered unifier of children within reach of a piano originate? Could the soloist have once included "Chopsticks" in his juvenile repertoire? Might we share not only Brahms but "Chopsticks"? Next to me an elegant young Chinese woman is holding a rose. Is she the wife of the soloist? I long to know such details in order to extend my appreciation of the Brahms concerto. As usual I am attending the symphony concert with my friend Oscar Belkov. Oscar played the violin for twenty-five years under Toscanini and has passed his priceless Cribari fiddle on to our concertmaster, who is Russian, like Oscar. Now eighty-five years old, Oscar lives for moments when he can hear the masters played on his Cribari. Papa Belkov and his brothers were violinists, too, and when they came from Vladivostok to Chicago in 1906 a violin chair was waiting for them in the pit at Minsky's. It was better than pogroms, anyway, and Brahms you could play at home. Whether Oscar played foolishness such as "Chopsticks" I wouldn't know how to ask, any more than I could ask the lady with the rose if she would permit me to touch her coarse straight hair. There is no language for such questions.

* * *

How the soloist merges with Brahms, their languages fused in the music itself. You would think they were twins. Bourgeois or not, Brahms, we know, slaved to perfect this concerto for us, that the drudgery of preparing to play it for us, the audience, held the soloist in a kind of bondage. Listening, each of us rapt, humbled, we are good wise children. Those of us who have to live with failed musicians within us are even embarrassed, if nostalgic for the musician we might have become.

* * *

And I remember the day when my brother came home during what would be the last piano lesson, trembling in fear and pain. He and Frankie Kleber had been shooting at each other in the tall grass beyond the baseball field with BB guns. That was the beginning of a long siege at the end of which he lost an eye. Mrs. Horowitz, our teacher, was expecting a baby anyway and would have given up the lessons. Mama was pregnant, too, and in the midst of it all a junior brother was born to us whom I babysat while Mama visited the New York Eye and Ear Hospital. There was no money to pay for surgery and treatment but a famous German specialist stepped in and tried to save the eye. The war was beginning and our Auntie Flo and Uncle Percy went back to England to do their bit as Air Raid Wardens. I finished up John Thompson's piano course book on my own and even learned some Mozart sonatas and Brahms rhapsodies. But soon Cole Porter, Sigmund Romberg, and company, with their promise of private bliss and playable by ear, usurped the dead masters.

Perhaps playing her songs was a child's attempt to pacify our mother in her permanent struggle with identity conflict. Dad, who later made his fortune on the war, would have staked me to any conservatory in the world. But "Chopsticks" and Vilia intervened, cluttering up my consciousness. Still, sitting here in Symphony Hall, with Oscar from Russia and the soloist from Taiwan, it seems clear that Brahms has served me well all these years, continuing to gild my days.

* * *

I wonder now whether the woman next to me with the rose is, in fact, Chinese. What emotions does a Taiwanese soloist inspire in a person of her persuasion? Has she come especially to hear Brahms or to please her escort, perhaps? She holds the cool rose with care. How did they discover Brahms, I find myself wondering. Certainly it must have been in circumstances very different from mine. A "Bell Telephone Hour" in Formosa? A Metropolitan Opera in Taipei? How did my father discover Brahms? Our Irish immigrant grandfather memorized long passages of the English Shakespeare, whom Brahms must surely have rated with *schlag* and roast beef. Grandfather, who murdered not his father but his father's religion and way of life–starvation included–must have substituted Shakespeare's sonnets for the comfort of ritual bead-telling. In his courting of urban secular life in the New World, he must have modeled for my father the right to an inner life, poetry or music for the pain, let the women take care of the chores. But we can only guess, as history sullied by trauma grows secretive. Yet the recent legacy of my grandmother's mother-of-pearl opera glasses suggests that Dad was somehow taken along to the opera, just as I was, when Mama would put her foot down at Wagner–after all, her real loves were Gypsy Kings or Student Princes or nomad bandits.

* * *

At what age would Mama have begun to exploit her lovely voice and look for solutions in operetta? In the severe depression of old age she would put on those damned Kern records and wallow in them. They failed her then; nothing but drugs, I suppose, could have lifted the thick disabling fog of depression that set in with menopause, divorce, an empty nest, and other signs of powerlessness.

* * *

Vilja of *The Merry Widow* and Bill of *Showboat* saw her through her middle years as books had seen her through the hapless misfortune of growing up poor, Irish, and motherless in the Mick-hating dockside streets of Liverpool. With her models, Flo and Percy—with their stiff-upper-lip loyalty to England during the Blitz when they could have been safe in New York—she never stopped admiring the English. Their culture, their porcelain and silver, their queen, their literature never let her down. And in the last ebbing weeks, near death, she could be persuaded to sing in the frail small voice that remained to her the English lullabies about golliwogs and the nursery rhymes that we loved as children and that she must have picked up to give herself a little history.

* * *

If Brahms had been an Englishman, Mama might have loved him. To get revenge on the Irish, who, she felt, betrayed her and caused her untold humiliation growing up in Liverpool, she loved everything English. It fell to me many years later to explore the source of our Irishness. Strange, but it was in County Clare in a pub with a fire of peat moss that I heard Brahms leider sung by an Irish contralto, Bernadette Greevy. Whether Greevy had known the meadows of Tyrol or had found Brahms through roast beef on childhood Sunday afternoons, she knew him to the bone. "*Wie bist du, mein Konigin?*" her rich velvet voice floated out over the firelight in the music's search for tenderness, and who could have guessed the Irishness that Brahms carried within himself. Yet he would be equally at home in London's Royal Albert Hall. For that matter, Brahms may have been a favorite of Hitler and his Reich.

* * *

As well as of Russians and Chinese, even those displaced by circumstance and living now in our un-Tyrolean southern California, which I, too, have adopted as my home territory, displacing in turn Indians and Mexicans. Mexican Norteño music has incorporated the polka and other influences of European culture generously imported and shared by Maximilian. But I have yet to discover if Brahms with his universal message has arrived in the hearts of these, my co-Californians. Perhaps the cello yields to the brass and shimmer of the mariachi as he exalts Mexicanidad, assuaging the pain of living so far from God and so close to the United States.

* * *

But the crescendo of the final movement is at hand, preempting contemplation. Such gorgeous tones in carefully measured intervals and progressions, how they must have challenged the chest capacity of Brahms. We vibrate, too, our egos, our status, our ethnicity, the very labels of the designer gowns erased by the exquisite sawing of the little horsehair bow, the small Taiwanese man from the small island in the shadow of a huge Brahms-like continent. Fairly spastic now, his hand is wobbling itself into a final spiral of smoke and we are melting one by one into a great sea of humanity as the coda rises up into the ceiling of the American city's downtown hall with its plush seats, from which we jump forth and fire our salvos of applause. It is Brahms, the essential bourgeois but rooted in the folk, who makes a community of us, Brahms the obedient son who eschewed risk and rhetoric, who worshiped Bach and Bismarck, Brahms, who never bought the tragedy of freedom and never left home, who has fused us transients and run-a-ways, or children thereof. We are English and Irish, Chinese and Russian, Croat and Serb, no doubt, Latin-American and African-American, refugee and conquering tycoon—we don't know what we are, other than a sea of humanity, a Brahmsian river flowing down the aisles of the symphony hall, and to the small, humble, exhausted man on stage, the tide is bearing a single and perfect red rose.

Contributors' Notes

SIV CEDERING, born and brought up near the Arctic Circle in Sweden, is bilingual and has written half her books in Swedish, half in English. She is the author of twenty-one books, including two novels, six books for children, and several collections of poetry. She has received prizes and awards for fiction, poetry, screenwriting, and visual art, including Pushcart Prizes for both poetry and fiction and fellowships from the New York Foundation for the Arts.

REGINA DE CORMIER, born of a Swedish mother and a French father, is the author of two books, *Growing Toward Peace* (Random House), which has been translated into fifteen languages, and *Hoofbeats On The Door* (Helicon Nine Editions). Her poetry has won the Pablo Neruda Award, the Ruben Dario Poetry Award, and has been published in *American Poetry Review* and *The Nation.*

DIANA DER-HOVANESSIAN is a New England born author of twelve books of poetry and translations with work in *American Scholar, Agni, Graham House Review,* and *Nation.* She has awards and fellowships from the Massachussetts Council of Arts, N.E.A., Fulbright Foundation, and P.E.N./ Columbia University Translation Center.

HEID ELLEN ERDRICH grew up in North Dakota where her mother, a member of the Turtle Mountain Chippewa tribe, and her father, a German immigrant born in Minnesota, taught at a BIA boarding school. She attended Dartmouth College and John Hopkins University, and she moved to the Twin Cities in 1992. She is a founding member of Native Arts Circle Writers, a group editing an anthology of Native American writing from this region.

ARLENE GRALLA FELDMAN teaches seventh grade English in the New York City public school system and is pursuing a Master of Fine Arts degree at Brooklyn College. "The Right Way" is an excerpt from her novel-in-progress, *My Best and Dearest.*

SESSHU FOSTER, author of *Angry Days* (West End Press), grew up in Chicano barrios of East L.A. where he lives and works. *Invocation L.A.: Urban Multicultural Poetry* (West End Press) won an American Book Award.

KIP FULBECK is an hapa artist based in Southern California and Hawaii. His personal narrative work explores his experiences as Asian American and Amerasian man in this country. Fulbeck's use of vernaculars range from SoCal slang to pidgin English to broken Cantonese. A performance and video artist whose work has been shown at the Whitney and the Museum of Modern Art, Fulbeck is also an Assistant Professor of Art Studio and Asian American Studies at the University of California, Santa Barbara.

DIANE GLANCY teaches Native American literature and creative writing at Macalester College in St. Paul. Her second collection of short fiction, *Fire Sticks*, was published by the University of Nebraska Press. Her collection of essays, *Claiming Breath* (University of Nebraska Press), won a 1993 American Book Award. Her third collection of poetry, *Iron Woman*, was published by New Rivers Press, and a fourth collection is *Lone Dog's Winter Count*, published by West End Press.

BETH HARRY has lived and studied in Jamaica, Toronto, and Trinidad. She is the founder of a school for children with disabilities and currently teaches special education at the University of Maryland.

PENNY HARTER attributes her strong feelings for the natural world to her Carolina Cherokee heritage. She now lives in Santa Fe, New Mexico.

CATHERINE HOUSER is an associate professor of English at the University of Massachusetts Dartmouth.

SUSAN ITO is a half-Japanese American (and half unknown) fiction writer living in Oakland, California with her husband John and daughter Mollie. She is an MFA candidate in the Creative Writing Program at Mills College. She teaches an Asian American Women Writers' Workshop and is working on a collection of stories called *Filling in the Blanks*.

IAN GRAHAM LEASK was born in Twickenhaum, West London and is now a resident of Minneapolis. He has taught fiction writing, literature, mythology, and composition for the University of Minnesota, the COMPAS Writers-in-the-Schools program and the Loft. His first collection of fiction, *The Wounded and Other Stories about Sons and Fathers* was published by New Rivers Press in 1992.

NANCY LEE grew up on the West Side of Cleveland (land of a thousand polkas). Her family background is Korean, Japanese, and German Mennonite. An artist as well as a writer, she recently illustrated *From Africa to the Arctic* for Ananse Press. She lives in Seattle.

JOAN LINDGREN, a translator of Contemporary Latin American Poetry, has taught cross-border translation and writing workshops in schools and prisons in the San Diego-Tijuana area.

LISE McCLOUD grew up at and is presently an "intensive residential guidance counselor" at Wahpeton Indian School in North Dakota. She received her M.S. in health sciences from Mankato State University, where she won the 1993 Robert C. Wright Minnesota Writers Scholarship Competition.

VICTORIA MANYARROWS, Eastern Cherokee and Italian, grew up in reservation border towns and foster homes in North Dakota and Nebraska. Since 1981, she has worked with community arts and alcohol/substance abuse programs in the Bay Area, and has a Master's degree in Social Work. She plans to continue writing and working with Indian people, devoting her energies to promoting a positive, Native-based world view.

TARA L. MASIH has published fiction, poetry, and essays in various national magazines and anthologies. She is the recipient of several awards for her work, and was nominated for a Pushcart Prize in 1991. She works in Boston as a freelance book editor and writer, and she contributes to *The Indian-American Magazine.*

BEVERLY MATHERNE grew up in Cajun County, a few miles west of New Orleans. She taught drama at Kansas State University, was a technical writer in the San Francisco Bay Area, and now teaches poetry, playwriting, and technical writing at Northern Michigan University. Her work appears in anthologies and magazines such as *Bay Area Poets Coalition Anthology, Cottonwood Review, Great River Review, Kansas Quarterly,* and *Louisiana Review.*

BARBARA MUJICA is a bilingual writer who combines elements of her Chilean and Jewish backgrounds in her fiction. Raised in Los Angeles, Mujica is deeply involved in Hispanic culture. Her articles on issues relevant to Hispanics have appeared in many newspapers, including *The New York Times, The Los Angeles Times, The Dallas Morning News,* and *The Miami Herald.* She is the editor of four critical anthologies of Hispanic literature published by Harcourt Brace Jovanovich, and she currently teaches Spanish at Georgetown University in Washington, D.C.

JULIA OLDER has worked and studied in France, Italy, Mexico, and Brazil. She is the author of several books, including *Blues For a Black Cat: Ten Stories by Boris Vian* (University of Nebraska Press), *The Ultimate Soup Book* (Plume/Penguin), and *Menus a Trois* (Viking/ Penguin). She currently lives in Hancock, New Hampshire.

SHARON OLINKA will have a book of poems published by West End Press in 1994. She also writes for *American Book Review.*

ANA L. ORTIZ DE MONTELLANO received a Loft Creative Nonfiction Award in 1990 and was named Loft Inroads Mentor for Emerging Hispanic Writers in 1993. Her works have appeared in *Looking for Home* (Milkweed Editions) and in numerous periodicals, among them *Sing Heavenly Muse!, The Hungry Mind Review,* and the *Star Tribune.*

SHEILA ORTIZ-TAYLOR has taught at Florida State University for nearly two decades. A transported Californian, she writes fiction and poetry. Her novels include *Faultline* and *Spring Forward/ Fall Back.* "La Frontera" is from a memoir-in-progress called *Home Movies.*

WALTER PAVLICH's latest book, *Running near the End of the World,* won the Edwin Ford Piper Poetry Award and is published by the University of Iowa Press. It also received the Joseph Henry Jackson Award of the San Francisco Foundation. Other work can be found in the issues of *The Atlantic, The Yale Review, American Poetry Review, Poetry, The Iowa Review,* and *The Antioch Review.* He divides his time between California and his native Oregon.

MAGGIE PENN is an attorney presently employed as the Human Rights Specialist for Saint Paul Public Schools. Prior to becoming an attorney, she worked in alternative Indian Education at Red School House in Saint Paul for ten years and another two years as a workshop presenter for Northern Plains Resource Center of United Tribes. Penn grew up in Devils Lake and Bismarck, North Dakota and is one-eighth Turtle Mountain Chippewa.

SIMONE POIRIER-BURES has received several awards for her writing and has published poetry and fiction in over a dozen literary magazines. She grew up in Halifax, Nova Scotia in a French Acadian family. Many of the characters who appear in "Ten" also people her novel *Candyman*, which will be published by Oberon in the fall of 1994. Poirier-Bures presently teaches in the English department at Virginia Tech University in Blacksburg.

JAMES RAGAN's books of poetry include *In the Talking Hours* (Eden-Hall, London), *Womb-Weary* (Carol Publishing) and the plays *Saints* and *Commedia*, produced in New York and in the Soviet Union. He has been Fulbright Professor of poetry at the University of Ljubljana, Yugoslavia and at Beijing University China. He currently directs the graduate Professional Writing Program at the University of Southern California.

NORA REZA likes painting, writing, travel and conversation. At present she commutes between Paris, where she recently had an exhibition of her paintings, and Minneapolis, where she enjoys time with her daughters, Ahna and Sarah.

LILIANE RICHMAN was born in Paris, France of immigrant parents and moved to the United States in 1959. Her work has appeared in magazines and anthologies such as *Blood To Remember* (University of Texas Tech Press), *Movieworks* (Little Theater Press), *Aileron*, *The Texas Maverick*, and *Black Bear Review*.

ELISAVIETTA RITCHIE is the author of seven collections of poetry and one fiction collection *Flying Time: Stories & Half Stories* (Signal Books), which includes four PEN Syndicated Fiction winners. The United States Information Agency has sponsored her travels as a visiting poet throughout the Far East, the Balkans, and Brazil. When not traveling, she lives in Washington, D.C. and Toronto.

JULIA PARK RODRIGUES is a poet and freelance journalist with a BA in journalism from San Francisco State University. She teaches poetry to elementary and junior high students, and she writes regularly for Bay Area publications. She now lives in San Leandro, California.

W. R. RODRIGUEZ is the author of *the shoe shine parlor poems et al,* narratives and lyrics of the South Bronx (Ghost Pony Press). He has completed its sequel, *the concrete pastures of the beautiful bronx* which includes the poem "democracy."

NICHOLAS SAMARAS was raised in Foxton, Cambridgeshire, England and Woburn, Massachusetts, and later settled in New York. His first book of poetry, *Hands of the Saddlemaker* (Yale University Press) received the Yale Series of Younger Poets Award, and his individual poems have been featured in *The New Yorker, Poetry,* and *The Paris Review.* A student of Classical languages, he is a Teaching Fellow at the University of Denver, where he is completing studies for his academic PhD. in English Literature.

CHERYL SAVAGEAU is of Abenaki and French Canadian heritage. Her first collection of poetry is *Home Country* (Alice James Books), and she has been awarded fellowships in poetry by the N.E.A. and the Massachusetts Artsists Foundation. She works as a writer-in-the-schools and as a storyteller. She lives in Worcester, Massachusetts with her husband and son.

THELMA SETO is a bi-racial, multi-cultural Japanese-American born in Syria, raised in Lebanon and Iran, whose primary loyalty is to the Middle East. In 1991 her short story "Vacancy" won first prize in a contest co-sponsored by the Japanese American Citizens League and the Association of Asian Pacific American Artists.

LAIMA SRUOGINIS was born in Teaneck, New Jersey and has studied in Lampertheim, Germany and Vilnius, Lithuania. She is a poet and an artist and is presently in the MFA program at Columbia University's School of the Arts.

DEBORAH STEIN was born in West Virginia, grew up in Seattle, and now lives in Minneapolis. She is the author of *Colors: Inspirations For a Cul-*

turally Diverse World and editor of *From Inside Volume 1, An Anthology of Writing by Incarcerated Women.* The recipient of numerous local and national grants, she conducts creative writing workshops for youth and incarcerated women in alternative settings like prisons, halfway houses, alternative high schools.

THOM TAMMARO is co-editor, with Mark Vinz, of *Inheriting the Land: Contemporary Voices from the Midwest* (University of Minnesota Press), an anthology of poetry, short fiction and essays, and a poetry chapbook, *Minnesota Suite* (Spoon River Poetry Press). He lives and works in Moorhead, Minnesota where he is Professor and Director of the New Center for Multidisciplinary Studies at Moorhead State University.

MARCELLA TAYLOR grew up in the Bahamas of African, Seminole and Scottish descent. Her poems have appeared in forty journals and anthologies, in a collection, *The Lost Daughter,* and in a chapbook, *Songs For the Arawak.* She was a Loft Mentor winner and has been awarded half a dozen residencies including The Helene Wurlitzer Foundation in Taos and The Camargo Foundation in Cassis, France. She currently teaches at St. Olaf College.

SUSAN TIBERGHIEN, a native New Yorker, married a Frenchman and has lived in Europe ever since. Her stories and essays have been published in periodicals and anthologies and have been read on the radio in both America and Europe. She is an active member of International PEN.

NATASHA TRETHEWEY was born in Gulfport, Mississippi. She received a B.A. from the University of Georgia, and M.A. from the Hollins College Creative Writing Program, and is currently working on a M.F.A. at the University of Massachusetts-Amherst. Her work has appeared in numerous journals, including *Agni, Callaloo,* and *The Seattle Review.*

LEWIS TURCO was born in Buffalo, New York, the son of an Italian Baptist minister who was a native of Sicily; his mother was a Midwestern Methodist missionary from Superior, Wisconsin, of Danish and Yankee extraction. He is the author of twenty-five books and the founding director of both the Cleveland State University Poetry Center and the Program in Writing Arts at S.U.N.Y. Oswego, where he has taught for twenty-eight years.

BARBARA UNGER is the author of a short story collection and five poetry books, most recently *Blue Depression Glass* (Thorntree Press). Her poems appear in *The Nation, NY2, The Massachusetts Review, Southern Humanities Review,* and in anthologies from Milkweed Editions and Negative Capability Press.

TERESA WHITMAN is the winner of a Loft-Mentor Award in fiction, an AWP Intro Award in fiction, a Loft-McKnight Award in poetry, and an Academy of American Poets Award. She lives in St. Paul with her two children and writes poetry and stories.